RECEIVED

NOV 0 7 2005

BY:_____

MAIN

D1218563

The
Gate of Gods

Also by Martha Wells

The Wizard Hunters
The Ships of Air
The Death of the Necromancer
Wheel of the Infinite
City of Bones
The Element of Fire

The Gate of Gods

Book Three of the Fall of Ile-Rien

Martha Wells

An Imprint of HarperCollins*Publishers*

HarperCollins books may be purchased for educational, business, or sales promotional use. For information please write: Special Markets Department, Harper-Collins Publishers, 10 East 53rd Street, New York, NY 10022.

FIRST EDITION

Eos is a federally registered trademark of HarperCollins Publishers.

Based on a design by Elizabeth Glover

Printed on acid-free paper

Library of Congress Cataloging-in-Publication Data has been applied for.

ISBN-13: 978-0-380-97790-1
ISBN-10: 0-380-97790-7

05 06 07 08 09 JTC/RRD 10 9 8 7 6 5 4 3 2 1

To Lisa Gaunt and Katrien Rutten

Chapter 1

T his isn't a good idea," Tremaine said under her breath. She was aware she had said it before but she hadn't been counting.

"Do you really think so?" Radiating annoyance, Gerard was cleaning his spectacles with his handkerchief in a way that could only be described as aggressive. "I'm afraid that wasn't made clear to me the first seven times you said it."

Gerard, evidently, had been counting. "All right, fine." Tremaine folded her arms, looking around the meeting room foyer. She resented being here. This building, part of the Capidaran Senate, was prized for its age and historical significance rather than its comfort or utility. Cold and not well lit, the foyer was lined with dark wood and the high coffered ceiling had yellow patches from old water damage. Colonel Averi and several dignitaries, including the Rienish and Parscian ambassadors to Capidara and members of their staffs, were waiting too, standing about in small groups, pretending to chat amiably. Gerard was the only Rienish sorcerer present; safety decreed that the *Queen Ravenna* remain crewed and ready to leave Capistown harbor at any time. At the moment Niles was on board with one of the spheres he had constructed, so the ship could defend itself from Gardier spells and be taken through the etheric world-gate at will.

They were all here in the Capidaran Senate to discuss the plan to liberate Lodun, the Rienish city where dozens of sorcerers, plus hundreds of other townspeople and students, had been trapped behind the town's defenses in a magical Gardier blockade since the beginning of the war. And with all their past and ongoing problems with Gardier spies, Tremaine felt any discussion in a virtually public forum was an incredibly bad idea. But while the Capidarans had lost some of their merchant ships, they hadn't yet come under direct attack, and it was hard to convince them of the immediate danger.

Tremaine could almost understand why. Up until a few weeks ago they had all believed the Gardier had come from a hidden city somewhere in the empty ocean between Ile-Rien and Capidara. Discovering that the Gardier came from another world entirely, that they used an etheric world-gate spell to transport their military vessels to a place they called the staging world, inhabited mostly by primitive peoples with no sorcery or modern weapons to protect them, and from there to Ile-Rien and Adera, had been hard enough to swallow, let alone explain.

And when it came down to it, Tremaine felt her presence here was useless. Not that her presence anywhere else would have been particularly helpful. There was plenty of work for sorcerers; the Capidaran and the expatriate Rienish and Aderassi sorcerers who had been trapped in Capidara when the war started had all been conscripted to build Viller spheres, the only real defense against the Gardier. The Viller Institute researchers were busy examining the prototype airship brought back from the Gardier world, but Tremaine really didn't know enough about mechanics and engines to help with that.

She grimaced and looked around again, impatient. Everyone wore sober wool or broadcloth suits, except for Averi and the other military men present, who had on their dark blue dress uniforms. She noticed Averi's uniform hung on his thin frame, making it obvious he had lost weight since it had first been issued. Tremaine wore a new outfit of dark wool serge, and the narrow skirt and long-waisted jacket might be fashionable, but she found it constricting and drafty. She didn't think the cloche hat did anything for her either, but Capidaran polite society insisted women wear something on their heads. On her bad days, she felt as if a dead albatross might be more appropriate headgear for her, suiting her mood and her apparent role in life. Since they had arrived in Capistown, nothing seemed to be going right, or if it did go right, it moved at a snail's pace.

"Where the hell is your father?" Gerard muttered, pulling out his pocket watch to check the time. Again. The watch had been one of the first things he had purchased in Capistown, a replacement for the one broken during an attack by the Gardier's mechanical disruption spell. The same spell that Rienish sorcerers couldn't defend against without the help of the spheres. The spell that had devastated Rienish and Aderassi military forces.

"Oh, come now, Gerard. Considering what you sent him out to do, does either one of us really want to know the answer to that?" Tremaine said dryly, and considered him paid back for the "seven times" comment.

Gerard gave her a brief glare, putting his watch away. "If we can just get this nonsense over and done with so we can get on with the experiment—" He stopped, relieved. "There he is."

Tremaine looked at the double doors standing open to the dark marble-floored hall. Nicholas Valiarde was just stepping into the room, nodding cordially to Colonel Averi, who nodded back with a closed and somehow wary expression.

Tremaine regarded her father with as much suspicion as Colonel Averi did. Nicholas wore a black suit and overcoat, managing to make the impeccably expensive cut look rakish, despite the gray in his hair and the beard he had recently grown. He didn't look as if he had been robbing a bank; but then, he wouldn't.

Then the door to the inner chamber opened and Tremaine followed Gerard inside.

No weapons were allowed in the meeting and had to be handed over before anyone entered. This produced quite a collection. Everyone expected Colonel Averi and the other military men to be armed. A few eyebrows were raised when Tremaine produced the pistol she had been carrying for the past two weeks, and Gerard surprised everyone by emptying his pockets of a flick knife and a revolver. Nicholas was the only one unarmed. Tremaine snorted to herself in derisive amusement, knowing weapons or lack thereof was no measure of who was dangerous and who wasn't; if the Capidarans had any inkling, they would never have allowed Nicholas inside the building.

The meeting room was as drafty as the foyer and the hall, with a dark marble floor and dark paneling lightened only by electric sconces, newly installed in the old building. Rows of long, finely carved tables and uncomfortable benches faced a dais with a table and chairs for the principal figures.

Tremaine was making her way toward a seat, already feeling the room's damp chill penetrate her bones, wishing she was back at their refugee hostel with a cup of coffee, or in bed with Ilias, or better yet on the *Ravenna* in bed with Ilias and coffee, when Gerard grabbed her arm. This was not something Gerard normally did, not unless he strongly suspected they were about to be killed. Instinct freezing her into immobility, Tremaine hastily surveyed the room.

She had noted in a general way the several well-dressed men and women taking seats at the head table, shuffling papers, addressing casual comments to one another. Now she saw that the man seated quietly at one end of the table was Ixion.

Oh, for the love of God, she thought, mostly disgusted with herself. *I should have expected this.* The sorcerer was wearing a gray wool suit with high pointed lapels in the latest fashion; for some reason this made Tremaine's skin crawl. None of the other Syprians would wear Rienish clothing except for a coat against the cold.

There was no hint now to show that the body Ixion was wearing had been grown in a homemade vat on the Isle of Storms; his brows and eyelashes had grown in and his hair was dark, if too short for fashion. His face was ordinary, that of a reasonably handsome older man.

Beside her, Gerard echoed her thought, quietly furious. "I should have known this was coming."

Tremaine turned to him, appalled, then read his expression. "Don't walk out," she said sharply. If ever a man looked as if he was about to take his sphere and go home, or at least back to the *Ravenna*, it was Gerard.

Count Delphane, highest-ranking Rienish noble in Capidara, and representative of the Queen and Princess Olympe, took his place at the table. He was tall, sharp-featured, with carefully cut gray-white hair. He met Gerard's gaze steadily, as if letting the sorcerer know his reaction hadn't gone unobserved.

Gerard pressed his lips together. "No, I won't walk out. They would know it for an empty gesture." They would know Gerard wouldn't desert the people who depended on him, no matter how great the provocation.

Nicholas stepped past them, commenting dryly, "This surprises you?"

Tremaine set her jaw and studied her feet in her uncomfortable new shoes. She supposed it made a horrible kind of sense. They were desperately short of sorcerers, and only the most skilled were able to successfully build Viller spheres, the only things that made resistance to the Gardier possible. Even with every available sorcerer at work constructing them, there were still far fewer than they needed to repel an invasion of Capidara, liberate Lodun and the rest of Ile-Rien and protect their ally Parscia. To people who didn't know Ixion's history, it must seem mad not to make use of him. Ignoring Nicholas, she said, low-voiced, to Gerard, "The request to give up our weapons takes on a new aspect."

"Yes, doesn't it," Gerard agreed, his expression grim. Nicholas had moved on, finding a seat at the front row of tables, near the outside aisle. Tremaine caught Gerard's sleeve, hauling him to an empty place in the middle row, anxious not to be the only ones left standing. She wanted to give Gerard time to recover.

As everyone found a place, the Capidaran minister, a grim-faced older man, stood on the dais, saying, "I don't think I need explain the gravity of our situation to anyone here. The Low Countries, their colonies in the Maiutan islands, Parscia and Bisra have all suffered terrible losses. Adera, and now Ile-Rien, have fallen."

Unexpectedly, Tremaine felt her stomach clench. Was this the first time someone had said it aloud? The minister paused, staring inquiringly at Tremaine. She stared back blankly, then realized he was actually looking at Gerard, seated next to her, who had raised a hand. The minister asked, "You have a comment?"

"I have a question," Gerard corrected, and Tremaine rubbed her brow to shield her expression, hearing that tone in his voice.

"Yes?"

"What is he doing here?" The question was pointed and obviously directed at Ixion.

The minister threw an unreadable glance at the Syprian sorcerer. It was Count Delphane who answered, "He's offered to help defend Capistown from the Gardier."

Gerard shook his head slowly, incredulously. "You must be out of your minds."

Ixion spread his hands, the picture of reason. "I have never done anything but defend myself." He spoke Rienish with less of an accent than Ilias and the other Syprians did; he had learned it from his captors the same way he had learned the Gardier language on the Isle of Storms.

Gerard lifted his brows. "By concealing your identity so you could murder three young women in their own home, among other crimes too numerous to list."

This gathering was too orderly to actually stir or murmur, but Tremaine detected a sudden shift in interest and a new alertness around her; she suspected that the members of the Rienish Embassy to Capidara hadn't known this.

Three young women. Ilias's cousin, Giliead's sister and stepsister. Tremaine hadn't known them, couldn't remember the names she had been told. But she knew how close Syprian families could be and how painful that loss must have been. Not the least because Giliead and Ilias both felt responsible for failing to see through Ixion's deception. And since Giliead's sister had been all that had stood between the Andrien household and the more acquisitive branches of the family, it was a loss that continued to have repercussions. Tremaine knew why Gerard had brought up that crime rather than any of the many others that could be laid at Ixion's door. Ilias and Giliead had seen it happen, and if the Capidaran government could be persuaded to hold a hearing, they could testify to it.

Ixion, of course, seemed impervious to the accusation. He said simply, "I was angry. I felt I needed to revenge myself. Something you could perhaps understand in your current circumstances."

Gerard sat back, his lips thin with distaste. But he had made Ixion's character public and it would be impossible for the Capidarans to ignore.

A voice, quiet but amused and clearly audible to the entire room, said, "It's been my experience that such 'indiscretions' are invariably committed by men who are enraged by their own sexual inadequacy."

The room went silent. Tremaine choked on an indrawn breath and clapped a hand over her mouth to keep from ruining the moment by gasping for air. The speaker had, of course, been her father.

Ixion contemplated Nicholas in bemused silence. Nicholas, slouched on the bench, chin propped on his hand, gave him back a thin predatory smile.

Ixion lifted a brow. "You find such behavior cruel and immoral, of course."

"No," Nicholas answered with a slight shrug. "I find it dull and unimaginative. As well as enormously predictable."

Ixion's brows drew together. Tremaine read that look with unexpected clarity. Nicholas wasn't what the sorcerer expected and Ixion couldn't decide if he was facing an opponent or a kindred spirit, and it clearly intrigued him. He said slowly, "That could be construed as a challenge."

"A challenge?" Nicholas didn't bother to seem innocently surprised; he said mockingly, "To an entirely reformed character such as yourself?"

"That's enough." Delphane cut off Ixion's response firmly, throwing a forbidding look at Nicholas. "We have much to discuss and little time for it." He glanced at the Capidaran minister and got a nod to continue. "You all know that we're here to discuss the plan to use the etheric world-gates to liberate the Rienish sorcerers trapped by the Gardier in the city of Lodun. If you've studied the notes at all, you realize there is some protection against materializing inside solid objects written into the gate spells, but creating gates on land is still problematic, at least for us. We originally thought Lodun's wards must be keeping the Gardier out, but we don't know if that's the reason the Gardier haven't entered Lodun through a world-gate, or if they were unable to establish any spell circles in the corresponding location in the staging world, or if . . ." His expression hardened. "They have entered Lodun, and have simply allowed the barrier to remain in place to keep whoever remains alive inside imprisoned." Tremaine winced. The Gardier used large crystals they called avatars in place of the spheres, but all were inhabited by the displaced souls of sorcerers, none of which had gotten there by accident. The Rienish still had no idea how the Gardier did this, or what happened to the captured sorcerers' bodies, or the answers to a number of unpleasant questions. "None of our prisoners can shed any light on this." Delphane paused to look around the room, his eyes hard. "But if any of those inside are still alive, we have to attempt a rescue. The spheres now make this more feasible."

No, really? Tremaine thought, rolling her eyes. There were some quiet comments exchanged in the audience, then Delphane continued, "Of course we know now the barrier must be maintained through use of the crystals. Now if anyone has any thoughts . . ."

After an interminable period, the meeting broke up for a short interval. Tremaine suspected it was to give the older members of the Capidaran delegation a chance to retreat to one of the retiring rooms where there were working radiators. She noted that Ixion had guards who conducted him away, burly young men in Capidaran dress militia uniforms of red and gray. There was also an older man with old-fashioned muttonchop whiskers, dressed in a well-tailored civilian suit, who would be a sorcerer, and a correct young woman in a dark dress who must be his assistant or apprentice. Tremaine snorted to herself in disgust. Small use that would be if Ixion decided to make trouble.

She caught up with Gerard out in the foyer in time to hear him tell Averi, "I think that demonstrated that Ixion's claims are completely false. Even under mild provocation, he couldn't keep himself from making a threat."

"Yes, but I hardly think what Valiarde said was mild provocation," Colonel Averi pointed out wearily. "The man is impossible."

Well, yes, Tremaine mentally agreed. She looked around, noting that Nicholas was not only impossible but absent, off on his next mission. It looked suspiciously as if he had only shown up for the meeting to invite Ixion into that confrontation. She stopped abruptly, letting Gerard and the colonel draw ahead of her, wondering if that were the case. *He would have had to know that Ixion would be there,* she thought, annoyance turning to anger. *And he didn't tell us. . . .* But she didn't see how he could have known; they had only been in Capidara two weeks, surely not even Nicholas could have set up a spy network in that time. *Unless he already had one in place, and he just had to find it again. . . .*

"Tremaine, if you have a moment." Giaren stepped up to her, opening a brown cardboard portfolio. He was a young man, dressed very correctly, with his hair slicked back. He was Niles's assistant in the Viller Institute, though he wasn't a sorcerer himself. "I thought you might want some of these."

The portfolio was filled with photographs. Tremaine took the first he handed her, diverted. "You took these?"

"Yes." He paged through the others, selecting a few. "I've been using the camera to help catalog the Institute's experiments with the spheres and it seemed natural to take some exposures of the *Ravenna.* Though," he admitted, apparently realizing just how many photographs were in the portfolio, "I seem to have gotten a bit out of hand."

The black-and-white image Tremaine held was grainy but she recognized the *Ravenna*'s boat deck immediately. It had to have been taken when they were disembarking at Capistown port; the long hulls of the lifeboats that nearly made a roof over the deck were swung out in their davits and a crowd of refugees and sailors milled around the railings. Back against the wall, Giliead was seated on the steps that led up to one of the hatches, Ilias at his feet. Many of the other figures were a little blurry as the camera had caught them in motion; the two Syprians, sitting still, were in sharper focus.

There was a hard edge to Giliead's face and his expression was guarded and suspicious. Ilias looked more relaxed but still watchful. His hair had come mostly loose from his queue and hung down past his shoulders in a mane of curls and tangles. The lack of color muted the effect of their Syprian clothes, but the sleeveless shirts and jerkins, the leather boots and braid, armbands and earrings and the pants with lacing rather than buttons still looked exotically different from the dungarees or tweed or pullovers that everyone else seemed to be wearing.

From this distance the curse mark branded into Ilias's cheek was just a glint of metallic light against his skin.

She sorted through the other photographs, finding one of the ship's officers posed rather stiffly in the wheelhouse, and one of Gerard and Niles, Gerard's dark head bent down near Niles's sleek blond one, their backs half-turned toward the camera and their attitude that of conspirators. *So the last great sorcerers of Ile-Rien will be remembered to posterity,* she thought dryly, *if there is a posterity.* But the next was of Arites, sitting cross-legged on the floor of a lounge she didn't recognize, his parchment sheets in his lap and his wooden pen in his hand, gazing earnestly up at someone standing over him. His braids were loose and his hair was falling into his eyes, making him look much younger than he was. Had been.

Giaren must have read her expression. He said quietly, "That's the young man who was killed, isn't it?"

Tremaine let out her breath, ignoring the tightness in her chest. "Yes. One of them."

Giaren cleared his throat and sorted through the folder of photos again, changing the subject. "I thought I had one of your father, but it didn't develop."

Tremaine nodded ruefully. "It's the silver nitrate in the film stock. He doesn't show up on it."

Giaren stared at her blankly.

"That was a joke," she added belatedly.

"Oh." He sounded relieved.

Ilias was waiting for Tremaine out in the drafty hall, sitting on a wooden bench. He wore a borrowed dark blue naval officer's greatcoat that mostly concealed his Syprian clothes: a sleeveless shirt, dark-colored pants and boots of dyed and stamped leather. He also wore a white gold ring on a thong around his neck, a wedding gift from Tremaine. The copper and leather armbands were hidden by the coat and the copper disk earrings were buried in his hair.

Seeing him under the brighter electrics of the hallway gave Tremaine a slight shock. He was pale and there were bruised hollows beneath his eyes, and he looked ill. Or more correctly, he looked like someone accustomed to living his life outdoors in hard physical activity who now had little to do, was trapped inside most of the time, couldn't sleep for the noise, hadn't seen the sun in days and could hardly breathe the bad air.

The Syprians hated Capidara. Capistown was crowded onto a hilly narrow peninsula that sheltered the large harbor, so land was at a premium. Buildings of brown brick or weathered stone, crammed with businesses or flats, stood several stories tall, blocking out the winter daylight from the narrow streets. And, unlike Vienne, there had been no room to expand and no great building projects in the recent past to widen the main avenues and turn old byways that had been little more than footpaths into real roads. The streets here were perpetually crowded with wagon and automobile traffic and a constant din of shouting and engines and horns.

The *Ravenna* wasn't the most aromatic of transports but the cool clean wind of the Syprians' world had swept the steamship odors away through most of the trip. Even Tremaine, used to cities and automobiles, could smell the stink of smoke here; it was making all the Syprians ill and the cold and damp didn't help either. Gyan, oldest of the Syprians who had followed them from Cineth, had been unable to stand it and was staying on the *Ravenna*, where the air was fresher and the ship's heating system kept the cold at bay. Danias, the youngest Syprian, had been sent with Gyan, partly to get him out of the city and partly because Syprians couldn't contemplate going anywhere alone. Pasima and the rest of her contingent—Cletia, Cimarus and Sanior— had separate quarters in the Port Authority, which kept the interfamily fighting to a minimum.

The *Ravenna* was anchored near the mouth of the harbor, as Capistown's deep-water docks were crowded with their own big ships, unable to leave port because of the Gardier's attacks on their regular routes.

Another Rienish Vernaire Solar liner, the *Queen Falaise,* was docked there also, having been trapped here by the war. She was now being loaded with supplies and weapons for the embattled troops in Parscia, and had had one of her grand ballrooms turned into a circle chamber for the etheric world-gate spell.

Tremaine dropped down onto the bench next to Ilias, saying, "Don't laugh at the hat."

She didn't manage to provoke a smile, though Ilias leaned against her, close enough to rest his shoulder against hers for a moment, a Syprian gesture that could be a greeting or an offer and request for reassurance. "Well?" he asked. "How did it go?"

"That depends on which side you're on."

He lifted a brow. "That badly."

"Yes." She hesitated. "I need to tell you . . ."

"Ixion's found himself a lawgiver who thinks he can use Ixion against the Gardier," Ilias interrupted grimly.

"That's . . . exactly it."

Ilias just looked tired and resigned. "We've been expecting it. He manipulates people. Even without curses, he's good at it."

Tremaine took a deep breath, searching for reassurance to offer and not finding any. Giliead, the god of Cineth's Chosen Vessel and the only one who had been capable of communicating with the single Gardier crystal they had captured, had already flatly refused to help unless Ixion was executed. What this was going to do to the fledgling Rienish-Syprian alliance Tremaine didn't want to consider. Given the way Syprians hated and feared magic and sorcerers, it had been a miracle the alliance had even progressed this far.

Two women passing down the corridor, dressed in the height of Capidaran fashion, were staring at them with sharp critical expressions. Capidarans could be astonishingly provincial at times, even here in their largest city, and many seemed to regard the Syprians dubiously. Perhaps because they were too like the native inhabitants of this area, forced out to make way for the Capidarans. Tremaine stared back, widening her eyes slightly, and was rewarded when both women looked hurriedly away. She turned to Ilias to find him watching her quizzically. He asked, "How do you do that?"

"What? Oh." She shook her head slightly. *Things you learn in a mental asylum.* "It's a talent."

Gerard stopped in front of them, preoccupied and harried. "Hello, Ilias. Tremaine, we're starting again."

"Oh, goody," she said mock-brightly, and got to her feet.

★　　★　　★

Ilias watched them go. The hall was cold, but he didn't want to go back to their room in the building across the street. It was cold too.

He wasn't used to having nothing to do. Even when he and Giliead were home at Andrien, there was always something that needed to be done. A fishing boat with a leaky hull, a fence to repair. There seemed to be so much that needed doing here, but none of it could be done by him. He felt useless.

Then he saw Pasima coming up the corridor and felt worse. She was a tall woman from the coastal Syprian strain, wearing a dark-colored stole pinned at her shoulder, mostly concealing the colors of her Syprian clothes. Her dark hair was braided back from her face, and while her features were a little less finely cut than those of her beautiful sister Visolela, men still turned to follow her progress as she walked past.

Ilias knew she would sail by him without a glance, so it took him a moment to realize those were her boots with the red-stamped leather planted on the floor in front of him. He looked up at her, startled and wary. Her face was set in hard lines and white from long days of tension. She sat down on the bench, almost close enough to touch. Startled, Ilias shifted away, just to make it clear he didn't find her presence any favor. "Someone might see you," he told her, making no effort to keep the sarcasm out of his tone.

She watched him critically, long enough to make the back of his neck prickle, though he just looked back at her and refused to break the silence. Then she said, conversationally, "You really think this foreign woman wants you?"

He could have done without that. He said dryly, "Curse marks don't make any difference between the legs." The silver brand on his cheek, given to any Syprian who survived a wizard's curse, made him a pariah in the Syrnai. His status was a little better since Tremaine had married him, but not in the eyes of people like Pasima.

She shook her head, as if he hadn't spoken. "You aren't like their men, you don't know the first thing about living in a city like this. The only reason she took you was to get Giliead's help. If he continues to refuse to help her people, you should ask yourself how long you'll have a place here."

Arguing with her was pointless. Saying she was right that he couldn't live here but that for the rest there were some things you had to take on trust was worse than pointless. He said through gritted teeth, "What do you want?"

Pasima took a sharp breath. "I want you to talk to Giliead."

Ilias looked away, tightening his jaw. Of course she did. "You can talk to him yourself."

"He won't listen to me." She shifted forward, lowering her voice, though there was no one in the corridor who could understand Syrnaic. "You know what will happen if he goes back to Cineth."

"What could happen," Ilias corrected, unable to help himself.

"I don't want him to be hurt."

He snorted and eyed her skeptically.

Her face tightened with offense. "He's my brother by marriage. If you don't believe I have any concern for him, at least believe I don't want the disgrace to fall on my family."

Ilias met her eyes. Maybe it was true. Family honor was vitally important to Pasima. Grudgingly, he said, "What do you want to say to him?"

She took a deep breath. "That he should stay here. Not return home."

Ilias stared at her, his brows drawing together incredulously. He had said the same thing to Giliead himself already, and though they both knew it wasn't possible, he still couldn't quite get it out of his head. Hearing Pasima echo it was unnerving. "He can't do that."

She shook her head as if he had made some silly emotional protest, not understanding. "He would be safe. Safe from the god's punishment, at least," she amended, perhaps remembering that none of them were safe, now that the Gardier could cross worlds wherever they wanted.

"He has to know what will happen," he told her, annoyed. Surely no matter what she thought of Giliead, she could understand that.

"He should accept it, stay here, and let the god choose another Vessel," she insisted.

Oh, now I see. Ilias smiled sourly. "The god won't choose another Vessel while Giliead lives."

Pasima frowned in disbelief. "How do you know that?"

"It's in the Journals." Gathered by various poets through the years, the Journals told the stories of all the Vessels, their life histories, the wizards they had fought and killed, details about the different curses they had encountered. Everything they knew about the gods. Most people didn't bother to read the whole text, as the poets usually excerpted the more entertaining stories. But Ilias had had to do something on all the long nights Giliead had set himself to study, so he had read them too. "There's a story about Liatres, a Vessel from Syigoth. He was injured in a battle on the Outer Islands and couldn't walk. He lived for years after, but the god didn't choose the Vessel to replace him until he died." Arites had been writing Giliead's journal, Ilias recalled suddenly. He didn't know if the older parts had been copied and sent to the poets in Syrneth yet or not. The newest part must be mixed up with the story Arites had been writing of the *Ravenna*'s voyage. Though if things went the way they feared, Giliead's journal might not be a story Arites would have much wanted to tell.

Pasima sat back, her brows knit. Ilias felt a flash of pity for her. He said, "There's nothing anyone can do about it now. We have to wait and see what the god will do."

Her face set, the lines of strain around her finely shaped mouth deeply etched. "There's a reason our ancestors decided to mark the cursed. Maybe it's Giliead's continued association with you that made this happen." She stood abruptly. "You should stay here and let him return alone."

Pasima didn't stay to take in his stung expression, already turning on her heel, striding away down the cold corridor. Ilias looked at the mud-stained stitching on his boots, gritting his teeth until his jaw hurt. *Why did you even talk to her? What is wrong with you?*

When he looked up, Nicholas Valiarde was standing over him. He wore Rienish clothing, all in black, most of it concealed by a long black coat. *Oh good, it's my crazy father-in-law,* Ilias thought in resignation. This day was just getting better and better. Nicholas said, "Come with me."

Ilias eyed him. "No."

An eyebrow lifted slightly. "You only take orders from my daughter?"

Ilias lifted a brow right back at him. "Yes."

Unexpectedly, Nicholas's mouth quirked in amusement. He sat down on the bench, sweeping his coattails out of the way. "I see."

A test, Ilias thought sourly. That was about all he needed. Then he realized Nicholas had spoken Syrnaic. "You got the god-sphere to give you our language." It came out sounding like an accusation. The special sphere, the one that the wizard Arisilde lived in, had given Tremaine, Gerard, Ander and Florian the ability to speak Syrnaic when they had first come to Cineth. They had discovered later how to get it to give the ability to speak Aelin, the Gardier language. At least Nicholas had learned that one the hard way, by living among the Gardier.

"It seemed easiest." Nicholas regarded him for a long moment. "I have an appointment to view a house in town. Do you want to accompany me?"

Ilias frowned, not certain he understood. "A house?"

"Gerard needs a place to make further experiments with the sphere. And I'm assuming you and the others find the accommodations in the refugee hostel as uncomfortable as I do." He watched one of the Capidaran warriors with a shooting stick propped on his shoulder stride down the hall.

Ilias thought it over, considering briefly the idea that Nicholas might mean to kill him. At this point, anything would be a welcome distraction. He shrugged. "I'll come."

Ilias had walked along the harbor with the others, usually to look wistfully at the *Ravenna,* but he had only gone into the city a few times, and not very far. The noise and stink of smoke was bad enough inside the port.

Nicholas didn't lead him toward the building's outer court, but down the polished stone stairs and through an unobtrusive door in the wall at the bottom. It led through a series of dingy corridors and into a low-ceilinged noisy room filled with wooden cabinets and steam and cooking smells. People in white clothing stared at them as they passed but no one tried to stop them; Nicholas pushed through a heavy wooden door at the far end and they were suddenly out in gray daylight, in a small dirty stone-paved court. It was sunk below the street, walled by an iron-barred fence, with a stairway leading up to an alley between high brown brick walls. Following Nicholas up steps that were still damp from a recent rain, Ilias was aware this was probably not the way most people left the building. As Nicholas paused to close the barred gate behind them, Ilias asked, "Are we prisoners here?"

Nicholas hesitated, then let the gate latch drop. "Not as such." He took a pair of small round glass eye-lenses out of a pocket, like the ones Gerard wore. But when he put these on, Ilias saw the glass was tinted dark rather than clear. He turned down the alley, walking toward the noise of the street. "I'd rather not give anyone the opportunity to restrict my movements."

Ilias could understand that. They reached the walk bordering the street in front of the heavy stone façade of the Port Authority. It was fairly broad but awash in mud, with a narrow stone verge for people

to walk on. The passersby hurried along, dodging water and mud
spray from the wheels of the horseless wagons. Most were dressed in
the same kind of clothes the Rienish wore, dark blues or browns and
grays with only a touch of color in a neckcloth or scarf. Ilias wrinkled
his nose at the stench of smoke and stagnant water and worse. He
didn't understand how these people could have horseless wagons and
wizard lights like the Rienish but have failed to master the elementary
skill of draining their city of human waste.

Ilias had been to a Rienish city with Tremaine, the one the Gardier
now occupied. The smoke and the noise had been nearly as bad but
there had been marvelous things to look at: windows with jewel-
colored glass, huge stone buildings heavy with carvings of strange
creatures. These buildings were all brown brick or a weathered dun-
colored stone, none as imposing, and the windows were just dusty
glass. The people here spoke mostly Rienish but other languages were
mixed in as well, making it confusing.

Ilias knew from past ventures out that the people here would still
stare even if he tied all his hair back, so he hadn't bothered. People did
stare, not in the idly curious or sometimes appreciative way that the
Rienish did, but as if they were affronted at seeing someone different
from themselves.

Nicholas stepped around a mud puddle, and said, "Why did you
ask if we were prisoners?"

Ilias shrugged, at first not meaning to answer. Then he found himself saying, "Tremaine says they're listening to Pasima. If she's told
them that when we go back to Cineth, the god will kill Giliead for what
he's done . . ." He shrugged again, torn between the anxiety that made
him want to talk about it and a reluctance to drag the whole thing out
before Tremaine's enigmatic father.

Nicholas threw him a sideways glance, his eyes invisible behind the
opaque lenses. "I hadn't realized your situation in Cineth was quite
that serious."

"We don't really know what the god will do," Ilias admitted. "But
no Chosen Vessel ever used a curse before."

"But it has punished Vessels for transgressions in the past."

"Our god hasn't." Cineth's previous Chosen Vessels had all led
fairly unremarkable lives, except for the one a few generations ago
who had somehow managed to acquire two husbands and a pack of
children in between ridding her territory of several particularly vicious
wizards. Her descendants still had their farms to the south of the city.

"Other gods have. They refuse to see the Vessel, and then he kills himself." Gunias of the Barrens Pass had fallen on his sword when his god had denied him, though no one knew what Gunias had done. Eliade of Syrneth's crime had been more obvious: she had been sent away from her god when she had killed her own sister out of jealousy over a man; she had drowned herself.

Nicholas was silent for a few steps before he replied obliquely, "There are better ways of getting rid of unwanted individuals."

Ilias thought he meant that it was no good overreacting, that there was no proof the gods had caused deaths that might well have come out of guilt. But because he wanted to get something out into the open, he said, "Like me."

Nicholas stopped to regard him directly, the stream of people impatiently circling around them. Ilias still couldn't see his eyes but his voice was dry and faintly exasperated. "That aside, if anything happened to you, Tremaine would of course assume that I had arranged it. No evidence I could produce of my innocence, no alibi no matter how ironclad, would convince her otherwise, and I could shortly expect an unpleasant surprise." Turning away to continue up the street, he added, "If you raise a daughter to be both independent and an excellent marksman, you have to accept the fact that your control over her actions is at an end."

They reached a quieter street finally, though the buildings here were just as ugly. Nicholas stopped in front of one with steps leading up to a door a little way above street level. Ilias supposed with the city so crowded they had to take advantage of every space, but he didn't understand why half the people didn't just pick up and go build another city somewhere else. It seemed ridiculous to let a place grow so large that it became unpleasant to live in. *And it's not like they have to look for a spot with a god either,* he thought, watching Nicholas climb the steps and pull at a little brass handle to one side of the door.

Ilias heard a bell ring dimly within. After another moment's wait, the door opened to reveal a thin man with dark hair and narrow features, dressed in the same jacket and pants that many of the men seemed to wear, except his was a dark brown and the cloth tied around his neck was bright red. Nicholas spoke to him in Rienish and Ilias didn't bother to listen, looking around to see if there was anything on the street to keep him occupied while Nicholas conducted his business. The man replied, moving back out of the doorway and making an expansive gesture. Nicholas glanced back, gesturing for Ilias to follow.

Ilias hesitated a moment, surprised, then remembered the only good thing about this place was that they had no more idea what a curse mark was than the Rienish. He went up the stairs after Nicholas.

The entry hall was high-ceilinged and dark, despite the wizard lights in glass shades mounted on the walls. Four doors opened into other spacious rooms, and stairs at the far end led to the upper floors. It was a relief to be out of the cold, though Ilias suspected that once he got used to it this house wouldn't feel warm either. It was a little like the house that Tremaine had lived in, the one he had seen in their brief trip to her land, except this one smelled of damp rot. It made him miss the *Ravenna* again; her insides were all light wood and colored glass, her colors ivory and gold and red.

The Capidaran man looked him over curiously as he shut the door, speaking to Nicholas in Rienish, "And this is your . . . ?"

"Son-in-law," Nicholas replied, stepping to one of the partly open doors to examine the room inside. Everything was dark and heavy, with dark colors in the carpets and the wall coverings, heavy dark wooden furniture with dark fabric cushions. "I'm taking this house for my daughter and her in-laws."

"Oh, I see." The man seemed to make some mental shift.

"The ballroom?" Nicholas prompted.

"Ah! This way." He turned to lead the way up the stairs.

Ilias trailed after, turning over the Rienish words *ball room,* and remembering it wasn't as interesting as it sounded. At the top of the stairs there were two double doors, and the room proved to be just a big shadowy chamber, the floor of once-fine wood set into squares, the different grains and hues used to make patterns. There were curse lights in pink crystal balls mounted on the walls, and the ceiling was figured into squares. Though the colors here were lighter pinks and creams, the paper wall coverings were peeling off, revealing plaster beneath that was green with mold. Ilias wrinkled his nose at the smell. But Nicholas looked at the polished expanse of floor and nodded to himself. "Perfect."

"So glad it suits," the Capidaran man said, though there was a note of incredulity in his tone.

The talk turned to coins and how much Nicholas was going to give for the house. Bored, Ilias wandered the length of the room, half-alert for lingering curse traps. Though he didn't have Giliead's god-given ability to see curses, there were things he knew to look for: blind spots in his vision, surreptitious movement, changes in the air. Giliead would have to check over everything, but Ilias suspected there was nothing here.

Through an archway at the back he found a much smaller room that was all glass, the long panes set into panels of wrought iron. It might have been a fine place except that the glass was covered with dust, turned to a thick sticky substance by the damp, and there were pottery tubs filled with dirt and the dry remains of dead plants. He rubbed at the glass with his coat sleeve and found it looked down onto a garden paved with stone, with overgrown beds choked with weeds and dead brush and a fountain with stagnant green water. He sighed, leaning his forehead against the cold glass. Everywhere he looked there were reminders of death.

Nicholas wandered in and studied the windows with an air of dissatisfaction. The Capidaran man followed him, hesitating as Nicholas wandered out again. He stepped over to Ilias, and asked, "Valiarde— it's a noble Rienish family, yes?"

Ilias shrugged. "I don't know." He wasn't sure what *noble* meant.

"I see." The man nodded, still bewildered. "But wealthy?"

Ilias thought about it, trying to answer honestly. "They paid a lot for me."

The man just looked more bewildered, until a shouted question from Nicholas sent him hurrying out of the room.

Ilias left the dead plants to their slow degeneration and went back through the big chamber. He found a wide stairway in the hall and climbed it, finding two more floors of cold musty-smelling bedchambers. Above that there was another stairwell, this one narrow and cramped, the wood paneling giving way to yellowed plaster halfway up. The hallway it led to was also narrow and cramped, with a low ceiling and only one bare wizard lamp for light. He opened a door and the wan light from the corridor showed him a small dark room with a bare iron bedstead and a washbasin on a stand. A thick layer of dust coated every surface and it smelled of must and rats. It looked like a cell, except the door didn't seem to have any kind of lock. He left it open, moving down the hall to check a few of the other rooms. They were all the same.

He heard Nicholas's quiet step on the stairs and glanced back at him, asking a little suspiciously, "What are these rooms for?"

"They're servants' quarters," Nicholas said in Syrnaic. He glanced into one of the rooms as he came along the corridor. "Fortunately I wasn't planning to hire live-in help. Other than that, I think this will do."

Ilias started to ask what it would do for when at the far end of the hall, one of the still-closed doors slowly started to swing open. Nicholas saw his expression change and turned, one hand moving to the pocket of his coat, but it was obvious no one was there to move the door. Fully open, it hesitated a moment before slowly and deliberately closing again; Ilias heard the latch click as it shut. Nicholas sighed in annoyance and looked at the Capidaran man standing in the stairwell, who smiled apologetically and made a helpless gesture.

"Shades." Ilias squinted up at the yellowed plaster ceiling, considering. Probably angry shades, since the quiet ones never knowingly drew attention to themselves. "Gil can take care of those."

"So he can." Nicholas had fixed the Capidaran man with a gaze that should have melted the skin right off him. "Then this will still do—for half the price."

Chapter 2

It was evening and cold with mist-drizzle when Tremaine arrived back at the refugee hostel. She was tired, thirsty, and had the strong sensation of an impending headache. Reaching the hostel was not much of a relief.

The place had been a commercial traveler's hotel, right up until the Capidaran authorities had conscripted it to hold refugees, so it was actually in much better condition than the dilapidated seaside hostelry at Port Rel that the Viller Institute had once taken over for its headquarters in Ile-Rien. There was no fallen grandeur here; there was in fact no grandeur of any kind. Crossing through the pokey little lobby with its bad imitation Parscian carpets and floral upholstery and dusty potted palms always brought back memories of waiting for trains in small villages along the Marches.

The people sitting around on the hard wooden benches and understuffed couches made the place look even more like a station waiting room. *Except no one's going anywhere,* she thought, depressing herself further. They spoke quietly, calm but with signs of strain showing in tired eyes and worried voices. They were Rienish, Parscians and Aderassi who hadn't enough funds to find a place in the city or who had no relatives or friends here to support them. The Maiutans, all of whom were ex-prisoners of the Gardier, would have been in even worse straits, without even an overworked Embassy to appeal to. But some of the freed prisoners had been Lowlands Missionaries who had known which local charitable organizations to alert, and several contingents of volunteers had managed to hurry off the Maiutans before the Capidaran government had been able to stop them. The others were supposed to have dual citizenship with Capidara, so they could leave if they wanted, but employment was scarce and most had nowhere else to go. The lobby smelled of must and dust and fear sweat.

Tremaine had almost reached the stairs when one of the harried desk clerks hurried over, holding a folded slip of paper. "Madam Valiarde! A message for you."

As one of the few people still in the hostel who could actually afford to tip, Tremaine usually got extra attention. She exchanged the hoped-for Capidaran coin for the message and unfolded the paper. There was nothing on it but an address. She stared at it blankly, then realized what this must be. *He found a house.* She wondered how. Accommodation was supposed to be nearly impossible to get in the crowded city, and Gerard had needed a large room for experiments with Arisilde's sphere. "Did they clear out our rooms?"

"Yes, madam." The man sounded relieved. The entire staff was somewhat nervous of the Syprians, and Giliead in particular was in no mood to be friendly. Tremaine counted the staff lucky; it would have been much worse if Pasima's group had been staying there as well. "They said we could give the space to someone else."

"Yes, that's right." She tucked the address away in her pocket with a mental sigh. There was no telling what shape the house would be in and she suspected real food and real rest were a long way in the future.

Preoccupied, she turned back toward the front door, hoping she could find a taxicab driver who knew the street. Her path blocked, she looked up to find herself facing Ander Destan.

Ander was dressed as a civilian, in a tan pullover and a leather jacket. The shopkeepers and market stalls had been doing good business with the refugees who had money, all of whom were buying clothes, blankets and other items that would quickly become scarce once the bombing started here. Smiling, Ander said, "You look lovely. That outfit suits you."

Tremaine regarded him blankly. She distrusted compliments on her appearance in principle, but she really couldn't find anything in that statement to object to. It made an interesting contrast to what Ilias had said when she had gotten dressed this morning, which had been "Why do you wear clothes that hide your breasts? It's not as if anyone's going to think you don't have any." Come to think of it, she hadn't been able to muster a suitable reply to that one either. "Are you waiting for Gerard? He's going to be trapped in the meeting for a while longer."

"I was waiting for you, actually," he said, and gave her that slow warm smile that had worked so well on her and so many women in the past.

Tremaine eyed him, unimpressed. "Really."

Ander let out his breath, the smile turning wry. "I suppose only the truth will do."

"Some people prefer it," she acknowledged that warily.

"I know Gerard and the others have some sort of plan afoot—"

Tremaine rolled her eyes, annoyed. "And you thought you'd get it out of me with a few compliments. That's a new interrogation technique. 'My, what a nice hat. Give me the secret plans—' "

"Tremaine! You know that's not what I—" He eyed her. "Maybe you don't know. Can we start over?"

Starting over would take years, and she didn't have any to spare. "What do you want?"

"I'd like to help."

Tremaine lifted a brow. "Don't you have anything better to do?"

"At the moment, no. I've been assigned off the *Ravenna*, but the Capidarans are handling most of the duties." He added bleakly, "There's nothing to do except wait."

Watching his face, seeing the new lines of anxiety and strain that she didn't remember being there before, Tremaine felt a reluctant surge of empathy. She rubbed her forehead wearily. *I hate it when I do this.* "All right, come on. But you're paying for the taxicab."

The shade in the top of the house was not only angry, it was actively hostile. Braced against the door to keep it from slamming and trapping them inside, Ilias hoped the battle at least gave Giliead a chance to work off some of his temper. "I'm just telling you what she said," he repeated for the third time. He hadn't even gotten to the part yet about just who Pasima thought was responsible for all this.

The wan yellow illumination came from the curse light in the narrow attic corridor, revealing that the floor of the long room was littered with odd fragments of metal or wooden rubbish and rat droppings.

Giliead paced the confines of it, his face set in grim lines. He was a big man, even for a coastal Syprian, and nearly a head taller than Ilias. Outraged, he seemed to take up even more space in the relatively small chamber, his light brown hair frazzled in its braids. "I just don't understand what she expects to gain out of it," Giliead said in frustration. He had tracked the shade back to this room and the first brush with it had left long light scratches across his chest and neck.

The old wooden door, propelled by the shade's anger, shoved against Ilias's shoulder with renewed vigor; he leaned into it more firmly, bracing his feet in the doorjamb. The shade's turbulent presence made the room deadly cold; their breath misted in the air and his fingers were going numb. "Why do you think she wants to gain something?"

"Why else would she care?" Giliead demanded. "It doesn't do her any good if I die. Whoever the god picks will be a child; does she want Cineth to have to rely on other cities' Vessels for the next score of years?"

"No. I think she was being sincere. For her, anyway." It was what worried Ilias the most. The door whacked him in the back again and he grimaced, saying impatiently, "Look, just calm down. Forget Pasima. You're not going to be able to convince this motherless shade to rest if you're angry."

Giliead snarled, "I know that." Then he pressed his hands over his eyes, taking a deep breath.

Dust stirred across the room, lifting in a curtain, then gently dispersing. Ilias found himself holding his breath, and not just to keep from sneezing. *It doesn't mean anything if he can't do it. Some shades never rest and this one is a real bastard.* But he still held his breath.

The room was calm, silent. Ilias felt the pressure of the door against his back ease, then it squeaked as it swung gently back. He straightened up slowly, relieved.

Further down the corridor, another door banged. Then again. And again. Giliead opened his eyes, swearing. "Well, at least it's not haunting this room anymore," Ilias said wearily, standing back to let him stomp out. It was going to be a long evening.

Dusk was gathering and a light rain had started when the taxicab deposited Tremaine and Ander in a broad residential street. It was lined with three-story brown brick town houses. Unlike such houses in Vienne, most had steps leading down to basement entrances for servants under the front doors, and there were no ornamental iron-work fences, window boxes or potted trees. Despite that, the street seemed clean and open. Tremaine could see warm yellow light behind drawn curtains, and men in overcoats or women carrying market baskets hurried up to welcoming doorways. There was something odd about observing such ordinary activities, as if seeing people who weren't enslaved, weren't fleeing death or warily waiting for the next bombing was unusual. *Well, for me it is,* she thought tiredly.

Tremaine looked down to consult the address again and decided it should be in the middle of the block. "This doesn't look so bad," she said cautiously as they walked along the damp pavement.

"What were you expecting?" Ander asked, sounding amused.

Tremaine thought of trying to explain Nicholas's taste in houses, or Nicholas's taste in general, and decided against it. She also thought of saying *I shot a man in cold blood to get a truck, Ander, so please get that tone that says "you silly little girl" out of your voice when you speak to me.* "Nothing," she muttered. *Nothing changes. You shouldn't have let him come.*

These houses looked about the size for families of professional men with room for children and a cook and housemaid; some even seemed to be broken up into flats. She had thought Gerard wanted something with a room large enough to draw a spell circle in. Though maybe— She stopped suddenly, as the house occupying the middle portion of the block came into view. "Oh, God."

It was a huge hulking structure, its brick leprous with mold, with no ground-floor windows and a pair of badly proportioned pillars flanking its entrance. There was no carving on the eaves and the proportions were subtly off; it looked like a small and incompetent copy of a badly neglected Vienne Greathouse. The neat town houses to either side of it seemed to stand in silent reproach. Ander took the address away from her, saying, "That can't be it."

"Of course that's it," she snapped. "The place has 'Valiarde' written all over it." It had probably been built years ago as part of an estate by some Capistown land baron and the city had gradually encroached on its grounds until only the house was left.

She stamped up the steps, reflecting that at least it looked big enough to have a ballroom, and tugged at the bellpull.

Nicholas, who must have noted their approach, opened the door almost immediately. He eyed Ander with enigmatic disfavor, greeting them with, "Why did you bring him?"

Tremaine regretted it now herself but she wasn't going to admit that. "Because he asked," she said flatly, stepping in past Nicholas to look around. The entrance hall was high-ceilinged and dingy, the wood floor showing evidence of past water leaks. Four sets of double doors opened off it, and there was a staircase at the end, but it was all a little too small and badly balanced for a true grand entrance. Whoever had built the place had been struggling between elegance and parsimony.

"Evening, Valiarde," Ander said with cautious reserve, stepping inside.

Shutting the door, Nicholas answered with a noncommittal grunt. Years ago when Tremaine and Ander had first met, she had been immersed in Vienne's artistic community and Ander had been a feckless young noble who liked slumming. Nicholas had met him twice, managed not to speak directly to him on either occasion, and now appeared to be trying to stay consistent.

For his part, Ander seemed to be fooled by Nicholas's portrayal of an eccentric gentleman-adventurer, though with Ander it was always hard to tell. In contrast, Ilias and Giliead weren't familiar enough with Rienish society to be taken in by the façade. They treated Nicholas with wary respect, and when they were in the same room, they always seemed to reserve a part of their attention for him, alert for any sign of aggression. It was a wariness they didn't show with anyone else in their group, an almost instinctive understanding that Nicholas was dangerous; they weren't willing to trust their safety to his goodwill.

Kias seemed to sense it as well; he avoided the whole issue by trying to never be in the same room with Nicholas.

And Nicholas . . . *Appreciates the honesty.* Well, she had thought he might be tired of hiding what he was.

Tremaine went toward the only set of doors that stood open, stopping in the archway. There was a fire in a large and ugly brick hearth and the electric sconces were lit, chasing shadows back into the dark wainscoted corners. Calit was on the floor by the fire, dressed in dungarees and a bulky blue pullover sweater that was too big for him. Spread out on the floor around the boy were an array of toys, all of the kind that could usually be bought from street peddlers in Ile-Rien and presumably here as well: a few crudely carved wooden animals, picture cards with famous sights in the city, some polished stones and three brightly colored tops. Calit was arranging the collection with the concentration of an explorer surveying artifacts of a foreign land; which, in a way, he was. He was an Aelin, one of the people who the Rienish called Gardier, and had come back with them from their brief involuntary visit to the Gardier's world. He glanced up, nodded a solemn greeting to Tremaine, and regarded Ander with suspicion.

Tremaine advanced cautiously into the room. "Where is everyone?"

"The attic appears to be haunted," Nicholas said, following her in, Ander trailing behind. "Ilias is with Giliead, dealing with it. I think Kias is shifting some empty barrels out of the pantry."

Tremaine nodded slowly. "So we're living here, then?"

Nicholas gave her a raised eyebrow. "Temporarily."

"Right. Did anyone tell Gerard and Florian?"

"They'll be along later tonight, once they finish at the Port Authority."

"I can go pick them up, if you like," Ander offered blandly.

Nicholas regarded him with equal blandness and apparently decided to take his relationship with Ander to a new level by actually speaking to him. "I suspect Gerard is capable of making his way here unescorted."

Considering that Gerard was capable of world-gating an eighty-eight-thousand-ton passenger liner, he was probably right. Leaving them to it, Tremaine went down the hall and started up the stairs. The second-floor landing gave on to another hallway with a sitting area at the far end beneath a curtained bay window. There were four doors off the hall, all open, and all the lights were on. She looked into rooms until she spotted her carpetbag, a couple of Syprian leather packs, Ilias's sword in its scabbard and one of the wooden carved cases that held arrows and a goathorn bow, all piled on a dark bureau.

She wandered inside. The carpets and upholstery were all dark, the furniture of a heavy wood in a bulky style out of fashion even for Capidara, and there was a fire in the hearth. There was also a radiator in the corner, but it was cold. She supposed she should feel lucky for the electricity, such as it was. *God, I wonder what the plumbing is like.* She buried her face in her hands. Best not to find out just at the moment. But it was better than being one of the poor bastards at the refugee hostel, with nowhere to go.

Needing to distract herself, she checked the carpetbag to make sure her journal and the folder with Arites's papers were all there, but someone, probably Ilias, had packed it carefully. She had left most of Arites's writing stored on the *Ravenna*, since it would need to return to Cineth, but she was using his partially complete dictionary to teach herself to read Syrnaic. She shut the door and quickly changed out of the new but uncomfortable dress suit and into Syprian clothing. The shirt she pulled out of her bag was a faded gold and the pants a soft dark blue, each with block-printed designs along the hem and with seams reinforced by braided leather. It was the first time she had worn this shirt and she discovered it had ties to allow the sleeves to be looped up and secured at the shoulder, leaving the arms bare. A sensible arrangement for a garment that might be worn on a fishing boat, but it was too cool to wear like that now. She pulled a Rienish wool sweater on over it, put on her comfortable old boots and sighed with relief.

She took the back stairs down to the kitchen to discover actual food being delivered through the service door under Kias's supervision. The kitchen walls were dingy brick, the room furnished with a long plank table and a few chairs. A couple of old wooden dressers held a random assortment of cracked china plates and stained copper pots, all probably judged too worn for the former owners to haul away. Distracted by the sight of a bag of coffee beans and two bottles of wine on the sideboard, Tremaine almost didn't recognize the white-jacketed man placing warming pans on the old-fashioned monster of a range. He nodded to her affably and she squinted at him, racking her memory. "Were you on the *Ravenna?*"

"Yes, I volunteered in the kitchens," he answered with a smile and an Aderassi accent. "I am Derathi, late of the Hotel Silve. I have been hired as chef in a restaurant a few streets over, and your father has made arrangements with us to feed you."

Tremaine lifted the lid of the warming pan, her stomach contracting at the appetizing scents. "This looks wonderful," she murmured.

"If you need anything, please send to us, at any time." Derathi paused at the kitchen doorway. "This is a good city, but . . . I would like to return to Ile-Rien, and then Adera again someday."

Tremaine looked up, meeting his solemn gaze. *We both know, but let's not say it.* "Someday."

Derathi took his leave and Kias stepped out of the pantry, asking without much hope, "Any news?" Kias was Giliead's father Ranior's sister's son. He was big like Giliead, olive-skinned, with frizzy dark hair falling past his shoulders.

"Nothing good," Tremaine told him. She supposed he already knew the news about Ixion from Ilias.

With a resigned shake of his head, he filled a couple of plates and carried them out of the kitchen, calling for Calit. Not feeling sociable, Tremaine sat down to eat at the battered kitchen table; the old range still radiated heat, making this the most comfortable room in the house. Ilias wandered in when she was nearly finished, standing in front of the still-warm range, with his arms tightly folded across his chest. He looked worn down and tired, more so than he had this morning. She knew that dealing with Giliead, who had been shuttling between rage and despair over what he saw as Ixion's release, wasn't easy. Tremaine had been on the verge of asking about it several times, but she was reluctant to broach the topic. She asked instead, "House still haunted?"

He shook his head, casting an annoyed glance up at the ceiling. "I think Gil scared it away."

Tremaine hesitated. "Because he's a Chosen Vessel or because he was really angry?"

He snorted wryly. "Guess."

Tremaine winced. She thought for a moment he would go back to rapt contemplation of the rusting iron range but he turned to the table, hooked a chair out and sat down. He pulled her plate over, investigating it for scraps.

Tremaine rescued the last hunk of bread. She eyed Ilias for a long moment. "Homesick?" she asked him finally.

He glanced at her with a lifted brow, not understanding.

She was surprised Syrnaic didn't have a word for it. She gestured with the bread, clarifying, "You miss being home."

He shrugged, but looked away. "It's summer there. We'd sleep outside in the atrium at night, or out in the fields."

As opposed to being stuck in this moldy cold house, or the crowded cold refugee hostel. Watching him crack the leftover bone and render it free of any shred of edible material as methodically as a wolf, she said, "We're not going to be here that long."

He frowned down at the plate and started to speak. Then Ander walked in. Searching for an uncracked cup on the sideboard, he nodded politely. "Ilias."

Ilias looked up sideways, regarding Ander for a moment in silence, then looked at Tremaine. She could tell from his expression that this was about the cap to his day. She said brightly, "Ander's here."

Ander poured coffee from the enamelware pot resting on the stove, giving Ilias a thoughtful look. "I hope you and Giliead don't still blame me for Ixion."

Ilias let out his breath. "We don't blame you." He glanced up at Ander again, his expression just this side of irony. "All you did was let him out."

Ander's mouth twisted in annoyance. Tremaine took a sip of coffee and pointed out mildly, "If you didn't know, Ixion has managed to convince the Capidarans that he can help them against the Gardier."

Ander stared at her, his brows drawing together. "You're joking. . . . You're not joking. What do they think they're doing?"

She watched him over the rim of her cup, trying to decide if she thought he was telling the truth. It had suddenly and belatedly occurred to her that that might have been why Ander had sought her out, that Gerard's open hostility during the meeting had worried the Rienish command enough to send someone to keep an eye on him.

Ander was shaking his head. "I wonder what they think Ixion can do for them? He doesn't have a sphere. They'll have to . . ." He hesitated.

"Get Niles or one of the others to make one for him, unless they're stupid enough to let him learn how to do it himself," Tremaine finished his thought impatiently. The new spheres weren't as powerful as Arisilde's, not being inhabited by the living soul of a sorcerer, but they did allow Niles and the other Rienish and Capidaran sorcerers here to use the gate spell, fight the Gardier crystals and cast far more elaborate spells of their own. If Ixion got a sphere, he would probably kill all of them. "The new spheres actually work, unlike—" She stopped, blinking. "Oh, that's perfect."

"What?" Ilias demanded, sitting up, suddenly alert. "You've got that look."

Ander regarded her suspiciously. Maybe he recognized the look too. "You can't mean—"

"Before they found out how the world-gate spell worked," she explained to Ilias, "several sorcerers tried to build spheres to use it. The spheres couldn't take it and destroyed themselves—and the sorcerers using them."

"So Niles could build him a trap god-sphere?" Ilias asked, rubbing his chin speculatively. "Would Niles do that?"

"Mm. Good point." Tremaine tapped her fingers on the table, thinking it over. "To save our lives, yes." She shook her head, disappointed. "But when Ixion hasn't done anything yet . . . I don't think so. We could broach the idea, but if we got caught by the Capidarans . . ." She looked thoughtfully at Ander, who had his arms folded.

Ilias jerked his head toward the other man, his expression sour. "He'd tell everyone it was our idea—"

Ander frowned at him, "Hey, I know as well as anyone that—"

"And if Ixion gets a god-sphere and dies of it, everyone will think it was our doing even if it wasn't," Ilias finished.

Tremaine stared at him. She could recognize that brand of logic anywhere. "You've been talking to Nicholas."

"Yes," Ilias answered warily. "How did you know?"

"It was a lucky guess." She rolled her eyes in irritation, whether at herself, Ilias or Nicholas she wasn't sure, pushed her chair back and left the kitchen.

The service corridor was dark and Tremaine blundered through a couple of traditional baize servants' doors and ended up in the salon. Nicholas was sitting in one of the armchairs, reading the Capistown newspaper, and Calit was still playing with the wooden animals on the hearth rug. Before she could form an ironic observation on the domesticity of this scene, Nicholas said dryly, "You should be more careful."

"What?" Tremaine said, startled. She realized a moment too late she should have said "Undoubtedly" and walked out of the room. Whatever he had to say, it wasn't going to do her any good.

"As civilized as the Syprians' behavior is, you have to remember that their society is run on different principles than ours." Nicholas turned a page of the paper, rustling it into a better position. "If Ilias continues to see Ander as a threat to his relationship with you, he may act to remove the threat. And he may not feel the need to announce his intention first."

Tremaine snorted. She thought this was wishful thinking on Nicholas's part. "Ilias isn't in love with me."

He lifted a brow, not looking up from the paper. "As I said, their society is run on different principles than ours."

Tremaine flung her arms in the air, aware she wanted to argue but having nothing rational to say. She stomped out into the cold hallway, feeling about twelve years old and angry at herself for it. The clunky ring of the front door's bellpull stopped her.

Picking up a rickety chair near the door to the parlor, she dragged it over so she could stand on it and peek through the dusty fanlight. In the dim illumination of the streetlamp, she saw it was Florian and Gerard.

She hopped down and shot back the door's bolt, pulling it open. "Ah," Gerard said in relief as he saw her. "So this is the right place."

"Who else would live here?" As she stepped back to let them in, Nicholas appeared in the doorway to the salon, demanding, "Did you look to see who it was first?"

"Yes," Tremaine snarled. *God, does he think I'm that stupid?* "Somehow I failed to let Gardier spies with guns into Coldcourt the entire time you were gone."

Nicholas narrowed his eyes at her and vanished back into the salon.

"I see everything is as usual. Everyone here?" Gerard said briskly, helping Florian off with her coat. Florian, not having had a worthless meeting to attend, was dressed comfortably in canvas pants and a faded brown sweater, her red hair tucked up under a man's cap.

"Yes. Oh, and Ander's here," Tremaine added. She saw that Gerard had a leather bag over his shoulder that had been hidden by his coat. The sphere, Arisilde's sphere.

"I see." Gerard pressed his lips together briefly, then shook his head. "Well, I suppose it can't hurt."

"Colonel Averi is the only other one who knows about this, isn't he?" Florian asked, looking around the foyer with a distracted expression. "The house is . . . Uh . . ."

"Ugly, and it smells bad," Tremaine supplied, taking the wet coats from Gerard and draping them over the battered hall bench. "It's also violently haunted, though apparently Giliead's monumental bad temper scared whatever it was into temporary submission."

"Niles knows as well," Gerard answered Florian, ignoring the rest as they stepped into the salon.

Nicholas was moving chairs up to the round table in the other half of the room. "Any trouble?" he asked, flicking an opaque glance at Gerard.

"No, we weren't followed." Gerard answered the question that had actually been asked, setting the sphere down on the scratched surface of the table.

Nicholas nodded, looking down at the little device. It was about the size of a croquet ball, formed of copper-colored metal strips, filled with tiny wheels and gears. He reached to brush a droplet of water off the somewhat tarnished surface, and a blue light sparked deep inside the copper depths. Nicholas lifted his brows. "Does it do that often?"

Gerard watched Nicholas's face. "Yes. He often responds to people he knows."

Nicholas didn't react to the "he," at least not visibly. He regarded the sphere a moment more, then turned away. Speaking in Aelin, the language of the Gardier, he said, "Calit, go up to your room now."

The boy looked up. Calit was slowly learning a few words of Rienish and Syrnaic, with Kias and the other Syprians' help, but he couldn't understand much of either language yet. Gardier believed that learning other languages was somehow beneath them, and even if Calit overcame that, he hadn't had any formal schooling. "Can I take these things with me?"

"Of course you may take your things with you." Nicholas placed a slight emphasis on the *your*. It had also been hard to convince Calit that when they gave him anything, whether it was clothing, a toy, or even food, it was his to keep.

Tremaine watched the boy carefully gather the cards and trinkets. "How is he doing?" she asked Nicholas in Rienish.

"As well as can be expected." Nicholas watched the boy leave the room. "I'm going to have Kias take him back to the *Ravenna* tomorrow. For his own good, I don't want him to see too much of what we do here."

Though he hadn't had any noticeable problems aboard ship, in the refugee shelter Calit had persisted in sleeping under his bed. Tremaine said only, "He likes the *Ravenna*."

"He may be of some help in questioning the prisoners," Gerard put in. "The woman Balin seems to know a good deal more than she should, as a member of the Service caste. Not that she's revealed any of it voluntarily." As Ilias and Ander came in from the hallway, he told Nicholas, "Colonel Averi is beginning to think you're right about her."

"Right about what?" Tremaine took the chair next to the fire, trying to ignore the musty puff the upholstery exuded. Ilias settled on the floor at her feet, a gesture she suspected was solely for Ander's benefit.

Giliead entered, throwing a disgruntled glance at Ander. He consulted Ilias with a look. Ilias responded with an eye roll. Capistown hadn't seemed to affect Giliead's health the way it had Ilias's, but maybe that was just because he had concealed it better. And since he spent most of his time angry or simply not talking, it was harder to tell.

"That Balin is not Service caste, but an observer posted either by Command or Science," Nicholas was explaining, "Meant to evaluate the performance of those officers on the base."

"So they spy on their own people?" Florian took a seat on a footstool near the hearth, folding her arms and huddling into her sweater for warmth. "That makes sense, considering what else we've heard. But she doesn't have one of those little crystals?" A tiny crystal fragment implanted in someone's body could allow the Gardier to temporarily take control of that person's mind, without his or her knowledge. It was nearly impossible to detect, as they had discovered on the voyage here.

"No, none of our prisoners were Liaisons, either voluntary or involuntary ones." Gerard looked around the room, gathering everyone's attention. He spoke in Syrnaic, since there was no one here who couldn't understand it. It also meant their conversation was private, whether it was overheard or not, since as far as they knew the Gardier couldn't translate the Syprians' language. "There are various plans for freeing Lodun, most of them involving landing troops, either by sea or by using a world-gate. But I feel we can use a world-gate to still greater advantage."

"You want to use one to go from the staging world to Lodun, to inside the barrier?" Ander asked, frowning. "I thought Command decided that wasn't feasible."

Gerard frowned back. "It isn't feasible with the mobile circle, the one the *Ravenna* and the Gardier airships use. But I think more can be done with the circle symbols." He glanced at the sphere, sitting quiescent on the table. "We need to find out more about the inner workings of the spheres and the circles. To do that, I feel we need to find out what happened to Arisilde, how he became trapped inside this sphere. We know Arisilde left Nicholas on the Isle of Storms, intending to return to carry the word that the Gardier were preparing a massive assault."

Tremaine grimaced. Nicholas had told them he and Arisilde had stolen the gate spell from Gardier agents in this world and used it to follow them to the staging world, the world the Syprians came from. The first time they had tried it they had ended up in the ocean, with the Isle of Storms distant on the horizon, much the way she and Gerard had. Arisilde had been able to sense the etheric activity around the island so they had returned to Ile-Rien and obtained a small sailboat for their next trip. With it they had managed to reach the island. They encountered the Gardier, who were scouting with the intention of turning the old abandoned city there into one of their bases of operations against Ile-Rien. Nicholas had decided to infiltrate the Gardier, talking his way into joining them.

"If we had gotten that word, if we had had Arisilde's knowledge of the world-gate spell from the beginning . . . I think we can assume that the course of events would have unfolded in a very different fashion." Gerard cleared his throat and continued more briskly, "We also know that Arisilde had resolved to discover the origin of the Gardier gate spell. He believed, even before Nicholas had discovered the . . . acquisitive nature of the Gardier's explorations, that the spell had been created by someone else."

"He said the gate spell had a different flavor," Nicholas contributed, leaning against the mantel and watching with opaque eyes. "He said that it had a weight and an elegance of design that gave the impression of a different mind than the one who had created the crystal he accidentally destroyed." Years ago, before he had disappeared from Ile-Rien, Nicholas had discovered Gardier agents and stolen the gate spell and a crystal avatar, though he had had no idea at the time that he was dealing with anything other than a criminal organization of sorcerers. Arisilde had killed the avatar, but discovered his sphere could substitute for it and make the spell work.

"He destroyed it accidentally?" Giliead asked quietly. It was the first time since arriving in Capistown that he had revealed any interest in their situation, and Tremaine found herself staring blankly at him, along with Florian and Gerard.

Nicholas shifted to face him, explaining, "He was horrified at finding a living mind inside it. I think he meant to release it but didn't stop to consider the consequences." He shrugged slightly. "I suspect if he had stopped to consider, he would have done the same."

Tremaine could believe that. They knew now the living minds imprisoned in the crystal were captured sorcerers, Rienish, Aderassi, Maiutan and whatever others the Gardier had managed to seize.

"That aside," Gerard interposed, "I think—I hope—that if we can discover how Arisilde's consciousness was transferred into the sphere, it will contribute another piece of the puzzle. To that end, we're going to attempt to directly contact Arisilde."

"You can't just ask him?" Ilias wanted to know. Tremaine was glad he had asked, since she was thinking the same thing.

"I tried that," Gerard admitted. "Without result. But his attempts to communicate have all been through etheric means. He allowed Giliead to see the etheric traces of his spells, he spoke to Tremaine in a dream, and before that he conveyed to her some details of events that had occurred to Ilias and Giliead in the Syprian's world, implying that he had contact at some point with the Syprian god of Cineth."

Tremaine saw Ander frowning thoughtfully and grimaced, glad no one knew the outcome of Arisilde's empathic communications to her at Coldcourt. She had been unaware of them, but they had fed her own melancholy and depression to the point of suicide. If she hadn't been such a lousy planner, she would have done away with herself long before Gerard had come to ask her for the sphere for the Viller Institute's experiment.

"So we're going to try a method commonly used to speak to etheric beings," Gerard finished, adjusting his spectacles and clearing his throat.

Ilias twisted around to look up at Tremaine, brows lifted inquiringly. She didn't get it either, but before she could ask, Florian said tentatively, "A séance?"

Gerard frowned at her. Apparently he had hoped to get through this without anyone using that word. "I wouldn't describe it as that, though the underlying principle is the same."

Ander snorted and said dubiously, "Using spiritualism? Isn't that a little . . . odd?" Contacting the dead through spiritualism had most often been used in Ile-Rien as either a confidence game or a pastime of people who should know better.

Gerard eyed Ander in a way that should have dropped him dead on the spot. Remembering what kind of day Gerard had had, Tremaine interposed in Rienish, "My uncle lives in a metal croquet ball and I'm married to a man from another world—maybe you should consider redefining 'odd.' "

Ander took the point with a wry smile and Gerard managed to take a calming breath. Florian said hastily, "Don't we need a medium? How does that work?"

"A medium isn't necessary," Gerard said with some asperity. "We have here the people whom Arisilde was closest to."

While Gerard set up a few precautionary wards, Tremaine borrowed a couple of table knives from the pantry and demonstrated table rocking and other tricks of the spiritualism trade. Nicholas was pacing with his hands in his pockets, watching with an imperturbable expression. She supposed he would correct her if she got anything wrong. Crouching to watch how she was making the table move, Ilias said, "So . . . no one just looks under there?"

"It's misdirection," Florian tried to explain. "They think they have looked under the table."

"But they look at the wrong time," Tremaine added, though her mind wasn't really on it. Her palms were sweating, though she wasn't sure why she should be nervous. *What are you afraid Arisilde will say?* She remembered Colonel Averi's not-so-subtle suggestion that Arisilde might be dangerous, that he might have gone mad inside the sphere. She didn't believe that. *But maybe I don't want to be proved wrong.*

Gerard came back into the room, carried the sphere to the table and carefully set it down again. "Very well. The wards I've placed around the house should prevent any outside influences from intruding. This doesn't include the etheric entities that are currently inhabiting the place, but they should be easy to discourage."

Tremaine put the knives on a side table and rather self-consciously took her seat. Nicholas took the chair opposite her and Gerard gestured Florian to the other seat, saying, "We need at least four people to make the circle."

Tremaine noticed he wasn't inviting Ander. She almost expected Ander to make an arch comment but he just said, "So the holding-hands part isn't just stage dressing?"

"Holding hands is not necessary," Gerard said repressively, taking his seat. "You could make yourself useful and turn out the lights."

Ander dutifully pressed the wall switch and the room was left in the flicker of firelit darkness. "Put your hands flat on the table and focus your thoughts on Arisilde," Gerard instructed.

They sat in silence for a time. Tremaine slumped in her chair, stifling a yawn. Ilias, Giliead and Ander were standing a few feet behind her so she couldn't see them, and it was a little too dark to make faces at Florian. Then the fire went out with a faint whoosh, as if someone had thrown a blanket over it. Tremaine flinched and shivered at a sudden cold draft of air, noticeable even in the none-too-warm atmosphere of the parlor. *That was definitely something,* she thought, a little unsettled. "Everyone all right?" Gerard asked sharply.

There was a general murmur of agreement. "I didn't see anything when it happened," Giliead put in, sounding intrigued, "so it wasn't one of the shades."

"Good," Gerard muttered.

Tremaine heard a chair creak and someone shift impatiently, someone else take a sharp breath. Time stretched and she was about to ask how much longer they had to wait when Giliead made a startled exclamation. "What is it?" Gerard demanded.

"Something just brushed past me," Giliead answered, sounding wary. Tremaine could sense him moving behind her, trying to find whatever it was, though he stepped so quietly he didn't even make the floorboards creak.

"Turn on the lights," Nicholas ordered suddenly.

Tremaine blinked at the sudden glare of electric light. She heard a startled curse from Gerard, and Nicholas said, "Tremaine, don't move."

"What?" She looked down at her hands. Her jaw dropped. "Oh . . ."

The table was covered with writing scrawled in black, spiraling out from the sphere in the center and crossing her hands where they still lay flat, crossing Nicholas's hands. It had just missed Florian and Gerard. Ilias was at her side suddenly, tense with alarm, asking, "Does it hurt?"

"No." Her breath misted and she realized the room was still icy cold. "I didn't feel it at all."

Ilias looked at Giliead, who stood back from the table, his expression fascinated as he watched something invisible drifting through the air. He said, "I didn't see it when it happened, but I can see it now; the whole room is filled with curses."

Florian pushed back from the table, fumbling a pair of aetherglasses out of her pocket and putting them on as Gerard shoved to his feet. "There's ether everywhere."

Gerard circled the table, his expression rapt. "Those are the same symbols as on the circle— No, no, they're similar, but different."

"This isn't ink." Nicholas leaned down to peer at the table's surface, the writing scrawled across his own hands. "It's soot from the fireplace."

Gerard was already digging a pen and a battered notebook out of his coat pocket to copy the symbols. "It would be better if we had a photographic record. I don't suppose there's a camera in the house—"

"Giaren has one, he gave me some photos today," Tremaine said, leaning down to study the marks scrawled across her hands. There was a sweeping curve on the back of her right hand, part of a circular symbol that had something like a curlicue on the top. On her left hand was half of a pair of lopsided triangles. Nicholas was right, the broad strokes had been drawn with a finger, dipped in soot from the hearth. "Do we have a telephone?"

"Yes, but careful what you say. This isn't something that could be trusted to an exchange. In fact, I'll—" Nicholas looked around in annoyance, realizing he couldn't move without disturbing the delicate writing. "Damn it."

Tremaine controlled a snarl, instead commenting to Ilias, "Yes, I was planning on confiding the entire episode to the operator while she was making the connection."

"I'll telephone," Florian said hastily, getting to her feet, "I'll just tell him to come here, I won't say why. Where is it?"

As she hurried to place the call, Gerard started on Tremaine's side first, copying enough of the design to allow her to leave the table. Standing up, she was able to see the roughly circular pattern of the markings. That, taken with the similarity in the symbols Gerard had noticed, meant only one thing. "So this is another spell circle." She lifted her brows at Gerard. "Maybe he heard you, about wanting a circle that could take us from the staging world to Lodun safely."

Gerard glanced up, straightening his spectacles. "I don't know. But the original spell circle opens etheric gateways between worlds. This one . . . might open something else."

Chapter 3

Several hours later, Tremaine sat in one of the spindly chairs at the door to the second-floor ballroom, yawning profusely. She had finally been able to wash her hands once Giaren had arrived with the camera and careful photographs had been take to supplement Gerard's notes. The Syprians had all retreated out of the room as the first flashbulb popped; despite the explanation, she didn't think they quite understood what the camera was doing. She remembered she hadn't shown them the photographs from the *Ravenna* yet; that might be an interesting experience.

After that, while Gerard and Florian studied the symbols and Giaren turned the pantry into a temporary darkroom, she and the others had worked at sweeping and scrubbing the ballroom floor to get it ready for the circle's inscription. It was a big room, suffering from water leaks down through the walls and rather horribly lit with pink crystal sconces. The ceiling was coffered and figured with plaster and the pink-and-cream flowered wallpaper was coming off the mildewed walls in long shroudlike strips, making the room look as if it had a skin disease. The once-fine parquet floor had been cleaned about as well as any of the others in the house to prepare it for sale, but for the glyphs to be properly inscribed the old coats of wax had had to be removed. Tremaine tiredly pushed her hair out of her eyes, wondering if she could get the large kitchen range to heat water for coffee again without setting anything on fire. It would probably be easier to use the hearth in the salon.

Gerard was now crouched on the floor, carefully painting in the chalk-marked symbols with Florian's help, being observed by Ilias, Ander, Giliead and Giaren. Kias hadn't objected to the magic but didn't want to be a part of it or witness to it; he was downstairs, tending the fire in the salon and dozing. *Coffee,* she reminded herself, getting wearily to her feet.

As she went down the stairs, she heard Nicholas in one of the rooms off the hall, and paused long enough to ascertain that he was talking to Niles on the telephone. Again. Niles, who had to remain on the *Ravenna* with his sphere so the ship could world-gate if there was an attack, had been telephoning using the ship-to-shore line every half hour. He was attempting to supply Gerard with all the assistance that Gerard didn't require and giving the impression that he felt they were all having fun without him.

In the hallway she heard a hesitant knock at the door. It was the middle of the night. *And we aren't expecting anyone,* she thought grimly. *Fantastic.* As she dragged a chair back to the door, she heard Nicholas hanging up on Niles. Taking a cautious peek through the fanlight, she stared at the two people standing on the stoop, visible in the light from the street lamp. Recognizing them, she grimaced in resignation.

She turned to find Nicholas and Kias in the hall, Kias with his sword drawn. "It's Cletia and Cimarus," she reported.

Kias muttered something inaudible, sheathed his sword and retreated down the hall. Tremaine jumped down, setting the chair aside. "Kias," she asked sharply, "how did they know where we were?"

"I told Gyan," he admitted from the doorway to the salon.

Nicholas regarded him sourly. Tremaine pinched the bridge of her nose, thinking, *Gyan must be out of his mind.* She told Kias, "Why don't you go up and tell Giliead they're here."

Kias winced but headed for the stairs. Resigned, Tremaine drew the bolt and opened the door.

Both Syprians were standing back from the threshold as if they expected something unpleasant to leap out at them. They were sister and brother, and Pasima's cousins. Cletia was slight and had a deceptively delicate appearance, with long blond curls that fell past her shoulders. Cimarus was tall and dark-haired, with long braids neatly tied back, and had some resemblance to Pasima in the handsome cast of his features. Water dripped off their hair and the dark-colored wool wraps they wore over the more colorful fabric and leather of their Syprian clothes. Tremaine sighed. "Well, come in."

They stepped into the hall cautiously and Tremaine shut the door on the rainy night. She saw they both had their swords tucked under their wraps, which didn't surprise her, but as Cletia let the wet wool slip off her shoulder she saw the other woman also had the leather packs and bags they carried their belongings in. *They came to stay?* she wondered, startled. She had thought they had just come to argue.

Giliead came down the stairs, his face set and angry. "What do you want?" he said, not sounding as if he was particularly interested in the answer. Ilias trailed behind him, watching the two visitors with suspicion.

Cimarus looked up, shaking his hair back, and Tremaine saw his cheeks were red from embarrassment. "We quarreled with Pasima."

Giliead hesitated. That obviously wasn't the answer he had expected. But he said, "And why should we care?"

"We quarreled over you, you arrogant ass," Cletia snapped.

Silence stretched. Giliead glanced down at Ilias, who shook his head slightly in response, as if he wasn't sure whether to believe them or not. Giliead advanced another few steps down the stairs. "Did she tell you to leave?"

"No. We left on our own," Cletia answered. She looked at Tremaine pointedly and, with the air of someone performing an unpleasant but necessary duty, said, "It's our right to ask for lodging at another Andrien household."

So much for staying out of the middle. Tremaine looked at Ilias, lifting her brows, though she knew Cletia wouldn't lie when there were others present to contradict her. He gave her a reluctant nod. "Oh, good." She looked at Nicholas. "Well, do we have the room?"

He eyed the two newcomers thoughtfully. Cletia weathered his gaze but Cimarus shifted uneasily. In Rienish, he asked Tremaine, "I assume they can be trusted?"

"They won't betray us to the Gardier," she replied in the same language. Unlike the others, Cletia and Cimarus never made attempts to speak Rienish, though she suspected they knew enough to understand most conversations. Nicholas almost certainly knew that too, and his question had been more of a warning to them than anything else. *But I don't want them here.* She let out her breath and rubbed her eyes. "But they'll fight with the others and argue about everything."

"Ah. Then I should feel quite at home," Nicholas said pleasantly, and with that left the hall.

Tremaine stared after him, feeling her face heat. She took a deep calming breath. *I don't want him here either. In fact, I think I'm going to go to the mountains, find a cave and become a hermit. No relatives allowed.* "Kias, why don't you show them to a room." She turned to a frowning Cletia, saying brightly, "By the way, the attic is haunted, and Gerard is about to do a curse in the ballroom. I'll be in the kitchen."

Tremaine found the coffee beans in a cabinet and a grinder, and proceeded to take her frustration out in manual labor. Ilias appeared after a short time, boosting himself up to sit on the sideboard next to where she was working. He watched her for a moment, then picked up one of the beans, sniffing it thoughtfully. "And how are they settling in?" she asked him.

He shrugged, apparently indifferent. "I don't know." He bit into the bean, winced and spit it out.

Giliead wandered in at that point and leaned on the sideboard, watching Tremaine. After a moment of stiff silence, he said, "We owe them hospitality. There's nothing I can do about that." There was a definite chill in the air. Tremaine felt the urge to intervene and managed to squash it, pretending to give the awkward coffee grinder her full attention. She knew both men well enough by now to realize that they would either get over it immediately or have a fistfight and then get over it immediately.

Ilias gave him a sharp stare. "Did I say there was?"

Giliead glared back. "No." He appeared to wrestle with himself for a long moment, then admitted, "When we go back, it might help with the council if they're honest about what happened. It would make it easier on Mother and Halian. And you."

Ilias rubbed his face, looking as if his annoyance was suddenly spent and he was just tired again. "Will that help you?"

Giliead seemed surprised, as if that thought hadn't occurred to him. "I don't see how it could," he said honestly.

Ilias swore, hopped off the sideboard and walked out, banging the door on his way. Giliead watched him go, his face troubled, and Tremaine grimaced in sympathy. "Is it really going to be that bad?" she asked, giving up on the coffee grinder.

He leaned against the sideboard, taking a deep breath. "It will either be that bad, or it will be nothing. It's impossible to tell until we get there." He looked down at her, smiling ruefully. "If the waiting doesn't kill us first."

Tremaine nodded. "Waiting is what makes me . . . crazy." The beings the Syprians called gods didn't have many rules, as far as she could tell. They didn't make moral judgments or hand down pronouncements; they didn't answer questions, except those posed by the Chosen Vessels relating to magic or sorcerers. Their presence in a cave or a hollow tree would drive off the most dangerous of the etheric entities the Syprians were troubled by and seemed to lessen the effect of inimical spells. They didn't seem to attack sorcerers directly but in the few historical cases that Giliead had spoken of where sorcerers had ventured to attack a god, the sorcerers had reputedly not fared well.

Gerard's theory, which Giliead was coming around to, was that the gods only objected to hostile spells. That that was why Giliead had found it difficult at first to see wards and other protective Rienish spells; the god ignored those and so Giliead had never learned how to spot them. And the god must have communicated with Arisilde at some point, before he had gotten into whatever situation it was that had led to his being trapped in the sphere.

Tremaine had pointed it out before, but she felt obliged to say again, "But the god didn't object to Gerard or Florian, and it acted sort of friendly to Arisilde in the sphere. And it didn't interfere with any of the spells they cast in Cineth. So maybe . . ."

"Maybe," Giliead agreed quietly.

Tremaine could tell he was humoring her now. "But Gerard's not a Chosen Vessel. I know, I know," she snapped. She seized the recalcitrant coffee grinder again. "You two just be pessimists; I'm going to be an optimist from now on."

Giliead actually snorted in amusement. "That will be a change." He took the coffee grinder away from her. "What are you trying to do with this thing?"

Giliead was much better at making the coffee than Tremaine, once she had explained the principle. This did not help her mood any.

There wasn't much else to do after that than sit around and watch Gerard work on the spell circle. A dusty sofa and a couple of chairs hauled in from another room made the waiting a little more comfortable.

Tremaine had taken a seat there with Ilias sprawled next to her. Florian was still sitting cross-legged on the floor near the developing circle, taking notes for Gerard, though she looked more than half-asleep. Giliead sat on the floor, watching thoughtfully, and Ander was pacing. Giaren had finished developing the photos and had taken over Nicholas's task of talking to Niles on the telephone, leaving Nicholas free to stalk the upstairs hall in what was probably an unconsciously sinister manner. Cletia and Cimarus had retired to elsewhere in the house, and Kias was supposed to be keeping an eye on them and on Calit, who was asleep.

Ilias was dozing on Tremaine's shoulder, though this was probably the most uncomfortable place in the house to sleep. Dust floated in the air from all the floor cleaning and the room was still uncomfortably cold and damp. But Ilias was very warm against her side and Tremaine was on the verge of drifting off herself, when Gerard got to his feet with a grunt of effort. She sat forward, waking Ilias with an elbow. "Is it done?" she demanded.

"Yes." Gerard massaged his lower back with a grimace. He glanced up, saw everyone watching him expectantly and sighed. "I can tell it's meant to take us to the Syprians' world, but I have no idea where. It's not like the circles we've used before, that can only take us to our current location in the next world over. It has many of the same characteristics of the original spell circle, though many of the key figures and glyphs are different." He bent down again to collect his scattered notes.

"But we know Arisilde wanted us to go there," Tremaine pointed out, getting to her feet. She went to the edge of the circle, standing next to Florian. It didn't look much different from the other circle to her, but then she didn't know the symbols well enough to recognize most of them, or even to know if they were in the right order. Ilias had followed her, pacing along the edge of the circle thoughtfully. Giliead came over to sit on his heels near the edge, examining the symbols. Tremaine noted nobody touched it, or stepped inside, though it would take the sphere to make it work.

"But we don't know why," Florian put in around a yawn. "It might be because there's something incredibly dangerous there that he wants us to know about."

Nicholas stepped up behind Giliead, his hands in his pockets. "I don't think the danger or lack of it is worth debating; it's obviously something he felt it was vital for us to know."

Tremaine bit her lip, considering it. She glanced at Giliead. "What does it feel like to you? I mean, does it seem any different from the other spell circles?"

She thought an instant later that that might not be the most politic question in the world, especially coming from her. She was the one who had talked Giliead into using his ability to speak to their captured Gardier crystal, leading to his working an actual spell with its help. But he just frowned in a preoccupied way, holding out a hand above the carefully written symbols. "I can tell it has power, that it's . . . waiting for something. But that's how the others feel." He shook his head. "It's a little different, but every one I've seen has been a little different; they never feel identical."

Florian was nodding, looking a little more alert. "That makes sense. I bet the circle on the *Ravenna* changes as the ship moves. That it would feel different to you here in Capistown harbor than it did when we looked at it on the voyage here, in your world."

"Right." Tremaine folded her arms. "So we need to test it." They all knew testing it meant using it, sending someone through. The Viller Institute had tried the first circle a few times before successfully making it work. Of course, it had been the badly constructed spheres that had killed the sorcerers involved, not the circle itself. Though somehow she didn't find that very comforting at the moment.

"Those experiments were a little expensive, if you recall," Ander pointed out, his expression dry.

"Yes, Ander, oddly enough I do recall Riardin's dying before my eyes as his sphere destroyed itself in an etheric explosion," Gerard said, still looking distractedly around for his scattered notes. "Nevertheless, I'll be making the experiment myself."

"I'm not sure that's wise," Nicholas said, watching him with a trace of concern. "If Arisilde was trying to show us how he became trapped in the sphere, and this circle has something to do with that—"

"Oh, hell." Tremaine stared at Gerard, horrified. She hadn't thought of that. "You shouldn't go, Gerard."

Florian pushed to her feet, alarmed. "She's right, Gerard. There's dangerous and there's . . . *dangerous.*"

"I'll go," Ilias said suddenly.

"No, you won't," Tremaine said, startled, at the same time as Giliead, sounding aghast, said, "What?"

Ander stepped forward, as if no one had spoken. "I'm obviously the one to go."

"Why?" Ilias demanded, turning to glare at him. "I've done it more than you have."

Ander rounded on him impatiently. "You don't understand the spell. You don't have any idea what happens when—"

Ilias snorted derisively. "And you do?" He flung an arm in the air. "Explain it to us, then."

Not sure which one of them she wanted to argue with, Tremaine pointed out, "Hey, I've done it more than both of you put together—"

"Children, quiet," Nicholas snapped. In the sudden startled silence he lifted a brow in ironic comment, and added, "Let's listen to Gerard, shall we?"

Gerard gazed at the ceiling as if asking it for patience. "I'm going because I'm the sorcerer and it would rather help to be able to return."

"But I could—" Florian began.

"No." Gerard told her, pausing to look at her over his spectacles. Florian could use a sphere to make a circle work, but her results hadn't always been ideal. "I appreciate the offer, but no."

As Florian subsided reluctantly, Ander put in, "Of course, but you'll need someone to—"

Gerard interrupted, "And I accept Ilias's offer to accompany me."

"And me," Tremaine added, alarmed that she might actually be left out. It wasn't fair. Going through strange circles was one of her few accomplishments.

"No." Gerard told her. "I want to keep the first expedition to a minimum."

First expedition? Now Gerard was being a rampant optimist, to assume there would be a second. "But I always go. It's . . . lucky," Tremaine finished self-consciously as everyone stared at her.

"Not this time," Gerard said firmly.

Now that the decision was made, Ilias was impatient to get it over with. "Shouldn't you take some more time?" Florian asked, looking over to where Gerard stood near the circle. The wizard was still going through his papers but he had put on his coat, apparently the only precaution he was going to take. The other men were waiting with him, except for Giaren, who was still using the talking curse box to speak to Niles. Florian turned a little hopelessly to Ilias. "To make more preparations?"

"Like what?" Ilias slung his baldric over his shoulder and checked the set of his sword in the scabbard. He knew from what Gerard had said, and his own past experience, that either all would go well and they would quickly return, or it would go badly immediately.

Tremaine folded her arms, pacing impatiently. She had been running her hands through her hair, disordering it as if she had just gotten out of bed—which made him want to be in bed with her right now. "This is going to drive me crazy," she said, sounding more angry than anything else.

"Now you know how we felt when you made that first experiment with Gerard," Florian told her sharply.

Tremaine was unimpressed. "Yes, that's why I always go. Then I don't have to feel this way."

Giliead had been standing at Ilias's elbow, radiating increasing impatience. Finally, he said, "I need to talk to you."

"I don't— Hey!" Giliead seized his arm and hauled him into the cold hall, then through the first open door to one of the empty bedchambers. Ilias banged into the door and grabbed it, planting his feet to halt himself. "What?" he demanded, jerking his arm free.

Giliead planted his hands on his hips, glaring at him. "You don't know where this thing will take you. Think what happened last time—"

"Either the sphere has a god in it or it doesn't. And either we trust it or we don't," Ilias said, his voice flat with irritation. "If you've got another choice, I'd like to hear it."

Giliead grimaced. "Why are you doing this?"

Ilias took a deep breath, trying to actually answer the question and ignore the peremptory tone. "If I don't do something, I'll go crazy. The only thing useful I've been able to do in days is help clean a floor." He shook his head in frustration, shrugging. "Besides, he can't go alone. If that thing takes us to the middle of a Gardier outpost—"

Giliead gestured in annoyance. "Have you not noticed that he is a wizard? He can take care of himself."

Ilias stared at him, then said through gritted teeth, "So I'm useless. I'm still going."

"Hey, that's not what I—" Ilias cut him off by slamming out of the room, managing to bang Giliead with the door in the process.

He stamped down the hall and back to the ballroom, where everyone was gathered. Gerard was standing inside the curse circle now, the god-sphere tucked under his arm, still reading the sheaf of paper in his other hand.

"Hey." Tremaine caught Ilias's baldric as he passed her, forcing him to stop or strangle himself. She was frowning but instead of speaking she pulled herself forward and kissed him. The kiss deepened until their teeth scraped, then she released him. She still said nothing, but at the moment she didn't need to. He knew Pasima was right, that he couldn't live in Tremaine's world, and what was between them had been born out of expediency. He could admit to himself he still didn't know what it was they had together. And now he had to go off and hopefully not get killed.

He went to stand next to Gerard in the circle, conscious of everyone's eyes on him. Giliead had followed him into the ballroom and stood next to Tremaine now, arms folded, watching him worriedly.

Gerard glanced up, folding the paper and tucking it carefully inside his coat. He said, "Ready?" He looked as if he just wanted to get it over with. Ilias felt the same. He nodded tightly.

Nicholas said in Rienish, "Good luck, gentlemen."

Ilias was braced to fall into water. Every time he had been through the world-changing curse, it had been over water. Sometimes very cold water. The sphere sparked blue and spun, and the room vanished. His stomach lurched from a sudden drop and he felt the floor fall away under him. An instant later he landed on hard stone, staggering to keep his balance and stay on his feet.

Heart pounding, Ilias looked around wildly, reaching for his sword hilt. They were outside, in gray daylight, under the partial shelter of a soaringly high rocky overhang. Nothing moved nearby except Gerard, shakily getting to his feet a few paces away.

Ascertaining that they weren't dead and weren't about to be leapt on by anything, Ilias took a deep breath and actually looked at the place.

The ledge they stood on extended some fifty paces beyond the shelter of the giant overhang, ending in a jagged cliff. Beyond it was a sweeping view of a cloudy morning sky and the wall of a canyon. A dark green band of forest topped the buttressed cliffs directly across the gorge and clumps of greenery clung in pockets up and down the rock, all wreathed in drifts of mist. The air was fresh and cold and the roar of falling water echoed off the rock. Ilias moved forward, far enough to peer over the edge, and saw there was a broad river several ship's lengths below. Further away, a cluster of toweringly high falls at the end of the canyon fed it, the water plunging dramatically in cascades of spray. Despite the cloud-streaked sky, it was a beautiful sight, the dark green against the gray of the rock, the whitecapped rush of the water.

Behind him, Gerard swore softly in awe. Ilias glanced back at him and saw the wizard wasn't reacting to the view. He turned to look.

The gray-veined walls of the overhang were carved with square columns, narrowing as they arched up to gather in a domed circle on the rock high overhead. The floor had been smoothed by human hands and etched with strange symbols— Ilias skipped back away from the markings on the stone, realizing they were from the world-changing curse and formed a large circle.

"It's all right," Gerard said, though he sounded a little over-whelmed. He was looking around at the symbols, the sphere tucked under one arm. "It won't—shouldn't hurt to touch them."

Ilias let his breath out, nodding. He looked around at the overhang again, following the line of columns. "Look, it's broken off." The right-hand wall was missing a last column entirely and the other had only the jagged remnants of one. "The end of the chamber is sheared off." He carefully stepped over the curse circle and crossed the distance to the end of the ledge to look directly down, stepping cautiously as he drew near the edge in case it crumbled. He sat on his heels, leaning out to see the gray-green surface of the river below.

"My God, yes," Gerard said, following him. "If these columns were evenly proportioned, there was at least another section of about this size extending out over the water."

"Maybe more than that." Ilias could see huge chunks of stone thrust up out of the water all along the rocky bank so far below, each creating whitecapped waves and eddies as the water rushed past. If that amount had fallen on the bank, no telling how much littered the deeper water toward the center.

A flock of birds flew by, white with long thin bodies and large grace-ful wings. Ilias stood and backed away from the edge. The cold was making the scars on his back ache, but at least it was clean air, fresh as the morning of the world. "Do you know where we are?"

Gerard shook his head. "I have no idea. I know we're somewhere in your world, but that's all I can say."

"It looks a little like the Wall Port, like the same people built it," Ilias pointed out, then found himself unable to say exactly why he felt that way. As Gerard stared at him expectantly, he gestured helplessly. "The way it's so big. Or something. I don't know."

But Gerard frowned, looking over the chamber. "Perhaps you're right. But this is clearly a spell circle and these symbols match the new ones Arisilde gave us. Though I don't see any specific spot for the antagonist—the sphere or crystal—that controls it."

Ilias headed toward the back wall, slowing his steps to let his eyes adjust to the shadows. The stone was darker back here as well, making it harder to see the carvings. Gerard stopped, tracing a band of faded figures with his fingertips. Following the curve of the wall, Ilias felt the faint rush of air from the doorway before he saw it. Closer, and he could see the narrow opening, set between two of the pillars. He paused in it, squinting to see. It was carved back into the cliff, and dim daylight filtered down through cracks in the rock, illuminating a wide passage with more rooms opening off it.

"It doesn't appear to have been recently occupied," Gerard observed, stepping to his side.

Ilias took a deep breath, tasting the breeze. The air held stone dust, moss, water, bird droppings, with no scent of human presence, at least not nearby. "Not this part of it, anyway." He glanced at Gerard; he knew they had found something important. "The people who lived here, they made the world-changing curse."

Gerard nodded grimly. "Yes, that spell circle carved into the rock is at least as old as the rest of this place."

Ilias moved down the passage to the first door, taking a cautious look inside. It was a big room, dimly lit by an old crack in the high rocky ceiling, roughly squared off, with a circle of low stone blocks in the center. The circle was about the right size for a fire pit. Ilias stepped inside, but it was too dark to make out old burn marks on the stone or soot stains on the rock above it. This might have been a room for living in, though there wasn't a stick of furniture or scrap of cloth left to prove it. There were carvings on the walls, in parallel bands, and half columns carved out to make it look as if they were supporting the rock overhead.

He went back out to the passage. Gerard had made a light, a little floating ball of yellow-tinged illumination, drifting along after him as he investigated a room across the way. Ilias had to shake his head, thinking of how a little wizard light like that would frighten people back in Cineth. He snorted to himself. That was the least of their problems. Gerard glanced up, asking, "Find anything?"

"Just another empty room." This one was bigger and lacked the fire pit, and had an opening into the next empty chamber. Like the other, it was clean except for drifts of dust and blown leaves.

Gerard frowned thoughtfully, running a hand through his hair as he looked around. "We'll have to come back when it's evening here. If those clouds abate, we can get a look at the stars and have a better idea where we are in your world." He stepped back out into the passage, the wizard light bobbing along after him. He stood there a moment, looking down the shadowy corridor. "Unless we can find more writing, or more significant carving, back there. . . ."

Ilias drew breath to suggest they explore it now, then thought of how Tremaine and Giliead would feel, waiting and worrying. "We should get back, tell the others what we found. And that we're not dead."

"Yes. Yes, of course." Reluctantly, Gerard moved back toward the main chamber. As they came out into the wan daylight, he made the wizard light vanish with a distracted wave of his hand. "We'll need to come back with a larger group, and—"

"Wait, wait. I saw something." Ilias crossed to the side wall, studying the half column there intently. "Something flashed in the light, like metal."

"Where?" Gerard demanded, hastily following him over.

It was too dark in the corner formed by the column to see it, whatever it was. Wary of curse traps, Ilias didn't want to feel around for it. He stepped back, motioning to Gerard. "Make the light again."

Gerard made a preoccupied gesture and the light sprang into existence above his head, banishing the shadows from the dark corner. Ilias spotted it immediately, pointing. "There."

Gerard stepped close, squinting, lifting the glass pieces over his eyes to peer at it. "Good God," he whispered, startled.

It was a squiggle of what Ilias could now recognize as Rienish writing, marked on the stone with some white substance. Near it, wedged into a small crack in the carving, was a round metallic disk, like an ornament or a game counter. "What does it say?" he asked impatiently.

"It says 'The Scribe' in Rienish." Gerard sounded incredulous. "And this . . ." He scraped at the object with his thumb and managed to push it free. He turned it over on his palm and Ilias leaned to look, seeing it was of a light-colored metal incised with the delicate little figure of a flower. "Is a button."

Ilias nodded, seeing it was like those on Gerard's coat, though the design was different.

"But why back in this corner and not in a more obvious place?" Gerard said, half to himself.

Ilias jerked his head toward the opening. "Rain and dust gets blown in here and might have worn the writing away, if it was any closer to the opening. It's sheltered back here." He cautiously dabbed at one of the strokes forming the words, figuring Gerard would have warned him if it was a curse trap. A white powdery substance came away on his finger.

"Yes. Yes, that must be it. It's written with chalk. I suppose we're lucky it lasted this long." Gerard shook his head slowly. " 'The Scribe' is vaguely familiar. I think it's the title of something, a book or a play." He lifted a brow ironically. "I strongly suspect Nicholas will be able to tell us."

"Why?" Ilias demanded.

"Because this button is made of white gold, a metal that can't be used to conduct etheric activity, unlike silver. It's a sorcerer's coat button." Gerard closed his hand around it, his expression intent. "And it can only belong to one person."

Yes." Nicholas studied the button, turning it over on his palm. "Arisilde must have left it there."

Tremaine had shouldered her way in between him and Gerard to see. She picked up the button. "So he was there." It only made sense. *Why else give us the circle to go there? But what did he want us to see?* Whatever it was, it didn't seem as if Ilias and Gerard had found it.

She hadn't known just how worried she had been until both men had appeared in the circle again, no worse for wear. A gust of cool outdoor air from the other world had accompanied them, with a scatter of dead leaves that had drifted to the ballroom floor like torn paper fragments. She had seen Giliead rub his face to conceal his expression and look away, and Florian fan herself with a sheaf of notes, and knew she hadn't been the only one. The initial experiments at the Viller Institute with the spell circle had had immediately fatal consequences for the sorcerer involved, but that had been without Arisilde's help and without a correctly assembled sphere. She hadn't worried about that. *Well, not much anyway,* she admitted to herself. But there had been no telling where this circle was meant to go and what they would find waiting for them.

"How can you be certain?" Florian asked, standing on tiptoe to look over Tremaine's shoulder. She sounded a little skeptical. "I can't remember what Gerard's coat buttons look like and I'm standing right next to him."

"Because it comes from one of my old coats, the one Arisilde was wearing when I sent him back," Nicholas told her.

Tremaine nodded, remembering. "He never bought clothes. He just wore whatever he could find."

Ander lifted a brow. "He sounds like he was a little . . ." He glanced at the sphere, sitting nearby on the table, and obviously decided to choose another word. "Unique, for a sorcerer. I wish I'd met him."

Nicholas slanted him an opaque look, but Tremaine was willing to concede that compared with Gerard and Niles, Arisilde had looked like a mad ragpicker. And in his case, it wasn't for an intentional effect, as it was when Nicholas assumed that guise.

"What did the writing mean?" Ilias asked, watching Nicholas. " 'The Scribe'? It was a message to you?"

"Yes." Nicholas glanced at him. "It's the title of a painting in my collection, one of my favorites. Years ago Arisilde constructed a spell for me, using the painting to . . . keep an eye on an acquaintance of mine."

Gerard was nodding, lost in thought. "I thought it sounded familiar. But did he mean it to suggest that he was spying on someone? That he had followed someone there?"

Nicholas was staring at the coat button, his brows drawn together. "I think it may mean . . . that he felt he was being followed, or watched. By some method he couldn't discover."

Tremaine looked from Gerard to Nicholas. "Was it me?" she demanded. "Were you using the painting to spy on me?"

"What? No!" Nicholas stared at her, startled into showing honest affront. "For the love of God, Tremaine, it was years before you were born."

"Oh." Tremaine subsided, aware she was being a little overwrought. "Maybe he just wanted you to be sure it was he who left the message."

Ignoring them, Gerard continued, "Nevertheless, this is an important discovery. These new symbols, compared with the original circle, can tell us so much more about how the individual elements that make up the spell actually work. It could allow us to manipulate them, to choose our destination, so we could construct another circle that could transport us to Lodun from any point in the staging world, or even from our own world—"

Ander nodded. "It means we can get inside Lodun and get the people out, without the Gardier knowing until it's too late."

"If we can devise the right circle," Gerard added, giving Ander a repressive look. "I'll report to Colonel Averi, and I suggest the rest of you get some sleep."

Chapter 4

The next morning dawned far too soon, at least for Tremaine. It had been well past midnight when she went to bed but she woke after only a few hours, her mind retracing yesterday's events in exhausting detail. Seeing the gray line of daylight under the door didn't help.

She crawled out of the still–faintly musty bed, cursing as her bare feet touched the cold boards. Fumbling along the wall, she found the switch for the wall sconce and pushed it, blinking at the dim glow of the shaded electric light. She gathered her clothes up from the chair where she had left them but the cold was funneling right up her cotton nightgown as if it was a chimney, and she made a run back for the bed.

Ilias was lying on his stomach, arms curled around a pillow, watching her blearily. "What are you doing?"

"It's cold," she said through chattering teeth, pushing her feet under the blankets to warm them against his side. He gasped and woke up a little more. His queue was unraveling and his hair was a mass of frayed tangles and curls, spreading out over the muscles of his shoulders, the two long lines of scar tissue showing through the strands. The scars were a souvenir of Ixion, of a transformation spell that had reversed when Giliead had cut Ixion's head off. The spell was the reason Ilias had gotten the curse mark. Absently she picked up one of his smaller braids, picking it apart to redo it.

He eyed her a moment. "Are you nervous about something?"

"No," she said firmly, deciding to ignore the hint. "Why do you ask?"

"No reason." He buried his face in the pillow again. But after a moment, he asked, "We're going back to the cave with the circle today?"

We? Hah! Tremaine thought, her mouth twisting bitterly. She didn't think she was likely to be included. *And if you were, what could you do?* "They have to have a meeting about it first. Before I came up last night Gerard had telephoned Averi, who said the Capidarans want a piece of it too." She tried to keep her annoyed snarl subvocal. "I don't know how much use we're going to get out of it. We already knew the Gardier steal everything they can find and use it for their own purposes. And we already knew they must have found the spell circle somewhere else; so we found one of the places where they could have stumbled on it. In your world. Somehow."

"Yes," Ilias said dryly into the pillow. "They stumbled on it, and they thought, Here's gibberish scratched on the ground, let's pop a wizard into a piece of pretty rock and see if it takes us to another world."

Tremaine lifted her brows, giving the braid a deliberate tug. "Damn, you are a sarcastic bastard. No wonder Giliead is so intimidated by you."

Ilias turned his head just enough to regard her with one eye and an air of deeply affronted suspicion. She clarified, "Yes, I am making fun of you." She took the point, though. They did have much more to find out and the new circle and its destination were just a single piece of the puzzle. *You're being a pessimist again,* she reminded herself with asperity, *you gave that up, remember?*

She finished the braid, retying the end and reaching for the next. But he pushed himself up on his elbows, tossing the other braids out of her immediate reach. He took her hand, absently running his thumb over her bitten nails. "Why did you bring Ander here?"

"Oh God, good question." She shook her head. "Because I hate myself."

He cocked an eyebrow at her, unimpressed. Tremaine gave in and explained, "He still sees me the same way he saw me five years ago, as a silly little girl. Oh, maybe he's condescended to elevate me to plucky little girl. And I have enough problems with trying to figure out who I am." She shrugged helplessly. "I can't help wanting to give him opportunities to—I don't know, prove me wrong. Or prove himself right.

It might be nice to be the plucky little girl who is absolutely sure what's right, who doesn't have blood on her hands, who's never made decisions that got people killed."

Ilias shook his head. "Maybe he just wants something to stay the same as it used to be," he said, sounding intensely reluctant to make this concession. Then he looked up at her through the tangled fringe of his hair. "I like grown women."

Tremaine eyed him for a moment. "All right, I take back the sarcastic bastard remark," she conceded. "It was true, but I take it back."

Later, Ilias sat at the big table in the kitchen with Tremaine and Giliead. He was having trouble deciding if he was still angry at Giliead, but the food Derathi had brought that morning was rapidly improving his mood. Gerard and Florian had gone to meet with the Capidaran wizards at the port, Ander accompanying them, Giaren had gone to report to Niles, and Kias had taken Calit back to the *Ravenna*. Cletia and Cimarus hadn't made an appearance yet this morning, a situation Ilias hoped would continue. He felt he could get along fine without ever seeing them during their entire stay in the house.

The talking curse box kept ringing shrilly from the front room and Tremaine kept getting up to answer it, returning in a state of increasing annoyance. Nicholas was here somewhere, but apparently he was no longer bothering to respond to the box's incessant demands.

She returned yet again, muttering, "No, no one's here. No, that hasn't changed in the past five minutes. Yes, I do believe they are perfectly capable of placing a call once they do get back here, if they want to talk to you, which frankly, I can't imagine why they would." She dropped into a chair, rubbing her face.

Giliead winced sympathetically. Ilias picked up one of the heavy little buns filled with sweet cream, asking Tremaine, "So has anybody said when we go back yet?"

"No." She propped her chin on her hand, sounding resigned. "I'm betting it will be this afternoon when the Capidarans come. Gerard can get a look at the night sky in the other world then, if it's not cloudy." She lifted a brow ironically, turning her cup around on the table. "You can imagine how thrilled Nicholas is about the Capidarans."

Ilias nodded, lifting his brows. To say Nicholas was somewhat protective of his privacy was a vast understatement. It was like saying Pasima was somewhat worried about her status in Cineth.

Giliead leaned forward, poking at one of the buns. "We need to decide what to take." He glanced a little self-consciously at Ilias. "You said it was cold there?"

That trace of hesitancy, and the sign that Giliead meant to help them after all, got Ilias over the last of his pique. He shrugged, feeling guilty over letting it drag out this long. "It wasn't bad while we were there, but it would be much worse at night. We'd need warm clothes, blankets if we stay there any time. And water. There should be a way down to the river from those passages, but we didn't see one. I'd rather not take the chance."

"Yes, it would be nice to be prepared this time," Tremaine put in, picking up her cup. "Like with a sphere and a sorcerer." The curse box shrieked again and she swore, thumped the cup back down and stamped off to answer it.

Giliead picked up a cloth, absently mopping up the liquid that had slopped out of her cup. He said slowly, "You know I didn't mean—"

"I know," Ilias interrupted. He wasn't exactly happy with how he had reacted. It was a stupid thing to do in the middle of a battle, and even if they weren't fighting right at the moment, this was still the middle of a battle.

Tremaine returned, but though she was frowning, she looked considerably less irritated. "That was Colonel Averi. He wants me to come down there. It's something about that damned Gardier woman they've been questioning forever."

"I'll go with you." Ilias got to his feet. Since there was nothing more to do here at the moment, he might as well.

Since she was going to talk to a Gardier prisoner, Tremaine didn't change out of the Syprian clothes she had put on earlier, the dark pair of pants and the gold shirt with the sleeves that tied back. Her battered boots, an overcoat and a cap made it a comfortable and convenient outfit for tramping through the cold and muddy streets. She knew from speaking to Balin before that the Gardier woman found the signs of alliance between the Syprians and the Rienish disconcerting. Not disconcerting in a "my enemies are allying with each other" way, but disconcerting in a "my enemies are intimate with animals" way. The Gardier had never seen the Syprians as people.

Tremaine briefly considered a taxicab but automobiles made Ilias ill, so she decided to walk to the Port Authority. It wasn't a long way and would give her a chance to work off her excess energy.

"We didn't come this way before," Ilias said, as the street she had chosen expanded into an open circular plaza. It wasn't large by Ile-Rien's standards, but it was almost palatial given Capistown's lack of space. It was paved with a gray-veined stone that gleamed in the overcast light. In the center, surrounded by bright beds of early-spring flowers, was an oversize statue of a female figure swathed in robes and holding a sword.

"Nicholas likes back alleys," Tremaine explained, turning onto the covered promenade that ran around the perimeter of the plaza. It was fronted by expensive shops, the local telegraph office and several cafés. The inclement weather had caused the café patrons to withdraw inside, but as she and Ilias passed an open set of double doors, Tremaine heard a mandolin chorus and smelled sweet bread. She sighed. She thought the Syprians would enjoy Capistown more if they had a chance to explore the places where people actually lived, and not just the refugee hostel and the government buildings they had been trapped in so long. She had heard of a confectionery somewhere in this district that sold chocolates shaped like seashells; maybe on the way back she could find it.

Ilias nudged her elbow, asking in a low voice, "Who are they?"

Craning her neck to get one last sniff of the café, Tremaine hadn't seen the small group of people sitting on the paving stones just off the promenade, dangerously close to the motorcar and wagon traffic circling the plaza. They wore ragged cloaks over skirts of braided grasses and brief leather tabards, and both women and men had cropped dark hair with tribal scarring and tattoos decorating their sallow skin. None of them looked healthy, and the children and elders were close to emaciated. They had clay bowls set out on the pavement and were ostensibly selling jewelry made of polished stone and braided hair, though they were probably doing more begging.

"They're Massian natives, they lived here before Capidara was colonized." *And if we don't stop the Gardier, that's better than what will happen to the Syprians,* she reminded herself. The Gardier would simply exterminate the inhabitants of the Syrnai. *And if by some miracle we do win the war, are they any better off?* her self retorted. The rich forests around Cineth would tempt any number of land barons, eager for new territories to exploit, and the rest of the city-states were probably just as lush. The Capidarans already had the secret of building the spheres and what was left of the Rienish government couldn't even protect its own people, let alone its otherworld native allies.

Ilias frowned, probably baffled at why the Massians were sitting in the street. "What's colonized?" he asked, stumbling over the unfamiliar Rienish word.

She shook her head, tugging at the sleeve of his borrowed coat to get him to move along. "It's not important." *And I hope you need never find out.*

A light rain had started by the time they reached the Port Authority. One of Averi's corporals met them in the foyer, a large echoing space floored with dark marble and occupied by the usual contingent of Capidaran bureaucrats and businessmen hurrying back and forth. As was apparently standard for Capidaran public spaces, it was too cold in the building for Tremaine to bother leaving her coat at the cloakroom and Ilias kept his as well.

The corporal led them up the back stairs to the floor of the rather cramped and dingy offices given over to the Rienish authorities. Strangely dressed Rienish and Syprians were a more familiar sight here, and a couple of Capidaran naval officers and a woman secretary Tremaine recognized from the various meetings she had attended actually said hello to her. They reached Averi's area, where there were more familiar faces and even a few officers Tremaine knew in passing from the *Ravenna,* most contemplating some naval charts and captured Gardier maps tacked up on the wall.

Averi appeared almost immediately out of the back room, greeting them brusquely with, "I heard about the experiment last night. You were lucky you didn't kill yourselves, going through a gate into some unknown place." Colonel Averi was the highest-ranking Rienish army officer in Capidara; if there were others who had taken evacuation transports, none had made it here. He was an older man, with a grim face and thinning dark hair. He and Tremaine had had their problems when they first met, but they had managed to achieve an almost accommodating working relationship. Capistown hadn't improved Averi's health any either; he still looked thin, pale and more like he should be lying in a hospital bed than planning an attack on Ile-Rien's occupied coast.

Tremaine nudged Ilias, who was craning his neck to see the charts, saying pointedly, "He's talking to you."

"What?" He looked startled, then shrugged, telling Averi in Rienish, "We had to find where it went. It's lucky every time we go through and don't die."

Averi didn't seem satisfied with this answer, but he didn't pursue it either, just shaking his head and gesturing for them to follow him back to the inner room.

It was more private but not any better appointed, with wooden filing cabinets and a table covered with papers, most weighed down by a large book of standard nautical charts. "I've had Balin brought here from the cells in the Magistrates' Court," he said. "There's a room we use on this floor for questioning."

"Why did you want me to talk to her?" Tremaine asked, looking distractedly around for a place to sit and seeing there wasn't one; the straight-backed chairs all seemed to be a vital part of some arcane filing system.

"I wanted to confront Balin with someone who has been to the Gardier world. I know she's become increasingly uneasy with our new knowledge of the Gardier—the Aelin." Averi glanced at Tremaine with a thin smile. "I know she wasn't pleased the first time one of us was able to speak to her in her own language, but you should have seen her face when we asked her about the Liaisons."

Tremaine nodded. "Liaison" was the closest the Rienish could come to the Gardier word for the men who had had small crystals implanted in their bodies, who passed along orders from the Gardier's upper echelons. Though Nicholas had lived among them so long, he had never been able to find out just who the Liaisons were liaising with, or why. "And you think she's some kind of observer, sent to spy on the other Gardier by Command or Science or whichever."

"Yes. There's apparently a deep distrust between the Command and Science classes." Averi picked up a sheaf of papers, frowning absently. "She can write and read, which makes her too well educated for their Service class."

They had found out so much about the Gardier in such a relatively short time, going from knowing next to nothing, not even what they called themselves, to actually visiting their world and one of their cities, stealing a new prototype airship, and to having all Nicholas's accumulated knowledge after spending the last few years as one of them. They also had a few old Aelin books, scavenged out of an abandoned library. Nicholas had read them for the Viller Institute researchers, and the books had turned out to be novels, adventure tales of explorers and traders of some earlier age, bearing little resemblance to the Gardier life Tremaine and the others had glimpsed in Maton-devara. *But speaking of Nicholas. . . .* Tremaine asked carefully, "Why did you want me to try, though? Hasn't Nicholas already spoken to her?"

"Yes, but—" Averi hesitated, his brows drawing together, and Tremaine looked down to hide her sudden realization. *He meant, "I wanted to confront Balin with someone who has been to the Gardier world who I don't distrust as much."* It was something of a revelation.

Averi finally finished, "You had quite an effect on her the first time you spoke to her. I think she's afraid of you."

Tremaine glanced at Ilias, who lifted an ironic brow, and said in Syrnaic, "He's talking to you this time."

The room used for questioning was bare, with stained plaster over battered wainscoting, but it had a working radiator and was warmer than the hall outside. The only furniture was a scarred table and two straight chairs. The Gardier woman was already seated in one, and two guards, one Rienish and one Capidaran, stood back against the wall. It wouldn't matter how large the audience was, as Tremaine would question her in Aelin, the Gardier language, something only a few members of the Rienish command knew.

Balin was a tall woman and lean, dressed in a loose white civilian shirt and pants. Her hair was growing back from the bare fuzz that seemed to be regulation for Gardier Service people, probably because she hadn't been allowed access to a razor or scissors. The color was a muddy brown and it fluffed out around her ears in a particularly foolish way. She looked up, her plain face changing from a kind of weary defiance to watchfulness. "Oh good, you remember me," Tremaine said, with a patently false smile. She took the other chair, slouching into it casually.

Ilias went to lean against the wall behind Tremaine, and Balin's eyes followed him with cold disgust. Her gaze came to Tremaine again, and she said in her husky voice, "You. What do you want of me now?"

"The same as I did before. Nothing," Tremaine replied in Aelin. The sphere had given the language to her the same way it had given her Syrnaic, so she knew it nearly as well as Nicholas did. She shrugged, idly examining her fingernails, surprised to discover that she still hated this woman. When Balin had been captured on the island, squatting on the ground, bound with the chains the Gardier had used on their slaves, she had demanded that her captors surrender. Tremaine would have shot her if Giliead hadn't taken the rifle away. She said, "But the others have some idea that you were sent to the island to spy on Command for the Scientists or on the Scientists for Command. That you're not as stupid and useless as we assume."

Balin didn't betray any surprise at Tremaine's knowledge of her language, but she must be used to it now from Averi and Niles and the others who had questioned her. Gardier considered learning other languages as an activity only pursued by a lower order of beings. Balin's thin lips twisted in amusement. "I know what you want."

Tremaine met her gaze, a renewed stirring of rage making her eyes narrow and her jaw tighten. She had the realization that she really, really disliked people telling her they knew what she wanted, knew what she thought, when she didn't know herself and they couldn't possibly know. She smiled thinly, recognizing that Balin had an unerring talent for saying the wrong thing to her at just the right time. "I'm all attention."

"You want to know how we make the avatars. This is obvious. The others think you want to make them for yourself." Her face hardened with contempt. "I know you want to unmake them, to get those inside—out." She snorted. "You are pathetic. You could make hundreds of avatars but you will never defeat us because you are afraid to do what must be done." Her gaze flicked to Ilias again. "You sneer at us for our contempt of the primitives, but you let them serve you—"

Tremaine wasn't sure what else was said. She was on her feet, standing over Balin, gripping the woman's chin hard enough to feel the bone under the flesh. Through the roaring in her ears she was conscious of the Capidaran guard caught flat-footed and taken aback, the Rienish guard startled enough to drop one hand to his sidearm. Balin looked up at her, eyes wide, her pose of world-weary contempt forgotten. Her voice coming out in a harsh rasp, Tremaine said, "Do you know how to get them out?"

"No." It was a pitch above Balin's usual husky tone.

"Were you an observer?" Tremaine asked, but she knew she had lost the benefit of surprise.

Balin's eyes flickered. "No."

Tremaine let her go, making her expression deliberately bored. "Yes, that was very convincing." She headed for the door, ignoring the guards. Ilias followed her out, shutting it after her.

Tremaine stood in the corridor, running her hands through her hair. She was trembling with rage, ready to hit something. Preferably Balin. Ilias watched her with concern, then said, "So she still thinks she knows everything."

Tremaine took a deep breath to calm herself, and her mouth quirked wryly. "That came across through the language barrier, did it?"

He shrugged. "She's awfully arrogant for someone who was just an ordinary warrior. The prisoners from the Wall Port outpost aren't like that. I think you're right that she's a spy on her own people."

Averi came out of another doorway, from the room where he had been listening in on the questioning. He was frowning, and Tremaine said quickly, "We think she is an observer spy, for what that's worth. But it doesn't mean she knows anything about the Gardier that Nicholas didn't already find out."

Averi let his breath out, nodding. "I can't imagine they would send a particularly high-level member of either Command or Science on a mission like that. But all the other prisoners have broken down and talked fairly openly. The fact that she won't, and that she was part of that original group the Liaison seemed so anxious to dispose of on the *Ravenna*, makes it seem as if she has some important information."

Tremaine nodded, relieved he wasn't going to mention her outburst. Maybe it had looked planned rather than spontaneous and heartfelt. "Niles's confusion charms aren't helping?"

Averi's lips twisted ruefully. "They only help when we know the right questions to ask." He glanced up, his frown clearing, and Tremaine saw Lady Aviler advancing up the corridor toward them.

Lady Aviler had organized the refugees on the *Ravenna* and continued to do so in Capistown, finding them accommodation and using her influence with the wealthier Rienish and the upper-class Capidarans to provide employment for them. The extraction of the Maiutan ex–prisoners of war from the refugee hostel by the Lowlands Missionaries had gone very smoothly; Tremaine had suspected Lady Aviler's well-manicured hand in it. She was a slender older woman, wearing her graying dark hair in the latest appropriate style for matrons and a well-tailored blue wool suit.

"Colonel, Ilias." She nodded a cordial greeting to Averi and bestowed that special smile on Ilias that Rienish noblewomen of a certain generation saved for handsome young men whose normal style of dress displayed bare arms and chest. Ilias gave her a brilliant smile back. "Tremaine, I wonder if I could have a word."

"I'll be back," Tremaine said over her shoulder, as Lady Aviler had a firm grip on her elbow and was walking her down the hall.

As soon as they were out of earshot of the offices, Lady Aviler said, "I wanted to ask if you could give your father a message for me."

"Probably," Tremaine agreed cautiously, unwilling to commit to anything where Nicholas was concerned.

Lady Aviler didn't argue about the qualification. "If you can, please let him know Lord Chandre has been to see the Princess Olympe again."

Tremaine frowned at the unfamiliar name. She hadn't ever been much interested in the personalities at Court and had no idea now where most of them had ended up after the evacuation. "Lord Chandre? Did he come over on the *Ravenna*?"

"No." Lady Aviler's lips pursed, as if she had just tasted something unpleasant. "He's been here for some time and he's apparently made himself a power in the Rienish expatriate community here in Capistown."

Tremaine's brows lifted. "I see." She did see. Rienish nobles who had abandoned ancestral estates to flee Ile-Rien early in the war weren't exactly well regarded. In many ways it was an unfair judgment; many Rienish travelers had been trapped abroad by blockades and the sudden danger of any kind of overseas travel. But she could understand why Lady Aviler, whose husband and son had stayed to the very last to accompany the royal party to Parscia, might not see it that way. Lady Aviler would be there too, if she hadn't been sent here with the Princess Olympe. "And that's not a good thing?"

Lady Aviler gave her a sharp sideways glance, then evidently decided to be forthcoming. "I knew his family before the war. He alternated between being an idler and starting a number of failed speculations and businesses. His father had to continually supply capital to buy him out of financial disaster, and he also has some unpleasantly close financial ties to a number of Bisran nobles. Now he has many business interests and a great deal of property here in Capidara, and great . . . financial influence with the Capidaran Ministry."

"And he wants to be an advisor to the princess?" Tremaine snorted. Olympe Fontainon was still a schoolgirl, barely out of childhood. She had been sent here as a precautionary measure, in case the Queen and the prince didn't reach Parscia successfully. *That's all we need, a worthless royal favorite.*

"I'm not sure advice is what he has in mind." Lady Aviler sounded thoughtful. They had reached the end of the hall, where it opened into a gallery looking down on the drafty foyer. Men and women in business attire still hurried back and forth below. A Capidaran Magistrate, dressed for criminal court in elaborate blue robes and trailing a shoal of black-suited solicitors, passed by below them. Lady Aviler leaned on the polished railing, tapping her fingers on it. "His continued visits to the princess give him an appearance of being involved in the war effort. It could give him even more influence on the Rienish here in Capidara."

Tremaine didn't think she had much of a head for politics, but this sounded . . . distressing. She was aware of an unpleasant sensation in her stomach. She didn't have any particular trust in Count Delphane, but he had been an advisor to the Queen and involved in the upper levels of the Ministry since she could remember; he was a known quantity. And she didn't want someone who hadn't taken the risk on the *Ravenna* making decisions for those who had. "There's a reason she can't refuse to see him?"

"She can't afford to offend him, at this point. She isn't the Crown Princess. Not as far as we know." Lady Aviler's lips grew thin and her expression bleak.

No word from Parscia then, Tremaine thought, feeling the sinking sensation grow worse. They had an heir safely ensconced here, so it shouldn't matter whether the Queen and the prince survived or not, but Tremaine found that after considering herself apolitical at best all her life, she now feared change worse than anything. There had been so much of it, and all for the worse. "Do you want me to tell Nicholas to take care of Lord Chandre?"

Lady Aviler lifted a brow, and said wryly, "Good God, child, that wasn't subtle. No, just tell him Chandre's been to see her."

Giliead heard Gerard outside and opened the door. The wizard was standing on the step while down in the street, several people were climbing out of a pair of dark-colored horseless wagons. "The people we were waiting for?" Giliead asked, eyeing them thoughtfully. The clouds had closed in and a light rain had started, spattering on the dusty pavement.

Gerard glanced back. "Yes, the Capidaran delegation to examine the new circle. Florian will be a little later, she was detained at the ship."

Nicholas had reached the door by that point, standing next to Giliead to look out. At Gerard's words he growled something under his breath in Rienish that Giliead didn't understand but could guess the import of.

Nicholas retreated back into the house. Giliead had actually spent the morning talking to him, answering a lot of questions dealing with Syprian wizards in general and Ixion in particular. It had been an interesting experience, to say the least. Nicholas wasn't a man who revealed much of himself, but Giliead could tell enough to know that he was even more ruthless at heart than Tremaine.

Giliead stepped back to let Gerard in, noticing the familiar bag the wizard had slung over his shoulder. Except what was in it wasn't so familiar. "That's not the god-sphere."

"No, this is the sphere Niles made. He wanted to work on the *Ravenna*'s illusion charms and Arisilde is much better for that, so I went out to the ship and traded spheres with him," Gerard explained. His brows lifted and he added in exasperation, "I also think Niles is feeling left out, but there's nothing we can do about that. One of us has to stay with the ship."

Giliead waited in the cold entrance hall of the old house, arms folded, as Gerard conducted the Capidarans in. One of the men was a wizard, but small, stooped and much older than any wizard Giliead had ever seen, with long graying hair and a wrinkled face. He walked with a limp and had the delicate pale paper-thin skin of the very old or very ill. He looked more like someone who should be at home by the hearth being looked after by his grandsons, especially on a wet gray day like this.

As the group milled in the dingy hall, shedding coats and decorative walking sticks and other items, Gerard brought the old man over, saying, "Giliead, this is Kressein, the former Capidaran Ministry sorcerer who has come out of retirement for the war. Master Kressein, this is Giliead of Andrien, the god of Cineth's Chosen Vessel."

The old man looked up at him with clear bright blue eyes, saying in Rienish, "I have been very curious to meet you."

Giliead lifted his brows, keeping his expression noncommittal. Despite the man's age, he could tell Kressein was wrapped in curses. Like the Rienish curses he was getting better and better at sensing, these were passive curses, not meant to be harmful. He wondered if they were there to help sustain the old man's health. Kressein, apparently undaunted by the cool reception, continued, "I've heard much about your ability to see etheric traces. You can truly tell someone is a sorcerer simply by looking at him?"

Giliead let his breath out, recognizing the request for a demonstration. His eyes flicked over the rest of the group. Two men in the red and gray that Capidaran warriors wore, three in the dull brown or blue clothes of most men in the city. The youngest one carried a large leather bag slung over his shoulder. Two women, both in the confining clothes and little caps favored here, like the ones Tremaine wore when she went to the council meetings. He nodded toward the younger sharp-featured one who wore her long dark hair pulled back into a bun. She had done a curse recently; he could still see it on her hands, though he couldn't tell what it had been. "She's a wizard." He had spoken in Syrnaic, but the woman looked up sharply, startled. "And you made a sphere." He rested his eyes on the leather bag carried by the young man. "But it doesn't have a god." Not alive, it wasn't able to conceal itself like their sphere-god. It was like the sphere Niles had made; Giliead could see it through the material of the bag, its curses swirling inside, tinted with the same aura as its creator.

Gerard translated his answer, and Kressein laughed, startled. "I see there was no exaggeration. You're correct, of course."

"Of course," Gerard echoed with a slight smile.

Kressein gave him a sideways glance. Giliead thought he saw rivalry but couldn't tell if it was friendly or not. He wondered if Gerard hadn't just been making him known to the other wizard, but had been making the point that Giliead could see any curses Kressein might cast. But the old man only smiled. "So, let's see this new gateway of yours."

Waiting for Tremaine, Ilias wandered back into the entry room, where people were working over the maps. He felt his own frustration easing as he watched all these preparations, even if what they were preparing for was the trip back to the other side of this world, that would take them through the world-gate back to Cineth. When they returned to the Syrnai, the god would pass judgment on Giliead, and at least the waiting would be over. He was more than ready for the waiting to be over.

The door to the stairwell opened and Ander entered, exchanging greetings with the other men. *Oh, good, him again.* Ilias made an effort to look bored and not disgruntled, casually moving to a table to look at the map spread there, though he had no idea what place it depicted. It did no good, as Ander spotted him and strolled over, saying in Syrnaic, "Hello, Ilias. What are you doing here?"

Ilias glanced up, taking his time. He said in Rienish, "Averi asked us to come."

Ander lifted a brow. "Us?"

Just then Tremaine returned from down the hall, looking thoughtful. She saw them standing together and her expression took on a certain sardonic cast. "Tremaine." Ander greeted her with a nod. "What brings you here?"

"Just doing a favor for Averi," she replied. She eyed him for a moment. "Have you heard from Gerard?"

"About the second trip through the new circle?" He nodded. "The Capidarans are sending a contingent to the house to get a look at the circle for themselves. Afterward we're going to assemble a small group to go through and look at the night sky. We'll probably stay at least until morning so we can search the place thoroughly."

We this, we that, Ilias thought, looking down at the toes of his boots to hide his disgusted expression. It would have been interesting to hear Gerard's reaction to that. Tremaine must have thought so too. She put on the smile that Ilias thought of as her fake one, saying mockearnestly, "We'd better get back then so we can get ready."

Ander lifted his brows. "Don't you think you should stay here?" he asked.

Tremaine frowned, glancing around. "Why? What could I do here?"

He smiled. "I didn't mean here in the office, I meant here, in Capidara."

Tremaine's frown was reaching the point where if Ilias had been on the receiving end, he would have seriously considered keeping his mouth shut unless he was in the mood for a fight. Her tone clipped, she said, "And again I have to ask: and do what?"

"Be safe."

Ilias stared, then rolled his eyes.

"Safe?" Tremaine's laugh was derisive. "There isn't anywhere that's safe. Not anymore. Besides, what's the point in . . ." Her expression stilled and Ilias knew she had seen it now. She said softly, "The point is that I wouldn't be getting in the way. Is that it?"

Ilias read the anger under that deceptively mild tone, but he wasn't sure if Ander did. Ander shook his head so reasonably. "I didn't say that. But this trip, and the one to Lodun . . . If we do manage to get in, it's going to be a long hard fight. We need sorcerers and soldiers. There wouldn't be anything for you to do," he pointed out gently.

Tremaine's expression was like brittle glass. Watching her, Ilias lost his sour sense of triumph over Ander's misstep. It wasn't just an insult; it had struck her to the heart. He tried to interrupt, "Tremaine—"

But she was still looking at Ander. "And I'd hate to be in the way," she snapped, then walked out of the room.

Ander smiled ruefully. "I was afraid she would take it like that." He slanted a challenging stare at Ilias. "You're welcome to come along. And Giliead. We could use your help."

Ilias took two deliberate steps to pass just a little too close to the other man, saying as he walked away, "If I thought you didn't know exactly what you were doing, I'd feel sorry for you."

Giliead paced the hallway outside the ballroom, listening with half an ear to the Capidarans' conversation. He wasn't as quick with Rienish as Ilias, but he could understand most of what they said, despite their strange accents. They were carefully copying down the symbols that made up the curse circle and discussing Gerard's description of the chamber it led to. Giliead had given up trying to look interested after only a short time and come out here to pace, wishing Ilias and Tremaine would return. He would rather see the place himself than hear about it again. He had already consulted with Gerard about what they would need for a longer stay there and a thorough search, and Gerard had sent a list to Averi. There wasn't much to do until the supplies arrived.

He heard a step on the squeaky floorboards and glanced up to see Cletia cautiously peering out of her room. Brow lifted ironically, he told her, "It's all right, they're just talking."

She gave him a glare and stepped out into the hallway, folding her arms. She wore a loose yellow tunic over pants and boots, and rubbed the sleeves briskly as if she was cold. "This is a very unpleasant place," she commented.

"I noticed." He wasn't going to point out that she didn't have to be here. Cletia's break with Pasima still surprised him. He wasn't entirely sure what had brought it about. He thought part of it might be that Cletia was more than old enough to be making her own household now and that Pasima might not be willing to acknowledge that.

Karima had been careful to give his older sister Irissa room to grow, encouraging her to build her own home across the field from the old Andrien house. But Karima had thought her family would increase as her daughter, stepdaughter, and Ilias's cousin Amari all brought home husbands. Thanks to Ixion, that hadn't happened. "We won't be here long."

Cletia nodded. "We were told the *Ravenna* would go from this world to Cineth, then back again to the Ile-Rien land."

"The second part isn't quite that easy." The plan to try to use a curse gate to get into the city where the other Rienish wizards were under siege was all well and good, but Gerard still didn't know the right symbols to make the curse circle go where they wanted it to.

She was watching him thoughtfully, frowning a little, but he had known Cletia since she was a child and seldom seen her do anything but frown. Then she said, "Will you go with them?"

Giliead hesitated, both from surprise that she had bothered to ask and the fact that he had no idea how to answer that question. Despite what had happened with Ixion, he didn't want to abandon this new part of their family at this dangerous time, and he knew Ilias didn't either. And somebody had to be there when Ixion inevitably turned on the Rienish and the Capidarans. But that wasn't a decision he was free to make at the moment. "It depends on what happens in Cineth."

She took a deep breath. "I thought—" The not-so-distant boom of thunder interrupted her and she glanced toward the little round window that lit the stairwell, startled. "That was close."

His head turned toward the circle of grimy glass, Giliead felt a cold chill walk up his back. There had been no flash of lightning. In the ballroom, Gerard had been speaking but all the voices abruptly stilled. The thunder crashed again, and this time Giliead knew it for what it was.

He turned to the ballroom, almost colliding with Gerard in the doorway. The frozen expression on the wizard's face would have told Giliead all he needed to know if he hadn't already guessed. Gerard said, "It's the Gardier. They're bombing the city."

Tremaine was on the stairway down to the foyer when Ilias caught up with her. He didn't say anything, for which she was grateful. She wasn't sure what he thought; she knew that as the nominal head of a Syprian household she was doing a lousy job.

They crossed the foyer and reached the outer doors, the cold gray day greeting her as she stepped out on the walk. It had rained lightly while they were inside, making the paving slick and treacherous and giving the brownstone office buildings across the way a damp gloss. She made it two steps down the road before Ilias's lack of comment got to her and she turned to him and demanded, "Well?"

He shrugged, looking annoyed. "He does that whenever he talks to you."

Tremaine was already starting to regret her outburst. What was the point, anyway? She shook her head, feeling tired of it all. "He just wants me to be safe."

Ilias stopped abruptly, startling the businessmen who had been walking behind them into hurriedly veering around. Exasperated, he said, "I want you to be safe. Gil wants you to be safe. Florian wants you to be safe. Gerard, your father, Averi the warleader, they all want you to be safe. When did any of us say it to you in a way that made you seem like a fool?" He gestured helplessly, upset and frustrated. "You said you let him stay around because you hate yourself. That's true. You want him to punish you." He took a deep breath, maybe afraid he had said too much. He finished a little lamely, "And you shouldn't do that."

She stared at him, mouth open, then managed to shut it and look away. "I . . ."

Ilias grabbed her arm. Startled, she saw he was looking up, his expression aghast, and followed his gaze.

Stark against the gray clouds was the giant black shape of a Gardier airship. Tremaine stared for a long heartbeat, trying not to believe her eyes. The jagged ridge along the back that led down to the cluster of knife-edged tail fins, the black swell of the balloon, the control cabin tucked up under it. *It's our airship,* she tried to tell herself. The one they had captured at such high cost in the Gardier world. *It isn't our airship,* common sense told her a moment later. The cabin was smaller, without the second level; it was one of the older models. Then sound and motion returned and she pointed, yelling a strangled warning to the others on the street as Ilias hauled her toward the shelter of a doorway.

The first explosion crashed as Tremaine slammed back into the closed door, Ilias shielding her with his body. Tremaine knotted her hands in his coat, waiting for flying debris; their shelter was only a step and a brick archway, fully exposed to the street. But though she could hear screams and shouts there was no whoosh of fire and shrapnel.

Her brain ground into gear and she stood on tiptoe, looking over Ilias's shoulder to see smoke rising above the buildings across the street. *It hit two— Three streets away,* she realized, judging it with senses honed in the bombings of Vienne. The Capidaran style of public building wasn't as elaborate as the Rienish and the Gardier might have trouble picking out the Port Authority from the air. She knew they were aiming for it. If Gardier spies in Capidara had scouted the targets for this force, they would be aiming for the refugee hostel, the Port Authority, the Magistrates' Court, the Ministry, anywhere the new spheres might be.

Another booming crash, and another, echoing from behind them. . . . "The harbor," she breathed. The *Ravenna.* "Oh no." She pounded Ilias's shoulder and he stepped back. Keeping hold of his sleeve she pushed out of their inadequate shelter and ran down the walk back toward the Port Authority. Instinct said to take the opposite direction, away from a potential target, but the side street was the shortest path to the harbor front.

People were running, screaming, motorcars speeding past as smoke from the bomb bursts belched into the sky. A siren belatedly started to howl as Tremaine reached the corner and ran toward the harbor. She stopped at the end of the short side street, where it opened onto a raised promenade that ran alongside the waterfront. Ilias jolted to a halt beside her.

The view opened up from here into the curve of Capistown's harbor, framed by the mountains that bordered the town on the left and the long arm of land that reached out into the bay on the right. Over the masts of the small fishing boats and pleasure craft that were docked along here, she could see the larger ships that lay farther out at anchor. One of them was the *Ravenna.*

The great liner, painted gray for camouflage in the open sea, dwarfed the military ships and the smaller *Queen Falaise* moored nearby. The abstract outline of an eye was still visible on this side of her prow, painted there to make her more acceptable to the Syprians when she had been docked outside Cineth harbor. There were three huge smokestacks on the topmost deck, and Tremaine couldn't see any sign of steam from even one. "Go, go, go," she muttered. "What are you waiting for?"

Then a black airship blinked into existence above the liner.

Tremaine felt her gorge rise. "Oh, God." *This can't be happening.* She couldn't remember who was on the ship, Niles and Gyan for certain, maybe Kias and Calit. . . . She saw the dark shapes fall from the airship and held her breath.

The moment stretched forever, long enough for her heart to start beating again. The bombs must have missed.

Then fire blossomed up from the liner's upper decks and the ship shuddered, heeling sideways as it started to vanish under the surface. Tremaine made a strangled noise in her throat.

"No." Ilias shook his head, his expression baffled. "There's something— She's not going down like— And there's no sound!" Then he caught her arm, pointing urgently. "Look at the water."

"What?" Tremaine shook her head, sick.

"There's a bow wave, over there." He was bouncing on his toes in anxiety, pointing toward a churning V of white froth midway across the harbor.

Tremaine squinted. It did look like a bow wave. A large one just like a giant liner should produce. *What the hell. . . .* The water the *Ravenna* was sinking into was flat, undisturbed. "God, you're right!" She pounded Ilias on the shoulder, bouncing up and down herself. Now that she knew what to look for she could see a haze of steam in the air far above the apparently shipless bow wave. "It's an illusion." That explained the hesitation after the bombs dropped; the sorcerer controlling the illusion had had to rapidly adjust it to make it look as if they had struck a solid target. It was Niles, of course. *It's sneaky and subtle,* Tremaine thought, jubilant. It had Niles written all over it.

Distant pops sounded as a Capidaran battery on the far side of the harbor fired at the airship. Its wards deflecting the shots, the airship dropped more bombs. But the *Ravenna* illusion wavered; Tremaine could see water through it now, the tremendous splash as the bombs hit the water, a cloud of rapidly vanishing fire and smoke. She looked again at the empty bow wave to see the real *Ravenna*'s stern shimmer into existence as the illusion cloaking it dropped away.

The Gardier aboard the airship must have realized their mistake as the illusory vessel beneath them faded. The airship turned, angling toward its real target. But fiery orange lines crept over the black surface of the balloon, flowing over it like liquid light; Tremaine knew it was the gas inside the hydrogen cells, ignited by a sphere. "Niles can't take much more," she said, thinking aloud. "Those two illusions— some of that he could do in advance but—"

The real *Ravenna* released another cloud of steam, then disappeared, turbulent waves radiating out from the spot it had just occupied. Niles had made a world-gate for the ship, probably right before he collapsed. Ilias swore, startled. "It's different when you see it from outside," he said under his breath. He had gone through world-gates several times but Tremaine didn't think he had ever seen the *Ravenna* perform this feat from a distance.

She nodded rapidly. All the boats along the dock rocked madly as the waves from the ship's abrupt disappearance reached them. "Let's hope there was nothing waiting for them on the other side." Then another bomb burst from inland made her reflexively cover her head.

Ilias pulled her back to the shadow of the warehouse behind them, saying, "We've got to get out of here."

"Yes, we have to get back to the— Shit." Seeing the *Ravenna* escape seemed to have freed her stunned thought processes. She went cold with dread, realizing what the airship's exact targeting of the *Ravenna* meant. "They knew exactly where she was. They gated right on top of her. Or what they thought was her."

Ilias nodded, flinching as another explosion sounded. Tremaine could smell smoke on the wind now. He said, "Right, there's spies here too."

She turned back to the side street, making for the main road again despite the danger. "We have to get to the house. The Gardier will be heading there, that's what all this is for." No one had known about the house and the experiment with Arisilde's sphere except themselves, until this morning when Gerard and Ander had informed the Capidarans. The timing of the attack might be coincidence, but Tremaine didn't much believe in coincidence anymore.

She was halfway down the side street when she heard the distinctive whoosh-thump of a falling bomb. She hit the cracked pavement, instinctively covering her head as Ilias threw himself on top of her. The explosion reverberated through the street and she heard the dull roar of fire. Ilias rolled off her and she pushed herself up, realizing she and Ilias were covered with dust and plaster flakes. The bomb had struck the Port Authority.

"Damn," Ilias muttered, sitting up on his knees, looking up at the building. Tremaine could see that the brick wall looming over them didn't look damaged but smoke streamed up from the roof.

There was an airship nearly right above them, moving off now but it would be coming around for another pass. Tremaine grabbed Ilias's arm, hauling herself up. "It'll be back. We've got—" She inhaled a lungful of acrid smoke and doubled over, coughing.

Ilias pulled her onward, glancing up to keep track of the airship's progress. They reached the street to see a building had collapsed less than a block away and the air was filled with dust and smoke. The street was empty of fleeing pedestrians but a motorcar and a truck had been trapped in the debris, the motorcar crushed under a fall of bricks and the truck trapped by a beam across its steaming engine.

Ilias hesitated, scanning the street, then started toward the collapse. Tremaine had been hacking up dust trying to clear her throat enough to tell him to do just that; the airship was targeting the larger public building behind them and wouldn't waste another bomb on the far end of the street. She just hoped Averi and the others had had time to get to safety.

They made their way through fallen bricks and abandoned motorcars, coming within a few paces of the back of the trapped truck. Tremaine had just realized it was a Capidaran government vehicle when a gunshot, loud and close, made her jump nearly out of her skin. It had come from the truck, from the cabin over the back bed.

Ilias stopped, throwing her an inquiring look. Tremaine shook her head, baffled. The Gardier didn't land troops during bombings. At least, they hadn't in the bombings of Ile-Rien. Then the cabin door started to swing open and Ilias dived to one side and Tremaine scrambled to the other.

The opening door blocked Tremaine's view but she saw a lean form jump out. The door nearly thumped her in the head as Ilias hit whoever it was from the side, knocking him to the pavement.

Tremaine stepped around the door, saw the struggling figure on the bottom had a pistol in its hand and stamped on it, pinning the weapon and the hand to the pavement. A sharp cry of pain told her who this was and she swore bitterly.

As Tremaine stooped to grab the pistol, Ilias sat up, still pinning the struggling figure. It was the Gardier woman, Balin. "Guess who?" he told Tremaine, grimacing as the woman tried to knee him.

Tremaine stepped past him to look into the back of the covered truck. Two people in the red-and-gray Capidaran military uniform lay inside, the man in a crumpled heap against the front wall of the cab, the woman sprawled across the bench, a bloody wound in her chest, the silly little cap that the Capidaran Women's Auxiliary members wore knocked askew, still held to her head by hairpins.

Tremaine felt her lips draw back in a snarl. They must have been moving Balin back to her cell in the Magistrates' Court. From their positions, the man had been thrown forward and possibly died in the crash; Balin must have gotten his gun and shot the woman after a struggle.

Automatically chambering a round in the pistol, Tremaine looked down at the Gardier woman. Balin's face set but her eyes were afraid; she had a trickle of blood from a scalp wound running down her cheek. Ilias, keeping a wary eye on the woman, hadn't looked up. "What do we do with her?" he asked, breathing hard. "Take her with us?"

If I had to shoot someone in cold blood, I'd rather it be her than that idiot I killed for the truck in Maton-devara, Tremaine thought. Not that her blood felt particularly cold at the moment. If she could trade Balin for that poor dead Gardier man she had left to grow cold in a ditch, she wouldn't hesitate. *Unfortunately, it's not a trade.*

"We'll take her with us," she said. "Get her up."

Chapter 5

Giliead had given up counting explosions. The distant blasts were punctuated by the eerie wail of what Gerard said were warning sirens, though they sounded further away now. Sick with anxiety about the others, Giliead paced the front hall, where Gerard was trying to use the talking curse box to reach Niles on the *Ravenna*, or Averi at the Rienish headquarters, but the thing wasn't working properly.

Kressein, with the assistant who carried his sphere and the two Capidaran warriors, had left already, going off to try to do what they could to repel the attack. At least they could do something; Giliead felt trapped and useless.

Gerard spoke into the curse box with more agitation, then slammed the listening part down. "I've lost the operator." He loosened his collar, swearing. The sphere was still tucked under his arm. Giliead had noticed it never clicked and sparked to itself the way the god-sphere did. "The lines must be down."

Giliead didn't know what that meant but it couldn't be good. He looked away, gritting his teeth to keep from asking useless questions. *Fire is falling from the sky and Ilias and Tremaine are out in it.*

Gerard must have read the thought from his expression. He took a deep breath, saying, "Tremaine is . . . more than experienced with bombings. She was in Vienne through most of the worst— They should be fine."

"I know, but—" The crash of glass breaking from upstairs interrupted him. Giliead traded a startled look with Gerard, then beat the wizard to the stairs, taking them two at a time. He couldn't smell a new curse. As he reached the ballroom doorway he saw the remaining Capidarans were still in the big room, the two women, the other man, all of them looking around in a puzzled way for the source of the crash. Frowning, Giliead felt a draft of fresh damp air that shouldn't exist in the enclosed chamber. From here he could see straight through to the archway at the back, where a small room with glass windows looked down into the dead garden. He started forward; it had to be the source of the noise and the sudden draft. The Capidaran man, much closer to that end of the room than Giliead, was already moving that way. Giliead glanced over his shoulder, telling Gerard, "Something came through back there—"

From behind him, Nicholas shoved into the doorway, shouting, "Stop! Gerard, it's—" An explosion shuddered the floor. Giliead staggered, shocked, covering his ears and wincing away from the light and sound.

He saw fire roil out of the far end of the ballroom, enveloping the Capidaran man. Giliead started forward in instinctive reaction with no idea what he meant to do, but Gerard ran past him, flinging up a hand and speaking a spate of unintelligible words.

Giliead felt the curse grow outward from Gerard, saw it as a haze of yellow light spreading toward the back of the room, passing the two women who had fallen to the floor under the force of the blast. The fire met the curse, washing up against its fragile barrier. Then the flames and heat vanished.

Giliead fell forward a step, staring. The wall that separated the little glass room was singed and blackened, a hole blasted through it revealing broken wood, shredded paper and smashed plaster. Shattered glass and wood fragments lay in an uneven pile just at the foot of the nearly invisible curse barrier, as if they had been washed there by a flood. Beyond it the Capidaran man sprawled, his clothes half burned away, his skin bloodred.

Giliead gasped a breath, choked at the stench of burned human flesh, and ran toward the injured man. He passed through the barrier, feeling it pluck at his clothes and hair, and fell to his knees beside the Capidaran. He was breathing, but with a liquid rasp that meant burned insides. Behind him, Nicholas reached the curse barrier and bounced off as he tried to pass through. Stumbling back, he swore in frustration. "Quickly, they may throw another explosive any moment. Gerard—"

Giliead hadn't thought of that, but of course the Gardier would have more of the things. He gathered up the wounded man as carefully as he could, grimacing at the close view of burned skin showing through the gaping holes in his shirt and jacket. He said hurriedly, "Wait, don't take away the curse, I may be able to bring him through."

Giliead lifted the man and stood, mentally gathered himself, and stepped into the curse barrier. He felt it pull at him again, at the man in his arms, but after an instant it gave way and he stumbled through to the other side.

Cletia stood in the doorway, staring, a horrified Cimarus behind her. "Take him out in the hall," Nicholas ordered, just as glass crashed again from the windows behind them. "Excellent timing," Nicholas added under his breath.

Giliead agreed, feeling his stomach clench at the nearness of their escape. He carried the man out to the hallway, deliberately not looking back at the curse barrier, knowing the other weapon would explode any moment. The other two Capidarans were already out in the hall, the older woman collapsed on a chair, her face chalky with shock. "Get some wet towels," Gerard told the other woman sharply. "There's a bathroom just up one floor. Stay away from the windows." He had spoken by habit in Syrnaic and had to repeat himself in Rienish as the woman stared at him blankly.

Giliead laid the man down on a couch at Gerard's urging, just as the second blast went off, muffled behind the protective curse barrier. If someone needed better evidence that Rienish curses could protect people rather than hurt them, Giliead couldn't think what it would be. He threw a glance at Gerard, asking, "Those are the same weapons from the Gardier world, the ones that made the fire in the building?"

"Yes, an incendiary," Nicholas answered him, striding toward the stairs. "You, Cimarus? Get upstairs, see if you can spot them from the window on the floor above this one. Try not to open the shutters far enough to let them fire in."

Giliead looked at Cletia, opening his mouth to reinforce the order but she jerked her chin at Cimarus, telling him to follow Nicholas's instructions. As Cimarus bounded up the stairs, Cletia ducked back into their room and came out with her scabbarded sword, hurrying after Nicholas.

"Yes, careful," Gerard called after him. "They're sure to keep trying. Is the door to the back secure?"

"It was the last time I checked," Nicholas said grimly, starting down the stairs.

Gerard had knelt beside the couch to listen to the wounded Capidaran's labored breathing, trying to touch his ruined skin as little as possible. He sat up, taking a sharp breath, sweat staining his collar. "This man's going to die unless I do a healing."

"You can fix this?" Giliead asked, trying to keep the incredulity out of his tone.

Gerard gestured, distracted. "Burns aren't difficult to heal. It's simply a matter of encouraging the skin to grow back, something it's already inclined to do on its own." He shook his head slightly. "But it's a complicated spell, I don't know if I can hold the wards. . . ." His jaw set. "I have to try."

Giliead got to his feet, realizing he couldn't help here. As he started up the stairs, the younger Capidaran woman appeared again, her arms full of dripping wet cloth, passing him on the steps. The older woman staggered to her feet and came over to help her lay the towels on the wounded man.

Giliead heard Gerard ask urgently in Rienish, "Meretrisa, do you have any experience with major healing spells?"

She shook her head, her face anguished. "No, I've never— I don't think I can."

Giliead moved quickly up the stairs, going to the room where he had stored their bowcases, selecting one hurriedly and taking a handful of hunting arrows. He found Cimarus struggling to open the window at the end of the hall. "Move that metal clip over, then you can push the top part up," Giliead told him, tossing the arrows on a handy chair and pausing to string the bow. It was a fine one made for him in Cineth, of polished goathorn, wood and bone.

Swearing in frustration, Cimarus got the glass window pushed up out of the way and cautiously eased the shutter open. "There they are," he murmured. "Down in the garden." Giliead looked over his shoulder and saw three men in the brown Gardier clothing confidently crossing the winter-dead garden court toward the back of the house. All carried the long black shooting weapons. "Go get a bow," Giliead told Cimarus grimly, shouldering him aside and nocking an arrow. He drew, taking careful aim on the Gardier in the lead. These men might not be wizards but he had never felt any regret in killing those who used fire as a weapon. And it would help clear Ilias and Tremaine's way back to the house. "There's going to be more of them."

Tremaine brought the taxicab to a halt, cursing. The end of their street was blocked by an automobile jammed into an ancient horse-drawn omnibus. Someone had cut the horses loose and taken them away but no attempt had been made to clear the blocked street. "Idiots," she muttered, throwing the motorcar into reverse and only belatedly remembering to look behind her.

Braced in the back, keeping a hold on Balin, Ilias pointed out rather desperately, "We can walk from here."

"I know, but—" But the neighborhood was too empty. She didn't want to hurry down that street under the gaze of all those windows. And the bomb blasts were getting closer, following them the whole distance from the harbor.

She jolted the motorcar back into gear, turning down the street that ran behind their house, remembering that Mr. Derathi had made his deliveries through the back door so there had to be a passage through to it. This street was much like the other, lined with brown brick town houses, some with shops in the bottom floors. It was empty, quiet, as everyone huddled in terror indoors. She braked at about the spot where their house was in the opposite street. Craning her neck, she was rewarded with the sight of a narrow alley running between the two brown brick buildings into the center of the block.

Tremaine bailed out, pausing as Ilias dragged a struggling Balin out of the back. The smell of smoke was strong here, but the breeze must be coming from the harbor. Balin glared at her, spitting a curse, but Tremaine was too occupied to surrender to the impulse to kill her. She led the way down the narrow alley, carrying her pistol down at her side, concealed by a fold of her coat. Dirt had drifted over the paving and weeds and determined flowers had taken root, but there was a flattened path down the center. At the end was a battered wooden gate in their house's garden wall, standing open. She was willing to bet Derathi hadn't left that open this morning.

She waved for Ilias to wait and he pulled Balin to a halt, covering her mouth when she tried to shout. Tremaine turned back to her to put the pistol's muzzle right under her nose, saying quietly in Aelin, "If you bite him, three guesses what I'll do to you."

Ilias lifted a brow in appreciation. Balin looked convinced, so

Tremaine turned back to the gate, carefully peering inside. There was no real spot for anyone to hide in the small walled yard. She spotted the first brown-clad body crumpled in the weedy dry flower bed and twitched, raising her pistol. An instant later she saw the feathered arrow shaft standing out of the man's back and knew he wouldn't be causing trouble anytime soon. She eased a little further through the gate and spotted another Gardier floating in the stagnant green water of the fountain, and several more sprawled on the dirty stone flags. *Looks like we had company, and company regretted it,* she thought, grimly pleased.

She glanced up at the house, grimacing as she saw the second-floor windows in the conservatory had been broken out. She looked down again, realizing that broken glass littered the paving. "That's not good," she muttered, stepping forward. The windows must have been blown out in an explosion. Glass cracked under her boot and she held out her free hand, in case there was a—

"Dammit!" Tremaine leapt back, gritting her teeth, shaking her numb hand. Her fingers pricked and tingled from even brief contact with the ward. She glared at the house, hoping the ward had also announced her presence as well as zapping her with what felt like an electric shock, but no one appeared at the door or windows.

"Tremaine," Ilias said quietly.

"It was a—" She turned, saw he had his hand clapped tightly over Balin's mouth, that he was looking at the far wall of the garden. Not the wall, she realized a moment later, but the three sets of bootprints in the dirt beside it. *Illusion,* she realized with a sick sensation, *they can't get past a ward set with a sphere's help, so they're waiting for Gerard to drop it to let us in.* "—a ward, right, you know how we always—" *Say the leader's the one in the middle, say he's holding the crystal maintaining the illusion about chest level—* She twitched her pistol free of her coat, raised it and fired.

The report rang out as the illusion shattered between one blink and the next. Two Gardier flung themselves away and one fell to the ground, crystal shards spattered with blood scattered around him. The telltale remnants of liquid light pooled on the ground, all that was left of the sorcerer who had been trapped inside the crystal. *Guessed right,* Tremaine thought, already scrambling for cover behind the raised edge of the fountain. A shot into the coping sprayed her with stone chips and she rolled away, feeling gravel and broken glass grit under her back. With the crystal broken the Gardier couldn't destroy her pistol with their mechanical disruption spell, but that didn't stop them from shooting.

Ilias had flung Balin aside and tackled the nearest Gardier, taking the man to the ground before he could bring up his rifle. Tremaine popped up to take a shot at the other, missed as he fired at her. The bullet hit the dead man in the fountain, making the corpse jerk horrifically. Two more Gardier vaulted over the wall. Ilias had killed the one he had tackled and now crouched behind the gate, taking cover from the gunfire. Balin, knowing the Gardier might not realize she was one of them, had flattened herself into the weeds across the court. Or she might just remember what had happened to some of the other Gardier prisoners, killed by a Liaison to keep them from talking.

Damn it, this could be a problem, Tremaine thought desperately, crawling through the gravel, trying to keep the fountain between her and the Gardier. Knowing she only had three shots left, she risked her head to fire again, just as a feathered shaft suddenly slammed into the nearest man's chest. The Gardier choked as he fell, blood foaming at his lips.

Tremaine shot the other one as the last tried to go back over the wall, only to be dragged down by Ilias. She heard a door bang and turned, just in time to see the other Gardier who had been creeping quietly up behind her. Before she could even get her pistol up, Giliead suddenly appeared behind him, his sword biting into the man's shoulder.

Tremaine pushed to her feet, watching Giliead finish the Gardier off with a thrust to the chest, uneasily fascinated. She tore her gaze away, looking back to make sure Ilias was all right. He was just retrieving his knife from the body of the Gardier who had tried to escape.

Giliead spotted Ilias and his whole body relaxed, though he didn't do more than nod to him in relief. Ilias gave him a tight smile back, then dodged sideways to recapture Balin as she ran toward one of the fallen Gardier rifles.

"We need to get back inside, there's more of them," Giliead told Tremaine, turning back to the house.

"Right." Tremaine started after him, and flinched back with a curse as she walked into the ward again. She shook her stinging hand, gritting her teeth. "Hey, can we do something about that?"

Giliead looked back in consternation. "Sorry, it doesn't work on me."

The servants' door at the side of the house opened and Nicholas stepped out, motioning them to come toward him. "Hurry, Gerard's opened a passage in the ward."

"Are you sure?" Tremaine took a cautious step forward, feeling the air in front of her.

"No, it's a cruel joke," Nicholas snapped. "Get in here."

Snarling under her breath, Tremaine followed Giliead across the littered pavement to the doorway, Ilias hauling Balin along after her.

"Why on earth did you bring her?" Nicholas asked as they reached the house. He shut the door behind Giliead and shot the bolt, throwing a suspicious glance through the inset window.

"Bring who?" Tremaine's expression was too acid for mock-innocence. She went through the little entryway and into the kitchen. Cimarus was in the doorway to the pantry, his sword hung over his shoulder, watching worriedly.

"She was escaping," Ilias replied, pushing the Gardier woman ahead of him. Balin snarled at Nicholas, who ignored her.

Tremaine decided to give up on the sarcasm battle. "What happened to the windows? The bombing is still several streets away."

"We've been attacked by two groups of Gardier." Nicholas turned away from the door impatiently, leading them through the kitchen. "They're obviously after the sphere or Gerard or both."

Tremaine snorted derisively. "That's suicidal of them. Arisilde's not going to—"

"Unfortunately, Arisilde isn't here," Nicholas cut in. They came out into the front hall, which seemed undamaged except for a lingering odor of smoke. Nicholas started up the stairs. "Gerard took him out to the *Ravenna* last night, so Niles could work with him. He brought Niles's sphere back here to carry on the experiment."

"Oh." Tremaine bit her lip, taken aback. That explained the simultaneous illusion and gate spell. Niles had had powerful help.

Gerard met them at the top of the stairs, saying in profound relief, "Thank God you made it safely."

"Do you know where Florian is?" Tremaine asked. She had been hoping the other girl would be at the house with Gerard, but surely she would have come out to see them by now.

"I left her with Niles on the *Ravenna* this morning, with Kias and Calit." Gerard looked at her sharply. "Did you see if—"

"The illusion worked, Niles was able to make a gate." Tremaine felt the tightness in her chest ease. With Arisilde and Niles and the

Ravenna between them and the Gardier, Florian and the other Syprians were better off than they were.

She saw two Capidaran women she didn't know, one young with dark hair done up in a bun, the other older and a little on the stout side, both leaning anxiously over a man stretched out on one of the fusty divans. There was a pile of towels and a large china bowl of water on the floor. Tremaine took a step forward to see who was hurt and suddenly realized the red and black marking his torso was burned flesh and blackened cloth, not just a rather ugly patterned shirt. Her gorge rose. "Who's this?" she asked, trying to clamp down on incipient nausea.

"Tremaine, this is Meretrisa and Vervane, members of the Capidaran party," Gerard said, preoccupied. "The injured man is Aras, with the Capidaran Ministry." He turned back to Nicholas. "We need to—"

A bomb blast shook the house, plaster dust raining down, windowpanes rattling in their casements, glass shields trembling in the sconces. Everyone flinched and Vervane, the older Capidaran woman, cried out, clapping her hands to her ears. Balin looked around hopefully, as if she expected the house to collapse. But the old building stayed upright. Tremaine looked around for a window to see how close the hit had been. Before she could take two steps for the stairs, another blast hit. She staggered, the vibrations making her teeth ache.

"God, what are they doing?" Gerard muttered, heading for the window with Nicholas.

Tremaine made it to the stair railing, looking out the window above the front door. In the haze of smoke she saw that the houses across the street were rubble.

Another bomb blast shook the house and she gripped the railing. How many people had died in the past minute?

As the sound faded, Nicholas said quietly, "They've realized they can't get past our wards."

"So they're just bombing the rest of the street?" Tremaine gestured in frustrated rage. She looked at Gerard. "Can you stop them?"

He shook his head slowly, his eyes not leaving the devastation. "Not with this sphere. I can't hold our wards and strip theirs simultaneously. If Arisilde was here—"

"If Arisilde was here, Niles wouldn't have gotten the *Ravenna* out in time," Tremaine told him, frustrated.

"Quite possibly." Gerard looked at Nicholas, grimacing. "The

Gardier must think Arisilde is with us. They won't stop until they find him."

"They'll bomb this neighborhood to the ground around us." Nicholas nodded absently, eyes distant as he thought it over. Tremaine bit the inside of her lip to keep from snapping at him. The worse the situation, the calmer Nicholas seemed to get, and it drove her mad.

Gerard lifted his brows suddenly. "We'll have to abandon the house, drop the wards, let them take it." He smiled thinly. "We'll go through the circle."

Tremaine blinked. *Of course.* The only value in the house was the sphere and the circle itself, and Gerard and Giaren had already taken enough notes on it to be able to re-create it anywhere. They could wait out the attack in the cave Ilias and Gerard had found, then return. She turned to Ilias and Giliead, waiting tensely behind her. "We're going through the circle—get anything we might need."

They were both moving before the words were all the way out, Ilias bolting for the stairs and Giliead shouting for Cletia and Cimarus. Tremaine turned back as Nicholas said, "Yes, it's the only thing we can do. I'll stay here and destroy the circle."

"What?" Tremaine's brows drew together, but a moment later, she saw it too. "Because the Gardier could follow us through."

Gerard's worried gaze never left Nicholas's face. "At the very least, they would be able to copy the new circle's symbols. We can't allow that."

Nicholas was nodding. "I recommend you wait there until Niles can re-create the new circle and send you word that the attack is over." He lifted a brow in ironic comment. "Really, Gerard, don't look so dramatic. I am planning on leaving the house before it's blown to bits."

Gerard swore, passing a hand over his face. "I realize that."

Ilias pounded back down the stairs, his pack and Tremaine's bag slung over his shoulder with his sword and one of the wooden cases the Syprians stored their weapons in under his arm. Giliead appeared with Cletia in tow, carrying their packs and weapons and the other cases. Cimarus came up the stairs from below, taking the packs Cletia passed over to him. Tremaine smacked herself in the forehead, knowing she should have been moving already. She started for the stairs. "Gerard, do you have any notes or books here, anything you need?"

He looked around, distracted. "Yes, in my case downstairs."

Nicholas took the pistol from her, moving to cover Balin while Tremaine hurried downstairs. She found Gerard's case on the table in the salon and as she grabbed it up another bomb blast reverberated down the street. Her jaw ached from gritting her teeth and she tried not to imagine the faces of the people she saw on this street, the women and children living in the houses, the people who worked in the shops. Remembering that Ilias had said it was cold in the other world, she grabbed Gerard's overcoat from the bench in the hallway, slid to a halt and caught up the coats that must belong to the Capidarans.

As she reached the top of the stairs Giliead was carrying the wounded man, wrapped in a blanket, into the ballroom, with Meretrisa and Vervane following uncertainly.

Tremaine went after them but stopped in the doorway, startled by the sight of the damage. The conservatory windows weren't just broken, the whole back section of the room was charred and blasted. A shoal of broken wood and plaster chunks had fetched up against an invisible barrier where a ward had stopped the debris from flying across the room. The air smelled heavily of smoke and sulfur.

Nicholas was covering Balin with Tremaine's pistol and Gerard was herding the others into the circle. Cletia looked stoic and Cimarus nervous, an attitude also shared by the two Capidaran women. Ilias just looked impatient and Giliead grim. Gerard told Nicholas, "The wards will linger a short time after we go, so you'll have a few moments."

Nicholas nodded, and as Tremaine dumped the case and her armload of coats inside the circle, he passed the gun back to her. "Wait a moment," he added, and pulled a handful of ammunition out of his coat pocket, dropping it into hers.

"Thanks." She threw him a look. He lifted a brow at her and she couldn't think of anything to say. She jerked her chin at Balin, telling her in the Aelin language, "Get over there."

She shook her head stubbornly. "I won't go."

Another blast sounded nearby, close enough to rattle the sconces and remaining windows, and cause a shower of plaster dust.

Nicholas moved before Tremaine could, catching the woman by the arm and propelling her into the circle. Tremaine hurried after, grabbing Balin by the collar and shoving the pistol into her side.

Nicholas stepped back. Gerard looked up at him, saying, "Good luck."

Nicholas just smiled. It was a particularly evil smile, and didn't promise well for the Gardier. *Bastard,* Tremaine thought. *He enjoys this kind of thing.* Somebody had to, she supposed. As Gerard whispered to the sphere she held her breath and felt the rush of vertigo, then the world turned dark.

Florian hurried down the alley and paused as she reached the street behind the old house, relieved to see its distinctive roofline over the shorter town homes surrounding it. *Nearly there,* she told herself. *See, I told you you could do this.*

The air had been heavy with smoke the whole way and it was much worse here; her lungs were starting to ache from coughing. The harbor launch she had ridden in from the *Ravenna* had just reached the dock when the bombing started. The Port Authority and the government buildings she was familiar with all seemed to be targets, which only made sense. As a victim of many Vienne bombings, she had decided to try what the Siege Aid people always told you never to do: to make her way across town back to the house.

Navigating rubble-blocked streets and dodging fire brigades, floods from broken water mains, patrols of Capidaran constables and soldiers as well as panicked civilians had been harder than she had thought. But the launch pilot had said the *Ravenna* had escaped and she had seen an airship crash into the harbor, and another go down near the Port Authority, so she told herself the attack couldn't last much longer.

Florian stepped out onto the walk, getting a better view of the empty street, and halted in shock. Half the buildings were piles of smoking rubble, leaving their house and a few of the town homes on either side standing like an isolated island. "Oh, no," she murmured, sickened by the sight. *They knew, the Gardier knew we were there.* They had to be looking for Arisilde.

She scanned the overcast sky hastily, but there were no airships in sight. She knew that only meant they might be hiding up in the clouds. Or that the Gardier had landed to attack the house from the ground. She whispered the words of her favorite concealment charm. It made her feel a little better, though not much.

Gritting her teeth, Florian darted across the street toward one of the few houses left standing, reaching the shelter of its set of stairs. She could smell gas and groaned under her breath; a broken gas main was all this situation needed.

Florian hesitated, knowing she was being stupid, but she had to see if the others were in the house, if they were trapped or . . . She started forward, hugging the side of this building, the rough texture of the bricks scratching at her clothes, and reached the edge of an alley. Overgrown grass came up through cracks in the pavement but it was free of garbage or rubble. She hurried down it, grateful for the shadows that hid her from above, nervous at how trapped it made her feel. This charm didn't exactly have a great record of success at fooling Gardier crystals or the smaller belt devices.

The heavy silence was making her ears hurt. She could hear the distant sirens of the Capidaran militia but no hint of movement or voices from the houses on either side of her. The inhabitants must have fled, but it was unnerving.

Florian reached a heap of rubble that had been someone's garden wall and edged around it, getting a view of the alley behind the old manor house's back court. The wooden gate was closed. She bit her lip, seeing that the conservatory windows on the second floor were broken out and the bricks around them singed. *Gerard must have been there, he could have warded the house against fire. They must be all right.* She needed to make sure no one was in the garden before she went through the gate. Glancing around, she stepped back to the rubble, putting one foot carefully on a broken pile of bricks and reaching to grab the part of the wall still standing. The rubble moved under her foot, making a loud chink of brick against brick; she froze. *Nobody could have heard that,* she told herself sternly, and started to boost herself up.

Someone clapped a hand over her mouth from behind and yanked her off the rubble, pinning her arms to her sides. Terror giving her extra strength, Florian didn't bother to try to scream, just bit down into the gloved hand with all her might, mentally fumbling for a defensive spell.

He dragged her back against the wall and an almost voiceless whisper in her ear said, "Florian, it's Valiarde."

Oh. Feeling like a fool, Florian released his hand. It was Nicholas, Tremaine's father, dressed in the dark overcoat and suit he had been wearing last night. She noticed irrelevantly that he had cut himself shaving that morning. He was also giving her a mildly annoyed look. She saw the teeth imprints in his glove and winced, whispering, "Sorry."

He held a finger to his lips, telling her to be quiet. Just then Florian heard movement on the other side of the wall and a low mutter of voices. Voices speaking Aelin, the Gardier language. She threw a frightened look up at Nicholas. They were standing close together, so the concealment charm probably covered both of them, but the men behind the wall must have a crystal and she was fairly sure they weren't deaf. She heard footsteps start along the wall, heading toward the gate at the far end.

Nicholas grimaced, releasing her arm and stepping away from her. He motioned for her to stay where she was and she nodded rapidly. She knew very little about Tremaine's father except what Tremaine had told her: that he was crazy and that it ran in the family. Knowing Tremaine, she found that oddly comforting at the moment.

Just as the man on the other side of the wall reached the gate, Nicholas called something out in Aelin. The steps hesitated, then the man asked a question in the same language.

Nicholas stepped to the gate, his boots soundless on the wet grass, standing just beside it. The gate jerked open and a man in Gardier brown stood there, suspicion etched on his features. His expression didn't change as his eyes passed over Florian and she knew her charm was working for the moment. Since the fallen brick had been enough to betray her to Nicholas, and she still hadn't a clue what shadow he had sprung out of, she held her breath and kept absolutely still.

It had been a while since she had seen a Gardier in person. This man had the cropped dark hair but his skin wasn't the unhealthy pale of the Gardier she had seen on the Isle of Storms; he was even a little sunburned. He wore the same roughly tailored brown uniform they all did, with some of the smaller spell devices attached to his belt, made from chips off the larger sorcerer crystals. He also had a pair of the Gardier version of aether-glasses around his neck. But he didn't step out of the gate into Nicholas's reach.

Nicholas waited just out of the man's view, his eyes narrowing with impatience. Frowning, the Gardier reached for the aether-glasses around his neck. *He'll see me anyway. Oh, what the hell.* Before she could change her mind, Florian gestured the charm away.

The Gardier started, staring at her, and took that fatal last step. Nicholas was on him instantly, an arm wrapped around his neck, and the man went down with a strangled gasp. Florian skipped out of the way, seeing blood splatter across the dingy gray stones. *God, I didn't see the knife either,* she thought, shocked. Nicholas had produced it out of nowhere.

Shouts from the house told her the attack had been witnessed. The

Gardier collapsed and Nicholas yanked something off the man's belt, not one of the crystal devices but a metal tube with a handle. He twisted the handle and flung it over the wall toward the house.

Taking her arm, he hurried her down the alley, saying calmly, "We had better report this to the Capidaran authorities. I don't suppose you know where there's a working telephone?"

"Was that a bomb?" Florian asked, not wanting to go through the whole encounter without at least getting a word in edgewise.

Nicholas didn't need to answer her: As they reached the alley the incendiary exploded.

Tremaine landed with a thump on solid stone. She staggered but managed to stay on her feet. The darkness was absolute and it was cold; someone jostled her shoulder, making her stumble. She kept her revolver planted firmly in Balin's back and tightened her hold on the woman's collar until she heard a strangled gasp. She didn't care; she didn't intend to be jumped in the dark by a Gardier. She just hoped she wasn't jumped in the dark by anything else. *Uh ... I hope we're in the right place....*

"Stay where you are," Ilias said sharply, cutting across murmurs of confusion and dismay. "There's a cliff nearby." He had spoken Syrnaic and Gerard repeated the command in Rienish, which caused the jostling behind Tremaine to stop abruptly.

A cold breeze brought her the smell of water and a clean mossy scent, and she realized that background rush was a river cascading over rocks, somewhere not so distant. Her eyes were starting to adjust and she could make out the arch of the overhang just as Ilias and Gerard had described it, where the opening to the gorge was outlined with a faint sheen of starlight. Then light blossomed behind her and she glanced around to see a misty ball of white sorcerous illumination forming over Gerard's head.

The light revealed the large domed cave, the half columns carved into the arching stone walls. Scanning the chamber with a preoccupied expression, Giliead said, "We need shelter for the wounded man."

"Yes, there are rooms back here that should be less exposed," Gerard said, his voice echoing oddly as the wispy light drifted toward the back of the overhang. "Everyone keep together," he added. "We didn't have a chance to search this place thoroughly."

Tremaine followed the light, prodding Balin along in front of her, only realizing they had gone down a corridor when she bumped against a cold stone wall. She groped her way through a door into a very dark room. Gerard gestured again and more wisps of light appeared, revealing a big drafty chamber with smooth stone walls marked by bands of geometric carving. There was a circular stone rim in the center about a foot high. Though the room was out of the direct path of the wind, a strong draft came from the doorway and cold seemed to radiate off the stone like one of the *Ravenna*'s refrigerated storage cabins.

Giliead carried the wounded man in, lowering him carefully to the smooth floor. Meretrisa and Vervane hurried after him, pulling their coats off to fashion a makeshift pallet.

"We need firewood," Gerard muttered, looking around. "And we didn't see anything combustible up here."

"There has to be a passage outside." Giliead stood, looking down at the unconscious Capidaran with a worried frown.

"There doesn't have to be," Tremaine had to point out, giving Balin a shove to get her further into the room. They should have brought some of the furniture from the house, since it was destined to end up as firewood anyway. "There could have been stairs leading up from the river that collapsed."

"Tremaine—" Gerard didn't sound in the mood for random speculation.

"Should we search the place now?" Ilias was at her elbow suddenly, Cletia behind him. "We know this passage is empty and there's room to hole up here for the night."

"No, you're right, we'll wait till the morning," Tremaine told him. It would be ridiculous to wander around here in the pitch-dark when they could fortify this room. Then she hesitated, Ander's words echoing in the back of her brain. "Is that right?"

Ilias snorted and gave her a light thump on the head, apparently the Syprian gesture that meant "don't be stupid." He headed back for the door, calling for Giliead, Cletia following him.

Tremaine looked around, trying to decide what to do with Balin, who was standing in sullen and merciful silence. Cimarus approached then, carrying his and Cletia's packs, asking, "Should I give them the blankets we brought?"

Tremaine saw that Meretrisa and Vervane were huddled on either side of the wounded man, trying to keep him warm. One of Gerard's light wisps hovered protectively over them. "Yes. No, wait, I'll do it, and you watch her." She nodded to Balin. "She's a Gardier, and she's already killed her guard and escaped once, so if she moves, gut her."

"I will, *daiha*— I mean, Tremaine." There had been a Syrnaic word in there Tremaine didn't know, and she eyed him suspiciously as he handed over the packs. He put a hand on his sword hilt, gesturing Balin back into a corner. The Gardier woman obeyed, watching him angrily.

Ilias paused in the corridor to tell Giliead, "We should post a guard at the stairwell."

Giliead looked up and down the stone passage, brows drawn together in thought. One of the floating balls of curse light had followed them, but Ilias saw it didn't provide much useful illumination. Shadows clung heavily to the corners and the other doorways were just cold black holes; they needed to find something they could make torches out of. "None of these rooms had other doors?" Giliead asked.

"No, just these out to this passage." Ilias gestured as they moved along the corridor, Giliead stopping to look into each room, using the curse light to make sure each was still as unoccupied as Gerard and Ilias had found it earlier. Cletia trailed after them. Ilias thought he had been fairly successful at ignoring her so far, and meant to continue.

Giliead found the end of the passage, where narrow stairs curled down a round shaft. Cold air flowed up it, but the draft wasn't as strong as the one that seemed to be blowing straight in off the snow-capped mountains across the gorge. "Let's put everyone else in that first room, and if anything comes up these stairs, there should be plenty of time to give warning."

Ilias nodded absently, looking around for a good spot for the sentries to sit. The corridor was a drafty place to rest in, the air damp and heavy with the scent of the river. "Nothing's getting up that cliff face. Not unless it can fly." He hesitated, thinking that over. "Or come through the curse gate," he added, frowning as he looked back down the passage. He could see Gerard there, studying the circle, another of the wispy balls of curse light floating around him.

Giliead lifted a brow, resigned. "We need a sentry there, too."

"What can I do?" Cletia demanded. She threw a look at Ilias, her features stark in the faint white light. "I want to help."

Giliead considered her for a moment. "Watch the stairs."

Ilias was already heading back up the passage. They needed to fix a blanket over the doorway to the overhang chamber or it would be too cold to sleep. If they had to stay here longer than one night they would have to find a way down to the forest; a good fire and a screen of brush for the doorway would make this place almost cozy.

Carefully avoiding the circle, Ilias went to where Gerard was standing near the ledge, staring up at the sky, paging through a sheaf of papers. He glanced up as Ilias stopped beside him, reflected starlight glinting on the glass over his eyes, and explained, "I'm trying to find out where we are."

Ilias squinted up at the sky, then lifted his brows in surprise. It was a clear night, the stars picked out like ice crystals against the dark void. "That looks like the Archers." He pointed to the constellation that formed the outline of two men with drawn bows. "And the Mother, and the War Galley. The sky looks like it did before the *Ravenna* made the world-gate and we docked at Capistown."

"That answers that question." With a sigh, Gerard tucked the papers back into a leather folder. "So we know we're somewhere close to the region in your world that Capidara occupies in ours. Hopefully by tomorrow Niles will send for us and we can bring more navigational instruments. We're rather badly prepared for an extended stay."

Ilias shrugged. "We've got weapons and blankets. If we can get out to the forest, we'll have everything else we need."

Gerard turned and one of the light wisps drifted over to him as he started back toward the circle. His face set in bleak lines under the white light, he said, "Yes. I suspect we're a good deal better off than our friends at Capistown."

Tremaine carried their other supplies in from the circle and sorted through them, but there wasn't much there. Her bag contained her clothes, the blanket Karima had given her and some more ammunition for her pistol. Gerard had only a couple of books, some personal items and an electric torch, which at least would come in handy. The Syprians were the only ones who had been able to grab a large number of practical things.

Cimarus still guarded Balin, Cletia had been sent to watch the stairwell down into the cliff, Gerard was in the outer chamber with the circle and Ilias and Giliead were trying to use Giliead's blanket to block the draft coming through the doorway. This involved using a couple of latchkeys from Gerard's pocket as nails driven through chinks in the stone and a rock for a hammer and a lot of mock-arguing about who was making the process more difficult by offering alternate suggestions.

Tremaine shook her hair back, looking at the Capidarans. Meretrisa was speaking quietly to the older woman, Vervane, who was watching the Syprians with a wary expression. Meretrisa caught Tremaine's glance and explained with a slight smile, "I was reassuring her that they aren't . . . as uncivilized as they look."

Tremaine lifted her brows. Giliead, the only one tall enough to reach the lintel of the doorway, had just responded to Ilias's criticism of his hammering method by elbowing him in the head. "It depends on your definition of uncivilized. When you see them kill someone, maybe that will give you a better basis for judgment." She glanced back to see the startled expression on Meretrisa's face. *Oops, time to put scary Tremaine back in the box.* She must be more tired than she thought. *Not everyone wants to know what you're really like, you know. In fact, nobody wants it.* "Sorry." She smiled, though it felt false and brittle, and got to her feet.

She made her way through the door-making exercise and out into the circle chamber. Gerard was sitting on the stone, wearing one of the Syprian blankets as a cloak, writing in his notebook in the glow of half a dozen balls of sorcerous light. "Is that a good idea?" she asked, gesturing to the lights. "Someone might see them from the cliffs. Even if we are in the Syprians' world, we still don't know—"

"I warded the opening against light," he explained mildly, without looking up at her. "No one will see it from outside."

"Oh." She sat on her heels, wrapping her arms around her knees and tucking her hands into her sleeves. It was probably colder out here, but she was numb now and couldn't tell. "Aren't you freezing?"

"Yes," he admitted. "Unfortunately, there's no ward that will affect temperature. But it isn't that much worse than the lodging halls at Lodun in the winter. Quite bracing, actually. It reminds me of my student days."

Tremaine lifted a brow. "That was forty years ago, Gerard."

He actually put his pen down to glare at her. "Twenty years ago, Tremaine, twenty—" He saw her lips twitch. "Very funny."

As he went back to his work, Tremaine sat for a moment listening to the river, organizing her thoughts. Finally, she said in Syrnaic, "The Gardier came right to the house, Gerard. They knew where we were."

He nodded grimly, not looking up from his notebook. "Yes, yes, they did."

She took a deep cold breath. "So . . . can they tell we're using this gate?" When they had first experimented with the original circle in Port Rel, transporting the Pilot Boat to and from the staging world to test the spell's abilities, the Gardier had been able to detect when the world-gates were opened. Of course, the Rienish hadn't known that at the time.

"The Gardier should only be able to detect us if they're nearby, in this world. Or if we use the mobile circle to gate to this corresponding location in the Gardier world." He lifted his brows. "Which I don't recommend we do. Ilias pointed out some of the constellations for me, and if I'm correct in my calculations, in our world we'd be closer to Kathbad than Capidara."

"Kathbad." Tremaine frowned. One of the first captured Gardier maps, the one Ilias and Giliead had managed to steal from the base on the Isle of Storms, had shown a major Gardier installation near Kathbad. Once they had realized the Gardier actually came from another world adjacent to the staging world, it had become apparent that the installation wasn't at Kathbad but at the same location in the Gardier world. Kathbad was a remote island nation, and even its nearest neighbor Capidara hadn't had any contact with it for the past three years. Since Kathbad was two world-gates from Gardier central, this wasn't surprising. Tremaine supposed there was nothing left of it by now. "So if we used the mobile circle, the one that takes us to this same physical point in either our world or their world, we'd either be in Kathbad, which is probably a Gardier slave state now, or near a huge Gardier stronghold."

"Yes." Gerard shrugged, still occupied with his notes. "Exactly."

No, I'm fine, really, thank you." Florian handed back the mug of stewed tea, her voice holding a thin edge of impatience. Everyone seemed to think she was about to have a hysterical collapse and kept trying to give her a blanket or a cup of tea or coffee. She understood it was Capistown's first bombing, but she had lived through so many in Vienne she had stopped counting them.

After the bombing had stopped, she and Nicholas had reached the Port Authority to find it still mostly intact. Two bombs had struck the building but one of the Ministry sorcerers had helped the fire brigade extinguish the blaze. The wounded were being carried to the court-rooms next door, the dead still lay where they had fallen. The Rienish offices were in the part of the building now too dangerous to enter and marked by fallen beams and a haze of plaster dust. But Florian had caught a glimpse of Colonel Averi and several other officers she knew, still alive and well. When Nicholas had vanished in search of information, Florian had been swept into the ground-floor offices of one of the steamship companies with a cluster of other refugees, most of whom actually were in a state of hysterical collapse.

Now she was sitting in one of the fine leather chairs of the office's well-appointed waiting room, surrounded by weeping secretaries, office workers and shop girls, with a couple of clerks and a woman Magistrate trying to keep them calm. *This is ridiculous. I know Nicholas said to wait, but I've got to get out of here.* Just as Florian got to her feet, Nicholas appeared in the doorway, saying, "The *Ravenna*'s back, come along."

She hurried after him, relieved he hadn't abandoned her entirely. The office door opened into a little court, once elegantly decorated with potted trees and a little fountain, and now packed with more confused and hysterical people. Florian followed Nicholas's black-clothed back through the crowd and out onto the harbor front. The salt air was heavy with smoke, streaming up from the warehouses and the wreck of an airship that had gone down in the dock area. Out in the harbor a large cargo ship had sunk, its bow still visible above the waves. Like a gray mountain on the horizon, the *Ravenna* was just dropping anchor at the mouth of the harbor, steam belching from all three of her stacks. The great ship looked whole and unharmed, and it was like seeing a piece of home. Florian took a sharp breath that almost turned into a sob. Frustrated, she wiped tears away, breaking into a run to catch up with Nicholas. *Stop it, this is no time to blubber,* she told herself sternly.

Nicholas led her to a dock where a tugboat was being commandeered by Colonel Averi and several other Rienish. She climbed aboard, accepting a helping hand from one of the Capidaran sailors. Nicholas had already made his way up to the bow and Florian found Colonel Averi on the starboard side.

"Florian," he said absently, and put a hand on her shoulder, as if making sure he kept track of her. Looking over her head, the wind ruffling his graying hair, he called to one of the sailors, "All aboard? Let's go."

She stood next to Colonel Averi as the boat chugged into motion, heading out into the gray water of the harbor. The wind was much cooler here and Florian shivered, glad that she had put on a thick sweater this morning. One of the *Ravenna*'s accident boats met them halfway across the harbor and they transferred onto it, the two small craft bobbing in the choppy water.

Soon the *Ravenna*'s giant gray wall loomed over them as the accident boat pulled alongside. Florian clung to a bench as the boat was winched up to the height of a four-story building; she had always hated this part. They reached the boat deck, the davit holding them close to the side, and a female Rienish sailor opened the gate in the railing, ushering them aboard.

Niles was waiting for them on the deck. "All right?" Averi demanded.

"Yes," Niles answered. He was hollow-eyed and hollow-cheeked, his normally sleek blond hair disarrayed. He carried Arisilde's sphere under his arm, apparently unperturbed by the fact that it was spinning rapidly and throwing out blue sparks. "There was a Gardier ship waiting for us when we made the gateway to the staging world, but unfortunately—for them—they were too close to our stern when we materialized and well within Arisilde's range. There were no survivors. There were other Gardier vessels in the area, so we returned as soon as possible."

Florian folded her arms to conceal a shiver, looking away. The gate spell was supposed to have built-in protections against opening a gate where another solid object was already present, but she didn't think those protections had ever really been tested.

Averi nodded sharply. "This changes our timetable rather dramatically. I need to speak to Captain Marais immediately."

As Niles and Averi strode off down the deck, several officers and sailors in tow, Florian stayed where she was. She felt a little lightheaded and wanted to find Kias, Gyan and Calit. She realized Nicholas was standing next to her, and told him, "Don't forget to tell Niles we need to do the new circle to get the others back."

"I will," Nicholas answered seriously, just as Florian had time to realize that was an incredibly stupid thing to say. Of course he would remember. She swore silently at herself, feeling her cheeks redden, as he asked, "You'll be all right here?"

"What? Oh, yes." The *Ravenna* was as familiar to her now as the block her old flat had been on in Vienne. On impulse she asked,

"They're going to talk about leaving, aren't they? I mean, the ship is leaving Capistown soon?"

"Yes." Nicholas looked out over the city, the familiar view of the brownstone town nestled between the sea and the mountains, now marked by plumes of smoke. His expression was distant, his brows drawn together in worry. "It's time to go back to Ile-Rien."

Chapter 6

Tremaine woke huddled against the corridor wall with Ilias's coat over her, cold, aching and cramped. She scrubbed her eyes, wincing at the bright dawn light filtering in around the blanket over the doorway to the circle chamber. Last night Ilias and Giliead had stationed themselves here to watch the circle, and Tremaine had squeezed in between them for warmth and finally fallen asleep. She dimly remembered that the two men had gotten up earlier when it was still dark, presumably to relieve whoever was watching the stairwell. Groaning, Tremaine shoved to her feet, staggered, and limped into the main room.

Everyone else was awake and stirring. Balin glared from her corner and Tremaine ignored her. It was too early in the morning to deal with Balin. Aras, the man with the burns, still lay quiet, Meretrisa sitting at his side, and Tremaine made her way over. "How is he?" she whispered.

"Better," Meretrisa told her in a normal voice. She lifted a fold of the blanket, revealing the man's arm and shoulder, and Tremaine leaned over to see. The skin was pink and new in blotchy patches where the burned areas had been. Meretrisa tucked the blanket back around him. "I don't think he'll wake for a while yet. This kind of healing takes a lot out of both the sorcerer and the patient."

"Right." Tremaine pushed her hair back, frowning absently. That meant Gerard would be worn and exhausted, even more so than usual. She straightened up with a wince. She felt creaky and about a hundred years old herself; she couldn't imagine how he felt.

She turned to find Cimarus standing beside her. He said, rather pointedly, "We have some herbs and grain, but we need water and wood for a fire."

Though the Syrnai was a matriarchy, Syprians organized themselves by family groups, in a system that had little or nothing to do with rank or gender, and seemed based on the fact that everyone knew what everyone else's best skills were. Knowing this told Tremaine absolutely nothing about how they decided who would scout, who stood guard, who steered the boat, who was the leader for that hour and who had to cook. Obviously right at this moment it was Tremaine's duty to organize the group to find water and fuel and Cimarus thought she was lying down on the job. She made vague placating gestures. "I know, I know. But we might be going back this morning." She headed for the hallway and the outer chamber, still limping. If they could return to Capistown soon, there wouldn't be much point in looking for a way down to the forest to forage, though they still needed to explore the place.

She ducked past the blanket curtain into the big chamber. Sunlight flooded it and the cool breeze carried the clean scent of the river and the distant rush of the waterfall. It was almost enough to wake her up. The jagged rim of the cave mouth looked out on a panoramic view of deep green forest cloaking the cliffs on the opposite side of the canyon.

Gerard sat on the stone floor near the circle, notebooks scattered around him, contemplating the symbols with a dissatisfied expression. He looked pale in the bright light, his face drawn and marked by dark circles under his eyes. The sphere sat next to him, quiescent. But since it didn't have Arisilde's active personality, that meant nothing. Ilias and Giliead both stood nearby, contemplating Gerard worriedly.

Tremaine frowned, pushing a hand through her hair again. "No word yet?"

Gerard looked up with a sigh. "No, nothing."

She bit her lip, uneasy. It would have taken Niles some time to draw the new circle on the *Ravenna*, once the battle was over. If the battle was over. If Niles was alive. If the *Ravenna* wasn't at the bottom of Capistown harbor or its equivalent in the staging world. "It's night there now, right? Maybe they decided to rest first."

"Perhaps." Gerard shook his head, gesturing in annoyance. "If we don't hear from them soon, we'll have to try to return. In the meantime, we might as well explore this place." He glanced at the doorway to the corridor, though they were all speaking Syrnaic and only Cletia and Cimarus could have overheard. "You all realize, someone in the Capidaran delegation must have communicated to the Gardier where the house was and what we were doing there. That was no random bombing; they were determined to stop us."

Giliead nodded, grimly unsurprised. Ilias looked thoughtfully at the corridor doorway, asking, "One of them?"

Tremaine shrugged, rubbing her eyes. "Who knows? I don't think a spy would let himself—herself—be trapped in the house with us, but there's no guarantee it's a professional spy and not just a lucky amateur."

"Aras walked toward the firebomb," Giliead pointed out. "He didn't know what it was. A spy would have been expecting some kind of attack."

"Unless he has a little crystal stuck in his skin, and doesn't know he betrayed us, like Niles did," Ilias pointed out.

"I can check Aras when I examine the healing on his burns, but I don't think he has one," Gerard said, thinking it over. "I think I would have noticed it during the healing spell." He glanced up at Tremaine. "You'll have to make an excuse to search the two women."

"God." Tremaine buried her face in her hands. "It could be anywhere, Gerard, and I'm not going to be able to think of an excuse to search anywhere." They could simply force the two women to allow a search. Though if they found nothing, all that would accomplish was letting a voluntary spy know that they were onto her. "Weren't the Capidarans supposed to be checking for Liaison crystals?" she demanded.

"Yes, but 'supposed to be' is the key phrase. They have little experience so far with how effective Gardier spies can be, and I don't know how careful they were," Gerard told her with some asperity. He sighed, gesturing helplessly. "Just be careful, all of you, and keep an eye on them no matter how helpful or innocent they seem."

In the gloom of the stone passage, Tremaine checked her pistol, wishing she had brought more ammunition than just the handful in her bag and what Nicholas had stuffed into her coat. She returned the weapon to her pocket, making sure she had Gerard's electric torch in the other. She paused, brow lifted, to take in the sight of Ilias, wearing his dark blue greatcoat over his Syprian clothes, with his sword belt slung over his shoulder. He caught her smile and demanded self-consciously, "What?"

"Nothing." She glanced at Giliead, who had tossed his dun-colored wrap over his shoulder to accommodate his heavy leather baldric. "Ready?" she asked him.

Cletia folded her arms, eyeing them with disfavor. "I should go too. I've done nothing but watch that door all night and nothing has come through it."

"Then you must be doing a good job," Tremaine told her brightly. Giliead gave Cletia an ironic eye as he stepped past her into the stair-well. "Keep it up," Tremaine added.

She followed Giliead, Ilias bringing up the rear. The stairs curved down in a spiral and the rock walls were streaked with moss, fractured sunlight from the cracks in the rock above lighting the way. Tremaine noted the steps were a little too tall for her and Ilias, but seemed ex-actly right for Giliead's longer legs, like the steps in the Wall Port and the deserted city under the Isle of Storms. A random thought re-minded her and she looked back up at Ilias to ask, "What does *daiha* mean?"

Ilias cocked his head. "*Dai*— You mean *daehan*?"

"Yes, Cimarus called me that."

"Huh." He nodded to himself, his expression hard to read.

"What does it mean?" She poked him in the stomach, but she might as well have poked the wall.

He seemed to take the question as a challenge. "I can't tell you what it means if you don't have a word for it."

"Don't be difficult."

Giliead sighed, apparently seeing his hope for peace and quiet quickly vanishing. "It's what you call a woman warleader, but only when you're in battle."

"Oh." Tremaine wasn't sure how she felt about that. Cimarus didn't strike her as being as unyielding in his attitudes as Pasima. Syprians didn't like to be alone, and Cimarus might find that Ilias's curse mark and Giliead's recent experience with magic didn't matter much when the other choice was near isolation. But Cletia was an unknown quan-tity. She had chosen to leave Pasima's company, but Tremaine wasn't entirely sure what that meant.

As they continued down, she saw there were also square niches cut into the walls, some high enough for lamps, some at waist height or only a few inches above the steps. She tapped one as they passed. "These are just like the ones in some of the walls in the old city on the Isle of Storms."

"All the dead cities we find look alike," Ilias said from behind her, pausing to examine a niche. He sounded like he thought it was a conspiracy. "What does that mean?"

They were the only unifying characteristics of three fairly dissimilar places, but that didn't tell them much about the original inhabitants. "Beats me."

"You're not supposed to say you don't know," Giliead told her, his voice echoing faintly in the well. "You're supposed to come up with a bad idea and then argue about how you're right all day."

"Hey," Ilias protested, obviously the one the comment had been aimed at. "I don't do that, you're the one who—"

"Fellows, don't start . . ." Tremaine trailed to a halt, staring at the wall. This step was wider than the others, turning it into a small landing. On the inside wall, at about her eye level, was an arrow scratched faintly into the stone, pointing up the stairs. She touched it, deciding it had been made with the edge of a coin. *Or a coat button,* she thought, nodding to herself. *Arisilde.* Lost in thought, she became aware that Ilias and Giliead were standing on either side of her, having seen the arrow and obviously expecting elucidation.

She shrugged, irritated that she couldn't give them an explanation. "We're still in the right place?" she suggested.

Ilias snorted in annoyance. "He could have left a more revealing trail sign. He doesn't want us to go down this way? Why?"

Giliead turned, starting down the steps more slowly, saying with grim emphasis, "I'm almost afraid to find out."

"Almost?" Ilias said under his breath, as Tremaine followed.

The stairs took one more turn, the light from above growing dim with distance. Giliead stopped and Tremaine leaned around him to see, brows lifting at this new discovery. Shade-dappled sunlight shone in from gaps in the rock, illuminating another big domed room, a mirror of the circle chamber above.

The gray-veined walls had the same square columns, narrowing as they arched up to meet in the dome overhead, the same bands of carving, broken by the cracks in the stone. And where the other chamber had been cut in half by the rockfall that had sent a portion of it down the cliff into the river, this one was bisected by a wall of cut masonry blocks. "What the hell?" Tremaine said aloud.

Ilias stepped past her to follow Giliead out into the chamber, scanning the area cautiously. "At least we found the way out."

Giliead's mouth twisted wryly. "I wouldn't say 'found.' There's nothing else down here." He moved toward the largest crack in the rock, an irregular opening just wide enough for a man his size to squeeze through. Just past it Tremaine could see green-shaded sunlight and a flat stretch of ground with tufts of dry grass.

Slowly, Tremaine looked around the big chamber, then followed Ilias and Giliead outside, climbing through the rough-edged opening to see an evergreen forest glade. The trees were some kind of giant pine, stretching up tall enough to easily tower over a sizable two-story house. Fallen needles made a soft carpet underfoot and the ground sloped down to a shallow winding ravine where a stream played over tumbled rocks and gravel. The air was fresh and clean and cold with the early-morning chill.

Giliead was already down by the stream, pacing along it, looking for signs of human occupation, or possibly curse traps. Ilias had taken up a position on a slight rise in the ground, keeping watch.

Tremaine climbed the slope to stand beside him, pine needles scrunching underfoot. She looked vaguely around for any more signs from Arisilde, but without any idea of what she was looking for, it was a fruitless search. "You think it's dangerous here?"

"Could be." Ilias jerked his chin down toward the stream. Tremaine looked, then looked again, her eyes widening. What she had taken at first for a collection of sun-bleached white rocks was actually a pile of bones, the carcass of some large animal. Very large, she realized, spotting the skull, which was a good two feet across the raised browridge. It had large eye sockets and teeth that were at least as long as Tremaine's forearm. "But maybe those only come up here in the winter, for the caves," Ilias added with a half shrug. "If we can catch one, that's a lot of meat."

"Right." *Catch one. Occasionally I forget that Syprians are crazy.* Tremaine found herself losing the urge to wander. At least the cave entrance was too small for anything like that to get inside. "I think I'll go back in," she told Ilias, and headed down to climb back through the gap into the cave again.

Dusting off her hands, she went toward the wall, staring at it. "I don't understand this," she said aloud. The chamber up on the cliff looked as if it had simply given way to time or some weakness in the rock face. This wall . . . didn't make any sense.

She studied the floor, scraping at the accumulated dirt with her boot heel in several places, but there was no sign of the symbols of a circle, or anything else, etched into the smooth stone. Turning back to the wall, she thought it looked just as old, but she was no stonemason. She scraped away at the dirt that coated the mortar between the blocks, then stopped, frowning. *Mortar?* The rest of this place had been carved right out of the rock. The city under the Isle of Storms had been constructed without mortar; she was sure of that. The long log-shaped stone blocks had been distinctive, piled together and attached to each other in ways that were inexplicable to her untrained eyes. *Did the Wall Port city use mortar?* The quality and color of the stone had been different, which made sense, as far away from the island as it was, but she couldn't remember if she had seen mortar or not. She thought not. *So it looks like somebody else put this wall here.*

Lost in thought, Tremaine became aware that Ilias was standing at her side, trying to hand her a grubby green-stripey object covered with dirt and dangling bulbous roots. "What? No." She fended it off with an elbow. "What is that?"

"A sava. You don't have those?" He brushed off some dirt and took a bite. It made a crunching noise, like a very ripe apple. As Tremaine eyed it skeptically, he added, "They grow all through these kinds of woods." Still chewing, he frowned at the wall. "Why is that here? It doesn't look like the rest of the room."

"I don't know." She gestured helplessly. "Nothing makes sense."

He lifted an ironic brow. "You just noticed that?"

"A little help here," Giliead grumbled from the opening as he tossed in an armload of fallen branches and kindling, and Tremaine, distracted by the idea of a fire and hot food, mentally put the wall aside for the moment.

While Ilias helped Giliead carry up several loads of wood, the others used the first bundle to get a fire started in the raised hearth in the main room. On the second trip Ilias saw that Cletia had unloaded the contents of her pack, producing a small cooking pot, a folded-up waterskin, some dried herbs rolled up in a leather pouch and what was left of her packet of boiling grain, which was almost enough for him to be glad she was here. Almost.

After they had brought up enough firewood, Ilias went back outside to cut some fresh branches, hauled them back up and used some leather cord from Giliead's pack to make a windscreen for the door into the cliff chamber. It took him a while to make it both easily movable and heavy enough to block the strong wind, but after it was done he wandered back into the main room, shaking pine needles out of his hair and clothes, to find the place seemed almost homey now.

The fire had nicely warmed the chill stone room and from the smell someone had made tea. Cletia was tending the fire now and keeping an eye on the Gardier woman Balin, and Cimarus had gone to watch the outer entrance. The Capidaran women were asleep; not surprising, as they had been up most of the night watching over the still-unconscious wounded man. Several of the sava had been washed and peeled and were now cooking in the coals. His stomach rumbled at the smell, reminding him he hadn't eaten since this morning. Which had been late last night, here. Realizing it was afternoon now, which meant it was deep into the night back in Capidara, he went back out to the cliff chamber, shifting the screen aside to pass through the door.

Tremaine, Giliead and Gerard were all seated on the floor, staring at the curse circle with varying degrees of consternation. "So it's been too long," Ilias said, uneasily considering the consequences.

Tremaine pushed to her feet, throwing an arm in the air. "It seems like a long time to us, because we've just been sitting around staring at it. Niles had to redraw the circle somewhere else from your notes—"

Gerard removed the glass pieces over his eyes to wipe his forehead with his sleeve. "My notes were very clear." He sounded testy about it. "It shouldn't take as long as it did to draw it for the first time. And a Gardier bombing has never lasted this long. With the spheres allowing an active resistance—" He stopped, shaking his head.

"We can go back to see what's happened," Giliead suggested quietly. "Or one of us can."

Ilias eyed him. It was true one of them would have to go, but he didn't want Giliead to volunteer. When they had been captured near the Gardier city, the wizard with the crystal stuck in his head had seemed far too interested in Giliead. They knew now that the Gardier had some way to take wizards out of their bodies and put them in their crystals, that they had done that with Rienish wizards they had captured, that Arisilde might have lost his body through the same process. If the Gardier thought a Chosen Vessel was the same thing as a wizard, they might have meant to try it with Giliead. Ilias would just rather not give them the chance.

"That sounds like a very bad idea," Tremaine said, unconsciously echoing his thought. "If they haven't come after us, there's a good reason."

Gerard paced away a few steps, thinking it over. "If Niles and Kressein were both killed. If Nicholas didn't make it—" He threw a look at Tremaine but her expression didn't change. Ilias knew she would never betray herself that way, not even in front of her family. "There may be no one who knows where we went." He took a deep breath. "Even if Florian survived, it may not occur to her that we fled through the gate."

Tremaine shook her head, frowning at the carved dome over their heads. "Niles, Kressein, Florian and Nicholas? Especially since we saw the *Ravenna* go through a gate. We might as well say the whole city's in ruins and everybody's dead."

Gerard stared at her in exasperation. "Tremaine, how many sides of this discussion are you on?"

She gestured erratically. "I'm just being the . . . devil's advocate. I don't know." She scratched her head, looking at the circle of symbols. "And we know we can't make a regular circle, because that would just take us to Kathbad and we know we don't want to go there."

Ilias nodded. He had been through enough curse circles by now to get the hang of it. "Besides, we're high up in the mountains. If we make the regular curse circle here, we could come out up in the air in the other place."

Gerard held up a hand for silence, saying carefully, "I'm aware of the difficulties of the situation." He rubbed his forehead, his frustration showing. "We'll have to try to go back through this circle."

Giliead shook his head, pushing to his feet. "We're all tired. We need to eat and sleep first. And if the worst did happen and the city's been destroyed, then it won't hurt to wait a little longer."

Tremaine watched Gerard thoughtfully. "He's right." Ilias knew it was mostly Gerard Giliead was thinking of. The wizard hadn't had any sleep in the last two days, and not much in the way of real meals. Gerard's eyes were hollow and he looked more exhausted than he had since the *Ravenna* had reached port.

Maybe Gerard realized it too. He gave in with a sigh. "Yes. Yes, he's right. We'll wait a little longer. At least it's giving me time to work on the problem of trying to get into Lodun."

*   *   *

Florian sat on the deck, rubbing her arms through her rumpled sweater. *I feel like I just did this,* she thought tiredly. They were in one of the *Ravenna's* Second Class lounges, and the electric lights were too bright for her tired eyes. Blackout cloth had been tacked into the fine wood veneer on the walls to stretch across windows that looked out onto the open deck. The blue and gold carpets had been rolled up and the couches, chairs and cocktail tables pushed back to the walls to clear the tile floor so that Niles could draw the symbols of the new circle.

He had been at it for some time now, the faint rasp of paper as he consulted his notes the only sound. Arisilde's sphere sat nearby on the floor, clicking occasionally as Niles drew the symbols.

Florian yawned. Her clothes still stank of smoke from the fires in the city and she longed to take a hot bath and collapse in one of the cabins, but she wanted to see the others back safe first. And Niles had needed her to confirm his reading of some of Gerard's notes, and later to help keep him awake and check his work. After all his efforts during the battle, he was still deeply exhausted. Giaren, who had made forays throughout the evening to the kitchens to obtain coffee and rolls, was sitting in an armchair on the far side of the circle, half-asleep himself. He had reported earlier that a detachment of Capidaran troops was coming aboard the *Ravenna* as planned, that Colonel Averi and Captain Marais had received word that the *Ravenna* could leave as soon as the supplies meant for the Rienish forces in Parscia were loaded, but that there was some problem that Averi was angry about. One of the officers had said he thought that the Capidarans had cut the number of troops they had promised at the last moment. In the quiet of this lounge at the ship's stern, it all seemed very far away.

The *Queen Falaise*, headed directly through the staging world for Parscia, had already left and Florian had watched from the Promenade deck as it had steamed out of the harbor, saluting the *Ravenna* with a blast of its horn as it passed. Ander was aboard, along with some of the other Rienish officers she had gotten to know here. With two Aderassi sorcerers and their newly made spheres, the *Falaise* had every chance of making the crossing safely and running the blockade to reach Parcia. That was what Florian kept telling herself, anyway.

Florian jerked awake as Niles sat back on his heels with a sharp intake of breath, rubbing his eyes. "That's it."

"That's it?" Florian straightened up. "We can get them back now?"

Niles got to his feet with a groan, one hand on the small of his back. "Yes. Just give me a moment." Giaren hurriedly stood, pouring a cup of coffee from the tray and carrying it over to Niles, who took it with a gasp of gratitude.

Florian pushed to her feet. "I can do it, if you're too tired. I mean, you must be too tired."

Wincing at the taste of the coffee, he glanced at her. "Are you certain? You haven't used this particular circle before."

"No, but I've done the other one, and I'll have . . . help." She gestured at the sphere. It clicked back at her, a blue light flickering briefly from inside. "He's done it before."

Niles hesitated but a voice from the furniture crowded against the far wall said, "She's right." Florian looked, startled, to see Nicholas sitting up from where he had been lying out of sight on one of the couches. He climbed over a chair, his black coat making him a rather graphic figure against the softer golds and creams of the upholstery. He reached the floor, shaking out his coat. "From what I understand, with Arisilde's help, I could attempt it as well."

Florian turned back to Niles, glad for the support. "Yes, so there's no need for you to—"

"Yes, yes." Niles waved her to silence. "Go ahead. But be sure to let the sphere set the parameters for you."

"I know." Florian hurried to grab the sphere before he changed his mind or recalled what had happened the first time she had tried to use the sphere by herself. It clunked as she stepped into the circle. Shaking her hair back, she looked down at its tarnished surface.

"It's different from working with an inert device," Niles continued, carrying his coffee over to a chair and easing himself down into it as if his back still pained him. "Just give it a prompt with the first few phrases of the adjuration and let it do the rest."

"Right." Florian nodded firmly. She tightened her grip on the sphere and began the adjuration.

A blue light sparked through the openings in the metal, but nothing happened. Florian frowned, and tried again. And again. She looked up, frustrated, to see Niles, Nicholas and Giaren watching her expectantly. *Damn it, why does this have to happen now?* she thought in despair. Yet another chance to show that she was useful, ruined. But maybe she was more exhausted than she thought, and that was why Arisilde wasn't working for her. Maybe she had simply messed up the spell so badly even he couldn't fix it for her. "Niles, I'm doing something wrong. The sphere isn't working for me."

Brow furrowed, Niles set his cup aside, getting to his feet. "That's odd. Usually it's a struggle to keep it from interfering." He joined her in the circle, taking the sphere and gazing down into it, his face going blank from concentration.

Florian waited, tensed in expectation of the sudden vertigo the gate spell caused, the sudden transformation into a new place. But there was nothing. The lounge remained the same, the electrics too bright, the furniture disordered.

Niles lifted his head, his expression incredulous and almost angry. "Something's wrong."

Tremaine was more conscious of the waiting now, and she hadn't any way to occupy herself. At least Gerard had been persuaded to lie down and try to sleep instead of poring over his notes trying to figure out a way into Lodun. Ilias and Giliead had gone foraging in the forest again, coming back with fish from the stream and a collection of nuts and berries. She had gone out with them earlier to explore the area around the bluff thoroughly, and though they had found more jumbled stone ruins and more signs that this had been some sort of ancient settlement, they had found no more tokens left by Arisilde. And there wasn't much of anything else left to find, just tumbled pillars, the remains of old foundations, scattered blocks from fallen walls. There was also no sign of current occupation, no trace of any other human inhabitants nearby. Tremaine was reduced to pacing the corridor.

The only good point in all this that she could see was that Ilias and Giliead had already benefited from being out of Capistown. After spending the morning out in the bright sun and brisk wind, Ilias had his color back and looked healthy again. Giliead was actually talking to people other than Ilias and hadn't lost his temper once.

The meal when it was ready was a welcome distraction. Cooked over the fire, the fish were good even without any kind of seasoning, and the sava turned out to taste a little like sweet melon once it was baked. "It's good country," Giliead said, spearing a piece of fish out of the coals for Cletia. With no plates, everyone was eating out of their hands. In a moment of generosity, Tremaine had even agreed to let Cletia give Balin a portion. "I'd hate to winter here, though."

"It's not winter now?" Tremaine asked him, only partly kidding. He lifted a brow at her.

Using his knife to cut up another sava, Ilias prodded her with his boot to tell her he didn't think she was funny. "We'd need half the year to lay in supplies," he added. "Without a good grain harvest, it wouldn't be much fun even then."

"We won't be here for winter." Cletia, more literal-minded, was eyeing them both a little suspiciously. "Will we?"

Ilias rolled his eyes. Annoyed, Giliead told her, "We're just talking."

I hope we're just talking, Tremaine thought, licking the last of the fish off her fingers. She thought the reason Giliead and Ilias had spoken of the possibility of being trapped here for a long time was because it was in both their minds. They had looked at the country around their mountain shelter with an eye to long-term survival, and she had the feeling they had decided that the prospect wasn't good, not without more supplies and time they didn't have. *Hell, even I can tell it's a little late to grow crops,* she thought dryly. *Especially on top of this mountain.* "You don't want to live here, Cletia? It's almost homey now."

Cletia gave her a somewhat arch look, acknowledging that this was not a friendly overture, then poked at the fire. "It's too bad we don't have Sanior with his laik," she said.

Tremaine frowned thoughtfully, remembering her Syrnaic vocabulary. A laik was a musical instrument, something like a harp and something like a guitar. Sanior had brought one on the *Ravenna* and played it occasionally, though Tremaine had never had leisure to listen to it.

Cletia added to Ilias, "If we did, you could dance for us."

Ilias regarded her with a lifted brow, as if he knew he was being taunted and was waiting for the punch line of the joke. *All right,* Tremaine thought, *with this one I have to take the bait.* "Dance?" she asked.

Giliead answered, "Young men of wealthier houses are supposed to learn things, playing the laik or the cyere, singing, dancing, for festivals and family celebrations." He had kept his eyes on Cletia through this explanation, a line between his brows, as if he couldn't quite decide what she was up to but he knew it was no good.

He had used another word Tremaine didn't know. "What's the cyere?"

Giliead thought for a moment, searching for different words. "Finger cymbals," he told her.

Still eyeing Cletia, Ilias said deliberately, "It's too cold here for dancing."

Cletia looked from Giliead to Ilias, pressed her lips together, then said in annoyance, "Don't glare at me, I was only looking for something to talk about."

Ilias snorted and put a piece of sava in his mouth, as if hoping that would end the discussion. But Tremaine, intrigued, had to ask, "Will you dance for me sometime?"

Ilias transferred the lifted brow expression to her, but this time without the suspicion. "Maybe," he said, around the sava.

After the meal, Tremaine glanced around, noticing that Vervane was sitting near the wounded man, drinking some of the tea, but Meretrisa was missing. Thinking that the woman had probably retired to the room they had designated as the latrine, Tremaine got up, stretched, and wandered out into the corridor.

The brush wind block still leaned back against the wall, and the sky outside the sheltering overhang was taking on the violet tinge of early evening. Trying to rub a kink out of her neck, Tremaine glanced up and saw Meretrisa seated beside the circle. The Capidaran sorceress was copying the symbols down in a small leather-bound notebook. Tremaine's mouth twisted. The Rienish command had given the mobile circle and instructions for constructing spheres to Kressein and the other Capidaran sorcerers as part of their alliance; did Meretrisa think they would withhold this new circle, that she couldn't trust them to pass it along as well? *And if we were going to withhold it, does she really think we'd be stupid enough to let the Capidaran Ministry know it existed?*

She strolled into the larger chamber, giving Meretrisa a casual nod as if she was encountering an acquaintance at the omnibus stop. But Meretrisa smiled self-consciously, as if aware she had committed a social gaffe, and put the notebook away in her jacket pocket.

Gerard walked in then, his hair disordered, in his shirtsleeves, eating a piece of sava and squinting at the sky. He said in Syrnaic, "It will be close to dawn in Capistown. This is as good a time to try as any."

Giliead and Ilias followed him, Giliead saying, "If any Gardier stayed to watch the house, they'll be weary of it by now and more easily taken by surprise."

"If Nicholas was able to destroy the circle, the Gardier should have had no reason to remain." Gerard looked around with a frown, absently patting the bag slung over his shoulder as if making sure the sphere was still there. "I'm still hoping our friends have just been delayed and the situation in Capistown isn't that serious."

Meretrisa hastily backed away from the circle as Gerard stepped into it. Giliead followed him. Ilias folded his arms and regarded him in a disgruntled way. Tremaine understood this was payment received for Ilias's accompanying Gerard on his first experimental trip here. *Men,* she thought, suppressing an annoyed snort. *Syprian men, in particular.* "Gerard, do you have a pistol with you?"

Gerard struggled into his coat, then took the sphere out of the bag, brushing lint off its polished surface. It was smaller than Arisilde's sphere and considerably less dented and tarnished. "Yes, but if there's a need for it, we'll be returning immediately."

Tremaine exchanged an ironic look with Ilias. Neither one of them needed to say, "You hope," but clearly they both wanted to.

"If they find the Gardier there, what will we do?" Meretrisa said, low-voiced. She folded her arms, tucking her hands into her wool jacket, and shivered. The breeze from the opening was turning cold again as the sun sank, but Tremaine suspected it wasn't the chill in the air that affected her. And Meretrisa did live in Capistown.

"Don't worry about that yet," Tremaine said, shifting uncomfortably. If Capistown had fallen so easily . . . *At least the* Ravenna *had a chance to fuel and take on supplies,* she thought pragmatically, but she wasn't going to say that aloud.

Gerard lifted the sphere and Giliead loosened his sword in its scabbard. Tremaine took a sharp breath.

And nothing happened. The moment stretched, and Giliead glanced at Gerard. Ilias frowned and Meretrisa looked puzzled. Tremaine cleared her throat.

Gerard swore, adjusted his spectacles, took a firmer grip on the sphere and obviously tried again. Again nothing. Tremaine's stomach tightened. *Oh, don't let this be what I think it is.* "Gerard . . ."

Gerard looked away, wiped the sweat off his forehead with his coat sleeve. "It's not working," he said grimly.

Ilias stirred uneasily. Tremaine protested, "But it's never done that before. Neither of them, that sphere or Arisilde. They always work."

Giliead was looking at the sphere, frowning. He reached out tentatively and Gerard handed it to him. Giliead held it while Tremaine held her breath. "Could you see the spell?" Gerard asked, his voice tense.

Giliead shook his head slightly. "It's harder to see the curses when it doesn't have a god."

"Test it," Tremaine urged. "Make it do something else."

Gerard had already reached out, laying a hand lightly on the metal surface. Giliead blinked, flinching a little, as half a dozen wisps of sorcerous blue light sprang to life just above their heads. "I saw that." He pulled his hand back, self-consciously dusting his fingers off on his shirt.

"It's not the sphere itself, then." Gerard cradled it in both hands, his jaw tight with tension. "Let me try again. Perhaps—"

"—it's just having a bad day," Tremaine finished under her breath when Gerard left the word hanging. There wasn't a personality in this sphere. It should work like the clockwork amalgamation that it was.

Gerard tried several times, even bringing Meretrisa into the circle and letting her try with the sphere, but nothing worked. Tremaine paced, Ilias wandered back and forth to the edge of the gorge and kicked loose stones over the precipitate drop to the river, Giliead stood with his arms folded and an increasingly grim expression. Vervane, then Cletia, came to stare worriedly at them and demand an explanation. But the circle refused to work.

Gerard kept trying, until the sky had darkened to an indigo-purple. The wind, blowing from the snowcapped mountains across the gorge, filled the chamber with an icy draft and the translucent balls of sorcerous fire clung to the pillars or were mashed up against the far wall by the force of the wind. Meretrisa had retired to the inner rooms, unable to stand the cold, but Tremaine's nerves kept her pacing, though her fingers were numb and her joints felt stiff. Giliead had taken a seat on the stone and Ilias had finally settled next to him, using the larger man as a windbreak.

Finally, Gerard stepped out of the circle, flung his notebook onto the stone floor and dropped down to sit beside it, burying his face in his hands. "Let's look at this logically," he began, his voice slightly muffled. "I'm using the adjuration in exactly the same way I used it for the first opening of this portal, our return, then our second journey here. There is, in fact, only one varying factor—"

Tremaine couldn't stand it anymore. She had thought of it earlier and was certain Gerard had as well, but she had been reluctant to say it aloud. "Nicholas was going to destroy the other circle."

"Yes." Gerard rubbed his eyes and took a deep breath, looking out toward the gorge. "Shit," he added succinctly.

Giliead nodded, weary and resigned. "This curse needs two circles, one there, one here."

"The symbols in the circle gave no indication that . . ." Gerard didn't finish the thought, shrugging helplessly.

Ilias shook his head, looking as if he was searching for something optimistic to say and not finding it. "The others . . . on the *Ravenna* . . . if we don't come back, they'll make another circle."

"Yes." Gerard sat up straight, making an effort to sound brisk. "They will, if they survived the attack." Then he swore, clapping his notebook shut. "If we don't return, they may abandon the plan to reach Lodun. The whole thing hinged on the success of this circle and how we could use it to create others!"

"Yes, but they'll come after us . . ." *Eventually. Which we all know they should have done already.* Tremaine scrubbed her hands through her hair with a moan. "Look, let's just— Go back by the fire, warm up before we freeze, get some food. Try again tomorrow." Gerard looked at her bleakly and she gestured vaguely, feeling hopeless and stupid. "We can't do anything about it."

Gerard shook his head, but reached up to her and she caught his arm to help him stand. Ilias was already on his feet, shifting the brush screen aside. Giliead stood by, waiting while Gerard collected the mostly useless sphere from inside the circle, slipping it back into its bag.

They trailed through the doorway into the passage and the welcome warmth of fire, Ilias wrestling the wind block into place behind them. Cimarus was out taking his turn at guarding the stairwell; he had constructed another fire pit from loose rock and sat next to it sharpening his sword, with a Syprian blanket wrapped around his shoulders. He looked up hopefully and Giliead shook his head, telling him there had been no further developments. Cimarus grimaced and ran the whetstone down his blade again.

Tremaine prodded Gerard on into their chamber; she knew this room would probably feel cold once she got used to it but at the moment it felt as warm as the beach at Chaire during high summer. Cletia and Cimarus must have collected more wood and more sava, as the fire burned high and there was a new collection of the striped melons roasting in the coals, next to the pot which steamed and emitted a fragrant herbal odor. Cletia sat on one side of the fire, the Capidarans on the other, huddled under their collection of coats and blankets, with a sullen Balin in her corner. The wounded man was awake and sitting up. He stood suddenly, wavered on his feet and had to be hastily steadied by Vervane. He demanded, "What's going on?"

Tremaine's brows lifted at the peremptory tone. She remembered that his name was Aras but not what he had been doing with the Capidaran party. The sorcerous healing had left splotches of new pink skin on his face and showing through the tears in his shirt and coat. His cropped dark hair looked singed. Ignoring him, she steered Gerard to a seat by the fire and draped his coat over his shoulders. That was the limit of her maternal instinct, so she was grateful when Cletia appeared at her elbow offering a warm mug of the tea from the cooking pot. Tremaine crouched to hand it on to Gerard, noting that the cup was stamped with the old arms of the hotel that had been conscripted as a refugee hostel. She wondered if Cletia had collected it as a souvenir or solely for pragmatic purposes. The Capidaran man demanded again, "What is happening?"

Returning to her seat, Cletia caught Tremaine's eye and grimaced. Tremaine took it to mean that even with the language barrier, the man had been making himself annoying. Tremaine looked at Meretrisa, asking, "Didn't you tell them?" She knew that after Meretrisa had left the circle chamber she had been ducking back in to check on Gerard and giving regular updates on their progress and lack of progress to the Capidarans, as Cletia had for Cimarus.

Vervane looked uncomfortable and urged the man to sit down. Meretrisa started to reply, hesitated, and Aras said, "I asked you."

Tremaine straightened up and eyed him, beginning that slide from annoyance into real anger. "Yes, you asked me." Ilias had been pacing the chamber, rubbing his arms and trying to warm up. He stopped abruptly, looking at Aras. Giliead was simply standing by the fire, arms folded, watching the man with an air of waiting for him to cross some invisible line.

"Tremaine, this is Langel Aras, speaker to the Capidaran Ministry," Gerard interrupted. He took a cautious sip of the herbal drink and winced. "Aras, this is Tremaine Valiarde. And you know as much as we do. The return spell won't work."

Aras stared at him, then sat down heavily, shaking his head. His disgruntled attitude that seemed to say loudly "I'm trapped with idiots" was worse than any cutting comment. And it gave Tremaine no opportunity to make a cutting comment back. She said only, "We're trying again tomorrow," and sat down next to Gerard, glaring grimly at the fire.

There wasn't much else to do. Meretrisa, Vervane and Aras eventually settled down to sleep, and with some persuasion, Gerard joined them. Cletia curled up on the other side of the fire and Giliead went off to relieve Cimarus at watch.

Tremaine just sat, her thoughts running in circles. *Arisilde sent us here for a reason and it wasn't just to see these rooms, this circle.* Ilias was right, this was hardly the place the Gardier had discovered the gate spell. Besides being in the wrong world, there just wasn't enough information here for anybody to discover much of anything.

Tremaine was starting to fume. It wasn't fair, damn it. There had to be something in that bottom chamber, but it was as empty as the rooms up here. *But why did Arisilde leave an arrow pointing away from it, as if he came from that direction?* Nothing there but a wall that bisected the chamber neatly at the point where the circle chamber had collapsed into the river. Nothing there but the way out, unless there was just something outside she and the Syprians hadn't ranged far enough to find. And if it was that far, it seemed as if Arisilde would have left a map or better instructions somewhere. *Maybe that's a fake wall,* she thought, planting her chin on her folded arms. Nicholas should be here. *Fake walls are his specialty ... Oh. Holy God.*

She leapt to her feet, causing Ilias, who had been lying asleep behind her, to scramble awake with a muffled curse. "What?" he demanded, shaking his hair out of his eyes.

Tremaine shushed him, found Gerard's pocket torch lying amid their small collection of supplies and headed for the door. Ilias shoved to his feet and followed her.

Out in the corridor, Giliead sat beside the smaller sentry fire. He looked up, frowning, at their approach. "What's wrong?"

"I want to go down and look at the wall," Tremaine explained, stepping past him.

"What wall?" Baffled, he looked at Ilias for help. Ilias flung his arms in the air in defeat.

"The wall, the wall that shouldn't be there." Tremaine flicked the torch on and started down the uneven stairs, one hand on the rough stone to steady herself. Ilias hurried after her and Giliead got up to follow. "The thing is, Arisilde was leaving these clues for Nicholas," she said, partly in explanation to them, partly gathering her thoughts. "He probably expected to show this to Nicholas himself after they met up again, but if something happened to him, he wanted Nicholas to be able to retrace his steps and find it. He didn't expect them to both be stuck. And whatever this was, exploring it kept him from going back immediately to give the warning in Ile-Rien, so it must be important."

As they neared the bottom of the stairs, Ilias shouldered ahead of her to reach the chamber first, stopping at the doorway. Tremaine flashed the torch over his shoulder, making sure nothing else was there. *A bear, or something worse, creeping in to use the place as a den would be just what we need,* she thought wryly.

The torch caught the gray-veined walls and the square columns, the bands of carving and the gaps in the rock that led outside. It was frigidly cold and quiet except for the muted movement of wind through leaves and branches, whispering in from the cracks in the outer wall.

Certain the chamber was empty except for themselves, Tremaine shoved past Ilias and went to the misplaced wall. She ran her hand along it, frowning. She could feel the rough texture, feel the cold that seemed to radiate off it. But Arisilde had been very good at illusions. She scrubbed at the stone, rubbing some accumulated dust off on her fingers. Focusing her torch on her hand, she stared at the smudge determinedly.

Giliead had come to stand beside her. She could sense doubt radiating off him with the same intensity that the stone radiated cold. "What are you doing?" he asked finally.

At least he hadn't said she was crazy yet. "It's an experiment," she told him. "I think the wall is a spell."

"But if it was a curse, Gil should be able to tell," Ilias said around a yawn.

Giliead studied the wall, his brows knit. "But if it's the man from the god-sphere's curse . . . I've always had trouble seeing its curses. It can hide them from me whenever it wants."

Ilias pushed at the wall thoughtfully. "So how do we tell?" He hadn't said Tremaine was crazy either. He gave the impression he was used to being dragged out of a sound sleep to humor people in the middle of a cold night and he simply couldn't be bothered to frame an objection to it anymore. *Maybe that's why I love him,* Tremaine thought, lifting an ironic brow at herself. Then she processed that thought. *I do what?*

She found herself staring at Ilias, inadvertently pointing the torch at him. Leaning on the wall, he winced, lifting a hand to shield his eyes from the light. "What?" he demanded.

Tremaine opened her mouth but before anything embarrassing came out, Giliead seized her hand. She flashed the torch back to her fingers. The smudge of dust was gone. "It is a curse," Giliead said, eyeing the wall with new respect. "How did you know?"

Ilias hopped away from it, startled. Giliead poked the stone again, then pressed his hand against it. Tremaine shook her head, forcing herself back to the problem at hand. "Arisilde knew my father used to use hidden compartments, fake walls. There's one fake wall at Cold-court. One that I know of, that is." She knocked on the wall, trying to think it through. "So Arisilde put this wall here because he wanted to temporarily block off what's behind it, but he wanted Nicholas to find it. And he must have wanted Nicholas to be able to get through it, even if Arisilde wasn't with him."

Ilias sat on his heels to examine the bottom row of blocks. "But Nicholas wouldn't be alone, he'd have to have a wizard with him to get here at all."

Tremaine nodded absently. Gerard would probably be able to break this illusion, but she didn't want to wake him. And she wanted to do it herself. She was certain there was a way that didn't involve magic. How had Nicholas said Arisilde had described the gate spell? That it had a weight and an elegance of design. That was how Arisilde preferred his spells. He had treated magic like an art form, not like a means to an end.

Giliead shook his head, still baffled. "I thought Gerard said that curses couldn't create something out of nothing, and a Rienish wizard couldn't do a transformation curse."

"Well, yes, but this is an etheric illusion," Tremaine explained. Lost in thought, she swung the torch back and forth, only realizing she was doing it when she noticed the light waving wildly around. "It's just a really good one. We're not actually touching it or leaning against it, we just think we are. That's why the dust disappeared from my hand when I stopped looking at it."

Ilias traded an uneasy look with Giliead and stood, falling back a pace from the wall. Giliead lifted his brows. "So there's not a wall here, there's just a curse that makes us think there's a wall here."

Tremaine stepped near the stone. "Right. So logically . . ." Turning her back, she closed her eyes and let herself fall backward.

She heard a yelp from Ilias and felt a hand brush her sleeve as someone made a wild grab for her and missed. Then her bottom hit hard cold stone with a bone-shaking jolt, followed by her back and skull. She swore, reaching back to grab her head. *Didn't expect that to actually work.* Ilias caught her arm and hauled her to her feet. "Tremaine, warn us next time! You didn't know what was back here. I didn't even bring my—" He stopped abruptly.

She blinked up at him but couldn't see his expression in the dim light. She had dropped the torch when she hit the ground and it lay on the floor, pointing into the part of the chamber that had been hidden by the illusory wall.

The light shone out in a broad triangle, illuminating an expanse of gray stone floor. Tremaine saw a broad curve of symbols carved out of the stone and thought, *Hah, another circle,* then realized she could see at least three more curves fading away into the shadows. *Unless they decided to make a gate circle into a giant curlicue for variety . . .* She grabbed up the torch, shining it across the floor.

She counted six circles, the symbols incised deeply into the stone, the carving filled with dust but still clearly visible. As she moved the light, she saw the chamber was bigger than she had expected. She had thought it would mirror the one at the top of the cliff, but it was at least four times the size. The half columns along the curved wall arched up to meet overhead in the dome, the stone so polished it threw back glitters of light, the design in the bands of carving more defined, without the wear of wind and rain. "It's like a train station for world-gates," she said, still finding it hard to believe. "Oh yes, I think this is what Arisilde wanted us to find."

Giliead stepped past her, leaning down to look at the first circle. "I think these are different than the others, the new one and the old one." He straightened up, scuffing his boot near one of the symbols. "This glyph is new."

"You memorized the symbols?" Tremaine demanded, startled. But she remembered the complicated system of Syprian trail marks and signs, a compressed form of their written language that allowed them to leave elaborate messages for each other with very few symbols. And both Giliead and Ilias had learned the directional signs on the *Ravenna* and how to understand Rienish far more quickly than she would have in their situation. She knew they didn't use writing much in their everyday life, preferring to leave that to their poets, so it must make their ability to memorize that much better.

From the other side of the room, Ilias answered her, "There wasn't much else to do today." He traced a path around another circle. "There's a different glyph in this one too. No, three different glyphs."

"After what happened at the Wall Port, it seemed like a good idea," Giliead admitted, moving to study the next circle. "You want to wake up Gerard now?"

Tremaine nodded slowly. "Definitely."

Chapter 7

Florian wearily slumped in a red leather club chair, her head in her hands. She had to keep stopping herself from asking what they were going to do; it was obvious no one knew.

They were in the opulent First Class smoking room, which on the voyage to Capidara had been taken over by Gerard and Niles as a work area and laboratory. The high ceiling rose to a dome and the walls were paneled in dark woods framed with strips of copper banding, the floor inlaid with stone tile. Two of the blocky tables had been pulled into the center of the room and were stacked with books, papers, glass beakers and flasks, jars of herbs and powders and crystals. Charts covered a surrealist seascape and an easel had been put up in one corner to support a chalkboard. Wooden crates were stacked against the opposite wall, all filled with books, sorcerous equipment and supplies. Arisilde's sphere sat on the table, idly spinning itself and clicking occasionally.

The *Ravenna* had left Capistown harbor before dawn. Capidaran ships sailing under concealment charms had sighted several Gardier ships and an airship near the coast, so they had had to gate early to avoid them. There had been some trepidation because of the problem with the new circle, but Niles had been able to take the ship through the original etheric world-gate using Arisilde's sphere, without any apparent problem. They were sailing on the sea of the staging world now, the Syprians' world, heading back toward a brief stop at Cineth, then world-gating back to their own world off the coast of Ile-Rien. Florian wasn't certain what the status was of the fledgling plan to help Lodun; so much of it had depended on Gerard and Niles making a new spell circle to get past the barrier.

Nicholas paced in front of the Parscian carved screens framing the marble hearth. Niles sat in another chair, his face pale and his eyes shadowed with exhaustion. He rubbed his temple, and said, "I'll re-draw the circle again. There must have been something I missed, some error."

Nicholas paused beside the table, picking up a spoon from the cof-fee service that sat there, carefully placing it in a line with the others on the tray. In his current state, Niles appeared to take this action as criticism. The sorcerer said sharply, "It's the only answer."

Florian winced, looking away. *We don't have an answer,* she thought. Niles had redrawn the circle three times during the night. Giaren had developed the rest of his photographs of the original circle from the Capistown house, and they had carefully compared them. As far as Florian could see, there was nothing wrong with the last circle Niles had drawn, or its two predecessors.

Nicholas regarded him with a lifted brow. "It may be the only an-swer, but it isn't the correct one."

Niles took a deep breath, contemplating the stacked crates and the books they contained. Useless books, for their purposes, Florian knew. They were in entirely new territory here. Niles said, "We could bring in Kressein, Avrain and Kevari, let them try."

Avrain was an expatriate Rienish sorcerer who had been studying magic with the Massians, the original native inhabitants of Capidara, and Kevari was an Aderassi sorcerer who had gone on a pleasure voy-age years ago just before the invasion of Adera and had been unable to return since. Both had volunteered to accompany the *Ravenna* back and to try to help Niles use Arisilde's sphere to reach Lodun. They were currently sequestered in a suite, trying to construct more spheres for Ile-Rien and Parscia.

Nicholas, still adjusting the positions of the spoons, threw a brief opaque look at Florian. She had the feeling he wanted her to dissuade Niles, but she didn't know what to say. "Niles," she began carefully, "all they can do is redraw the circle, based on Gerard's notes and Gi-aren's photographs. And I don't think anything was wrong with your circles."

She wouldn't have been surprised if Niles shouted at her, but he apparently wasn't inclined to it, even if he hadn't been too exhausted to shout. He shook his head wearily, saying, "Perhaps there's something—I don't know, off about me. My etheric aura. Maybe the Gardier crystal I was infected with has affected it and it's taken this long—"

Nicholas frowned. "Perhaps you're under a gypsy curse. Perhaps the ship will be struck by a comet and we needn't worry about it." He gestured abruptly in annoyance, disarranging the spoons. "Niles, this sort of speculation—"

A knock at the door interrupted him. Florian looked around to see Colonel Averi with another man of about his age, with graying dark hair and handsome regular features. He was dressed in a dark fashionable suit, and was glancing over his shoulder to say to someone, "—be of great help, I'm sure."

As he turned to face them Florian recognized him. He was Lord Chandre, a Rienish nobleman who had been living in Capidara. All she knew about him was that he had somehow gotten involved in the attempt to fight the Gardier. Behind him were a couple of men in Rienish army officer uniforms and another man in a suit— Florian sat up, staring in astonishment. It was Ixion.

Still slumped in the chair, Niles, hollow-eyed, hollow-cheeked, focused on Ixion. His eyes went hooded and he suddenly looked dangerous rather than defeated. "What is he doing here?" he said, his voice flat and quiet, cutting across Lord Chandre's attempt to speak. Florian saw Nicholas had casually stepped back against the marble mantel, one hand in his coat pocket and the other on the sphere. It was trembling on the table, its insides spinning with infuriated rapidity.

Chandre lifted his brows. He looked at Colonel Averi, who folded his arms and didn't seem inclined to be helpful. Chandre turned back to Niles, saying, "Ixion here has volunteered to assist you, so we'd like to discuss the situation." He smiled blandly around the room, ignoring the tension. "With Niles, that is. I'm sure you understand."

Florian looked in horror at Niles. "How very odd," the sorcerer said, apparently idly, "I'm to be assisted by a man whose prison I helped to construct? Or should I say a murderer whose prison I helped to construct. Yes, I should say that."

Ixion simply smiled, strolling further into the room, glancing around curiously. Florian thought his face was still a little too smooth and that there was something a little out of place in the way he wore the fashionable suit.

In a "we must be reasonable" tone, Chandre said, "Now, you must know about the arrangement the Capidaran Ministry had come to with Ixion. Let's just discuss this." He directed a more pointed look at Nicholas. "In private."

Niles lifted a brow. "Oh, I'd love to discuss this with you."

Florian took a sharp breath, feeling the air thicken, feeling the sphere shift from passive annoyance to active aggression. Ixion's face went still and his eyes narrowed. The heaviness in the air doubled and Florian knew if she could see etheric vibrations the room would look as if it was overflowing with them, charged with power, crackling with suppressed energy. Ixion smiled thinly, and said, "I do love a challenge. Pity you can't give me one."

Niles started to come out of the chair. Florian said sharply, "Niles, don't." His eyes flicked toward her. He hadn't lifted a hand but she felt the spells, his and Ixion's counterspell, trembling in the air, poised to strike. She wasn't sure anyone else in the room realized the danger. Except Nicholas. She said carefully, "That won't help."

"Yes," Chandre added, oblivious to the disturbance in the ether that resonated with the barely felt thrum of the engines and made the ship's metal bones sing. "Dissension in the ranks can't do us any good, you know." He sounded smooth and assured, but Florian sensed a certain satisfaction in his tone. He enjoyed wielding this power over the sorcerers.

Niles took a deep breath. Florian felt the spell dissipate and unclenched her fists in relief. Ixion's counterspell drifted away and his thin smile grew even more acidic. The sphere spit out a blue spark in disgust and subsided angrily.

Nicholas looked at Niles, lifting a brow in inquiry. Niles made a weary gesture of assent and Nicholas inclined his head. Grimacing, Florian pushed to her feet. She might be able to get them to let her stay, based on her knowledge of the circles, but she suddenly found that she didn't want to. Giliead had said this would happen and it made her sick at heart that it had. Actually, her sickness resided closer to her stomach.

Ixion said suddenly, "You would be so good as to remove that."

Florian glanced up, startled, but he was speaking to Nicholas. And he meant the sphere, now throwing off agitated sparks. Nicholas smiled with genuine amusement, telling Ixion, "If it affords you some sort of false sense of security, I'd be happy to."

He calmly collected the sphere and gestured politely for Florian to precede him, as the other men in the doorway made room.

Florian followed Nicholas, not sure what else there was to do. Sleep seemed impossible, despite the exhaustion that made her legs feel shaky. He led the way down the wood-paneled corridor, out onto the Promenade deck, a roofed expanse running the length of the ship. The broad glass windows revealed a sweeping view of the sun rising over the sea in orange and yellow glory, only a few clouds streaking the limitless horizon. There was a time difference between their world and this one, so that evening in Capidara was morning here. It added to Florian's floaty unsettled feeling.

Nicholas glanced at her, his dark eyes serious, assessing. "Could you tell what spell Niles was about to cast at Ixion?"

Florian bit her lip, thinking it over. "I didn't get much of a sense of it. I'd bet it was a variation of an unbinding."

"An unbinding?" He slid his hands into his pockets, frowning at the polished deck. "I thought that was only effective on magical constructions, like golems, for example."

Most laymen didn't know that much about sorcery, but given what Tremaine had told her of Nicholas's past, Florian wasn't too surprised at his knowledge. She explained, "Niles told me that he had been working a little on trying to figure out how Ixion had made his body, because of Arisilde, and the woman in the Gardier crystal. He said transferring consciousness at the moment of death, even if it's as dramatic a death as having your head cut off, would actually not be that difficult." Nicholas lifted a brow and she amended, "Comparatively difficult. He said Urbain Grandier actually did something similar, putting his consciousness in other people's bodies. Grandier was a half-Bisran sorcerer a couple of hundred years ago who—"

"I'm familiar with Grandier, and the historical context," Nicholas interrupted sharply. "Go on."

"Right, ah . . ." It took her a moment to get her train of thought back together. *This is as bad as the Lodun Entrance Examinations,* she thought in exasperation. "Niles said the difficult part is getting the body. Apparently Ixion really did grow it, like he grew the creatures the Syprians call curselings, and didn't just steal it from someone. And thank God for that, really, if you think about it." Nicholas still seemed unimpressed, and she hurriedly continued, "Niles didn't tell me what he was thinking of doing, but he may have been working on an unbinding spell, tailored to sort of disassemble whatever Ixion did to assemble the body. Because of the way the unbinding would work, there's a good chance it might keep Ixion from popping back into another body hidden on the island or somewhere." She shrugged helplessly. "That's what I'd do anyway, if I was him. If I could put together a spell like that, let alone cast it."

Nicholas nodded slowly, his eyes distant. "Niles's background is in etheric theory, correct? The philosophical aspects of sorcery?"

"Yes, that's right." Before the war, Niles had had more experience with researching dusty historical texts, experiments in manipulating ether and constructing Great Spells for other sorcerers. It made him an ideal choice for the Viller Institute. "It doesn't exactly make him a good candidate for a pit death match with a Syprian sorcerer who can do consciousness transference and transformation spells," Florian acknowledged ruefully.

"Is that why you stopped him?"

Florian halted, one hand on the railing. At the far end of the Promenade a few naval officers stood in a group discussing something animatedly, but other than that, they were alone. The ship had a different feel now, occupied with troops rather than refugees. Most of them were belowdecks in their quarters, or still in the First Class dining hall, and their mood was subdued. They knew they were going into danger, and they knew there were far fewer of them than Capidara had originally promised, even with the number of expatriate Rienish and Aderassi volunteers. "I— I couldn't let them fight it out, Ixion's been accepted by the Capidarans—"

"And if Niles, as a high-ranking Rienish sorcerer, killed a native sorcerer who had already been accused of murder, even if it was in an unprovoked fit of pique, do you really think he would get more than a stern talking-to?" Nicholas looked down at her, exasperated. "It was a perfect opportunity, Florian. The sphere was there to assist him, and there were even witnesses who could testify that it was a fair fight. Niles is not by nature a violent man, and he won't be easily pushed to this point again. Ixion is too clever to allow it."

"So you want Niles to murder Ixion?" With effort Florian kept her voice low. "I know Ixion is . . ." She knew how Giliead and Ilias would feel about this, but they weren't here. And no matter how she felt about it, realistically she wasn't sure they could afford to turn their noses up at any offer of help. "But he could help us. He has no reason to help the Gardier. In fact, he'd probably end up in a crystal if they caught him again. And Ixion hasn't done anything yet, not to us. Killing him now— It would be murder in cold blood."

Nicholas shook his head slightly. "I've never understood that attitude." While Florian was trying to get her mind around that casual and apparently entirely sincere statement, he turned, strolling down the Promenade again, hands clasped behind his back. Florian followed, feeling as if she were being drawn along like a wheeled toy on a string. He said, "Even if I didn't believe the Syprians' account of Ixion's past actions, his choice of alliance with Lord Chandre is proof enough that he has to be eliminated."

Florian frowned. "I'm not sure I understand."

He flicked an opaque look at her. "Chandre is more interested in positioning himself advantageously, whatever the outcome of this war, than he is in forcing the Gardier out of Ile-Rien."

Florian stared at him. "That's vague enough."

"I didn't have to give you an answer at all," Nicholas pointed out with deceptive mildness. They had reached a doorway to an interior corridor and Nicholas paused there, one hand on the door handle. "You've attracted Ixion's attention by showing him that Niles will listen to you. You may want to take care."

Watching him go, Florian grimaced. She had been ignored by virtually everyone else; she didn't see why Ixion should be any different.

Waking Gerard proved more difficult than Tremaine thought. Saying his name and laying a hand on his shoulder failed completely, and he responded to vigorous shaking by groaning and batting at her, so she decided to let him rest a little more. Meretrisa and the others were still asleep and Cletia was back on watch. Tremaine had told Cletia briefly what they had found and the Syprian woman had greeted the news with resignation. Apparently she was willing to use the circles to get to safety, but was not particularly thrilled with finding a treasure trove of them. There was nothing the Capidarans could do to help at the moment, so Tremaine was careful not to wake them. And she wanted Gerard to see the new circle chamber before anyone else did.

It was near dawn when Tremaine made another try and this time Gerard groaned, batted at her again, then actually opened his eyes and sat up.

"Guess what?" she demanded as he fumbled for his spectacles.

"What?" He got the spectacles in place after a couple of tries and gazed at her warily.

"We found something." She handed him a cup of the tea kept warm by the fire.

He took the cup, looking a little more alert. "Something helpful?"

Trying the different circles would either help them or kill them. Tremaine settled for, "Probably."

D ear God," Gerard muttered as he stepped off the stairs into the underground chamber.

"Nice, huh?" Tremaine moved past him, pleased with his reaction. Ilias and Giliead had brought in some wood from outside, building a fire in the narrow part of the chamber to make the cold a little more bearable and also fashioning some torches to light the place.

The firelight turned the gray veining in the stone to pure silver before the domed roof arched up into shadow. The circles etched into the smooth stone floor were each nearly twenty feet across. The new symbols from the circles were repeated in the carved bands along the wall, their looping curves intricate and mysterious. Gerard walked around for several moments, speechless, the sphere tucked protectively under his arm.

He paused finally, leaning close to the wall to study one of the bands between the pillars, adjusting his spectacles. "This is writing," he said softly, his voice echoing a little off the domed roof. "Is it a language used only for casting, or was their written language and their casting language the same?"

Tremaine assumed it was a rhetorical question. She rubbed her arms in her coat sleeves, trying to stay warm. The fire had taken the dampness out of the woodsmoke and pine-scented air, but if you stood still for any length of time it was still bone-achingly cold. Ilias and Giliead, once they had explored the chamber to their satisfaction, hadn't left the vicinity of the fire.

Gerard took a deep breath, turning away from the wall. "And you haven't found any other signs left by Arisilde?"

"No." Tremaine shook her head, gesturing in annoyance. She was sure they would find something, but there had been nothing to find. It took some of the excitement out of the discovery. "We looked pretty carefully."

"If he explored the curse circles, but didn't come back this way, he wouldn't have had a chance to mark the one he took," Giliead put in, explaining the pet theory they had discussed while searching the chamber. "The last one he took," he amended.

"We think he came in through one of the circles down here, mostly because the arrow in the stairwell pointed up," Tremaine explained. They hadn't done much else since finding the chamber besides come up with permutations of various theories. "So maybe the circle he gave us in Capistown was something he came up with specifically to connect with the one up there to get us here."

"But if each of these curse circles can only be used to go to one place, why doesn't the one up there still work?" Ilias pushed to his feet, stretching extravagantly. "Even if the one back at the house is ruined, that one up there should still go to its original place, right?"

"Yes, theoretically." Gerard nodded thoughtfully. "Unless the original counterpart has been destroyed as well."

Tremaine shrugged. "Which would explain why Arisilde sent us here, because he wants us to retrace his path, and it's the first step that still exists."

Gerard looked around again, brows knit. "He may have also sent us here simply to see these circles. With so many to compare with the one Arisilde gave us, I think I'll be able to isolate the series of symbols that controls the location. It should be similar to the symbols that delineate the world in the mobile circle."

Tremaine saw Ilias and Giliead exchange a thoughtful look. She lifted her brows. "So, which one do you want to try first?"

After Gerard copied down the symbols of all the new circles into his notebook, they retired back to the upper chamber for a conference and for breakfast, which had become an increasingly important issue for Tremaine as the cold morning wore on.

Ilias had been the one to cook, and had proved better at making the little graincakes than Cletia. Somehow when he did it, they actually had flavor. If not for the Syprians' ability to catch fish and find roots and nuts and identify what was edible, Tremaine knew they would surely starve. She didn't miss coffee as much as she thought she would, but now that they were almost through Cletia's grain supply, she found herself desperately missing bread.

Gerard explained the new find to the Capidarans while they ate the cakes, more of the cooked sava and some green nuts that Cimarus had found on his last foray for firewood. Meretrisa, Aras and Vervane listened with expressions of increasing doubt as Gerard talked. Giliead translated for Cletia and Cimarus while they smashed open nuts with a rock.

"I don't— Why should we risk it now?" Meretrisa asked, frowning in worry. After so long with no access to a brush or comb, her dark hair had come down from its bun and begun to look untidy, and Tremaine had helped her braid it while they were waiting for the sava to cook. It had given her a chance to unobtrusively check Meretrisa's neck and shoulders for crystals, but she had found nothing. Not that she had expected it to be that easy. She had no idea yet how she was going to get near Vervane; the older woman was as standoffish as Cletia, if not worse. "It's only been a day. Our friends could be delayed by any number of things—"

Tremaine and Gerard both drew breath to answer but Aras beat them to it. "That doesn't matter," he pointed out. "We have to explore these gateways anyway, the sooner the better, even if someone comes to us from Capistown in the next five minutes." Aras's mood seemed to have improved drastically now that he was presented with something useful to do.

"Yes, exactly," Gerard put in.

Vervane was nodding. The older woman had dark circles under her eyes and her skin seemed to sag. It made Tremaine wonder if the woman had actually slept or just pretended to. Her accent thick with a Lowlands tinge, she said, "Master Kressein would agree. The sooner we begin, the better. If the Ministry had any doubts . . . surely the attack has convinced them."

"I'm glad we're agreed," Gerard added firmly. Nobody mentioned the fact that Meretrisa hadn't agreed. Tremaine regarded the woman thoughtfully but Meretrisa let it pass, just sitting there with a faint line between her brows, as if she was thinking of something else. Gerard took a deep breath, gathering his thoughts. "The thing to remember is that we've had incidents in the past where a slight alteration of the gate spell led to a rather unpleasant and dangerous place."

He was talking about the world Florian had taken them to accidentally, the place where Tremaine and Arisilde had left the Gardier Gervas. Ilias grimaced at the memory and threw a look at Tremaine, saying in Syrnaic, "We don't want to go there again."

Tremaine nodded, giving him a thin smile. "I wouldn't want to disturb Gervas. I'm sure he's having fun with his new friends."

Ilias snorted in amusement and Giliead just lifted an ironic brow.

"The sequence of location symbols seems to indicate that these circles lead to places within this world, but there are still symbols we haven't encountered before, that we don't know the meaning of," Gerard continued, steadfastly ignoring them. "For this reason, I suggest we send only myself and one volunteer on each foray. Ilias and Giliead and Tremaine have volunteered." Gerard paused to give Tremaine a repressive eye. She smiled blithely back at him. They had had a discussion about this down in the circle chamber, where Tremaine had overridden Gerard's objections, pointing out it wasn't fair to ask Ilias and Giliead to take all the risk. And this was important. Since these circles led to other places in the staging world, they could help Gerard figure out how to gate straight to Ile-Rien from Capidara, or even how to gate inside Lodun.

Aras nodded. "I volunteer as well." He looked expectantly at Meretrisa. "And we have more than one sorcerer."

Meretrisa hesitated and Vervane looked a little alarmed, perhaps worried that she might be volunteered too. *Gosh, let's not be subtle,* Tremaine thought, disgruntled. She didn't mind volunteering herself for possibly fatal missions but volunteering other people was out of bounds. But Meretrisa said hesitantly, "I would like to learn the spell more thoroughly, perhaps test it once, if that were possible. I know it in theory, but—"

"There's no need to take unnecessary risks," Gerard put in firmly. "Once we discover a 'safe' gateway, Meretrisa can practice with it until she proves proficient. Until then, I'll perform the spell."

Back down in the lower circle chamber, Tremaine paced impatiently. Cimarus and Cletia had remained upstairs on guard over Balin and the other circle. Aras and Meretrisa had explored the chamber with Gerard but Vervane, though she had looked around curiously, had ended up staying near the fire. It was still chilly down here and Tremaine wondered why the older woman didn't just return to the upper chambers. But Vervane still seemed wary of the Syprians, and might not want to be alone with Cletia and Cimarus. Ilias didn't seem to want to be alone with Cletia or Cimarus either, but that was personal.

Gerard and Aras had picked a circle to try, the first one on the side of the room nearest the door. Aras, being far more helpful than

Tremaine would have given him credit for last night, suggested sending a useless object through and back first to make sure the circle
didn't open into solid rock. Gerard had explained that these point-to-
point circles used the spell language that apparently prevented them
from opening if there was a solid obstruction. The movable circles
used by the *Ravenna* and the Gardier airships were also supposed to
be obstruction-proof, but this was untested as they were only opened
in midair or over water to try to avoid the problem. Tremaine and
Giliead were the only ones who appreciated Ilias's suggestion that they
still send Cimarus through first, just in case.

Ilias had lost much of his sense of humor once Tremaine made it
clear that she was going with Gerard on this first test. "You're the only
woman in your house," he had pointed out, low-voiced, while the others argued about something else. "You shouldn't risk yourself."

"Yes, but it's a little too late for that now," she told him. "And it's
my turn." Her nerves were slightly abraded by Meretrisa's behavior
once Aras had recovered. She deferred to the man constantly, though
she was a sorcerer and Kressein's assistant, which should give her
some status in Capidaran counsels. Here, where having a competent
sorcerer with a sphere was the difference between getting home and
settling down to grow crops for the winter, it was ridiculous for her to
behave so diffidently. Every time Gerard turned to the woman to get
her opinion, Meretrisa hesitated and Aras answered for her. Tremaine
suspected it was annoying Gerard as well, though for different reasons. A competent colleague, someone to share the responsibility for
their lives, would have been a great relief to him; with Meretrisa hiding behind Aras, Gerard couldn't talk to her long enough to ascertain
whether the woman was competent or not.

Tremaine wasn't sure if Ilias and Giliead had noticed this. Ilias was
too busy trying to come up with a logical argument as to why he
should go with Gerard instead. Giliead was watching Gerard and the
Capidarans with folded arms and a closed expression, and avoiding
the fire because he could obviously tell Vervane was nervous in his
presence.

Aras had also volunteered to go with Gerard, dubiously eyeing the
pistol Tremaine intended to take. "Tremaine is a crack shot," Gerard
had told him firmly, forestalling her offer to prove it by shooting off
the Capidaran man's ear.

"But you don't need to go, there's—" Ilias started again.

"But it doesn't matter if I'm the only woman left in my house or not," Tremaine interrupted impatiently. "We don't have a house left standing in Ile-Rien, and if I die, it's not going to affect Nicholas one bit."

Ilias stared at her a moment, then pressed his lips together and looked away. *Oh, great,* Tremaine thought, watching his whole body stiffen with annoyance, more mad at herself than him. "What?" she demanded. He didn't answer, but she could sense him fuming as clearly as if she could actually see it in the cold air. Gerard, Aras and Meretrisa had finished their tour of the room and gathered around the circle they meant to try. Gerard was taking the sphere out of its bag. "Come on, we're nearly ready to go, tell me what I did wrong."

Ilias took a sharp breath and looked at her, saying deliberately, "Nicholas is not the only man in your family now."

Oh. She pushed a hand through her hair wearily. *Yes, that is your foot in your mouth; the taste should be familiar by now.* "You don't need me to take care of you, in case you haven't noticed. You've taken care of yourself and Giliead for years with no help from me." Giliead, standing almost in earshot and hearing his name, gave them a distracted look.

Ilias shook his head, but he looked more confused than angry now, which Tremaine considered a factor in her favor. "That's not . . . the point."

Gerard called her name and Tremaine turned to go. Ilias caught her arm, pulled her back and kissed her.

Gerard gave Tremaine a repressive look as she joined him in the circle. "What?" she demanded, taking her pistol out of her pocket and checking that it was loaded, even though she already knew it was. *I am not blushing. I am too old to blush.*

He shook his head wearily. "Nothing. Are you ready?"

"Sure." It wasn't the going there, wherever there was, that made Tremaine's stomach tighten with tension. It was the coming-back part. If this circle behaved the way the one in the upper chamber did and suddenly and inexplicably refused to work, it would strand them and leave the others without a sphere. *The other one won't work because Nicholas destroyed the circle in the house and Niles hasn't had time to make a new one,* Tremaine told herself, gritting her teeth. *It's the logical reason.* Unfortunately she had never considered herself a logical person.

Gerard turned his attention to the sphere and Tremaine braced herself. And nothing happened. After a tense moment, Gerard contemplated the stone ceiling in pure irritation, shaking his head, swearing under his breath. "Oh, you're joking," Tremaine said in disbelief.

"Yes, I thought a little humor would lighten the mood," Gerard snapped. "This circle isn't working either."

Giliead put his face in his hands and Ilias ran a hand through his hair, looking hopeless. Meretrisa stared in disbelief and Aras frowned. "But what does this mean?" Vervane asked helplessly.

"It's anyone's guess, at this point," Gerard answered, his voice showing the strain of trying not to bite the older woman's head off. "I assume the circle this one was meant to connect with no longer exists." He told Tremaine briskly, "Let's try another."

Tremaine followed him to the next circle, frowning. "You don't think it's the sphere, do you?"

Gerard threw her a dark look and she said, "Oh." *So he thought of that already.* But nothing had happened to it. This sphere hadn't been dropped or banged around, and no one had had any opportunity to tamper with it, not with the Syprians watching Balin and guarding the corridor while Gerard was asleep. And it still worked for other spells. "This is just great," she said under her breath.

"Right, brace yourself." With deliberate optimism, Gerard lifted the sphere. Prepared for another dud, Tremaine was caught completely by surprise by the sudden flush of vertigo.

The world went white and the next breath she took was icy cold.

Tremaine pivoted, staring, as Gerard made a startled exclamation. They were in a gray stone building, one wall tumbled down and covered with ice and snow. Through the gap she could see a cloudy gray sky and ruins spread out across an icy plain. Much of it was buried under white drifts, but Tremaine could see fallen pillars, tumbled blocks of stone, the remains of colonnades and avenues and elegantly proportioned buildings that seemed to go on forever. Icicles clung to half-collapsed pediments and the bases of broken statues, giving the whole scene a silver glitter.

This structure had a high ceiling and lofty dimensions, its walls covered with faded shapes of carved figures nearly worn away by time and weather. Tremaine could just discern the outline of a woman, lifting her arms toward a sun-disk shape, and a herd of antlered animals leaping a chasm. Her breath misting in the cold, she looked out again over the city. There were mountains in the misty distance, far past the ruins, huge and rugged as the ramparts of a castle, capped with white.

"Why do we never think to bring a camera?" she said in frustration. Studying the faded carvings, Gerard shook his head mutely.

Nothing moved but the falling snow, so Tremaine slipped her pistol into her pocket, then left her hand there. Her fingers were already starting to go numb. She took a step forward, shivering in her heavy coat, and felt the floor crack under her boot. Startled, she looked down to see it was covered with a solid sheet of blue-tinged ice. The symbols of the circle must be down there somewhere, but they were concealed under what had to be at least a foot of ice.

Tremaine exchanged a look with Gerard. He nodded grimly, saying, "It's good to know the factors in the spell that prevent materializing into a solid object actually work."

"That would have hurt," Tremaine agreed, her teeth chattering. In fact it hurt now. The cold was so intense it made her chest ache and taking a breath was difficult, even though the remains of the thick stone walls sheltered them from the wind somewhat. "If we need another ruined city, or snow, we know where to get it now. Can we go back?"

"Yes." He nodded, and she thought his nose was actually starting to turn blue. "An excellent thought."

He lifted the sphere and Tremaine closed her eyes, thinking, *Please work.* She felt the lurch, then her feet hit solid stone. She stumbled and caught herself on Gerard's arm, swearing in relief at the familiar sight of the firelit cave.

Ilias was beside her suddenly, brushing at her hair with a bemused expression. "Snow?" Brows lifted, Giliead studied the melting flakes scattered around them on the stone.

"Hold still," she told Ilias, and pushed her freezing hands under his shirt. He made a strangled noise but didn't protest, folding his arms around her and pulling her against his chest. Even huddled against his warm body, she felt like an icicle.

The others were clamoring with questions and Gerard was saying, his voice still rough from the cold, "A ruined city, buried under ice and snow. The circle itself was under a sheet of ice. If there are more circles there, I don't see how we could find them, or even survive the cold long enough to search."

"And we wouldn't want to get trapped there," Giliead added with unexpected firmness, glancing at Tremaine. She must look frozen.

Gerard nodded. "We have to keep looking." He took a breath which turned into a coughing fit. Clearing his throat as Aras pounded him on the back, he managed to say, "Though I think we have time to stop for a cup of tea first."

Ilias demanded, and got, his turn to accompany Gerard next. The wizard had wanted a rest first and had actually fallen asleep again for a time. They had been careful not to wake him. It made Ilias wonder just what the near-constant use of a sphere without a god, as well as using his other curses, was doing to Gerard. He had never known any wizards long enough to see if the use of curses took a physical toll on them or not. Noticing that Gerard, a lean man to begin with, looked thinner, with an unhealthy cast to his skin, and the flesh just under his eyes beginning to sink, Ilias thought that the answer was definitely yes, at least for Rienish wizards. And they still hadn't been able to discover if either of the two Capidaran women were spies, or if they had been innocently swept along on this journey.

He knew he hadn't been right to object to Tremaine taking turns at the curse circles with them. When it came down to it, she had been doing this longer than he or Giliead. It wasn't as if this was a marriage of anything but political convenience, as if they had a pile of children and unmarried relatives at home to worry about. But he didn't particularly want Giliead to try the curse circles either. He sighed to himself in frustration. *I think I'm an idiot.* Giliead just kept giving him looks that suggested he agreed with that assessment.

At least Ilias knew he had been right to take over the cooking today. He thought Cletia might be playing "I have to be matriarch and take care of you all" and he wanted to put a stop to that immediately. He wasn't going to have Cletia brooking Tremaine's authority in ways Tremaine might not realize.

After Gerard woke again, startled that he had slept so long, he quickly began to check through the papers he kept in the scroll's bag. Mostly to himself, Gerard muttered, "It can't hurt to have a second copy of the circle with us. Just in case."

"It would be nice to have another sorcerer, just in case," Tremaine added in Syrnaic, not looking at Meretrisa.

Gerard gave Tremaine a glare from under lowered brows, pointing out repressively, "She is a sorceress."

There was a faint snort from Giliead. As they all looked at him, he said, "She's afraid to do anything." Ilias, bouncing with impatience to be off, threw him an odd look and Giliead shook his head, gazing up in appeal to the dusty ceiling overhead. "I never thought I'd say that about a wizard."

"I wouldn't say she's afraid," Gerard protested. It was his turn to be stared at. He admitted, "Very well. She is very . . . tentative."

As the others started down the stairs, Giliead stopped Ilias, regarding him with a knit brow. "It'll be all right," Ilias told him lightly, not wanting to act as if he was going off to the outer reaches of nowhere, never to be seen again. Especially if it was true. "It's always been all right before."

Giliead's mouth twisted ruefully and he gave Ilias an affectionate hug that turned into a shove. "Just make sure it is."

Ilias went back down to the lower chamber, Giliead remaining in the upper to take his turn guarding Balin. Cletia and Cimarus climbed down the stairs with them, taking a couple of the bows to try hunting in the forest. Ilias began to wish they had brought more arrows. Cletia actually paused to look curiously around the circle chamber, Cimarus reluctantly trailing after her.

The Capidarans had come down with them as well, the older woman beginning to build up the fire again to help take the chill off the chamber, adding wood from the pile they had collected this morning. Ilias busied himself replenishing the torches that had burned out while Gerard looked through his papers and Tremaine waited, rocking back and forth on her heels. He lit the last one from the fire and got it wedged into a pile of rocks near the circle they meant to try next. Turning around, he found Cletia right behind him. The bow she was holding was one of his older ones, from when he was a boy; its lighter pull would be easier for Cletia's arm and its shorter length made it better for forest hunting. He thought she had some comment to make about the weapon, but she asked, "The first one took you to a world of snow and ice?"

"It wasn't a different world," he answered impatiently. "It was this one, just further into the cold country."

"Oh." Her brows drew together and she studied the ground at his feet, her blond hair falling forward to shield her expression. "It's . . . brave of you to do this, to go with the wizard."

Ilias stared at her, his mouth twisting in amusement. She must be desperate, whatever it was. "Tremaine went first," he corrected her. "What do you want?"

She looked up, frowning at him. "Nothing. I just—" Her gaze went to Tremaine, who was now watching them with a fixed expression Ilias couldn't fathom either. "Nothing," Cletia added sharply. Shouldering the bow, she turned and strode briskly toward the outer cave. Ilias saw Cimarus shake his head at the ceiling as he followed her.

Ilias snorted. *Whatever that was.* Turning to see Gerard tucking his papers away, Ilias moved to join him in the circle. Tremaine intercepted him halfway there. "What was that?" she asked, jerking her head toward Cletia.

"I have no idea."

Tremaine looked after Cletia, frowning. "I don't get her."

Ilias shook his head. He didn't understand Cletia now either. "Before she was trying to make herself into a duplicate of Pasima, now . . . I don't know." And he didn't care at the moment. "I wanted to tell you—" He took Tremaine's hand, shaking his head. "Our sister—Gil's sister Irissa—she wanted to travel with us, see new places, new people. She wanted to be a ship's captain and trade and explore. But because she was the heir to Andrien, she couldn't be risked and she had to stay at home for the sake of the land, and she never got to do any damn thing she wanted. And then she was killed in her own house."

Tremaine nodded, looking away a little, but her expression had turned rueful. "That's the point I was trying to make, I just did a bad job of it."

After that, there was nothing more to do except say what Ilias hoped was a temporary good-bye and go.

Ilias stepped into the circle as Gerard took out the sphere, rubbing a spot of damp off it with his coat sleeve. He asked Ilias, "Shall we?"

Ilias checked the set of his sword. "Yes."

Gerard regarded the sphere, and Ilias felt the world change.

He blinked and it was utterly black. There was no more light than if they had been suddenly transported to the belly of a leviathan. His startled intake of breath turned into a gasp and he realized the air was hot and dense and there was barely any of it to be had. Beside him he heard Gerard make a strangled noise. Ilias reached for him and caught his arm, keeping the older man upright. He was almost glad he couldn't see; this place had to be at least as bad as the red world Florian had accidentally taken them to. But the darkness pressed in and with each short harsh breath his head started to swim, prickles of pain in both temples. Something sparked blue in the darkness and the next instant he sucked in a breath of pure cold air, tinged only with woodsmoke.

Ilias and Gerard both collapsed at the same moment, slumping into sitting positions on the floor. Ilias had to fight to stay even that up-right; the urge to lie facedown and rest against that cool stone was hard to resist.

Aras swore in alarm and started forward, holding out a hand to Gerard. Tremaine sat on her heels beside Ilias, looking him over to make sure he was all right. She lifted a brow. "I take it we're crossing this one off the list too?"

"Indeed." Gerard accepted Aras's hand up with a resigned expression. Once on his feet he shook his head wearily. "It was . . . disturbing."

"There wasn't any air," Ilias elaborated, climbing to his feet with Tremaine's help and stepping out of the circle. He rubbed his forehead, glad to feel the pain receding with each full breath. He bit his lip, trying to remember what he could of the experience. He frowned at Gerard. "Were we underground?"

Gerard nodded. "I believe so. Wherever we were, I don't think it's worth returning to."

Ilias had no intention of arguing with that.

Florian ended up pacing the Promenade, wandering in and out of the main hall, and up and down the passenger stairs, fuming. *He's wrong,* she thought, remembering Nicholas's words. *A battle between Niles and Ixion—especially if Niles lost—couldn't do us any good.* And she was supposed to be helping Niles, and couldn't they have their damn meeting after Tremaine and the others were found? The fact that Niles had admitted their efforts to make the circle work had come to a dead end earlier didn't matter; the meeting was an annoying interruption.

She was on the Promenade, tapping her fingers impatiently on the rail, not seeing the brilliant blue sky or the limitless sea, when she realized the person standing nearby was Pasima. Florian blinked at her, startled. The Syprian woman stood stiffly, her mouth set in a thin line, dressed in a dark blue shirt over doeskin pants and boots. Before Florian could open her mouth, she said abruptly, "Have you found our people yet?"

Florian was fairly sure those were the first words Pasima had ever spoken to her, despite her being one of only a few Rienish speakers of Syrnaic. "No, not yet. I'm sorry, it's not working the way we thought—"

Pasima inclined her head, her eyes bitter. "So it always is," she said, turning away abruptly and walking up the Promenade.

"What's that supposed to mean?" Florian muttered, watching the other woman's retreat. "It usually works right, except—" *When it doesn't.* She rubbed her eyes wearily. There had to be an answer.

She heard a mild commotion from the open doors behind her and turned to see Lord Chandre's party, with Ixion, his guards and the Capidaran sorcerer Kressein, crossing the main hall toward the forward stairs. "Finally," Florian breathed, and hurried into the hall and back down the corridor to the First Class smoking room.

As she reached the doorway, Colonel Averi brushed past her, his face set. Florian stared after him, frowning, then cautiously looked into the room. Niles was seated at the table, his head in his hands.

Florian stepped inside, watching him worriedly. "What's wrong?"

Niles glanced up at her, his face pale and grim. "Ixion has offered them the spell he used to create his new body. As a show of good faith, he's going to . . . grow, I suppose, is the term, a body for the woman who is trapped in the Gardier crystal Tremaine and the others brought back from Maton-devara. Supposedly, if we can successfully free the woman from the crystal and transfer her consciousness to the new body, the spell will be used to free any other crystal-imprisoned sorcerers we encounter. I say 'supposedly,' because I remain skeptical, as you may have guessed."

Florian's jaw had dropped at some point and now she finally managed to make it work enough to say, "Here? On the ship? Now?"

"Yes." Niles gave her an ironic look. "He'll be under guard the entire time, of course. Even though Gerard and I, with Giliead and Arisilde's assistance, weren't enough to keep him contained last time. Oh, Chandre was good enough to admit that Ixion's original offer, to make the body for Arisilde, was probably a bad idea, since even with all the new spheres Arisilde is still our best line of defense. Averi believes the entire idea is mad, but Chandre pointed out that Averi was originally against using the world-gate spell, after the failed attempt killed Riardin." Niles slumped in his chair, his jaw set. "And if I find out who in the Viller Institute imparted that bit of information to Chandre, he's going to spend the rest of the voyage with an uncomfortable medical condition in his nether regions."

Florian dropped into one of the armchairs. Unfair, to hold Averi's original opposition to the world-gate spell against him. At that time they hadn't even known it was a world-gate spell. She shook her head, wondering now if Nicholas had been right. "I don't understand. How is Chandre getting away with this? Where did he get all this power? Didn't Count Delphane put Colonel Averi in charge?"

Niles took a deep breath. "Power is the key word." He glanced at her, his face weary. "Count Delphane is only a man, Tremaine. Just as Colonel Averi is only a man. Delphane, in fact, has less power than Averi, since the remnants of the Rienish military see Averi as their commanding officer and still obey his orders. Delphane's power rests only on the support of Averi and Captain Marais, and the others."

Florian protested, "But Count Delphane was one of the Queen's chief advisors. . . ." She let the words trail off, as she really thought about what Niles was saying. She said reluctantly, "But Chandre has more support in Capidara than Delphane. And the Capidaran sorcerers and military men have to pay attention to him because the Capidaran Ministry told them to."

"The only thing Chandre lacks is a sorcerer," Niles said, impatiently pushing things around on the table. "Kressein is his own man, and primarily loyal to Capidara. He may have to work with Chandre, but Chandre won't be able to lure him into his camp. That's why Chandre is courting Ixion."

Florian pushed to her feet, unable to hold still. "But he doesn't understand that Syprian sorcerers are different." She had thought Ixion might be of use, but somehow she hadn't envisioned this. "I can see why he thinks—We could free so many trapped sorcerers. But—"

Niles shook his head, gesturing in annoyance. "But is it a question of freeing a prisoner, or bringing the dead back to a kind of artificial half-life?" He leaned forward, tapping the table for emphasis. "We know what happens when a sorcerer tries to return a trapped soul to a body. It's called necromancy for one thing, and the result is one of the reasons that particular branch of sorcery has been outlawed in Ile-Rien for centuries."

Florian let her breath out, nodding. Necromancy was outlawed not only because of its primary concern of using the dead for divination, but because a soul returned to a dead body became little more than a slave for the necromancer. Or a ghoul or a lich, or other things even more frightening. She hadn't considered Ixion's body-changing spell in that light before, but maybe Niles was right. "I was thinking of something else, though."

Niles frowned warily, the look of a man who had had about all the bad news he could take. "What?"

"How do we know that what he's going to be growing is really a human body?" She leaned on the table, biting her lip in thought. "I'm not exactly certain, but he said he grew his body in a vat. That's the same way Syprian sorcerers make curselings." She looked up to meet Niles's gaze. "And that's what Syprian sorcerers do, how they take over villages, or try to. They make curselings."

Niles regarded her a moment in silence, then buried his head in his hands again. "Oh, that will be all we need."

Chapter 8

It was Giliead's turn to go with Gerard next, and Tremaine was beginning to feel the strain. It was like playing roulette, only you had
to win with each spin of the wheel or else.

And she found herself wanting a chance to talk to Ilias alone,
though it seemed like whenever she had a chance, she had no idea
what she wanted to say. She rubbed her eyes. *I give up.* She declared
herself officially hopeless.

Giliead, Ilias and Gerard had already gone back down to the lower
circle chamber, Aras following them down the stairs. As Tremaine
turned to head after them, Cimarus called her back. "She wants something," he explained, jerking his head toward Balin.

The Gardier woman was standing near the fire, her arms folded
tightly. "I want to walk around," Balin said, giving Tremaine an uncertain glare that somehow combined defiance and diffidence.

Tremaine started to say no, then groaned under her breath. She
didn't suppose it could matter. "All right, fine." She said to Cimarus
in Syrnaic, "Let her walk down to the circle chamber, but keep an eye
on her."

As Tremaine started down the stairs, Meretrisa joined her, saying,
"Only a few more circles to try." She sounded optimistic.

"Right." Tremaine disliked optimists at the best of times. And
Meretrisa had every reason to look cool and unaffected, since she

wasn't taking any of the risks and had no particular relationship with any of the people who were. As Tremaine stepped down the too-high stone stairs, careful in the dimming light, she added earnestly, "Too bad we don't have any other sorcerers to help Gerard."

Either the barb failed to land entirely or Meretrisa simply ignored it. "I understand you are not a sorcerer yourself? Yet we had heard the prototype sphere would only work in your presence the first time it was used."

"It got over that." The sphere Arisilde now inhabited had been an old one he had made as a gift for Tremaine. When she was a child, she had had just enough magic inherited from her maternal great-grandmother to use it to make colored light and find lost toys. She had never tried to use her small talent for anything else, and it had faded along with her childhood. It would mean an ordinary Viller sphere could do its automatic defensive spells if she held it, but she couldn't make it do anything else. But she wasn't going to elaborate on that to Meretrisa.

She persisted, "But Giliead is also a sorcerer, or perhaps the natives would call it a shaman?"

Tremaine glanced up over her shoulder, making sure Cimarus and Balin hadn't caught up with them yet. She didn't want to discuss whether Giliead could or could not use magic in front of any other Syprians except Ilias. And the idea didn't exactly make Ilias comfortable either. "Not . . . exactly."

"But I thought he was the one who was able to use the Gardier crystal to let you all escape from their world?"

"Yes, that was Giliead, but . . ." They reached the chamber, where Gerard knelt beside the circle, making a last few notes, and Aras had busied himself with building up the fire. Giliead was standing near Gerard, waiting patiently, and Ilias stood beside him, his back tense. Tremaine knew the risk of stepping into those circles was starting to affect him as well. She glanced at Meretrisa, who had stopped beside her, waiting for an answer. "It's complicated. Giliead is technically responsible to the god of Cineth, and the Syprian gods aren't keen on magic. With good reason." Tremaine didn't want to get into the fact that Giliead believed he had already irrevocably violated the god's trust.

"I had heard about their gods." Meretrisa looked across the room, studying Giliead for a long moment, frowning. "Is it true they think his power comes from it?"

"It's true." Tremaine sensed doubt, and felt her hackles rise. "I've met Cineth's god."

Meretrisa lifted her brows, her faint smile suggesting she knew she was being mocked. "Surely it isn't real."

Tremaine valiantly suppressed the urge to roll her eyes and sigh. *Yes, because I have nothing better to do with my time than invent elaborate jokes.* "It's very real. Gerard thinks the gods might be elemental spirits. Every city in the Syrnai—and some of the other places they have contact with—has gods. The gods help keep away the curselings, the creatures that wizards create, and other unfriendly etheric beings. The Syrnai is a very dangerous place to live without a god somewhere nearby. Just like Ile-Rien used to be, when the fay practically ruled the countryside." Crisscrossing the country with steel train tracks had broken the power of fayre in Ile-Rien, though the fay still lurked on coastal islands, in deserted ruins and deep forests. It hadn't been that different from the Syprians' situation, now that she thought about it. Before the trains, every village had had its priests and its family of hedgewitches to protect the inhabitants against fay. The Gardier were bound to encounter fay, as they were now supposed to be attacking the Bisran border. Tremaine sourly hoped they enjoyed each other's company.

Meretrisa nodded seriously. "I see."

Tremaine wasn't sure Meretrisa did, but she wasn't going to waste her time on further explanations.

Gerard stood, tucking his notebook away. "Ready?" he asked.

Giliead nodded. He looked down at Ilias, who said uneasily, "Just remember the way back."

Giliead didn't say anything, just ruffled Ilias's hair and gave him an affectionate shove, then stepped into the circle with Gerard.

Gerard took a deep breath, the sphere sparked faintly, and the two men vanished.

Tremaine bit her lip. *Right, now the real anxiety starts again.* Cimarus had drawn even with her and Meretrisa, watching the process in unwilling fascination. Tremaine realized that while he had been through world-gates a few times, he had never actually seen it from the outside. She started to ask him what he thought, then abruptly realized who was missing from their little group. "Where's Balin?" she demanded.

Startled, Cimarus scanned the chamber, then swore in guilty chagrin.

Tremaine clapped a hand over her eyes. "Great." There was only one place Balin could have gone, and that was outside through the crack in the wall. "I'll go after her." Tremaine started away, putting a hand in her pocket to touch her pistol.

"Wait," Ilias called sharply. He ran to catch up with her and they started toward the back wall of the chamber.

"It's going to be all right," Tremaine told him, not meaning Balin. Though considering they couldn't keep track of their one prisoner, she wasn't sure why anyone should feel secure in their competence to explore these circles.

He shook his head, giving her a rueful look, and climbed out through the narrow crack in the wall. Tremaine struggled out after him. The late-afternoon light was bright enough in the open areas, but it was dark and shadowy under the trees. Ilias went to the dirt flat just beyond the rocky outcrop, thoughtfully studying the ground. Tremaine looked, but there was no sign of Balin near the streambed or in the twilight fringes of the pine forest. "This way," Ilias said suddenly, turning back toward the rocks. "She went up here."

"Not toward the forest?" Tremaine followed him around the outcrop and up the rough slope, the gravel slipping under her boots. There were only a few straggly pines on this side, and clumps of dry grass sprouted in the sunny areas between. "Wouldn't that be the easiest way to lose us?"

He shrugged, still scanning the ground as they climbed. "Does she know how to live in the forest?"

Tremaine had to give him that one. "I doubt it."

Balin seemed to have found an old trail, or at least Ilias had. They hadn't explored this way before, simply because it hadn't looked as if there was anything up here. The path they were following wound up around the side of the outcrop, heading toward the cliff top. Warily watching the folds of rock above them, Tremaine kept half expecting Balin to tumble a boulder down, but there didn't seem to be a great deal of loose stones larger than pebbles.

They came around a knob of rock and were suddenly out on the cliff, a cool wind and the roaring crash of the waterfall accenting the view of snowcapped mountains and the woods across the gorge. Tremaine stopped, startled; there was something else up here admiring the view.

Stone statues, each about twenty feet high and with about that much distance between them, faced the river gorge. Their surfaces were smooth and dark, pitted enough by the weather to show a faint mottling of silver-gray. The bodies were just squat lozenges, details barely suggested, but the faces were round, serene and smooth, like those carved above the plaza in the Wall Port city. There were seven statues in all, and if Tremaine had the distances right, the collapsed half of the dome must have stood out from the cliff wall directly below the center one.

Ilias nudged her arm, jerking his head toward the cliff, and Tremaine saw the lone figure dressed in a dusty white shirt and pants. Balin stood in the yellow grass and wildflowers between two of the statues, looking out over the gorge and the mountains. She had her arms wrapped around herself, perhaps from the cold.

Tremaine sighed, scrubbing the sweat off her forehead. She made her way forward, careful of her footing on the uneven ground. She stopped far enough away that Balin couldn't suddenly grab her and throw her off the cliff. "So. Where are you going?"

Balin glanced back at her, with an expression that tried to be stoic but only looked forlorn. "There is nowhere to go."

"That was actually my point." Tremaine looked up at the nearest statue, knowing Ilias would intervene if Balin made a move toward her. She stepped close to it, feeling the slight rise in the ground that marked a paved platform under the layer of dirt, and put her hand against the stone. It was still cool, despite sitting all day under the sun, and rougher than it looked. *God, I wish she'd just jump and save us all this trouble.* She thought of the Capidaran woman Balin had killed, in the Women's Auxiliary uniform, and that stupid little cap. But it was superseded by an image of the young Gardier truck driver Tremaine had shot, who had died because he was foolish enough to stop and offer help to a supposedly injured boy. *God, I should jump and save us all this trouble.* But the thought was just an echo, with no force behind it.

Back on the Isle of Storms she had realized that Arisilde had been trying to communicate with her from the sphere, that he had somehow passed along fragments of Giliead's and Ilias's experiences, some of which had worked their way into her plays. That his unconscious melancholy influence had been partly responsible for fueling her need to kill herself. Realizing that had helped in many ways. Meeting Ilias, now waiting so quietly behind her, had helped in others. But at some point Tremaine had come to a place where even dying couldn't solve her problems.

She patted the statue. "Don't you think you've been gone too long?" she asked Balin, actually curious, looking at the woman standing stubbornly on the cliff. "If you did get back to them, won't they think you've been corrupted by us?"

"They would know I was loyal," Balin said stiffly, but the uncertainty was there.

"It doesn't matter if you're loyal or not, and you know it." Tremaine shook her head. "You've seen too much. Hell, I've seen too much. Of course, I think I'd seen too much before this ever started." She pushed away from the statue, deciding that when it came down to it, it was up to Balin. "Come back when you're hungry. Or go native. Or jump. Whichever seems appropriate."

She went back to Ilias, drawing him along with her, and they followed the rough path back down to the cave entrance.

About an hour later, Balin returned.

The sun was setting when Tremaine wandered the empty rooms along the corridor to the upper circle chamber, thinking, *God, I hate this*. One last circle to test, and then . . . She had no idea what came after that, if the last circle didn't lead anywhere either.

Giliead and Gerard hadn't been gone long. Their circle had taken them to a partially walled-off chamber. Giliead had been able to climb to a vantage point where he could see that they were in a city, bearing some resemblance to the Wall Port, but located in a desert with a mountain range visible in the distance. It hadn't taken Giliead long to realize that the city was actually inhabited, and that they were in the Barrens, and that they needed to get the hell out of there.

Tremaine had heard them talk about it enough to know that that circle was a dead loss. The Barrens had no gods, and had become the refuge of wizards and curselings. The only other people there were slaves, enspelled by the wizards. Giliead had never heard of an ancient city out in the Barrens either, so the chances were that it was deep in that hostile territory, far from the Syrnai.

Aras had tried to argue with Gerard about it, much to Giliead's teeth-gritted annoyance. "But surely much of this is just native superstition. The sorcerers there might know something of the circle," Aras had argued. "They might be able to—"

Ilias swore in irritation. "They won't talk to us. They'll just kill us. If we're lucky."

"We can't take the chance," Gerard had said firmly, putting a stop to the discussion before Ilias could elaborate on the probable fate of people who blundered into godless areas, or Giliead gave in to temper and punched Aras. "Besides, the stone used to wall up the chamber looked nearly as old as the city itself. The circle was probably walled up before the original inhabitants left. Which means the Syprian wizards inhabiting the place might not even have any idea it exists. And frankly, I'd rather they not learn about it. We have enough to contend with from the Gardier."

They had called a halt to the explorations for dinner, hoping that would restore everyone's nerves. Ilias had listened to Giliead's description of the Barrens with the appalled fascination of someone hearing a first-person account of a visit to Hell. Cletia had pretended to be completely unaffected, but Cimarus had volunteered to stand guard all night, probably because he was too unnerved to sleep. Then Gerard and Aras had taken the next circle.

They had been gone for nearly half an hour now and Tremaine felt as if her head was going to explode from tension. Giliead and Meretrisa were still down there waiting for the two men to return, but Tremaine was too edgy to stay in one spot. She wasn't sure if the delay was a good thing or not, if it meant they had found a place worth taking a careful look at or if they were trapped somewhere and it was all over. And there was only one more circle left to try.

Standing in an empty dusty room, staring at the enigmatic carvings, Tremaine glanced up just as Meretrisa passed by the doorway, heading toward the circle chamber.

Ilias and the other Syprians were with Vervane and the newly returned Balin, in the main room. Tremaine stepped out in the corridor in time to see Meretrisa pass that doorway and continue into the circle chamber.

Tremaine stood in the corridor, staring after her. *Huh.* She followed, moving quietly to the doorway of the circle chamber.

Meretrisa knelt beside the carved symbols, her small notebook in her hand. Her expression was intent, her brows knit, as she checked her copy of the symbols against the etched stone. This was the second time Tremaine had caught her alone with the circle, studying it. *The first time she was copying it, now she's making sure her copy is accurate.* She had to know that the Capidarans would get a copy. *So who is she copying it for?* And there was something about her face, something not quite guilt, but close enough. An awareness of a burden.

Tremaine took a few steps into the room, her rubber-soled boots silent on the windswept stone. She planted a smile on her face and said, "How did you come to be with the Capidaran delegation, Meretrisa?"

Meretrisa looked up, startled. "I . . ." She hesitated, and Tremaine's smile grew a little more saturnine. It wasn't exactly a difficult question to give an honest answer to. If one had an honest answer. *It's her,* she thought, certain suddenly. *Our spy.*

Meretrisa managed to arrange her face back into a polite expression. "The other Ministry sorcerer was ill and could not come, so I took his place. Several people were taken ill in his office that day."

"He just took ill suddenly." Tremaine nodded to herself. *That's not the oldest trick there is, oh, no.* It was easy for sorcerers to cause a minor indisposition, even to other sorcerers. Something just uncomfortable enough to make it difficult for the man to leave his home for a long meeting, but not bad enough to bother going to another sorcerer for healing. If a mild sickness charm had been attached to a letter or another piece of paperwork, it might affect any number of people, junior assistants, the boy who took in the mail, and look even more convincingly like a natural illness. "So what did they offer you? Is it blackmail? Did they tell you they have some relative of yours prisoner, because that's usually what they do." Meretrisa's expression had turned stony, but Tremaine saw her throat move as she swallowed nervously and knew it was guilt rather than outrage at being unjustly accused. *Oh, yes, it's her.* And Meretrisa wouldn't have a crystal implanted under her skin; an involuntary unconscious spy had no reason for excuses or guilt. "Or did they just tell you they would leave Capidara alone?"

Meretrisa looked away and Tremaine shrugged, taking a few more idle steps toward her. She wished Giliead was here, but he would probably feel any spell from down in the other circle chamber; she just hoped he could get up here in time. She suspected Meretrisa was a better sorcerer than she had pretended. Tremaine added the lie, "Oh come on, I knew from the moment the Gardier targeted the house. We all knew."

Meretrisa set her jaw, still looking away. Then she said, "They told me they had no plans to attack Capidara, they didn't need to, they had all they could manage with Ile-Rien, the Maiutan islands, Adera, the other places they had already taken. That they would send men to your house, to take the sphere and the new circle." Meretrisa gestured helplessly. "Of course, it was a lie." She pushed her hair back and Tremaine saw tears streaked her cheek. "It wasn't blackmail, there were no threats. They offered me money. And I took it. I have—had—a very low position in the Ministry. It's not like Ile-Rien here; the women sorcerers are not considered as useful or trustworthy as men. It was only money. And safety. I thought the sooner I gave them what they wanted, they would leave us alone."

Tremaine lifted her brows. She hadn't expected to get a confession so easily. "But you took a copy of the circle, just in case." Then she heard a faint sound behind her. She glanced over her shoulder.

Five Gardier stood in the ring of carved symbols, wearing the brown coverall uniforms, the small crystal devices hanging from their belts, four of them armed with rifles. The fifth was a Liaison, his face marked with two crystals, one set in the center of his forehead, the second in his cheek. Tremaine had one instant to be horrified, then she was dragging her pistol out of her pocket; but that one instant was already too long.

Pain exploded in her hand and she yelled, flinging what was left of the gun away. As she staggered the Liaison strode forward to seize her arm. Her hand was bloody and she felt her knees go weak. She couldn't tell yet if she still had all her fingers. Confused, she thought she had been shot, but it must have been the mechanical disruption spell, destroying her pistol.

Meretrisa was on her feet, staring in horror. A gunshot echoed off the stone and Tremaine flinched violently. Meretrisa fell backward, struck the wall and slid down into a tumbled heap, her notebook falling beside her hand.

"No shooting! We want them alive," the Liaison snapped.

"She is a sorcerer, dangerous," argued the one who had fired.

"She's not the sorcerer we want," the Liaison told him, annoyed. Tremaine had heard the descriptions but she had never seen a Liaison really close up before. He was a young man, perhaps early twenties, and must be relatively new; the puckered flesh around the crystals in his face was only just tinged with green and gray decay. He was holding the sorcerer crystal that must have brought the group here tucked under his arm. "Just get the others alive."

Stricken, Tremaine saw the officer make a sharp gesture and the other three start into the entrance to the caves, weapons at the ready. *Oh God.* Ilias was in the next chamber, but he must have heard the shot.

The Liaison gave her arm a shake; it jarred her throbbing hand and she gritted her teeth. He said to the officer, "Ask her what others are here, ask her about the sorcerer, the one making the circles work."

The officer turned to her, fumbling for the translator on a chain around his neck. It was a small metal disk with a crystal fragment, which contained the Gardier-Rienish translator spell that Arisilde had adapted for his own use. Before he could speak, a thump and a shout from the passage interrupted. Tremaine flinched again as a rifle went off, the shot ear-piercingly loud against the stone.

Something dark rolled into the room and the Liaison dropped Tremaine's arm, both men hastily backing away, obviously fearing an explosive. Tremaine shoved away from them, putting her back against the wall, thinking distractedly, *We don't have explosives.* The object rolled to a squishy halt and she saw it was a head with short dark hair, still wearing a set of Gardier aether-glasses. In the silence she could hear a strangled gurgling from the passage, the sound of someone else drowning in his own blood.

The Liaison and the officer stared at her and she stared back. "Syprians," she said in Aelin, answering one of the Liaison's earlier questions. "Lots of them."

The officer lifted his rifle but a long feathered shaft blossomed in his chest and he flung his arms wide, falling backward, his gun clattering to the floor. Tremaine flung herself for the weapon but the Liaison didn't move to grab it. He stepped into the circle and vanished.

Something bounced off the wall near where he had been standing and landed near Tremaine. It was another arrow, shattered from the impact on the stone. She stepped over it, grabbed the rifle barrel and pushed to her feet, cradling her injured hand. The officer with the arrow in his chest was still twitching a little, a spreading stain turning his brown uniform red around the long wooden shaft.

Ilias slammed into the room, sword lifted, lowering it as he saw the other Gardier was gone. "Tremaine?"

She stumbled to Meretrisa's side, thinking she was dead, but the woman had started to stir, whimpering a little, trying to push herself up. The blood was spreading down her sleeve, under her jacket and across her chest but Tremaine couldn't tell where it was coming from.

Ilias started toward her, but Tremaine shook her head rapidly. "One got away. Get our things, the food, everything, we have to go. Somebody get her, get her out of here."

Ilias turned back for the passage, shouting for Cimarus and Cletia. Cimarus appeared an instant later with a blanket. He knelt beside

Meretrisa, wrapping her in it, his face tight with tension. Tremaine pushed to her feet, getting out of his way as he scooped Meretrisa up and took her out of the room.

Tremaine glanced around, making sure she hadn't forgotten anything. That last dying Gardier was still looking at her, though his eyes were going vague. *Kill him, take him with us, leave him?* There was no time. She leaned down, dropping the rifle to unbuckle his belt with its pack of ammunition and a couple of the small crystal fragments that held individual spells. She pulled it off, slung it around her neck and grabbed the rifle again, straightening up. She snuck a look at her bloody hand and counted all five fingers. The pistol couldn't have exploded, or surely her whole hand would have been gone. The metal must have gotten hot, then started to come apart. Light-headed with relief, she stuffed her useless hand in her pocket and headed for the passage.

The other three Gardier were still there: the headless one slumped in the entrance to the first room, the gurgling one with an arrow in his throat in the opposite doorway and the last sprawled just inside the main room with an extremely ugly and fatal sword wound to the head. Giliead burst out of the stairwell so abruptly Tremaine yelped and flinched. He strode to her side, looking past her into the circle chamber with worried eyes, laying a hand on her shoulder. "They're gone?"

"For now. Meretrisa's shot." She remembered he could feel the circles and the gate spells when he was close enough. "We have to—"

"I know." He squeezed her shoulder and stepped past her into the room where the others were scrambling to grab weapons and packs and bags. Cletia, one of the Syprian goathorn bows slung over her shoulder, dumped out the water to stuff the pot in her pack. Balin was crouched in a corner, looking mutinous. *I should have shot that bitch,* Tremaine thought wearily. *We need to destroy the circle.* But she had nothing to do it with. And having her back to it was making her skin crawl. She looked around at the dead men again but couldn't see anything they had with them that looked like an explosive.

Vervane came out burdened with an armload of blankets and coats, her face set with distress. She tried to look into the circle chamber, but Tremaine caught her arm and turned her back around, sending her down the passage. The pain in her hand was making her head buzz. After a moment of trying to think, Tremaine followed Vervane. She could only carry the one rifle right now and would have to come back for the other weapons.

Climbing down the stairs just behind Vervane, she saw that the older woman's hand was bleeding. "Did you get hurt?" Tremaine asked her, then had to try twice to get the question out in Rienish.

Vervane glanced back at her, nodding, her face red from exertion. "It's nothing. That Gardier woman, I put my hand over her mouth so she couldn't call out and warn them, and she bit me."

Tremaine heard a commotion overhead and looked up to see Cletia hurrying down the stairs, carrying bags and packs, prodding Balin along ahead of her. They all reached the lower chamber to find Cimarus waiting at the bottom of the steps, Meretrisa bundled in his arms. "Outside?" he asked.

Tremaine hesitated, just as Gerard and Aras appeared in the circle on the far side of the shadowy room.

"Tremaine, you'll never believe what we—" Gerard began, stepping out of the circle. Then he took in their appearance. "Gardier?"

"Yes, from the other circle. One got away. Meretrisa's shot." Tremaine's hand was hurting all the way up her arm and all the way through her body until her back teeth seemed to be throbbing in rhythm with her pounding heart. "Gerard, we need to destroy that circle, or go outside, or—"

"Shot?" Aras interrupted, startled, staring at the limp form in Cimarus's arms. "What?"

Vervane was nodding urgently. "It's true, we must go—"

With a clatter Ilias and Giliead arrived at the bottom of the stairwell. Ilias was hauling Balin by the arm, his sword, a couple of packs and one of the bow cases slung over his shoulder. "They're back," Ilias informed them grimly.

"I felt the gate curse while we were coming down," Giliead agreed, his face set. He had the rest of the weapons and what Tremaine hoped was the last of their packs.

Gerard didn't hesitate, waving them over briskly. "We'll use this circle. Everyone get inside it immediately."

Aras strode forward, relieving Vervane of her load of blankets. "Yes, it goes to another junction like this one. We don't know if it's safe, but it's the best option."

Tremaine followed them, dragging the rifle along, not sure she was thinking clearly. "But doesn't someone have to destroy this circle, or won't they just follow us?"

Everyone assembled hurriedly in the circle. "We can destroy it once we get there," Gerard explained, lifting the sphere as he looked around to make sure everyone was accounted for. "There are hundreds more." Tremaine thought she could hear someone shouting in Aelin, the voice echoing down the stairwell.

"Here, down here!" Balin called out desperately.

"There's hundreds more what?" Then Tremaine gasped, her stomach lurching. They were suddenly somewhere else. *I will never get used to this.*

Tremaine got an impression of a giant cathedral-like space, blue-veined stone and sunlight slanting down from some great distance. It was cool and damp, but not as cold as the cave they had just come from. Then she had to sit down, clutching her swimming head and trying not to be sick.

Everything continued to swim, though she knew it was Ilias who pulled her to her feet, propelled her out of the circle and sat her down again a short distance away. After a moment the feverish sensation of impending nausea faded and she blinked sweat out of her eyes. Ilias was sitting in front of her, holding her injured hand, biting his lip in concern. She saw with surprise that among the bloody and burned skin there was a piece of rock stuck to her palm. She must have fallen on it in the circle chamber and it had stuck to the burned flesh. *Ugh, no wonder it hurts,* she thought with a wince.

Gerard was stooping over them, irritably demanding, "Why didn't you say anything?"

"I said 'ow,' " Tremaine told him, grimacing. She hadn't thought it was this bad. Then she looked up, and up, and up.

They were in a giant chamber, at least twice the size of the train yard at the central Vienne station. It was full of dusty sunlight from narrow slits of louvers set high in a soaring roof. The stone was light-colored, almost like a white marble with different shades of blue and gray woven through it. There were carved archways, leading off into other spaces, some sunlit, some shadowed. The floor was paved with a pearly gray stone and it was covered with circles, more than she could count. They seemed to be everywhere.

"Wow," Tremaine muttered. Giliead was standing guard over them, his sword resting on his shoulder as he watchfully scanned the area. Cimarus had taken charge of Balin, who sat in a sullen heap, and Cletia was nearby, sorting through the jumbled contents of their hastily packed supplies. Meretrisa lay wrapped in the blanket, Aras and Vervane anxiously leaning over her. "What about Meretrisa?"

"I've stopped the bleeding but the bullet punctured her lung," Gerard told her. "Now be quiet."

"Shouldn't we do something about the circle?" Tremaine wondered, feeling vague. "They're going to realize we went through one of them, so—"

"I already did," Gerard interrupted, digging a handkerchief out of his pocket. "I used the sphere to melt away a few of the key symbols." He handed the cloth to Ilias, and said, "Go on and pull it out."

"Pull what out? Ow!" Tremaine strangled a yell and glared at Ilias. He pressed the handkerchief over the now–freely bleeding wound, ignoring her. "It could have been stuck in a bone or something."

"It wasn't," Ilias told her repressively. "I pull things out of people all the time."

Gerard shouldered between them and took hold of her wrist, though Ilias didn't let go of her hand. She knew Gerard had already begun a spell because the throbbing started to ease immediately. She noticed Ilias still looked worried, his brow creased, sweat staining the open front of his shirt. And there was fresh blood spattered on his coat sleeves and caught in his hair. "That was very effective, that thing with the head," she informed him. He lifted a brow at her, and she amended, "I'm talking about cutting the Gardier's head off and throwing it at his friends. Who was shooting the arrows?"

He jerked his head toward the others. "That was Cletia."

"Of course it was," she said dryly. *Oh, good, I got saved by Cletia,* Tremaine thought, rolling her eyes. *That makes it all worthwhile.*

Ilias lifted the cloth at Gerard's urging and saw the wound in Tremaine's hand had already closed, though it looked new and raw. The burns were better and he could already see new pink flesh under the blood and damaged skin. He took a deep breath in relief and looked up at the wizard. "Thank you."

Gerard didn't seem able to speak and just patted him on the shoulder. Ilias knew he looked on Tremaine as a daughter. Apparently annoyed by their concern, Tremaine said in exasperation, "I feel fine."

"Just sit there quietly," Gerard told her with some asperity.

"Vervane got hurt too, go yell at her. Balin bit her, she probably needs a carbolic bath. And does this mean the Gardier captured the original circle, the one in the house? Or the notes on it you gave Niles? How else could they get here? I mean, there?"

Good questions, Ilias thought, looking at Gerard. Clearly not wanting to answer them now, the wizard said only, "It's a possibility."

Giliead glanced back at them. "We need to find a more defensive place to camp."

Ilias nodded. This place was so big this room might as well have been an open field; he felt exposed, as if he had a target painted on him. All the circles, each one a potential open doorway for their enemies, didn't help.

Gerard, already turning to go to Vervane and Meretrisa, paused to say, "Aras and I didn't explore very far. The place looks deserted but we only glanced into a few of those other chambers. Take great care; we don't know if the Gardier could get here through some alternate route, through another circle."

Ilias pushed to his feet, asking Tremaine, "You'll be all right?"

"Oh, sure." She blinked up at him. "I think I'm going to sit here for a while."

Ilias threw Cimarus a look that promised death if he didn't keep a good watch, then paused to shed his coat; it was too warm here for it. He avoided Cletia's gaze deliberately, knowing he needed to say something to her about her quickness with the bow. She had saved Tremaine, saved them all. But he couldn't deal with it just now. Pulling his baldric back over his head, he followed Giliead across the giant space.

They made their way between the circles, heading for the nearest archway. Giliead had left behind his wool wrap as well, and took a deep breath of the warm air. "What happened?" he asked quietly.

Ilias shook his head. The narrowness of their escape made his skin creep. "They would have had all of us, just like that, but Tremaine was in the circle chamber. I heard her scream when they made her shooting weapon break. I took two with the sword before they knew I was there and Cletia got the others with a bow before the last one escaped." It could have been Tremaine lying there instead of Meretrisa. *That last Gardier could have taken Tremaine with him.* The thought made him ill.

Giliead acknowledged what he hadn't said with a grunt, looking bleak. "We were lucky."

They reached the archway and got a view into the next chamber, and Ilias saw why Gerard and Aras had decided the place was deserted. This space wasn't nearly so large, though the ceiling was still a good two ship's lengths or so high and it was a long stretch to the next archway. There had been some kind of balcony along one side, but two of the supporting columns had collapsed, and the blocks that had formed it lay tumbled along the wall. No effort had been made to clear or repair anything and it all smelled damp and dusty and disused.

The openings slitted into the curved roof seemed to be everywhere, and the bright sunlight outside made it easy to see. The trickle of water falling led them through the next archway and into a smaller chamber that looked as if it had been carved right out of the blue-white rock. Water ran down a wall through a crack in the domed roof; the fact that it was caught in several carved stone basins before running out through a small drain in the floor made it obvious that it wasn't natural. Ilias let the water run over his hand and tasted it cautiously. It was clear and sweet. He glanced around the room again, frowning. There was something . . . artificial about it. "Why did they want a room that looks like a cave?"

"Who knows." Giliead made a helpless gesture, turning to investigate the smaller doorway that led off to the side. It turned out to be a corridor made to look like a rocky tunnel.

It had no openings in the roof and was dark, and one end ran only a short distance back the way they had come to the main circle chamber. But the other led to another larger room, dusty and empty, with more rooms beyond it. "This place is huge," Giliead muttered, sitting on his heels and using his knife to scratch a careful trail sign on the floor.

"We can get the others into that rock room for now. It's got water, and two doorways so we can't get boxed in." Ilias didn't have a bad feeling about this place; it didn't give off any feeling in particular, though its size was intimidating. He could see why Arisilde would have come here to investigate the circles, but searching for his oversubtle trail marks was going to be a chore. But he had never heard of a place like this in any story; the Wall Port had been an unthinkable distance from Cineth, but they had still heard tales of it.

Giliead nodded, pushing to his feet, his face weary. "We may be here a while. There's a lot to explore."

Ilias bit his lip, and had to say it out loud. "Do you think we're any closer to home than we were in the mountains?"

Giliead looked around again, his mouth twisted wryly. He rested a hand on Ilias's shoulder and pulled him into a one-armed hug. "I have no idea."

Florian found herself wandering the *Ravenna*'s main hall, where green marble columns flanked seating areas with couches and armchairs. The cherrywood-veneered walls were lined with the empty glass cases of the ship's old shopping arcade. This late at night, the only people around were a few officers and some researchers from the Viller Institute, all on their way to some other part of the ship. She missed the livelier company of the refugees, who had filled up all the *Ravenna*'s silences and given the long corridors a sense of noisy community.

Florian pushed through the heavy doors out onto the Promenade deck, but it was unlit except for the dim reflection of moonlight on the sea, the large windows looking out onto the limitless expanse of dark water and sky, and she retreated quickly.

It was well after midnight by the time Niles had finally been persuaded to rest. After the encounter with Chandre and Ixion, he had gone back to the Second Class lounge and drawn the circle again, with Florian and Giaren's help, with meticulous care. Again, it hadn't worked.

Florian had been surprised when Giaren, normally rather diffident, had slammed a book down on the table and shouted angrily that Niles was going to kill himself and what good would that do their lost companions? Niles had gotten huffy but had grudgingly agreed to go to his cabin and try to sleep.

With the blackout curtains and dead-lights carefully fixed over the windows and portholes, the corridors quiet, Florian perversely felt wide-awake.

Poking around in the corridors between the main hall and the closed doors of the Observation Lounge, she found the First Class library unlocked. On impulse she went in, scanned the shelves quickly and selected a gothic novel, meaning to sit down in one of the upholstered leather chairs in the main hall and read. But after a few moments the quiet, broken only by the hiss of air through the ventilators and the creaks and groans and thrums of the ship, began to feel creepy rather than restful. *Ixion's here somewhere,* Florian found herself thinking. Maybe not walking around loose, but would Lord Chandre's men and the Capidarans really keep as close a guard on him as Colonel Averi's men had? And she would bet he wasn't being kept in the specially warded chamber anymore. And if Nicholas was right about Ixion taking an interest in her . . .

Gah, you're going to make yourself crazy. She returned to the library, reshelving the gothic and instead taking a humorous story about the romantic adventures of a wine-bar dancer. She went out and down the passengers' stairs, past the portrait of Queen Ravenna and the First

Class Entrance Hall, the fine wood walls and the marble-tiled floor gleaming, and down to the smaller carpeted lounge where the steward's office, paneled in sleek wood with etched-glass windows, took up one wall. It had once been a command post for Lady Aviler's volunteers, but it was closed and dark now as well. Four large corridors led off from this lounge, two toward the bow and two toward the stern. She chose the one that led toward the First Class staterooms, hoping the Syprians would still be awake.

The quiet corridor stretched on forever, the distant end curving upward like an inverted horizon. The doors she passed, all set back in small vestibules, were closed and quiet, and she wasn't sure who, if anyone, was quartered here now. She tried not to succumb to the fear that something was about to dart out and grab her, but since something had, effectively, darted out and grabbed her on the voyage to Capidara, it wasn't easy.

Florian reached the right little vestibule and knocked lightly on the door. It moved in the frame a little, as Tremaine had been too impatient to wait for a key when she had first appropriated the rooms and had got one of the Syprians to break the lock. To her relief she heard a stirring inside.

Gyan opened the door, brows lifting in anxious surprise. "Florian." He studied her face a moment, then added ruefully, "I see you're not coming to deliver good news." He was an older man with a heavy build and a good-humored face, balding with a long fringe of gray hair.

"No," she said regretfully as she followed him into the suite. It was all red and gold, with a deep tawny carpet and red drapes covering the portholes in the far wall of the sitting room. The lights, all of which were on as the Syprians refused to touch the switches, were frosted crystal lozenges set into the cherrywood-veneered walls. A few small pieces of rough wood lay on a delicate marquetry side table, along with a scatter of wood shavings and a little knife. One piece of wood was in the process of being carved into the head and neck of a sea serpent. "Nothing's changed since this afternoon." Florian dropped down onto one of the gold-upholstered couches, the book in her lap, and said wearily, "It's so frustrating. I know we're doing everything right. We've done it exactly the same way we did it in Capistown, and Niles and I and the other Rienish sorcerers have all tried it, but nothing happens." She massaged her temples. "I know it'll turn out to be something simple that we're all overlooking."

Gyan took the other chair, letting his breath out. He looked tired and worn, the lines at the corners of his eyes and his mouth deeper, his skin tinged with gray under his tan. He had lived in the Andrien village with his foster daughter Dyani before it had been destroyed by the Gardier, and had been sent along on their trip here to be the Andrien family's diplomat, to counter Pasima's influence. "I hope so. Using these curse circles to travel . . . It just seems like no good can come of it."

At the moment Florian felt inclined to agree. She didn't see how the plan to get inside the Lodun barrier could go forward without modifying the new circle, and since the new circle wouldn't work, there seemed little point in that. And the others seemed to think Capidara hadn't given them enough troops to do much of anything, even with the new spheres. She saw a couple of the polished wood bow cases sitting on the dining table and asked, "Pasima's not here, is she?" Florian could do without being stared at accusingly.

Gyan made what looked like a warding gesture against the evil eye. "No, no, thank the god for that. She and Sanior and Danias moved down to the other room." He shook his head, leaning back in the chair. "Sanior isn't bad, he's young yet, but Danias has never had a thought in his head Pasima didn't put there. None of them took well to Cletia and Cimarus going off like they did, but of course it's their own fault. Sanior did tell me Pasima didn't like Cletia doing her own thinking where Gil was concerned."

"I just hope . . . Oh, I don't know." Florian scrubbed her hands through her hair. She supposed she should find somewhere to sleep but she still felt too keyed up. And she knew her belongings had been transferred from the refugee hostel back to the ship, but had no idea where they had ended up. Probably in Niles and Gerard's workroom, or locked up in the steward's office. "I don't mean to keep you up. Do you mind if I just sit here for a while?"

He got to his feet, gesturing around the room with a shrug. "Stay as long as you'd like. I'd prefer it if you'd quarter here with us. It's a bit quiet with just Kias and me and the boy."

"I'd like that," Florian told him in relief.

Gyan smiled, ruffled her hair, and went back through the dining room to the rear of the suite. Florian curled up on the couch and tried to read but it took an act of deliberate concentration to keep her mind focused on the heroine's adventures amid Vienne's *beau monde* and *demi monde*. Especially since she knew many of the characters had been based on real people and some of them had been killed in the war. She kept wondering where the others were, what had happened to them. If the theaters and cafés and Great Houses mentioned were still standing or had been bombed or burned out of existence. Shifting restlessly on the couch, she heard nothing, but felt a breath of cooler air from the corridor, as if the door had drifted open.

She looked up to see Ixion standing not two paces away. He smiled down at her. "We meet again, flower."

Cold shock washed over her, trickling down her spine like ice water. "What are you doing here?" *Arisilde's sphere,* she thought, frantic. Niles had it, in his cabin. *Telephone.* It was across the room, on the built-in writing desk. *Can I get to it?* The crew was so overworked, it could take time to reach a ship's operator. And Ixion wouldn't just stand there and watch while she did it.

Studying her almost clinically, as if watching every thought pass through her head, he said, "I wanted to see you." He still wore the well-tailored suit, and she could smell the faint scent of an expensive toilet water.

"You've seen me. Good-bye." Florian tried to keep her voice even, cursing the fact that she sounded breathless rather than firm.

He lifted a brow. "You don't scream for help?"

Her heart pounded, but she said, "I don't need to scream. If you think Arisilde doesn't know where you are, you're mistaken." Even if the sphere couldn't communicate directly, it would sense Ixion's presence. The thought let her set her jaw and regard him steadily. "Go away. Or tell me why you're here, then go away."

He strolled toward the open panel doors that led to the dining room, the bedrooms. Where Kias and Gyan and Calit were sleeping. "I can hear breathing. Shame if it were to stop." He tilted his head, watching carefully for her reaction.

Florian pressed her lips together, making herself stay calm. *Maybe screaming would have been a good idea.*

Ixion shook his head, still smiling. "And Giliead and Ilias are trapped in some far place, by your own curse circles. How I laughed to hear that."

She knew instinctively he wanted her to beg him to leave the others alone, and that begging wouldn't do any good. Perhaps he wanted her to try to run for the telephone, to give him an excuse to attack. "Did you laugh about it in front of Lord Chandre?" Her voice came out at too high a pitch but the comment stopped him in the doorway.

He looked at her, head tilted slightly, intrigued. She pushed on, "You've got him fooled, I suppose. He thinks you'll help us."

He lifted a brow. "But I will help you, flower." He moved back toward the center of the room, standing over her again. "I could help you make the recalcitrant curse circle work." His smile turned kind. Or she would have thought it was kind, if she didn't know what he was. "Bring your friends back."

That startled her. Florian swallowed in a dry throat. *If I thought that was true* . . . What if it was? "I don't believe you."

"It's simple, really. Something prevents the curse from completing itself." He gestured with a shrug. "Remove it, and the circle will work."

"What something?"

He shook his head sadly. "No, that's not the way of it. We bargain."

Florian eyed him. *He's lying. He has to be lying.* Ixion didn't know—shouldn't know—anything about the circles. "And what do you want?"

"Nothing of moment. Your assistance."

"In what?"

"In whatever I ask." He lifted his brows at her expression. "Only small things, I assure you. You could tell me if they speak of me, in any of your councils." He knelt suddenly, eye to eye with her. "You have power, but they neglect your teaching. When was the last time they let you perform a spell, or taught you a new one? They waste your talents in tasks any servant could do."

"There's no time—" She cut off the involuntary protest, biting her lip. *He was doing something there, something so subtle* . . . That he had echoed her own thoughts hadn't helped. She looked away, flustered and guilty. But if she refused, she knew there was no telling what he would do. "I'll think about it," she said flatly, feeling like a traitor and a coward. "I'm not promising anything, just that I'll think about it."

He pushed to his feet just a shade too gracefully, reminding her again that that body was only a few months old at most. He gave her an ironic nod, as if he knew she was lying and was only playing along with her. "Think hard, flower, and think fast. If I become impatient, someone might die."

Ixion walked out, as silently as he had arrived.

Florian sat there a moment, taking deep breaths. Her palms had sweated onto the cloth cover of the book and she set it aside, wiping her hands off on her pants, swearing in annoyance as she realized she was trembling. A sudden horrified thought struck. She scrambled to her feet and hurried through the dining room to the back of the suite, ramming her hip into the table as she passed. But even before she reached the main bedroom she heard the reassuring sound of soft snoring, and a glance inside showed her all was well.

Breathing a little easier, she went back to the sitting room and picked up the telephone receiver. After a few moments while she reflected that Ixion would have had leisure to kill her several times over had she tried this while he was here, one of the ship's operators finally answered. She cleared her throat. "Can you connect me with Nicholas Valiarde, please?"

Chapter 9

S o, you were right," Florian said, stirring her coffee with frowning concentration as she finished telling Nicholas about Ixion's visit. It was just before dawn and they were in the First Class dining room, at a table with Gyan, Kias and Calit. The giant room was paneled with gold-toned wood, with bands of silver and bronze along the top and bottom of the walls. There were private dining salons along the sides, separated from the main area by silvered glass panels, and blackout cloth was tightly tacked over the outside windows. Several dozen people were here now, officers and crew about to go on duty, men and women in Rienish navy uniforms, mostly concerned with the coffee and rolls being dispensed from serving trolleys near the baize doors. There were other civilians here too, mostly Viller Institute workers who had volunteered to return. The sea had been rough last night and everyone looked sick, weary or preoccupied, or all three. The ship would also be reaching the Walls of the World at some point late tonight or tomorrow, and they just had to hope the crossing would go smoothly. "I'm lucky I didn't get us all killed," Florian added, stabbing her spoon into the small supply of sugar. She couldn't believe she had been so stupid about Ixion.

"It wouldn't be your fault," Gyan told her, though he looked troubled. "It's just what happens around Ixion."

Kias nodded, resigned. "I've been waiting for him to kill us since he showed up on the Isle of Storms with his head back on."

Their table was near the center of the room, but the acoustics reduced the voices of the other diners to a murmur, and Florian was sure no one could hear them without coming closer and being obvious about it—which was probably the reason Nicholas had chosen this room to meet in. And they were speaking Syrnaic anyway, a fact readily explained by Gyan's and Kias's presence. Calit, who didn't know enough Syrnaic to get one word in three, was occupied with pulling his roll apart and flicking berries across the table. Florian added, "I thought about going to Colonel Averi, but even if he believed me, for Chandre and the Capidarans it would still be my word against Ixion's."

Nicholas had absorbed the information with a professional calm Florian found reassuring. "You're correct. Chandre wants a pet sorcerer too badly to allow anything to get in his way. Especially unpleasant facts about the sorcerer's behavior." He nodded to himself and pushed his cup aside, standing. "I'll take care of this. Just try to act as if nothing has happened. And don't mention anything to—"

"What, you're leaving?" Florian almost yelped, then hastily lowered her voice. "No, I want to help!" He looked down at her, lifting a brow. "I know, I know, but I won't mess it up again, I won't . . . waffle." His expression became even more ironic, and she felt her face reddening. "You'd let Tremaine help," she added, though she felt like a ten-year-old.

For the first time, Nicholas betrayed some real irritation. He sat back down, steepled his hands and said deliberately, "Tremaine would have kept her mouth shut and let Niles attack so Ixion could retaliate and the sphere could finish the bastard off."

"That would have been best, Florian," Kias informed her, though he managed not to sound reproachful.

"I know. That's a mistake I won't make again, believe me," she said firmly. "I know if we fail, we'll be in trouble—"

Nicholas took a deep breath, shook his head and contemplated the ceiling for a moment in grim silence. "Florian. If you don't think that's our predicament now, I'd truly hate to experience your definition of 'trouble.' "

"He's right, Florian," Gyan said urgently, leaning forward to lay a hand on her arm. "Killing a wizard, it's always a dangerous business, but this is Ixion. You can't risk yourself like that."

"But I'm already at risk," Florian protested, frustrated. It frightened her that Ixion had come to her, and she wanted to make that fear go away. She felt that if she was involved in the plot against him, it would give her back some control over the situation. But she couldn't think of a way to say it that made the least bit of sense. "It's me he came to."

"Florian." Nicholas eyed her. "The more people involved in this, the more difficult it will be. Men like Ixion have to be led to their destruction gently. Tell no one about this, not even Niles." He pushed to his feet. "And while I appreciate the offer, I don't need the help."

Watching him walk away across the big room, Florian said grimly, "I don't think he appreciated the offer."

"Don't take it badly," Gyan told her. His eyes followed Nicholas thoughtfully. "Some Chosen Vessels work alone."

"He's not a Chosen Vessel, he just . . . thinks he is." Florian poked at her crusty roll, biting her lip. "I have to help. If— When the others get back, what would Tremaine say if she found out I'd let her father get killed?"

" 'Thanks'?" Kias suggested.

Florian and Gyan both glared at him. He winced. "Sorry."

In the dim light of the grotto room, Tremaine woke stiff and sore, her mouth tasting like sandpaper. Her coat had been rolled up as a pillow and she lay on a folded blanket, but her back wasn't much appeased by that. Her dreams had been vivid images of Arites's death, the way he had jolted forward, knocking into her as the bullet had ripped into him from behind, the feel of his already lifeless body as she and Cletia had carried him up the airship's ramp. It took her a moment to remember why. *Right. Meretrisa.* She lifted a hand to shove the hair out of her eyes but stopped, peering closely at it in the dim light.

New skin, pale and tender, stretched across her palm and up her fingers and thumb. The dead burned flesh had all been neatly trimmed away; she supposed Gerard had done it while she was asleep. She flexed it and the skin felt tight and stretchy, like a wet glove that had stiffened when left too near the fire. Gritting her teeth at that image, she pushed herself up with a groan.

They had moved into the small grotto room Ilias and Giliead had found and sometime not long after that Tremaine had abruptly decided to lie down on the floor and sleep. She wasn't sure how long she had been out, but now their collection of packs and bags was piled against one wall, the other blankets folded and neatly stacked. Balin was in the corner asleep, with Cimarus seated nearby, his sword across his lap. Meretrisa lay against the far wall on a pallet of blankets. Tremaine could only see her face, pale as white paper, against the blues and golds of the weaving. As Tremaine sat up, Cimarus asked politely, "Is your hand better now?"

"Yes, actually it is." She cleared her throat. The muted daylight falling through the louvers in the roof seemed to be tinted more toward late afternoon, but it was hard to tell. She felt disjointed, out of sorts, disconnected from reality. Sleeping during the day usually had an unsettling effect on her, but not this unsettling. "How long was I asleep?"

Cimarus squinted up at the sunlight, thinking. "The night and half the day."

Damn. That's almost as long as Aras, and he was burned practically all over. She blinked, trying to wake up. "How is Meretrisa?"

Cimarus craned his neck to check on the Capidaran woman. "They say she should stay asleep, and not move. She has a healing curse on her, and isn't dying."

Tremaine nodded slowly. She vaguely remembered Gerard saying something about an injured lung. "Where is everybody else?"

"Searching the big room for the god-sphere wizard's trail signs, and copying things down." He shrugged one shoulder, his expression philosophical. "The same as we always do."

In the middle of the room someone had made a rough sort of square fire pit out of loose stone blocks and the smoke drifted up and out through one of the louvers. Vervane came in through the archway to deposit an armload of sticks and tinder next to it. Seeing Tremaine was conscious, she dipped a cup into the pot steaming on the fire and carried it over. Tremaine accepted it with a muttered thanks, startled to realize she actually was grateful. She was beginning to like this herb stuff almost as much as coffee. After a restorative gulp, she asked Vervane, "How's your hand?"

"Oh, it's fine." The older woman wiggled her fingers as she returned to the fire. "Master Gerard made it as good as new. But poor Meretrisa will take much longer to heal."

Poor Meretrisa the traitor. Tremaine vaguely remembered telling Gerard about that. "Did Gerard mention about—"

"That she told a spy about your new circle?" Vervane's expression was pained as she awkwardly took a seat on the floor. "Yes. I'm not sure Aras believes it completely, but . . ." She gestured helplessly. "The Ministry was warned, over and over again, but it was hard for them to believe it would happen in Capistown."

Tremaine nodded, feeling bleak. It had been hard for people to believe it in Ile-Rien, too. There wasn't much else to be said. "Is the fire a good idea? The smoke might tell someone we're here. Wherever here is."

Cimarus answered in Syrnaic, "Giliead and Ilias found a way to the outside, and said there's no one around as far as they could see."

Of course. That's where they got the wood, Tremaine thought, nodding to herself. She finished the drink and clambered to her feet, returning the cup to Vervane. "I'll go see if they've found anything."

"Tell Cletia it's her turn to watch the Gardier," Cimarus told her, then added plaintively, "And can't this lady learn to speak Syrnaic the way you did? It would be easier if we could talk."

Tremaine snorted, finding her new rifle leaning against the wall, carefully segregated from the Syprian's spare bows and arrows so it wouldn't contaminate them. She answered in the same language, "You could speak Rienish to her, you know. It wouldn't kill you." She had thought Cimarus and Cletia might have absorbed more Rienish than they pretended, and Cimarus had obviously understood the gist of her and Vervane's conversation. The Syprians seemed to all be quick with new languages, but Tremaine was fairly sure Pasima had made it a moral point not to speak Rienish and expected the others to follow her example.

Checking the rifle, she saw someone had unloaded it. She found the ammunition in a Gardier belt, coiled up nearby. It had a shoulder strap made of a mottled olive green leather with a texture like snake or lizard skin. Her pants didn't have any pockets and it was too warm to wear her coat, so she attached the brown canvas ammunition pouch to her own belt.

With Cimarus's parting plea "Remember to tell Cletia," Tremaine headed for the giant circle chamber, making her way through the long gallery with its fallen balconies and collapsed pillars.

She stopped in the archway, marveling again at the sheer size of the place, the cathedral-like shape of the roof. *Buttresses,* she wondered. *Are there buttresses on the outside? How does it stay up?*

Gerard and Aras were at the far end of the room, apparently examining and cataloging the many circles carved into the floor. Tremaine hoped Gerard's notebook had enough paper. Cletia, with a bow slung over her shoulder, was keeping watch near the center of the room.

Tremaine made her way over, the other woman warily watching her approach. "Cimarus says it's his turn."

Cletia took that in with a remote nod, still eyeing Tremaine. Then she said, "He didn't stay with you while you were ill. Did that surprise you?"

Tremaine, still playing mental catch-up, actually thought she meant Cimarus for a moment. Then she realized who Cletia did mean and went blank. The blankness didn't last long.

It had never occurred to her that Ilias would do anything except his job, which was to scout this new territory and watch Giliead's back while the Chosen Vessel looked for dangerous spells. The fact that Cletia saw her as the kind of woman who expected a man to stay at her bedside while she was sleeping off a healing spell instead of being out making sure they weren't about to be attacked was almost amusing. Amusing in an enraging sort of way. Tremaine's lips curved in a dangerous approximation of a smile. "Your estimation of my character is incorrect."

Several different emotions seemed to flicker under Cletia's calm façade, then she inclined her head in a gesture that reminded Tremaine of Pasima at her most annoying. She started back toward the archway and Tremaine watched her go. Then she gazed in irritation at the ceiling and told herself, *Look on it as a challenge.*

Gerard spotted her approach and straightened up from a circle, one hand pressed to his back. It might be the light, but he actually looked a little less exhausted. He must have taken time to actually sleep and eat last night. "How are you feeling?" he asked as she went to meet him.

"I'm fine. Find anything yet?"

"No, there's no sign of any message left by Arisilde. But I am finding more examples of the location symbols in the circles." He reached her, tucking his notebook into the bag with the sphere and taking her hand to look at the healing burns. "That's coming along nicely," he said with satisfaction.

Tremaine reclaimed her hand, flexing it experimentally again. "It feels better than it did when I first woke up. Less tight."

He nodded. "Working with it should help that, but be sure not to tear the new skin."

"Right, I'll work on that." Tremaine made a face at that image and changed the subject. "Where're Ilias and Gil? Vervane said they found a way outside?"

"They should be back soon." Gerard pulled out his pocket watch and squinted at it. "They've been exploring the area of the structure immediately around us and reporting in at fairly regular intervals. I can't persuade them to actually draw a map, but from what I understand . . ." He dug out the notebook again, flipping past pages of esoteric symbols to show her a rough diagram. "This part of the building is sort of a large oval, tucked in amid a mountain range. From the symbols and what we saw of the stars last night, we're at the western end of the Syrnai, in the inland territory occupied by people called the Hisians. Depending on where we are, Giliead estimates it would probably take two to three months to walk to Cineth from here."

"That's good." They could, at least, get back to Cineth, even if it took a long time. "So this is where we are in the building?" Tremaine peered at the map, trying to make sense of the little squares and circles and Gerard's cramped handwriting. "What's all this around it?"

"Empty rooms that could have been living quarters, lecture halls, meeting rooms." He shrugged, gesturing around at the huge room. "It's impossible to tell. This place has been abandoned for hundreds of years, like the city under the Isle of Storms and the Wall Port. The rest of this—" He traced a large amorphous shape that apparently indicated unknown territory. "Giliead says the building appears to go on for some distance, at least from the outside vantage point he and Ilias discovered. There's another large oval section down here, which is why I believe there's another circle chamber." He shook his head, closing the notebook. "They haven't advanced into that area yet. Giliead hasn't sensed any etheric activity, except for the circles themselves. But we've never been able to determine how well he can sense passive spells."

Tremaine nodded absently, frowning. They had covered a lot of ground in a day, but then if the rooms were all empty there wasn't that much searching to do, just making sure there was no evidence of a Gardier occupation. "Something about this . . ." She looked up at Gerard. "I didn't get the impression Arisilde had a huge amount of time when he was doing this."

Gerard's expression was blank. "When he was doing what?"

Tremaine gestured vaguely, shifting the rifle's strap on her shoulder. "Looking for whatever he was looking for after he left Nicholas. He was supposed to be taking the message back to Ile-Rien that we were about to be invaded by a foreign power from another world who had magic that we couldn't fight. I know he could be a little erratic— we never did teach him how to use the telephone—but this place would have taken days to explore, even for him." Tremaine shrugged helplessly. "He knew he didn't have days."

"Yes, yes." Gerard looked thoughtful. "I see your point. We should have found a signal or sign from him, like the coat button, as soon as we arrived."

"If we're in the right place."

Gerard nodded, his brow creased and his eyes distant as he considered all the implications. "If this isn't the place where he was . . . injured."

"Oh. That's a thought." An uncomfortable thought. Tremaine frowned at him. "Watch your back, all right? Don't do anything that, you know, Arisilde would do."

Gerard was still staring into the distance. "Yes, I—What?" He gave her an exasperated look. "How would I know—" His expression cleared. "Ah, they're back again."

Tremaine looked around, relieved to see Ilias and Giliead walking out from the center archway on the far side of the chamber.

Watching Ilias's lithe confident stride and the fine line of his jaw as he turned to say something to Giliead, Tremaine became aware that Gerard had been attempting to solicit her attention for some moments. He was now regarding her with a fond but weary expression. "What?" she demanded.

He smiled wryly, stuffing the notebook back into his bag. "Nothing."

The two men reached them and both had to examine Tremaine's injury before they answered any questions. Ilias took her hand, rubbing his thumb across the new skin on her palm while Giliead looked over his shoulder. "It's still hard to believe," Ilias said, glancing up at Giliead. Sorcerous healing had been the beginning of convincing the Syprians, or at least the Andrien Syprians, that not all magic was evil.

"Did your search turn up anything interesting?" Gerard asked hopefully.

Giliead rested his bow on the floor, saying, "There're no more circles in this wing. We did find a room with water basins big enough to bathe in—some of them are broken and the pipes aren't bringing the water anymore, but a few are still working."

Gerard nodded. "That may come in handy if we stay here any length of time. You're ready to advance into the other part of the building now?"

"Right after we get some food."

Tremaine saw Cimarus was arriving for his turn at watching the circle chamber and his respite from Balin. Telling herself Cletia's little sally had nothing to do with it, Tremaine decided it was time to get a private moment with Ilias. She looked at him pointedly, hoping he would get the message. "Gerard said you found the way out. Is it close by?"

"I'll show you." Ilias caught Giliead's eye and jerked his head back toward the hallway leading toward their camp. *That either meant "I'll meet you there" or "Make yourself scarce,"* Tremaine thought. From the suppressed amusement in Giliead's eyes, she suspected it was the latter.

Ilias led her back toward the archway he and Giliead had used, lifting a brow at Tremaine's rifle. "Are you going to keep that thing?"

"Until I get another pistol. I might talk Gerard out of his, but—" She recalled their recent unpleasant revelation. Not that anything but the sphere would do Gerard much good against a Gardier attack, but she felt profoundly uneasy at the idea of leaving him unarmed. "No, I think I want him to keep it."

He gave her a sharp glance. "Why? What's wrong?"

She repeated what she and Gerard had talked about, finishing with, "And I just don't think Arisilde would have spent much time here. I think he would have decided to come back later with help to search the place, and left. So if something happened to him here, it happened right away."

Ilias nodded, listening intently. "Or he came here first and went to the cold mountains from here." They reached the archway. It opened into a big corridor, similar to the one that led to their campsite but without the rubble from the collapsed balconies. It was dank and a little dusty, with some flowering creepers growing down from one of the louvers in the curving roof.

Tremaine considered that idea, frowning. "But then why did he give us the circle to take us there, not here?" Another smaller corridor led off into a darker section of the building; if she had interpreted Gerard's map correctly, that was the uncharted territory, the part Giliead and Ilias hadn't explored yet.

"Uh, he didn't remember it?" Ilias shook his head, obviously not pleased with that answer. He gestured down one end of the corridor. "This goes all the way around the circle chamber and connects up with the rooms behind it, the ones we already looked through. This other end goes to the way out."

As they started in that direction he added, "If we are on the wrong track, we've got to go back. And if the Gardier are still there, that's not going to be easy."

"It's not," Tremaine agreed. She shook her head, gesturing help-lessly. It was Arisilde they were talking about. Maybe attributing logi-cal motives to him was the wrong way to look at the situation. "I don't know, we've barely been here at all, maybe we'll find a mark or some-thing by one of the circles." The possibility that the Gardier had unim-peded access to the circle in their house in Capistown made her stomach hurt; she didn't want to think about it. And it did terrible things to their theory that the circle in the mountain's upper chamber had stopped working because Nicholas had destroyed the correspond-ing circle in the house. The other alternative was that the Gardier had captured a copy of either Gerard's notes on the new circle or Giaren's photographs, and had drawn it themselves, and that didn't bear think-ing about either.

Ahead at the end of the corridor, Tremaine could see a broad shaft of sunshine lighting up a heavy stone staircase. "So when whoever built this place went away, they just left the door wide open?"

"It's not an easy door to get to from the outside," Ilias assured her.

Tremaine assumed the corollary was that it wasn't an easy door to get out of either. The steps went up in stages, turning back and up into a stairwell that went through the curving roof. They started up, and up, and up. Tremaine's legs were aching after the first landing; the stairs were like those in the other ancient cities they had found and were a little too high for the comfort of normal-sized people. It was warm enough that she tied back the sleeves of her shirt, reflecting that in this climate bathing was going to be more of an issue than it had been in the mountains.

At the point where Tremaine judged they had climbed the height of a seven-story building and she was about to ask just how far there was to go, the next landing took them outside onto a broad open platform. She stopped, whistling softly.

The sun was bright in an intense blue sky dotted unevenly with puffy white clouds. It shone down on low mountains capped with a tangled jungle of deep emerald green and on a narrow gorge with dozens of tiny streams of water running down its rough sides. The platform gave way to a small grassy field atop a bluff, and a short slope led up to another small plateau covered with broad-leafed palms and shorter trees with twisty limbs and furry green leaves. The plateau was bordered by more tall cliffs, walling it off like a private garden.

Tremaine wandered out onto the bluff, stumbling on the remnants of broken and scattered paving, the sun warm on her face. Ilias took her elbow, steering her around to face back toward the building.

She shaded her eyes, swearing in disbelief. The structure was gray on the outside and enterprising vines and flowers had taken root in cracks and crevices, so unless you looked for the sculptured roundness of the different levels of roof, you might mistake it for a series of low hills. Their wing stretched off to her right, stone buttresses supporting the vastness of what had to be the circle chamber. Two more wings ran out for a much greater distance in front of her, the larger sections buttressed and apparently supporting themselves on the rocky cliffs that crowded close to the smooth stone sides. She couldn't see the smoke from their fire; it must be carried away by the fitful breeze.

Ilias stepped up behind her, wrapping his arms around her waist. She leaned back against his chest, grateful for the support after the long climb up the awkward stairs. He nuzzled her neck, saying into her hair, "We think we're inland from Syrneth, where the Hisians live."

"That's what Gerard said." And it seemed ridiculous to be standing here trying to think up a way to tell the man you were married to that you thought you had possibly fallen in love with him, so she turned around, making it a real kiss.

After a time, he sighed, resting his cheek against hers. She could feel the smooth spot in his beard stubble, where the silver curse mark marred his skin. Cletia had barely been willing to look at Ilias when she had first boarded the *Ravenna;* surely she hadn't been able to get past that in such a short time. *But if Pasima was trying to dictate your every thought, how long do you think it would take for you to want to do the opposite of everything she said?* she asked herself. *Not damn long.* Feeling a need to change the subject of her thoughts, she pulled back, asking, "How do we get down from here?"

He looked around with a shrug. "Climb."

"Climb? What, where? Down there?" Tremaine stared at the edge of the bluff. It was a long sheer drop down to the valley floor.

He jerked his head toward the cliffs ringing in their little plot of jungle. "Or up there. Or down onto the roof, then down the wall, but we think that would be too hard without ropes. And even with ropes, it wouldn't be easy."

"No kidding." Tremaine pivoted, studying the area again. "Climbing up the cliff looks like the best way, but I don't think Vervane could make that. Hell, I don't think I could make that."

"That's the problem," Ilias admitted soberly. "The people who lived here must have used the curse circles to travel in and out. That explains why they needed so many, anyway."

Tremaine nodded thoughtfully. There might be another entrance somewhere, one that didn't require climbing a sheer cliff, but there might not. "I think this is even more like a central train station than the chamber in the mountain. Whoever these people were, they must have traveled all over your world using these circles."

That led to an explanation of what a train was, what a station was, the principles behind the idea of switching stations, and the last train trip Tremaine had taken with Arisilde. While they talked, they gathered some more wood from the fringes of their patch of jungle and Ilias climbed a tree after some yellow fruit to supplement their limited supplies.

They started down the stairs, Tremaine carrying one bundle of wood and Ilias the other, having used his shirt to make a temporary bag for the fruit. Admiring the exposed view of his chest and shoulders, she asked, "Has Cletia said anything to you?"

He glanced at her, puzzled. "About what?"

"Nothing in particular."

He looked thoughtful. "Actually, she did say something when we were scouting the different circles back at the cold mountain." He shrugged, clearly dismissing whatever it was as nonsensical. "I couldn't tell what she wanted."

Tremaine lifted her brows. *That's interesting.* "I see."

She had meant for her tone to be neutral, but Ilias had sharper ears than that. "See what?" he asked, throwing her a suspicious look.

Tremaine drew breath to tell him what Cletia had said, and suddenly found herself assailed by doubt. She found the idea of expecting him to wait at her bedside like some character from a bad romantic novel hilarious, or possibly humiliating, or possibly both, but what if he didn't? What if he had intentionally stayed away to avoid giving her the wrong idea? What was the wrong idea?

While she still had her mouth open, trying to make a decision, he halted abruptly. Tremaine stopped an instant later, and in the sudden silence she heard the sound of soft-booted feet striking stone, heading rapidly away.

What the hell . . . Tremaine went cold, exchanging a startled glance with Ilias. None of their party had reason to eavesdrop or run away, except possibly for Cletia, and she would have had to leave Balin unguarded. And Tremaine was fairly sure she would have the sense to walk quietly away without alerting them.

Ilias hastily deposited his burdens on the steps and she followed suit, starting down the stairs after him as quietly as she could. They were about two landings from the bottom and Ilias made it in near silence, taking two or three steps at a time. Tremaine hurried after him, pulling the rifle off her shoulder and cradling it. *I really need to find a pistol,* she thought, her heart pounding.

Tremaine reached the corridor several steps behind Ilias. It looked undisturbed to her unpracticed eye, dust motes drifting in the shafts of sunlight, but Ilias crouched to examine the floor. "Someone's been here," he said quietly.

Tremaine's mouth twisted in rueful acknowledgment. "I was afraid you were going to say that."

He pointed to various scuff marks in the dust. "There's where Gil and I came and went when we found these steps, where Gil showed Gerard and Aras, then where you and I just came. Then there's that." He tapped the floor thoughtfully.

"That wasn't here earlier?" Tremaine tried to keep one eye on the now ominously empty corridor while trying to see what he was pointing at.

He shook his head, grimly certain, and carefully followed the track a few paces down the corridor. "He came after us, stopped just at the stairs—he must have heard us talking—then ran away." He crouched to look at the tracks again and lifted his brows. "It's not the kind of boot the Gardier wear, or like you wear. It's flat on the bottom, like our boots."

"That's something." Tremaine felt the tightness in her chest ease. If it was a native to this area who had been frightened off by unfamiliar voices in a place he had expected to find deserted . . . *That would be nice.* But somehow she didn't think so. "If you were out somewhere around Cineth, hunting or whatever, and you heard a man and a woman talking, even in a language you didn't understand, would you run away?"

"No." Ilias pushed to his feet, throwing her an ironic look. "Not unless I didn't want them to see me because I was planning to kill them."

Tremaine sighed. "That's what I thought."

Gerard frowned in concern, looking down the dark corridor into the unexplored wing. "Are you certain you don't want me to accompany you?"

"Yes, because getting our only sorcerer killed and spending the rest of our lives stuck here sounds like such a good idea," Tremaine told him, exasperated. "Now will you go back?" She adjusted the Gardier ammunition pouch on her belt and found herself checking the rifle yet again to make sure it was loaded.

At the intersection of the other passages, Ilias had found footprints in the dust where the intruder had turned into the other wing. Now Tremaine, Ilias and Giliead were going after him. Tremaine felt it would be at least as much fun as searching the *Ravenna;* in other words, dangerous and exhausting.

Aras had been sent back to watch Balin, Cletia to keep watch in the circle chamber and Cimarus had been moved to the corridor intersection, so he could watch for anyone attempting to enter their wing. He was armed with one of the bows and was uneasily surveying the dark corridors.

"I'll try not to let any strangers in, no matter how persuasive their arguments," Gerard told Tremaine, still repressively. "Just don't get hurt."

Tremaine snorted in derision as they started down the corridor. She kept behind Ilias and Giliead, who were walking a little apart, Giliead keeping his eyes on the corridor ahead and Ilias scanning the ground, following the tracks the intruder had left.

They had decided that the bows were better left to guard their camp, since Tremaine had the rifle. Both men distrusted the rifle on principle, but were willing to admit it was a necessary evil. And it might actually be useful, since the chances were that the intruder was not a Gardier.

Besides the distinct difference in boot soles Ilias had noted, Tremaine thought that if a Gardier had heard them he would have been back by now with more men to investigate. And the Gardier would have posted guards in this circle chamber.

They came to a little rotunda that formed an intersection of three corridors, two of them with lower ceilings and fewer louvers, leading off into shadowy depths. The third opened into a larger hall, lined with a double row of columns in an elegant hourglass shape that must be more to ornament the space rather than support the ceiling.

Ilias stooped to check a patch of dusty floor that to Tremaine's eyes looked no different from any other, and jerked his head toward the large hall. "That way." He kept his voice low.

"This looks like a main entrance," Tremaine put in quietly. The back of her neck was prickling, but in these long stretches with no debris to hide behind, she knew no one could be watching them. At least, she hoped so.

Giliead nodded, turning to scan the area again. Tremaine had noticed one of them was always on watch when the other's attention was distracted. When Ilias searched for faint footmarks on the dirty stone, Giliead was watching the corridor; when Giliead paused to look for curse traps, Ilias made sure nothing crept up on him from behind. They seemed to do it by habit, automatically, with never any need to discuss it. Giliead said thoughtfully, "Funny that it's here and not back where the outside doorway is. But they must have used the curse circles to come and go."

Tremaine, who was still hoping for a better outside exit, had to reluctantly agree. It did look as if visitors had been meant to enter the fortress through the circles, then proceed down here to the formal entrance hall. "So where did our mysterious stranger come from? Did he climb down the cliffs to get in here? The only thing we've seen so far that a scavenger could use is the loose stone, and he couldn't haul that up the cliff without a lot of help. Besides, with all these mountains around, it's not as if there's a stone shortage."

"We don't know he's alone," Ilias told her, taking the first cautious step into the hourglass hall, looking up to make sure nothing was about to drop on them from above. "And we don't know he didn't come through a curse gate like we did."

"But—" Tremaine was about to say that the man wasn't a Gardier, so couldn't have come through the gates. *Circular thinking like that is not going to help.* Following Ilias, she said, "You mean people besides the Gardier and us, who have the gate spell and a way to make it work without killing themselves."

Giliead threw her a wry look. "Why not?"

Tremaine protested, "Because it's complicated enough the way it is." But she could too easily see it. This place, like the Wall Port and the city under the Isle of Storms, was so old there wasn't a stick of furniture, a scrap of fabric or paper left behind. The people who built it had to be long dead, vanished into the past. The only attraction the place had was the circles.

They reached the end of the hourglass hall and Ilias followed the tracks through a maze of smaller corridors. Tremaine noted that at first she had found the fortress's large empty spaces grand and airy, but now they seemed ominous and menacing. Her nerves jumped at every whisper of wind.

The tracks finally led into a passage that was littered knee deep in rubble from a collapsed loft or gallery. Down its length, Tremaine could see entrances to several other branching corridors. As Ilias surveyed the expanse of track-concealing debris in disgust and Giliead watched the corridor, Tremaine asked, "So did he know we'd follow him like this? Did he come this way deliberately to try to lose us? Am I asking too many questions? Don't answer that one." She was half suspecting an ambush but the corridor was well lit by sunlight falling through the louvers and unless someone had buried himself under the heavy rubble, it was unoccupied.

"It's the natural thing to do," Ilias admitted, glancing back at her.

"Natural for you." Someone who wasn't an expert in tracking might not realize his passage could be read from the dusty stone floor almost as easily as in dirt or mud; Tremaine didn't think she would have thought of it, but she made a mental note now.

Tremaine ended up sitting on a rock in the middle of the corridor, keeping watch with the rifle across her knees while Ilias and Giliead cast back and forth, checking the branching corridors for revealing tracks. Her stomach was starting to grumble and she wondered how long this was going to take. If it turned out their intruder was just a Hisian who lived in the area and liked to explore the fortress, and who had lit out for home at being startled by strangers, this was all an appalling waste of time. But they had to make certain.

Finally, both men returned; Giliead with a thoughtful expression and Ilias frowning. "So you couldn't find his tracks?" Tremaine asked, trying not to sound hopeful.

Ilias shook his head, sharing a grim look with Giliead. "We found too many tracks."

Tremaine stared. "What?"

"People, a lot of people, have been passing through here, back and forth, for a long time," Giliead clarified. He glanced around again, brows drawn together as he considered the situation. "Their tracks are everywhere. You can even see paths in all this broken stone, once you know where to look."

"That's wonderful," Tremaine muttered. She couldn't see paths through the rubble, even when she looked. "But we didn't see any sign of them back in the gate chamber."

"They must get their food and water and wood somewhere else.

There has to be another entrance," Ilias pointed out. "They probably don't go to our half of the fortress often; there isn't anything useful there but those fountains."

"And those are probably all over the building. . . ." Tremaine suppressed a groan. "But they don't come to the gate chamber, so they must not use the spell—"

"Unless there's curse circles all over the building too." Ilias shook his head, distracted. He grimaced. "This makes it different."

"It could be a wizard," Giliead told Tremaine before she could ask. "Our kind of wizard. They find places like this to take over, like Ixion did on the island. These people that go back and forth through here, they could be slaves, apprentices. And if it is a wizard, there could be curselings."

Tremaine nodded slowly, getting to her feet, her palms sweaty on the rifle stock. He was right. They knew this place was in the Syrnai. And the Syrnai meant Syprian wizards. "And I don't suppose there's a god around here."

Giliead shook his head, still grim. "No. I'd feel it if there was one here. They don't conceal themselves like the god-sphere. There's nothing."

"That other tall section, which Gerard thought was another gate chamber, should be that way." Ilias jerked his chin toward one of the branching corridors. "If they use curses, that's where we'll find them."

Nicholas strolled along the *Ravenna*'s top deck, taking in the early-morning air and waiting for a chance to make trouble. He knew he wouldn't have to wait long.

One of the quicker ways to bypass the ship's long internal corridors was to walk along the outer deck and take the outside stairs, and on such a fine warm day as this, there was no reason not to. From his vantage point on the rail, Nicholas watched people pass back and forth on the open decks below. Lord Chandre had been assigned a suite on the Sun Deck in the *Ravenna*'s forecastle, where the officers and officials were quartered. Another sign that his influence was growing unpleasantly fast.

The cabin corridors in the forecastle would be crowded at this time, with Averi's staff, the Capidarans and ship's officers heading off for breakfast and preparing for the day's meetings. The meetings were mostly useless attempts to make the best of the small amount of reliable information on what was happening in Ile-Rien; Nicholas wasn't bothering to attend most of them.

As the morning activity gradually calmed down, he saw Ixion walk out onto the deck below, accompanied by a token pair of Capidaran guardsmen, the Capidaran sorcerer Kressein, and a Rienish man known to be a political ally to Lord Chandre. *Yes, that's charming,* he thought with a wry grimace. *Let's post two useless guards, an octogenarian sorcerer and a trained bootlicker to guard the dangerous prisoner.* Colonel Averi was probably about to go mad with exasperation.

Watching the group carefully, Nicholas decided Kressein did not look entirely happy with the situation either. The old man moved stiffly, both with age and with affront at his companion. *That's interesting.* Nicholas had never been too sure of Kressein, one way or the other, and there hadn't been much time in Capistown to remedy that. The Capidaran sorcerer might not like being forced to work with Ixion—*and who would?* Nicholas thought, suppressing a smile. *The man brings new meaning to the word* odious. *And also the word* obvious, *for that matter.* But Kressein's dislike for the Syprian sorcerer might not prevent him from siding with him if he thought it would help him defend Capidara. Personally, Nicholas would rather see Ile-Rien vanish from the earth than see it in the hands of men like Chandre. He lifted a sardonic brow, mostly at himself. *You, an idealist? Tremaine would be shocked.*

Wherever she was.

Waiting until the group disappeared into one of the doorways further down the deck, Nicholas took the outside passenger stairs down to the Sun Deck. He stepped in through the outer hatch into the corridor, dark after the bright morning outside. He nodded politely to a couple of harried Viller Institute secretaries carrying armloads of files. As soon as the two women turned the corner, he stepped into the steward's alcove, drawing the door shut behind him.

It was a small dusty recess, with a water tap in the counter, a gas ring and lights that were attached to call buttons for all the suites. Nicholas leaned back so he could look through the grille in the door, placed so that the steward could see most of the length of the special suite corridor. He didn't have to wait long before Chandre left his room and strode down the corridor, with two aides in tow to make certain no one mistook him for a lesser personage, like the captain or the chief engineer. He didn't pause to lock the door. Nicholas lifted a brow, waiting. *Yes, I thought the man would be vain enough to bring a valet.*

After another few moments, a young Aderassi man, wearing a very correct suit and with his long hair slicked back, stepped out of the suite, locking the door carefully behind him. He hurried away, probably to grab a hasty breakfast before returning to the room.

Nicholas waited until the valet had turned the corner, then slipped out of the alcove. A few moments with his lockpicks had the door to Chandre's suite open, and once inside he moved swiftly to the main bedroom, ignoring the dispatch cases and letter files lying about. He found the tortoiseshell brush set on the marble-topped dressing table in the bedroom, removed a few strands of graying hair from the brush, slipped the hair into an envelope and pocketed it.

He left the suite rapidly, pausing only to manipulate the lock until the tumblers clicked, so the valet would notice nothing wrong when he returned. Then he went down the hall to the room on the end, where Ixion was quartered.

There were no guards now and no one inside, though if there was that hardly mattered. This time Nicholas meant to be noticed.

He took a short prybar out of the inside pocket of his coat and used it to clumsily—though not too clumsily—jimmy the lock. Once he had the door open he stepped inside, but he only waited a few moments, long enough to make sure any ward the sorcerer had set would register his presence. He didn't bother to search, knowing Ixion would be too clever to keep anything incriminating where his captors, especially Kressein, might find it. The scent hanging in the air made Nicholas wrinkle his nose in disapproval. *But not too clever to experiment with an inferior variety of hair oil.*

He stepped outside, pulled the door until the latch clicked, then headed away down the corridor, humming an old music hall tune.

Huh. I'm not sure what that was about, Florian thought, from her position scrunched up in the corner of the corridor. Her concealment charm was carefully cast, but she hadn't dared to move once Nicholas had entered the corridor, barely breathing as he had moved from Chandre's room down to Ixion's. Nicholas was just too alert, too suspicious for anyone trying to use magic to sneak up on him.

Florian had no idea what he had done in Chandre's room; he had only been in there a few moments. And in Ixion's room he had done nothing but make it obvious that . . . *Oh, I see. At least partly.* He was drawing Ixion's attention away from her by provoking him deliberately.

Still deep in thought, she slipped along the corridor, passing Chandre's valet unseen as the man hurried back, carrying a mug of coffee and a couple of breakfast rolls.

She had the feeling Nicholas's plan would work. Her mouth twisted ruefully. *I just hope it doesn't get him killed.*

Chapter 10

All the tracks had given Ilias a vision of a wizard and a clutch of curselings, squatting in a second circle chamber like a nest of goat spiders, drawn by the curses in the symbols whether they knew how to use them or not. The wizards of the Syrnai usually preferred to kill each other rather than work together, but this place might well have drawn two or more to cooperate in order to exploit it. If it was only one wizard, there would still be a number of slaves cursed to obey him.

Giliead led the way through broad corridors that seemed too airy and full of sunlight to make a habitation for anything so dark. Ilias could tell he was listening and looking carefully for curse traps, from the way he held his head and paused frequently. But there was nothing so far, which might only mean the curse traps were outside the fortress.

Giliead paused at the next corner, making a sharp gesture. Ilias stopped, then leaned back to tell Tremaine in a bare whisper, "Stay here."

She nodded, lifting her brows and mouthing the words "Don't get killed."

Ilias just grimaced in reply. He stepped quietly to Giliead's side, leaning out cautiously until he could see around the corner.

There was a foyer with a broad archway, revealing another giant chamber, at least as large as the one with the curse circles. But framed in that archway, lit by shafts of sunlight from the louvers in the tall arched ceiling and outlined against the pale blue-white stone, there was a ship. Ilias blinked, staring, too caught by the sight for a heart-beat to even look for human inhabitants.

The ship rested on the stone floor, nearly the size of a war galley, but the prow and stern both curved up to points and the gray wood looked too thin to weather any storm. The tilted deck was nearly covered by cabins of different sizes, so there was little or no open space to move around, and Ilias couldn't see the mast or the tiller either. There was floral carving along the rail, not too different from something you would see in the Syrnai, but it wasn't painted like a Syprian vessel and there were no eyes. He spotted a long diagonal crack in the hull, probably made when it had struck the hard stone floor. *But how?*

Then he saw the square outline of a door, below where the waterline would be. Ilias bit his tongue to keep from swearing aloud. *It's a flying whale, a flying whale made out of wood.* The soft part, the great billowy body that caught fire so easily was gone, that was why it was so hard to recognize. And this body of wood looked more like something rational people might build than the bare metal bodies of the other flying whales. Near it, set out on the floor, he could see blankets, rough clay pots, other household goods.

Giliead thumped him on the back urgently, pointing at something on the other side of the chamber.

Slightly dreading the thought of what would be more worth staring at than a wooden flying whale locked inside this giant room like a beetle in amber, Ilias eased further out, trying to see what Giliead was pointing at.

He found himself swallowing in a suddenly dry throat. *Oh. Oh, no.* From this angle he had a limited view of the far wall of the chamber. It was covered with small alcoves, each barely large enough to accommodate a lamp or a jar. But inside each one was a hefty piece of rock covered with crystal. Just like the crystals the Gardier used to make the curse circles work, to protect their flying whales, to destroy the Rienish weapons, to kill. The crystals that contained the captive souls of wizards.

Ilias looked up to exchange an appalled expression with Giliead, then they both quietly retreated from the corner.

They moved back to where Tremaine waited impatiently. Keeping his voice to an urgent whisper, Ilias asked Giliead, "You think there's a Gardier wizard in every one of those crystals?"

Tremaine stared. "What?"

Giliead shook his head, lips pursed, deeply worried. "I can't tell. I have to get in there, I have to get close."

Tremaine was poking Ilias with increasing urgency. He told her, "There's a wrecked flying whale and a wall full of crystals in there, and a place where people have been living, but no circles."

She clapped a hand to her forehead, baffled and horrified. "That's . . . Here? I don't know what that means."

Giliead shook his head with a grimace. "It could be an ambush, but—"

"But let's do it anyway," Ilias finished, ready to get it over with. He knew what Giliead was thinking. They had to find out if those crystals were occupied or not. Ilias didn't think he could turn his back on them and walk away without knowing; he knew Giliead couldn't.

Tremaine nodded. "I'll cover you."

Ilias looked at her worriedly. If the long shooting weapon came apart like the small one had . . . "If they're Gardier—"

She grimaced, motioning for him to get moving. "I know."

Ilias went forward with Giliead, staying close to the wall, then he darted across to take the opposite side of the archway. Tremaine waited just at the shelter of their corner. From his position, Ilias had a better view of the crystal alcoves; he could also see that this half of the chamber was empty of human or Gardier occupants. He looked a question at Giliead and got a nod in return; Gil could see the opposite side of the chamber from his vantage point and it was empty as well. There still might be Gardier hiding behind the bulk of the whale, or inside it, but they had already decided to take that chance.

As Giliead drew his sword and stepped into the room, Ilias followed. He took a few paces forward, every nerve alert for any sound, any movement, the back of his neck prickling with the feel of being watched. Wasting no time, Giliead moved purposefully toward the wall of crystals.

He heard a faint step behind him and knew it was Tremaine, moving to the side of the archway to cover them with the shooting weapon. *I'm going to have to teach her to use a bow.* He would start as soon as they got out of there alive.

Scanning the chamber, he kept track of Giliead out of the corner of his eye, watching him cautiously approach the crystals. When he saw Giliead retreat, he fell back and they both reached the archway together. Tremaine lowered her weapon as they retreated back around the corner. "Well?" she demanded in a harsh whisper.

Giliead shook his head sharply. "All the crystals are dead, empty."

Still looking toward the silent chamber, Ilias frowned. "That doesn't make sense. Why are the crystals here? In our world? And how come the whale is made of wood?"

"Good questions," Tremaine muttered. "That looked like one of the old flying wha—airships—the Gardier had, like the ones we saw on that clock in Devara, in the books we found in the library." Her eyes narrowed in thought. "Was anyone in there? People, I mean, somewhere out of sight."

Ilias considered it, trading a look with Giliead, then said, "Yes. There's somebody watching in there, hiding. Probably more than one."

"The Gardier are hiding from us," Tremaine repeated. She propped the shooting weapon on her shoulder, gesturing in frustration. "Does that sound odd to anybody?"

"Well, yes," Ilias admitted. "They aren't cowards."

"And we know there's more than one of them," Giliead agreed. "Those tracks were recent." He looked thoughtful. "Going in after them is no good—they can pick us off easily. We need to lure them out."

Tremaine nodded, biting her lip. "Right. Let's leave them a message." She glanced around at the floor, finding a clear spot. Shifting the shooting weapon to her other hand, she crouched down and drew some symbols in the dirt with her finger.

"Is that a trail sign?" Ilias asked, frowning, then realized what it had to be. "Something in their language?"

She nodded, leaning forward to finish the string of symbols. "The spell only taught me how to speak Aelin, not read it. But if I'm remembering right, that says 'Paths of the Sky.' According to Nicholas, that was the title of one of the books we found. I'm probably not getting all the letters right, but if these people are Gardier, it should be close enough to make them curious."

"But that would make sense." Giliead looked back toward the enigmatic chamber. "And so far nothing else about this does."

That afternoon, Florian first made sure Nicholas wasn't doing anything more than consulting with the Capidaran officers about the Gardier. Then she went to the First Class smoking room, meaning to take some precautions of her own. The door was shut and locked and she knocked impatiently. She was certain Niles was in there; he had barely left the room since the ship had departed Capistown.

After a moment, Giaren eased the door open cautiously, lifted his brows as he saw her, and glanced back to say, "It's Florian."

She heard Niles grunt an answer and Giaren stepped back, opening the door and shutting it carefully again as soon as she stepped in.

Niles was seated at the table, looking into a china bowl half filled with water. *A scrying bowl,* Florian thought, intrigued. She moved to his side as Giaren locked the door again. Gerard had had dozens of these bowls on the voyage to Capidara, allowing him to keep track of individuals or to watch certain areas of the ship, wherever there was a reflective surface for the spell to exploit. And on the *Ravenna,* with all the glass, crystal and polished metal, there were more than enough reflective surfaces.

"What are you watching?" she asked quietly.

Niles reached out and took her hand. "Ixion's little experiment," he said, sounding preoccupied. Giaren, who didn't have enough magical talent to see into the bowl, even with assistance, settled his hip on the table at Niles's other side.

Florian leaned over, peering into the bowl. With Niles's help, she could now see a blurred convex image of one of the *Ravenna's* service corridors, a doorway, then a brief glimpse of a room.

Niles whispered something and the image of the room became larger, clearer. Florian could see metal walls painted yellow, so it could be any one of a hundred storerooms aboard the ship. There was a large drum or container that looked as if it had started life as something from the ship's innards somewhere. Steam rose out of it and Florian caught a bare glimpse of a hand tossing something in. The view retreated so abruptly it gave Florian a twinge of vertigo. She blinked, lifting her head. Looking carefully at the bowl, she saw a blue thread settled in the bottom. "Who are you following? Not Ixion, surely."

"No, I think he'd realize. This is Colonel Averi." Niles grimaced in impatience and rubbed his forehead as if the poor quality of the view was giving him a headache. "I think we're getting this through one of his coat buttons."

"Does Averi know? Isn't that—" Florian had started to say "immoral," but both Niles and Giaren were looking at her with nearly identical expressions of faint incredulity. She bit her lip, considering. *All right, all right, fine. I'm a stickler for rules and look where it's gotten me.*

Niles continued, "Ixion seems to have chosen a room with nothing reflective for the scrying spell to focus on." His expression grew sardonic. "Intentionally, I'm sure. He's learned far too much about our methods in the short time he's been with the Capidarans."

With a wince, Florian nodded. That she could agree with wholeheartedly. "Chandre's keeping you out because you refused to work with Ixion?"

"Yes." Niles leaned back in the chair, rubbing his temples. "Kressein hasn't been allowed in either. Apparently his critical regard affects Ixion's concentration, so Chandre has asked that he stay out as well. And Chandre's influence, financial and otherwise, in the Capidaran Ministry is so great, Kressein has agreed." He let out his breath. "God, I wish Gerard was here."

Florian nodded grimly. She wished they were all here. At least their friends were better off than they had been when the captured airship had taken them to the Gardier world. This time they had a sphere, and Gerard, and were probably just exploring the cave ruin. And being worried out of their minds as to why no one had come to fetch them yet.

She hesitated, wondering if she should tell Niles about Ixion's threat, despite Nicholas's instructions not to. She bit her lip, then decided against it. Niles would be made even more angry and distracted than he already was, and if he took it up with Averi and Chandre, it was still her word against Ixion's.

As Niles leaned forward again to study the bowl, Florian asked, "Is it all right if I go through the books?" Whatever horror or miracle Ixion was creating with that vat, she still had to prepare some kind of defense against him.

Niles waved assent and Florian found a spot on the floor near the crates and piles of books. Taking out her notebook, she pulled the nearest volume into her lap. Flipping through the delicate pages, she knew she shouldn't bother looking at complicated spells. She couldn't do anything too complex without the help of a sphere, preferably Arisilde; complex Great Spells like the massive unbinding Niles had devised were for experienced Lodun-trained sorcerers who were experts in etheric theory. But she knew Gerard always said that for attack and defense, simple spells were often best. He had rendered Ixion unconscious back on the island with a simple charm put together from hair, thread and spittle. But Florian didn't suppose that Ixion, now that he had more experience with Rienish magic, would be fool enough to let anyone hand him something again. Still, a charm was her best chance, and she concentrated on looking for simple ones that could be prepared in advance.

After several different books and copious notes, she looked up, startled to realize someone was standing over her. Fortunately, it was Giaren, not Ixion. Florian tried to look innocent; if Giaren asked what she was doing and she told him she was researching spells to defend herself against Ixion, Niles was going to want to know why, and she doubted he would accept random paranoia as a reason. But he only leaned down, tapping her notebook, and said thoughtfully, "Actually saltpeter works better in this one than sulfur. And try Montvarin's *History of Border Conflicts*, it has an entire section on defensive and offensive charms from the First Bisran War."

Florian blinked as he moved away. Though Giaren couldn't use magic, he was a researcher for the Viller Institute and probably knew almost as much about magic as any Lodun-trained sorcerer. "Right, thanks." *Of course, we're in a war. No one's going to wonder why I'm researching attack spells.* She rolled her eyes at herself and sat up on her knees to search the stacks for the book. *I think I'm overthinking this.* Tremaine would undoubtedly agree.

The afternoon light was just starting to fail when Tremaine and Ilias and Giliead returned to the circle chamber. The giant room was empty, disturbed dust glittering in the shafts of afternoon sunlight. Tremaine frowned, but then spotted Cimarus and Aras on guard in the archway that led to their camp in the grotto room. She could see why they had withdrawn back to that point. The large space of the circle chamber was too big to defend properly and once darkness fell it would be even worse.

"What did you find?" Aras demanded, as soon as they were within earshot. Tremaine smiled blandly at him. Gerard was already coming down the rubble-piled hall and she wanted to wait until he arrived, so she didn't have to repeat herself. With typical Syprian reticence, Giliead and Ilias both ignored the question.

"Did you find something?" Gerard asked as he reached them.

With a wince Tremaine shifted the rifle off her shoulder. The damn thing was heavier than it should be; gunsmithy was probably one of the skills the Gardier had chosen to inadequately borrow. "It's something, all right." Briefly she described the chamber they had discovered, the strange appearance of the early-model airship and the wall of empty crystals, while Gerard and Aras looked increasingly incredulous. Even Cimarus looked startled, and she wasn't sure how many of the words he understood.

Gerard nodded when she was done, his brows drawn in thought. "I agree, if they can read the message you left, they'll have to investigate. And if they've been trapped here for some time, as the wrecked airship and the living quarters suggest, they won't be able to resist. Whether they're Gardier or not."

"Why are you so sure they'll come?" Aras objected, talking to Gerard. "They ran away earlier. Why should they walk into a trap?"

"They don't know how many of us there are," Giliead said, patiently shifting into Rienish for Aras's benefit. He jerked his chin toward Ilias and Tremaine. "They must have seen the three of us when we went into their chamber, but they don't know about the rest of you."

Aras stared, startled. Tremaine folded her lips over a smile, realizing Giliead had never bothered to speak Rienish in front of the Capidaran man, or at least not to speak it quite so well, with a trace of Gerard's upper-class Vienne accent. Aras recovered rapidly, replying, "They could have been spying on us earlier."

Ilias shook his head. "No tracks. There was only the one, and he came no further than the outer hall."

Tremaine felt there had been enough pretend debate. They knew what they had to do, they needed to get on with it. "We already picked out the spot to wait for them." She handed the rifle to Aras to give him something to do and started briskly past him. "We need to get ready before dark."

Talking over the idea for the trap, they had tentatively chosen a room off the corridor on the opposite side of the circle chamber from their camp. Looking around it again, Ilias decided it was still a good choice. There was only the one corridor that led from the Gardier wing into this section, and anyone stepping out of it into the cross corridor would see the light from their fire immediately and hopefully be drawn toward this room. Aras was to be posted at the archway into the circle chamber, in case the intruders tried to use it to reach the other end of the corridor to work their way up behind them.

This room was larger than the fountain room they had chosen to camp in, but it was overlooked by an intact stone-pillared gallery that was reached by a narrow stairway up from the next room. The Gardier—or whoever or whatever these people were—would have to come in through the door from the circle chamber's main corridor, where they could be easily surrounded. At least that was how it was supposed to work. Ilias shook his head, reflecting grimly on how things didn't work as they were supposed to when curses were involved, even Rienish curses.

The late-afternoon light from the single louver in the ceiling was beginning to fail, and Ilias began to collect stones to build a fire pit. He could hear the others moving around, Gerard's and Aras's voices from the room next door. Giliead came in with his pack slung over his shoulder and an armload of firewood, Cletia following him with Ilias's pack and a stack of blankets.

Giliead deposited the firewood as Gerard stepped out onto the gallery above them, saying, "We'll need some kind of barrier up here or anyone coming in will be able to see me. If they are Gardier and using their crystal etheric detection devices, they'll be alert for any kind of sight-avoidance charm."

Giliead straightened up, regarding the gallery with a thoughtful frown. Some blue-flowered rock-creeper vines had worked their way in through the louver and spread across the ceiling. "If we brace a couple of branches against the wall and pull those vines down to cover them, that should do it."

As Giliead handed the branches up and directed Gerard's efforts from below, Ilias finished off the fire pit. His stomach was starting to grumble and he was glad Cimarus and Vervane, who were stuck watching Balin and caring for Meretrisa, were putting together a quick meal using the last of the sava and the fruit they had found up on the plateau.

Instead of depositing her burden and leaving, Cletia had stayed to arrange the packs and blankets in a way to suggest a camp, and was now trying to make the rolled-up extra blankets look enough like sleeping bodies to fool someone in bad light. Building the small fire in the newly constructed rock hearth, Ilias watched her efforts with growing irritation. It wasn't needed, as whoever walked through the door would have no time for close observation, and something about her manner was pricking his nerves even more than it usually did. "Don't worry about that, I'll do it later," he said, exasperated.

She glanced at him, then let the blanket she was fiddling with fall. She sat on her heels on the other side of the hearth. "I wanted to talk to you."

He snorted derisively, half thinking she wanted to reiterate Pasima's "convince Giliead not to go home" speech. "Go ahead. There's nobody important here to see you."

She winced and her cheeks reddened. "I wanted to say I was sorry."

That's a new one. Ilias frowned, not understanding. "For what?"

She pressed her lips together in annoyance, apparently thinking he was mocking her. "For treating you as if— I never knew anyone who had a curse mark before."

Ilias shoved at the wood, rearranging the branches unnecessarily. This made him far more uncomfortable than her contempt ever had. He had never much liked Cletia, even before the curse mark; she had always been one of Visolela's relatives, someone from one of the town families too worried about their own consequence for their own good. Then Halian had married Giliead's mother, Karima, and Visolela had married Halian's son Nicanor, connecting them all by marriage and inheritance. And Visolela had begun pressuring Karima to sell Ilias into marriage to a wealthy inland trader, which hadn't exactly given him any soft feelings toward her host of lovely and stiff-necked sisters and cousins.

Part of him didn't want to give Cletia the forgiveness she was asking for; he had been shunned by people whose opinion he cared about a great deal more than hers. Every time anyone had avoided him it had hurt, at least until he had gotten inured to it. But he didn't want to be childish either, not when they had to depend on each other to survive. Fighting his reluctance and bitterness, he shook his head and shrugged, feeling awkward. "It's not something most people know how to react to."

Cletia took a sharp breath. "And . . . I was angry, too. I heard the story that you didn't have to get the mark, that no one knew about the cursing but you and Giliead, that he told you not to tell anyone about it. And you did it anyway." She looked away, and he saw her swallow, as if the words were difficult. "I was angry that now my family wouldn't . . . That there would be no more possibilities between us."

Ilias stared at her, startled. Before the curse mark, he had never noticed Cletia, mainly because he thought she had never taken notice of him. And he had been too occupied with the women who were his friends to bother. Now with all the clear vision of hindsight, he had the sudden revelation that Cletia's standoffish behavior then could have been shyness and lack of confidence rather than disdain. "I didn't know. I—"

She reached out, catching his hand. Her skin was coarser than Tremaine's, her hand callused like his across the palm and the fingers from using a sword and bow. "Don't. You don't have to say anything. I just wanted you to know." She blinked, looking up, startled. Giliead was standing over them; they had both been so distracted they hadn't noticed his quiet approach. His expression was stony, his eyes on Cletia.

Her lips curved in a slight smile and she released Ilias's hand. She gave Giliead an ironic nod, stood and walked out, her boots crunching faintly on the scatter of dead leaves.

Ilias prodded the wood again, realized how many times he had rearranged it. He swore at himself, looking around for the tinder pouch.

Giliead sat down on the dusty stone, propping one arm on his knee and regarding Ilias expectantly. When Ilias refused to give in and say anything, Giliead demanded, "What are you doing?"

Getting flints and tinder out to light the fire, Ilias paused, lifting a brow. "What does it look like?"

"With Cletia," Giliead amended pointedly.

Ilias didn't know what Giliead was so indignant about; he had been the one who had agreed to let Cletia and Cimarus join them in the first place. Then Ilias stared at him, suddenly realizing this wasn't about possible truce making with the hostile side of the family. "What? That wasn't— She just—" Giliead shook his head, rolling his eyes to the shadowy ceiling. Ilias threw a look up at the gallery. A couple of long branches were wedged against the pitted stone balustrade, artfully draped with vines, but Gerard hadn't taken his place there yet. He lowered his voice and sputtered, "She talked to me. I can't do anything about it."

Giliead gave him a withering look. "When Tremaine beats you for being stupid, I'm going to help."

Glaring at him, Ilias flicked a pebble, managing to bounce it off his head. Tremaine came in just as Ilias was rolling backward to dodge Giliead's return buffet. She shook her head in mock disgust. "If you two are going to hit each other all night, I'm going to move to a quieter trap down the hall."

Tremaine propped her chin on her hand, poking at the fire with a stick. The dark settling in just beyond the limits of their small fire was a little daunting; she felt a persistent prickle in the back of her neck, as if something was creeping up on her. It was a relief to hear Gerard move occasionally in the gallery not far above their heads.

Giliead and Ilias sat to either side of her, both positioned so they could half face the door, which was just a square of darkness against the lighter wall. They weren't talking much so they could listen for the approach of their anticipated visitors. Ilias had been passing the time by methodically sharpening his various knives with a whetstone, and Giliead had that distant look that she had learned meant he was listening on a different level, alert for etheric traces that would mean spellcasting. They had arranged the blankets behind them in the darker half of the room to look like three sleeping bodies. *Or look sort of like,* Tremaine amended, *if you don't have long to look at them. And have bad eyes.*

Gerard had loaned her his pistol, which was a comforting weight in the ammunition pouch attached to her belt. She had the flap open so she could reach the weapon easily, but if these were Gardier, she wanted the layer of thick cloth between her skin and the gun. Aras had the rifle and was at the opposite end of the hallway, guarding the archway leading into the circle chamber; Cletia was at the other end with a bow. The other bow lay behind Giliead, already strung.

Besides their own small noises, the place was utterly silent except for the occasional chirp of an insect. Tremaine's ears felt sore from listening so intently. She shifted again, the tension making her shoulders ache. Ilias, most of his attention still on the leaf-shaped blade he was sharpening, threw her a sympathetic half smile. She studied him a moment, watching the firelight turn his unruly curls into a halo. Keeping her voice low, she said, "You never look bored. Except when we were in Capidara."

He thought about it, pausing to set the knife aside. "Cities are boring. There's nothing to do. This is like hunting."

He had a point, though Tremaine had always thought of hunting as a more active pursuit. But then she thought Ilias liked being the bait, fooling the prey into thinking it was the hunter. That she could understand. But she didn't want to turn the conversation to anything serious. Instead, she said, "There's lots of things to do in cities. You can talk to people you don't like, be run over by omnibuses, smell the sewers . . ."

Giliead made an amused snort. It didn't surprise Tremaine that he was both listening to them and concentrating on possible etheric vibrations; she knew he could talk to ghosts while simultaneously having a conversation with live people. Ilias cocked a brow at her and started to reply, then went still.

Tremaine held her breath; she had heard it too, a faint distant crackle of dead leaves under someone's boot. It could be Aras or Cletia, though there was no way to make sure of that without potentially ruining the trap. Sensitized to all the night noises after sitting in the quiet for so long, she knew it had come from the wrong direction to be Gerard.

Her nerves tensing and making her feel as if her feet were several sizes too large, Tremaine carefully began to stand. Acting as if they had all the time in the world, Ilias caught Giliead's eye, silently mouthing the word "Curses?"

Giliead shook his head, unfolding his long legs and reaching for the bow. Ilias stored his knives in various places and pushed to his feet, drawing his sword. Though they didn't hurry, they were already in position on either side of the door by the time Tremaine had finished her careful and silent creep to the shadows beneath the gallery. She swore mentally at them, sure they were doing it on purpose to annoy her.

She could clearly hear soft careful footsteps now and could tell there was more than one person, but fewer than the large group they had feared. Ilias held up three fingers. Tremaine eased down into a half crouch, drawing the pistol.

Then a form stepped out of the darkness into the open square of the doorway, the flickering light revealing him clearly. It was a man, older than Tremaine had expected, with gray hair and a seamed and lined face. He was dressed in dull-colored pants with ragged hems and an equally ragged shirt, with an incongruous patterned vest that glinted with silver and metallic blue in the firelight. His boots weren't boots at all, just leather wrapped around his feet and calves and bound with cord. He wasn't armed, though he wore a belt with little pouches hanging off it. What puzzled Tremaine was that his whole stance was tentative, not aggressive, as he squinted at the apparently blanket-wrapped forms on the far side of the fire. He didn't look like somebody coming to attack them, and he didn't look like a Gardier.

Giliead drew the bow smoothly, arrow already nocked. Tremaine said in Aelin, "Don't move."

She was so convinced by this point that he wasn't Gardier that she hadn't expected him to understand. But the man froze, his eyes alarmed, and there was a startled murmur from the corridor. Knowing he might just have been responding to a voice that came out of nowhere, she added, "Tell your friends to drop their weapons and no one will be hurt."

He hesitated, but she could see comprehension in his eyes. He lifted a hand, turning his head slightly to address his companions out in the hall, and said in low-voiced, oddly accented Aelin, "You heard her. Drop your weapons." Lifting his head, he addressed the room at large, "We mean no harm. We wish to talk."

Tremaine found herself sort of almost willing to believe that. If you were planning a triple murder of sleeping people, she was fairly sure you didn't send Grandpa in first, especially unarmed. She heard a clatter out in the hall, what sounded like something wooden being dropped, then the fainter noise of something metal—she was certain it was a gun—being carefully laid aside. She took a deep breath, ready to find out just who the hell these Aelin-speaking non-Gardier were. "Gerard."

Light sprang from a dozen different sources in the gallery above, wisps of etheric illumination whispering out to hover around the room, some darting out into the hall. The old man flinched, looking back and forth from Giliead to Ilias, revealed in the white glow of the sorcerous light. Tremaine stepped out, wanting his attention on her and not them. "Tell your friends to step inside here, please."

His hesitation was longer this time. Neither Ilias nor Giliead had moved. Ilias still stood with his back to the wall, sword held easily, watching the old man with his head cocked. His expression was very much that of a cat waiting patiently for a mouse to make a mistake. Giliead was still poised to let the arrow fly, calm as a rock. Impatiently, Tremaine said, "If they wanted to kill you, they'd kill you. Are we going to talk or fight?"

She could practically feel Gerard, still up on the gallery, glaring at her head, but it worked. The old man seemed to shake himself and stepped further into the room, gesturing for the two people she could now see out in the hall to follow him. They did, slowly and reluctantly, with wary glances at the two Syprians.

Once they were in the room, Tremaine heard rustling overhead as Gerard left the concealment of the gallery and started down. Both the newcomers were young, neither any older than Tremaine, dressed like the old man in an odd combination of dull-colored clothes that were almost rags supplemented with bright colorful fragments. The boy wore ragged brown trousers, though his shirt was in a little better condition. The sash around his waist was red with a gold sheen to it, fringed with beads. The girl wore a long skirt in a silky blue, her gray shirt obviously meant for a larger man, and a dull orange scarf over her hair. Both were dark-haired, too thin, though not to the point of starvation; both wary but with something almost eager about the way they looked around, as if they were also burningly curious. Craning her neck, Tremaine saw the weapons they had left on the dusty stone floor of the hall were a rifle with an oddly clunky trigger arrangement, a wooden spear with a metal head and a fish knife.

"Who are you?" the girl asked suddenly, looking from Tremaine to the Syprians. "How did you get here?"

They were honest questions and Tremaine found herself stumped for how to answer the first one without a lengthy explanation. She settled on "We're explorers. And we came here through one of the circles."

Tremaine had seen Gerard out in the hall, apparently signaling an instruction to Aras to keep his position on guard at the entrance to the circle chamber. Now the sorcerer stepped in, adding in Aelin, "As you did, I assume?" He had prudently tucked the sphere away in its bag; Tremaine agreed, there was no reason to advertise the fact that they had it, even though she was beginning to think it was unlikely that these people would have seen one before.

The old man exchanged a guarded look with the boy. "We did," he said reluctantly. "But it was not of our doing."

"Ask them why they came here," Giliead said suddenly, speaking Syrnaic. He hadn't lowered the bow, though he had eased the tension on the string. All three of their visitors looked at him, startled, as if they hadn't expected him to be able to talk. "Not to this place, but to us, tonight."

"Right," Tremaine answered in the same language, thinking she knew what he meant. He wanted her to find out their intent, what they had wanted to gain in coming here. "Are any of them wizards?"

"I don't think so. Not like our wizards. There're no curses around them at all that I can see." Tremaine caught the slight emphasis on the "that I can see."

Gerard had listened carefully. He looked at the old man again and said in Aelin, "Our friend would like to know why you came here tonight."

The old man spread his hands, his expression suggesting that he wasn't terribly clear on that himself. "We have spoken to no living souls—no one but ourselves—for many years. When we saw the writing in our language that you left, we knew we must find out who you were, even if you meant to kill us."

That's . . . not what I expected, Tremaine thought, her brows drawing together in consternation. There was one more thing she needed to know immediately. "Have you heard of the Gardier, then?" She tried not to make the question particularly pointed, but she watched all three of them carefully.

The girl was staring in uneasy fascination at Ilias and didn't even glance up. The boy was looking from Tremaine to Gerard, and didn't show any sign of recognition either. The old man, regarding Tremaine as carefully as she was watching him, shook his head. "No, I don't know that word."

She was a little shocked at herself to realize she believed him. It was one of the few foreign words, the word their enemies called them, that all the Gardier should recognize. Trying the other one, she added, "Or the Rien?"

Same response, or lack of response. The old man shook his head.

Tremaine let out her breath, looked at Gerard and shrugged. *You've got me. I don't have a clue.*

He nodded thoughtfully, then addressed the Aelin, "Let's sit down, shall we?"

Giliead slowly lowered the bow.

Tremaine sat on her heels, poking the fire up with a handy branch as the Aelin took somewhat uneasy seats around it. The drifting balls of spell light arrayed themselves in a circle around the room as Gerard maneuvered himself down to sit next to her, grunting as if his back hurt. Giliead and Ilias stayed beside the door, though Ilias had sheathed his sword.

The old man stirred, saying, "My name is Obelin." He indicated the girl and the boy, "This is Davret and Elon. We're of the Lehirin line, of the clans of Etara."

Gerard shifted the sphere's bag so it was behind him. "This is Tremaine, Ilias and Giliead, and I'm Gerard. First, I'd like to ask why one of your people ran from us earlier today, and why did you hide when we tried to find you?"

Obelin snorted, as if it was self-evident. Tremaine had to admit neither Ilias nor Giliead looked terribly friendly at the moment. They stood just at the edge of the firelight, which struck reflections off their armbands, the earrings buried in their hair and the cold glint of the curse mark on Ilias's cheek. Ilias had his arms folded over his scabbarded sword, the curved-horn hilt resting against his forearm. It didn't look like a position he could quickly draw it from. Then she realized he was holding it in such a way that Giliead, standing next to him, the bow propped on his shoulder, could draw it in a heartbeat. Obelin added, "It was one of the boys who came here today, to collect fruit from the patch just outside the staircase. He was afraid. It had been so long. And they didn't look . . . We had seen other people, something like them, from a distance. There is a place you can look down into the river valley, though the cliff is too steep to climb. We had seen them fighting with primitive weapons, like savages—" He hesitated, then gestured apologetically. "We were afraid."

Tremaine translated this for the Syprians, and Ilias didn't seem particularly perturbed by it. "If we're as far south as I think we are, they might have seen Hisians," he told her.

"They were right to be afraid," Giliead put in with a sardonic glint in his eye.

Gerard nodded, accepting Obelin's answer. "But why have you been here so long? How did you get here?"

Obelin shook his head, pushing a hank of graying hair out of his face. His hands were badly callused, reminding Tremaine of the hands of someone who had done hard labor in prison. "I don't know how much you have seen of this place, but there is no way to leave it on foot. There are various outside doorways, but all lead to small areas, once gardens perhaps, that are surrounded by sheer cliffs. We have ropes, and many of the younger ones have managed to climb down to the valley and back up, but the older people couldn't make it, and we were reluctant to separate. Then we saw the savages. . . ." He shook his head again. "As to how we got here, my people are explorers also, traders." He hesitated, glancing again from Tremaine to Gerard. "You may realize, this is not our world. The stars in this sky are different from ours—"

Tremaine cut off the attempt to explain. "Yes, we knew that."

He nodded, a little relieved. "So you know this. Before we came here, we didn't know such a thing was possible. In our own world, we were a trading clan, traveling out from our home in Etara across the seas, to trade with other peoples. We had traveled to the very distant reaches of our trade routes. In a small village, we encountered a man who called himself Castines."

Obelin's eyes turned bitter with memory, and he took Davret's hand. Tremaine sensed suddenly that telling this story to strangers was giving him a kind of emotional release that he had been denied a long time. "He had come out of the hills perhaps a month before we arrived, badly injured, and been tended by the people there, who were farmers. He had learned to speak our trade language somewhat, and told us that if we took him back to his land, he would show us a place of great interest, a hidden city, long abandoned by its builders." His mouth twisted ruefully. "It's the way of our people to compete for better routes, better trading goods, new and exciting things—luxuries, inventions—to bring home to the other clans. We were greedy for success at this, too greedy. So we went with him."

He shook his head at himself again. Davret squeezed his hand, and Elon looked grim. Obelin continued, "He boarded our craft and we followed his directions, traveling off our route and into the wilderness. At the point he had promised that we would see the city, there was nothing but empty forest. We challenged him. Then he showed us a crystal." He looked up, gesturing with his free hand. "It was about the size of a child's ball, like the ones in the wall of the room where we live." He nodded to Tremaine. "You saw them?"

"Yes, we saw those." Tremaine felt her skin start to creep; she had an idea where this story was going.

Obelin nodded. "He drew symbols on our craft, then used *arcana*." He glanced up at the wisps of spell light. "I see you know of this as well."

Gerard, listening intently, wet his lips. "We call it magic."

"It's not something our clan had much experience with," Obelin explained. "Those who are best at it tend to stay at home, in the clan strongholds, and don't travel the routes with the traders. Castines made the crystal do something with *arcana*."

"And you were here." Tremaine had to fight to keep her mouth shut, to not shout questions, to let the old man tell the story.

"Yes." Obelin laughed a little bitterly, and Elon winced. Davret patted the older man's hand. "Our craft was ruined as you saw, but we thought that this find was truly worth it. Castines showed us the crystal wall, and said they could be used for *arcana* that we had never heard the like of before. For us, *arcana* was just for simple tricks, or for controlling the winds. He said there were uses that we couldn't imagine."

"He was right about that," Gerard said dryly.

The man's brow furrowed, but he continued, "We stayed here for several days, exploring, then we decided to go back and report our find to our clan. Castines said he would take us back closer to Sivari, our trading center. That he could use one of the *arcana* spirals in the other big room to take us there. He took one of the crystals, a large one from the niche in the center of the wall, as proof of our find. But we decided some of us should remain, in case someone else came while we were gone to challenge our claim. We sent five others with him, to represent our clan's interest. Castines promised he would be back soon, within a few days, and bring the High Trader Clan's peers with him." He gestured helplessly. "We never saw him, or our companions, again."

Tremaine nodded slowly. "How long ago was this?"

He looked at Davret for help. She said, "My mother said the years don't seem the same here. But she's counted twenty-one rainy seasons."

Twenty-one years, more or less. Tremaine sat back, staring at nothing. In the Gardier world, Calit's mother had told him that before he was born, things were different. That the attack that the Gardier used for their rationale for invasion had not happened the way they said it had. *So whatever happened, happened when Calit's mother was a young woman who could remember the world the way it was.*

"But who are you?" Davret asked suddenly. "You use *arcana* to travel through the circles like Castines; was he one of your people?" She looked at Ilias and Giliead again, gesturing toward them with a baffled expression. "Are they your people too? They look so different."

"We're from—" Tremaine threw a look at Gerard, making sure it was a mutual decision to release this information. He gave her a barely perceptible nod. "—a place called Ile-Rien. We do use magic to travel through the circles. We're exploring them, sort of. We're trying to follow the path of a friend of ours, who we think came through here a few years ago."

"This is the first we've heard of Castines," Gerard put in, leaning forward. "As far as we know, he isn't one of our people. In fact, we'd very much like to know exactly who and what he is. I think that would help answer some questions we've had about the circles, and who uses them, where they originally came from."

Tremaine nodded toward Ilias and Giliead. "And you're right, they are different—they're Syprians. They come from this world, somewhere to the north of here, we think."

Obelin nodded, listening to all this intently. The old man seemed to have lost a great deal of his reserve. "We've seen no one, so I don't think your friend could have come here. If he had, we would have been glad to see him, I tell you."

"Tremaine." Ilias sounded impatient. Giliead was glaring at her. "What is he saying? What are you saying?"

"Sorry." She repeated the story briefly in Syrnaic, finishing with, "So twenty-one years ago a sorcerer returned to their world from here, with five of their people, taking one of those crystals with him."

Giliead winced and Ilias looked appalled at the probable fate of Obelin's friends. He said, "Tremaine, Castines could be a Syprian name. Are they sure he was one of their people?"

"No, they aren't sure. They said he had to learn their language." Tremaine chewed her lip, considering it. "If Castines was Syprian . . . Then how did he know about the circles?"

Frowning, Giliead prompted, "Ask him about crystals. The small ones, that they put into people."

"Yes," Gerard said grimly, speaking Syrnaic. "I was wondering about that myself."

Tremaine lifted her brows. "You think this Castines character was infected, like the Gardier Liaisons, and what they tried with Niles? But if he was Syprian, who or what infected him? Before they came, there was no one here but the crystals." She stared, thinking that through. "Are we saying it's not the Gardier who control the crystals, but the crystals who control the Gardier?"

"I'd rather not speculate on that without further information," Gerard told her firmly. "Frankly, this situation is terrifying enough." In Aelin, he asked Obelin, "Did Castines have anything odd about his face? Did he appear to have a piece of crystal embedded in his skin? I know it sounds odd, but it's something we've encountered before."

Obelin shook his head. "No, no, we saw nothing like that." He added grimly, "And I recall his face very well."

Tremaine translated the answer for the others and Ilias shook his head, saying, "That doesn't mean anything. We didn't know about the one they put on Niles until Nicholas found it."

Watching the Aelin carefully, Gerard asked, "Do you remember which circle Castines used to leave?"

Obelin nodded. "I have not looked at it in a long time, but I know where it was in the great room."

"Will you show it to us?" Gerard asked.

Obelin regarded Gerard for a long moment, hesitating. Then he said, "If we show you, will you help us?"

Tremaine lifted a brow. "Help you how?"

"Take us with you, when you leave."

"We can't stay here," Davret added urgently. "It's like inside prison walls. We would leave, go out into the forest no matter how dangerous it is, but half our family can't make it down the cliffs."

Tremaine looked at Gerard. Even she had to admit, it didn't seem an unreasonable request. He eyed them thoughtfully, saying, "We can't promise to take you back to your own people." He hesitated and Tremaine thought, *But the thing is, I have the feeling you wouldn't want to go back there, if you knew what you were walking into.* The gypsylike free-trading life Obelin had described was nowhere to be found among the Gardier today. If these people did turn up in Maton-devara or any other Gardier center they would probably be killed to keep them from reminding any others of their former lives. Or shunted into a labor camp, which amounted to the same thing.

Obelin added firmly, "As long as there are other people—we can make our own way, we're used to that. But we can't be mired here any longer."

Tremaine glanced around, her look taking in Gerard, Ilias and Giliead. "If this is a trap," she said in Syrnaic, "it's far more elaborate and crazy than anything Nicholas ever came up with, and that's saying something."

Giliead exchanged a look with Ilias, confirming that they shared the same opinion. "It can't be a trap. I think they're telling us the truth."

Gerard faced Obelin, meeting the old man's eyes. "We'll take you with us when we leave. If you show us Castines's circle."

That evening, Nicholas knew Ixion would be looking for him as soon as the sorcerer was free of Chandre and Kressein. The ship would reach the Walls of the World tonight and hopefully make the passage through without incident. But Ixion would know the voyage was half over and that he was running out of time. Nicholas made himself easy to find, choosing one of the writing rooms near the First Class dining room. It was close to the foyer where crew, civilians, and Capidaran and Rienish soldiers passed back and forth into the dining room; Nicholas didn't want to make it look as if he had deliberately sought a private spot for a meeting.

It was an interior room, so the shaded crystal sconces were lit, throwing enough shadows on the cherrywood paneling and the dark marble hearth for any number of sorcerers to hide in. Nicholas took a seat at one of the writing tables, careful to choose one on the far side of the room, where he wouldn't be easily visible from the open doorway. He rifled the desk but all the ship's stationery had been removed long ago, except for a scrap of desiccated blotting paper lurking overlooked in the back of the drawer. He hadn't brought anything to read because he suspected he needed reading glasses, and that was a concession to increasing age that he wasn't willing to make at the moment. He took a pack of cards out of his pocket and started to shuffle.

He didn't have to wait long. After only a short time, he heard a faint step on the plush carpet and looked up to see Ixion standing over him. Nicholas nodded a greeting. "Wandering around alone? How inconsiderate. I'm sure your guards will be looking for you."

Ixion's smile was a thin line. He was still dressed in the suit the Capidarans had provided for him, but there was something slightly off about the way he wore it, though it was a perfect accompaniment to his too-smooth skin and the new growth of hair on his skull. He said, apparently idly, "They have no idea I've left my room. You know, the one you visited this morning."

Nicholas had debated showing surprise and decided against it. Instead he tilted his head, as if conceding the point, and began to deal himself four hands of Three Card Sweep.

Ixion waited a moment, but when it became obvious that that was the extent of Nicholas's reaction, he pulled out a chair and took a seat across from him. Leaning his elbows on the fine wood, he said, "Lord Chandre has told me about you."

Nicholas smiled faintly as he finished dealing the cards, saying, "Of course he has. His spies in Vienne were very good, before he departed for Capidara."

"That you have concealed your identity, that you have killed wizards."

Nicholas frowned down at the cards, then used the seven of batons to capture the five of swords and the two of cups. "Only a few."

Ixion didn't like being ignored. There was a slight edge to his voice as he said, "I fail to see how we are so different."

Nicholas lifted a brow, still engrossed in the cards. "I do. I've never blundered so spectacularly that I got my head cut off."

"It was a minor inconvenience." Ixion leaned forward. "I know you want to kill me—"

"I imagine most people do."

"And returning to another of my host bodies would inconvenience me. It would also prevent you from learning the secret of making those bodies, to restore the wizards the Gardier have stolen from you." Almost gently, Ixion laid his hand down on the cards, preventing Nicholas from dealing again. Nicholas had a moment to study that hand, noting the smooth texture of the skin, unmarred by any sign of age or work, the perfectly formed half-moons of the cuticles and the nails, just a little too long. It was distinctly macabre. Ixion said precisely, with just a bare hint of triumph, "To restore your friend inside the sphere."

"Oh, is that what you're offering for your life?" Nicholas looked up, meeting his eyes for the first time, concealing his disgust for this half-alive thing in a makeshift body. Amused, he said, "I'm afraid you've come to the wrong man. Arisilde raised my daughter, but unlike the others, I know he's dead, and what's left of him is more use inside the sphere than out."

Ixion held his gaze, and Nicholas saw the moment when the man's opaque eyes accepted this as truth. Ixion drew back, mouth hardening. "I see." He pushed to his feet, his eyes hooded. "So you're determined on this course. No matter how self-destructive."

"Yes, you're very threatening. Now go away, please. It's the hair oil. Sorry, I'm sensitive." Nicholas gave the man a patently insincere smile.

Ixion eyed him a moment more, then walked out.

Losing the smile, Nicholas dealt himself the queen of batons from the middle of the deck, commonly thought to be the death card. "That ought to do it," he muttered dryly.

Chapter 11

Of course, the old man couldn't find it in the dark. Waiting in the circle chamber, Ilias propped his sword on his shoulder, swearing under his breath. But as impatient as he was, he could see the problem. Even with Gerard's curse lights, the chamber was vast and dark, the shadows all falling from the wrong directions, the shapes distorted. But standing with Giliead and Tremaine near the archway, watching Gerard pace back and forth with Obelin, the two younger Aelin trailing after them, Ilias still had to exchange a disgusted look with Giliead.

Aras stood with them, with Cletia still guarding the corridor. The Capidaran man watched with concern. Ilias didn't think he understood the difference between the Aelin and the Gardier, that these people were no more inherently evil than the people who lived in the village that had birthed Ixion. "You actually think we can trust them?" Aras asked Tremaine for about the third time.

Giliead folded his arms and looked away, radiating annoyance at the uselessness of the question. "Yes, no, I don't know," Tremaine replied, clapping a hand to her forehead. "I wish we couldn't."

Aras looked unsatisfied with this answer but Ilias knew what she meant. If Obelin's story was true, and he believed it was, it opened up some frightening possibilities. If something or someone had caused such a change in the Aelin, it might be able to do the same to the

Rienish or the Capidarans. *Or us,* Ilias thought, the idea giving him a chill in the pit of his stomach.

Gerard stopped to confer with the Aelin, then came over, distractedly wiping sweat off his forehead with his shirtsleeve. "We'll have to wait until morning. He simply can't see well enough to pick it out in this light."

"If we do find it," Tremaine demanded, "exactly where is it going to take us, Crystal Hell?"

"I think it will take us directly to a Gardier stronghold. Not that I think we should go there ourselves, but it will be a location of strategic importance." Gerard took a sharp breath. "But in the meantime I've asked Obelin to take me back to their camp. There's something about their aircraft I want to look at."

"We'll go with you," Tremaine said firmly, before Ilias could.

Giliead nodded agreement, throwing a grim look at Ilias. "We believe they're telling the truth, but there's no point in taking chances."

After a pause to let Cletia and the others know what they were about to do—and what course of action to take if they didn't come back—they followed Obelin through the dark corridors, Gerard's curse lights trailing them.

The white wispy lights sent odd shadows that chased each other through the ruins as they passed, making Ilias think of shades and curselings. To distract himself, he asked Gerard, "You want to see if the symbols for the curse circle are still on their flying whale?" He was walking beside Tremaine, keeping one eye on Elon, the one who might be in the best position to make trouble. Obelin had told them there were twenty-three of their people waiting back at the flying whale, that half were about his own age, the rest having been children when they came here or had been born since.

Both of the younger Aelin stared at them with open curiosity, but if their story was true, then neither was old enough to remember seeing any strangers before. And as much as Ilias would like to find things to hold against them, the fact that the younger members of the group had refused to leave the elders for the freedom of the outside world spoke well for them.

"Yes, I need to get a look at those symbols." Gerard, walking slightly ahead with Obelin, glanced back at him. "They said this Castines directed them to fly out into the wilderness before making the world-gate; I'd like to know if he was trying to find the right position for a mobile circle, or if he used a modified version of one of these point-to-point circles. Or if he did something entirely new."

"I'm tired of entirely new things," Tremaine said, keeping her voice low, though the Aelin couldn't understand her. "I don't understand most of the old things yet."

"That makes two of us," Ilias told her with feeling.

"Three," Gerard admitted ruefully.

"You people don't exactly fill me with confidence," Giliead contributed, throwing an ironic look back at them.

They reached the corridor that led into the Aelin's chamber and paused while Obelin called softly ahead. A startled voice answered and Obelin spoke for a few moments. Ilias could tell from watching Tremaine and Gerard that the Aelin weren't talking about killing the strangers, but he still checked the set of his sword, just in case some young idiot decided to act on his own.

Obelin motioned for them to continue. The healthier yellow glow of firelight flickered ahead and Gerard let the white curse lights gradually dim and vanish.

They reached the archway to see a wary young woman waiting for them, the flying whale chamber behind her now lit by dozens of lamps. The burning oil smelled musky, not like the sweet scent of olive oil that Ilias was used to. The battered hulk of the flying whale looked less strange in this half-light, as if it was only the old wreck of a ship washed up on a beach. More people waited cautiously just inside the room and others crept out from all over, staring at them in wonder. Obelin raised his hands to get their attention and began to explain who these strange newcomers were.

Ilias kept his eyes moving, alert for treachery. But Obelin had been truthful: most of these people were his age or older, their hair gray, their clothes ragged and threadbare, the fabrics dull with time, with occasional bright fragments they had saved as scarves or sashes. The younger ones looked almost incredulous at seeing strangers and there were a couple of dark-haired, wide-eyed children peeping at them from behind the keel of the flying whale.

Obelin turned to Gerard, speaking and gesturing around. An old woman, her white hair held back from her face in a frizzy tail, came to stand next to him, asking a bewildered question.

Tremaine wandered over toward the flying whale, where the door was open in the side. Following her, Ilias could see the thing wasn't made of wood at all, but of panels woven of a material like dried grass, painted over with some kind of lacquer to make it hard and waterproof. *Like a giant basket,* he thought, craning his neck for a look inside.

Davret had followed them, and now she spoke to Tremaine, gesturing toward the open door.

Tremaine glanced at Ilias, lifting a brow inquiringly. "She says we can go inside."

Ilias looked back at the others, and saw that Obelin, far from attempting to conceal anything, appeared to be taking Gerard and Giliead around the large room, gesturing and talking volubly. They were accompanied by the old woman, and several of the younger men and women trailed after them. Ilias imagined the old man hadn't had anyone new to talk to for so long, he couldn't stop himself. His gut still told him this wasn't a trap. He gave Tremaine a nod.

Davret led them inside, to an open chamber that seemed to take up most of the bottom portion of the thing. It was dark and close, the strawlike material of the tilted floor crunching slightly underfoot. No one seemed to be sleeping or living inside here now, probably because it was too warm and airless.

It was lit by colored glass jars that hung from hooks in the supporting beams, the light they gave off tinged with blue, though it flickered like firelight. Ilias eyed it cautiously, thinking it was a new type of curse light. Something inside the jars seemed to be moving sinuously.

Tremaine examined one and Davret gestured toward it, explaining. Listening to the girl, Tremaine's face screwed up into a half-intrigued, half-disgusted expression as she looked more closely at the jar. "She says they're worms, that you feed leaves to them and they make the light. After they've been here so long, the older ones have stopped breeding, so they're dying off and they have to make an oil from a plant they found out on the bluff."

Ilias leaned close enough to see the slimy white forms writhing in the bottom of the glass. "All right," he commented, thinking it wasn't any worse than using a curse light.

Davret was continuing to talk, gesturing as she led them around, answering Tremaine's questions. They were trailed by other Aelin, but all were children, none taller than Ilias's shoulder. Tremaine translated as they went along, pointing toward the folded piles of dull gold fabric stacked near the wall. "That's all that's left of the balloons. They don't have an engine like the modern Gardier airships. Their trade routes were all based on wind direction. Though she knows what an engine is, she just thinks there aren't any light enough to put in an airship. It sounds like they used a different gas for the balloons too. They never worried about things being flammable. Or maybe they just used hot air, I can't tell. They apparently did use some magic, but it sounds like fairly simple charms for guiding the balloon and protection against weather. She says the people who were able to do them were the ones who went with Castines."

Ilias nodded absently, taking it in as he looked around. He didn't think it mattered much how they had made the flying whale fly. The more he saw of these people, the more he thought they weren't warriors at all. They seemed to have no weapons except the one shooting weapon Gerard had confiscated; the rough spears they used looked more like something for getting fruit or nuts out of tall trees.

Davret led them through the cluttered interior, then up a ladder out onto the deck. The light material gave a little underfoot and the deck lay at a crazy angle; metal staves grew up into a half-broken structure that had once supported the rest of the whale. Huge piles of rope and cable lay everywhere. Davret and Tremaine climbed awkwardly toward the curve of a cabin dominating this end of the deck. Kneeling at the base of the woven wall, Davret pointed to a faint black mark.

Tremaine leaned down to peer closely at the mark while Ilias braced himself against the wall to stay upright. After a moment she pushed to her feet and he caught her arm to help her.

"It looks like a gate symbol, but I don't know how much that's going to tell Gerard," she reported. Davret blinked up at them hopefully, wispy dark hair poking out from under her bright scarf. "She says that's the best one that's left." Tremaine shrugged, looking weary. "It's more proof that they're telling us the truth."

Ilias nodded absently. He thought the story was too elaborate to be a lie, that no one except Tremaine and Nicholas would be capable of bringing off such a complicated deception. "But we knew that already. The thing they can't tell us is who Castines was, if he was Syprian or something else."

"He was something else, all right," Tremaine agreed, looking across the lamplit chamber toward the wall of crystal niches.

That night, while Niles worked on the world-gate again, Florian augmented her concealment charm with a few herbs and borrowed an extra pair of his aether-glasses without telling him. Then she went down a couple of decks to try to get a look at Ixion's work area.

The rooms Ixion had been given for his experiments were in the depths of the ship, in a maze of unused storage rooms. It was all bare metal down here, or yellow-washed walls. She slipped past two bored Capidaran guards in the outer room easily enough, passed through an otherwise empty chamber that seemed to be storing unneeded shelving removed from the other rooms, and put on the aether-glasses to check the next door for a ward. It was free of any etheric trace, so she used her set of master keys on the lock. She smiled to herself a little grimly, thinking how she had almost turned these keys in to the purser's office when they had arrived at Capistown, but Tremaine had convinced her not to. "You never know when they could come in handy," she had said, taking them out of Florian's hand and stuffing them under the clothes in Florian's bag. *Right again,* she thought, turning the key in the lock.

The door opened without even a creak.

Florian paused on the threshold, examining the next room cautiously through the aether-glasses. Nothing here was warded, but the doorway to the next room was surrounded by white pulsing energy, invisible to the naked eye but clearly revealed by the enspelled lenses. Florian grimaced. That had to be the room with the vat that Niles had managed to briefly glimpse with his scrying. *I'm not getting in there, not without letting Ixion know all about it. And I'd probably get turned into something awful into the bargain. Damn.*

She stepped into the room, slowly and carefully, her rubber-soled shoes quiet on the metal floor. *This chamber isn't warded, but that one is. Because this one is for show?* It was all perfectly normal, for a sorcerer's workroom. A wooden tool bench held an array of glass jars containing the usual herbal and alchemical materials, probably brought on board by the Capidarans, as Niles would no doubt have refused to share his store. The lead case that held the captured Gardier sorcerer crystal sat on the bench. Florian stared hard at it but couldn't see a trace of etheric activity either. No books, but then according to Giliead, Syprian sorcerers didn't use them, committing everything to memory. *Which is a little scary in itself,* she thought, her mouth twisted.

The jars of herbs and minerals were all as they should be, but . . . She stepped to the worktable, looking closely, careful not to touch anything. Some of the jars had been messed about with, perhaps in an attempt to make them look used. But it didn't bear any resemblance to the controlled chaos of the alchemical laboratories she had seen. And though Niles was scrupulously neat, even his work area wasn't as clean as this. *For show,* she thought, nodding to herself. *He doesn't use these things, he doesn't need them for whatever it is he's doing in there.*

Florian took a deep breath, unsatisfied, but there seemed little she could do here, unless she wanted to risk death and expose her activities to Ixion, probably with no result except for Chandre ordering her arrest for treason or something.

She turned to go but hesitated, looking at the silent metal box that held the crystal. She wondered if the woman inside was lonely; Giliead had been the only one able to communicate with her. *Well, maybe Ixion really will make her a body,* she thought, then sourly, *Oh, please. Not even I'm naive enough to believe that. Not anymore, anyway.*

They spent the rest of the night with the Aelin. At one point Tremaine sat down to lean her tired back against the lacquered side of the airship, closed her eyes to rest them, and woke up sometime later slumped over on her side with her head pillowed on Ilias's lap.

Far from being reticent, Obelin and the others old enough to remember had talked eagerly about their lost home and their time here, and had led them on a grand tour of their living arrangements, including the little fountain where they did the laundry. They had also talked a great deal about Castines.

Though they had basically fallen for what Tremaine would have considered a confidence trick, none of the Aelin were stupid. They knew they had been tricked, and with not much else to do with their time they had come up with every theory imaginable to explain why. The fact that their new Rienish friends could shed even a little light on this point was almost more valuable to them than the prospect of rescue.

"I'm really not certain what Castines's motive was," Gerard explained, when they had taken a seat around the substantial cooking hearth the Aelin had built in the back of the room. "We know he must have already had possession of a crystal powerful enough to open a gate; otherwise, he couldn't have reached your world to find you. The circle symbols he used must have opened a direct gate to the same location in the destination world. Unlike the point-to-point circles, the ones carved into the floor in the other large chamber, the mobile circle needs an air- or seacraft to operate, since it's difficult to use safely on land."

Obelin nodded slowly. "Before we agreed to his plan, it occurred to us that he might be a bandit who would lead us to a place where his

men could take our airship. This had happened before, to clans traveling in the wilderness." He made a weary gesture. "That we were prepared for, or so we thought."

The oldest woman, whose name was Eliva, sighed, and Obelin
threw her a reproachful look. Tremaine interpreted that to mean that
there had been debate about this decision at the time, and the faction
who had originally lost was still cherishing its vindication.

Gerard hesitated a moment, then asked reluctantly, "Apparently
your companions that he took with him . . . were able to use *arcana*?"

"Yes, two of them had learned how to do the *arcana* that helped us
guide the winds and protect the ship from storms," Eliva told him.
Gerard was trying to keep his expression blank, but Eliva wasn't
fooled. She told him simply, "We already know he must have killed
them all. We've mourned them for dead." It was her turn to hesitate,
looking at the fire with her gray brows drawn together, the flickering
light painting the seamed canvas of her face. "If you know how they
may have died, you could tell us. It would be no worse than anything
we have imagined."

Tremaine translated this quietly for Ilias and Giliead, wincing at the
picture it conjured. The old woman's words brought the Aelin's loss
and pain home to her in a particularly unpleasant way. How many
people had she known well, whom she was unlikely ever to see alive
again, whose fates she couldn't even guess at? What if Gerard and one
of the others tested a gate and never came back, and they were left to
sit stranded somewhere and wonder? All in all, she thought she preferred to be the one who disappeared.

Gerard cleared his throat. "This is something that we believe has
happened to many of our people who are sorcerers—users of *arcana*.
The Gardier use them to make the crystals work spells. . . ."

And Gerard explained who the Gardier were and what they had
done.

Now that morning had dawned and they were on their way back to
the circle chamber, all the Aelin following, Tremaine still wasn't certain
it was a good idea. Obelin and Eliva and the others had been reluctant
to believe it, insisting that their people did not go to war, that surely not
every clan could have been persuaded to such a bizarre course of action, no matter what rewards they were given. That not every part of
their land could be so changed from what they remembered.

Tell me about it, Tremaine thought with a trace of bitterness, as they reached the circle chamber. Aras and Cletia were waiting for them in the archway, their expressions both worried and frustrated, though Giliead had walked back earlier to report that all was well. But much as Tremaine would like, she couldn't blame these Aelin for the actions of the Gardier. It might be a characteristic of this particular family, like the way the Andrien family, saddled with a Chosen Vessel, were more open-minded about magic than other Syprians. But these people were open, candid, curious and gregarious, everything the Gardier were not.

Tremaine glanced at Davret, who was walking along beside her and Ilias, and asked, "Do your people have a rule about not learning other languages?"

Davret snorted in surprise. "No. How could we be traders if we couldn't talk to other people?"

"That's a good question." And Tremaine was willing to bet whoever had come up with that new rule had wanted to stop that open communication with anyone foreign. The Rienish had had some hints of this change from Calit's memories of the stories his mother had told him. It was chilling, that it had taken only a generation to turn a society based on trade and exploration into a killing machine meant only for conquering. *Benin,* she thought, remembering the Gardier Scientist Nicholas had worked with while pretending to be a traitor. *He was at least in his late forties, if not older.* Old enough to remember the change. *Did he actually think all this was a good idea?* Many Aelin remained who were old enough to remember the change, yet they could—or would—do nothing to stop it.

Watching Elon practically skip along, the older children dogging his heels and near frantic with excitement, Tremaine thought, *They can't go back to what they were.* It made her cold and heartsick. *Even if we win the war, stop whatever group of Gardier that make the crystals, they'll never get back to what they were before. And neither will Ile-Rien.* Her expression must have reflected her thoughts, because Ilias bumped his arm against hers, looking at her in concern. She shook her head slightly, telling him not to ask.

Gerard paused to answer Aras's impatient questions and the Aelin wandered past into the circle chamber.

Obelin shaded his eyes against the shafts of bright morning light streaming through the louvers. "Yes, it was toward this end. It was morning when they left, you see," he explained to Tremaine. "And I think we came through that door at the far end."

"Yes," Eliva agreed, looking around with a thoughtful frown. "You're right, we hadn't explored as far as this room, and it was a great surprise to see it. I couldn't think how they had kept the ceiling up without columns."

Tremaine managed not to launch into an explanation about buttresses just to relieve her own nervous tension. She didn't want to distract them now. Obelin was moving toward the center of the room, where the high ceiling came down to a triangular point, highlighting the bands of symbols carved into the blue-white mottled wall. She noticed most of the Aelin crossed over the circles, stepping on the symbols, unlike the Rienish and the Syprians, who veered carefully around them.

Cimarus and Balin had come out of the back, probably because Cimarus was dying of curiosity. Tremaine kept one eye on Balin but Cimarus was staying near her and the Gardier woman looked more baffled than angry. *She hears them speaking Aelin, but they don't look like her people.* Balin wasn't old enough to remember when Gardier were just Aelin, who preferred bright colors and traded for interesting gadgets and explored their world with avid curiosity. "Who are you?" Balin demanded, speaking to Elon, who happened to be closest.

The young man smiled at her, puzzled. "We're of the Lehirin line, of the clans of Etara. Who are you?"

Lifting a brow, Tremaine didn't think Elon realized Balin was Aelin; Tremaine and Gerard spoke the language just as well, and there was nothing particularly distinctive about Balin's appearance. Balin didn't answer him, retreating in confusion.

"This is it." Obelin waved to Gerard, and the sorcerer hurried over, the others following. Tremaine watched, only realizing she was biting a rough fingernail when she bit too hard and tasted blood. Ilias and Giliead had come to flank her, watching in silence while Aras demanded a translation and no one answered him. Obelin stopped at a circle at the further end of the room, directly under the point of the high roof, the louvers throwing half of it into warm daylight. At his side, Eliva nodded, her lined face dark with memory. He said, "I remember we walked to this end of the room, and Cherit told me they would return soon." He shook his head, looking away.

"Um . . ." Tremaine frowned at Gerard. *If this is the one I think it is . . .*

Gerard knelt to examine the circle's symbols, his face a study in confusion.

"That's the one we used to get here from the mountain," Giliead said quietly.

"Yes. That appears to be the case," Tremaine told him in Syrnaic. She looked and found the break in the circle, the rough patch of stone where Gerard had used the sphere to melt a few symbols away, so the Gardier couldn't follow them here.

Gerard looked grim. "You're correct. Well, this is a pretty problem." He got to his feet, passing a hand over his face wearily.

"So Castines used this circle to go to the mountain. That still leaves him here, in the staging world. How did he get to the Gardier world?" Tremaine demanded.

Gerard shook his head. "He must have used the mobile circle. Or there was something in the mountain ruin that we missed."

Tremaine's frustration bubbled over and she clapped a hand to her head, saying, "God, we'd have better luck playing roulette." She turned helplessly to Obelin, asking in Aelin, "You're certain? It was this one?"

A boy who had worked his way close enough to stare with rapt interest at Giliead's sword suddenly piped up, "That is the right one. It's right next to the one with the button."

Tremaine stared at Gerard, then the boy. "Button?"

He nodded, startled at suddenly being on the receiving end of so much concentrated attention by these strangers. He was small and thin, sharp-featured under a mop of dark hair, grubby and dressed in hand-me-down rags like all the others. Apparently he wasn't old enough yet to be awarded a scrap of the brightly colored fabrics they were hoarding. "It was right here." He pointed at the next circle over. It was only a few paces from the mountain circle, the morning light throwing it into shadow.

"Wait, wait," Gerard said, more to Tremaine, who had her mouth open. To the boy, he continued, "How did you know this was the circle Castines used to take the others away?"

"My uncle showed it to me. We found the button together. He said the people who built this place must have left it." The boy threw a reproachful look around. "Everyone else said it was one of our buttons, one of us must have lost it, but we knew the truth."

"Which one's your uncle?" Tremaine demanded, glancing around at the older men and trying to stay calm. Her hands itched to grab the boy by the collar and shake him.

"My brother," Eliva explained, frowning dubiously at the boy. "He died two years ago. His daughter was one of those who went with Castines. He would have remembered this spot well. What is this button? Why is it important?"

"What button?" Obelin demanded in exasperation, apparently of the entire group in general. "I don't remember this at all."

Half a dozen others did, and all spoke up to remind him. "Quiet!" Tremaine shouted, waving her arms. It was just as well the Syprians and Aras couldn't understand the conversation; they were all watching with various degrees of confusion and impatience. She turned to the boy, crouching to put herself at his eye level. "Kid. Yes, you. Did the button look like it was a kind of soft silver, with a flower etched on it?"

He nodded in relief, perhaps at a question that he could readily answer, which seemed to signal that his button evidence was now being accepted as fact. "I remember the flower. I could draw it—"

Tremaine motioned impatiently. "Where is it? Do you have it with you?"

He shook his head emphatically. "When my uncle died I made it my grave-gift."

Tremaine took a deep breath, asking Gerard in Rienish, "I don't think we need to talk them into digging up Uncle, do we?"

"No, no, we don't." He eyed the unobtrusive circle thoughtfully. "I suspect we will be making an expedition this morning anyway."

It didn't take them long to prepare to test the circle Arisilde had marked. By their previous arrangement it was Tremaine's turn; Aras protested but Gerard gave the impression he would prefer to have Tremaine with him.

The boy, whose name was Lomin, had been rewarded with a set of Syprian copper earrings ornamented with abstract stick figures spearing tentacled sea creatures, contributed by Cimarus. Tremaine had managed to head off the friendly offer to pierce the boy's ears; having had a close look at Ilias's during intimate moments, she suspected it involved something the size of a fruit knife and a lot of blood. Vervane had pinned the earrings to the boy's shirt instead. Now Vervane was back watching over Meretrisa, and the younger Aelin were wandering around the chamber, the elders sitting with Aras to watch the gate spell.

Ilias followed Tremaine to the edge of the circle, deeply worried. "Just . . . come back right away. If anything looks funny," he told her.

Gerard was already in the circle, paging through his notebook with an expression of concentrated frustration. She told Ilias, "It'll be all right. We know Arisilde came here from there, wherever there is, so this circle doesn't go to the place where whatever happened to him happened."

Ilias didn't look comforted by this. "Just come back right away."

Gerard glanced up at her, took his pen out of his mouth and said, "Ready?"

Tremaine nodded and stepped over the edge. "Ready."

He touched the sphere, and suddenly they were in darkness. Tremaine took a startled breath, vividly recalling the gate Ilias and Gerard had found to the place with no air. But there was air here, it just smelled of rotten eggs. And there was no crushing heat like Ilias had described; it was warm and damp, but not much worse than the fortress.

This is familiar. Tremaine blinked, trying to get her eyes used to the darkness. She could smell sea salt over the rotten egg odor, and that rushing sound wasn't the blood pounding in her ears, it was the sea crashing against rock.

Gerard, standing next to her, laughed suddenly. "Gerard—" she began uncertainly. This was a bad time for him to go mad. But gray light came from somewhere ahead, gradually illuminating rocky walls as her eyesight adjusted. And she knew this smell. "Oh, God. We're on the island!"

He grabbed her arm and shook it, jubilant. "Exactly! We're only a few hours' sail from Cineth."

Tremaine grabbed him too, bouncing excitedly, until she remembered this meant they were surrounded by a varied array of monsters created by Ixion's sorcery, for his own sick amusement. Gerard must have recalled this at the same moment, because he detached himself from her and gestured a spell light into life above their heads.

The pale white light lit up not a cave but a chamber constructed of the long black stone logs used by the builders of the abandoned city under the island. Drawing the pistol tucked into her belt and wishing she had brought the rifle, Tremaine pivoted, seeing the chamber was large and eight-sided, and the symbols of the circle were carved into the smooth floor. The spell light revealed that there was nothing hanging in wait from the ceiling. A large square doorway opened into a passage, but as Tremaine squinted suspiciously at it, Gerard gestured the light to move toward it. She saw it was blocked by a rockfall.

"At least we don't have to worry about something coming at us from that direction," Gerard said, relieved. He started cautiously toward the gray light. Tremaine followed and as they drew closer Gerard waved the spell light out of existence. Once it was gone, Tremaine could tell that was daylight ahead, with that gray tinge of sunlight filtered through the clouds and mists that perpetually hung over the island.

It came from around a half wall probably meant to block wind and rain from the chamber; as Tremaine carefully peeked around it she saw that the wall was perched on the ledge of a large sea cave. A wide staircase curved down to a gravel beach and a rolling surf. The cave had a low opening to the outside, barely a few feet above the waves. She looked around, frowning, for a way to the surface, and saw a smaller branch of the staircase curved up, climbing the rock to a narrow doorway high in the cave wall. She could just see gray clouds through it and a cluster of the purplish creeping vines that infested the island's jungle.

Right, she thought in relief, *if we can get to the harbor cave, maybe fix one of those wrecked boats, or build a raft or something, enough to get to the mainland and send a real boat back for the others . . .* Gerard interrupted her thoughts, saying with quiet satisfaction, "And that explains a great deal."

"What?" She stared at him, then followed his gaze. Farther up the beach, gray wood against gray rock, was a battered little sailboat. Even sheltered in this cave, the weather hadn't done it much good. Its anchor had kept it from washing away, but storms had pushed it up against the rock too many times, splintering the fine wood of the hull. The stained white sails lay in a tangle of lines in the bottom and the little mast had broken, probably from being thrown against the cave walls by high waves. *Anchor,* Tremaine realized abruptly, starting down the steps, *white sails.* Syprian boats used carved stones as anchors and their sails were all dyed. "That's a Rienish boat."

"Yes, remember Nicholas said that he and Arisilde took a small boat through their first circle, so they could reach the island," Gerard said, following her. "After Nicholas left him, Arisilde must have been drawn here somehow and stayed to explore."

Tremaine reached the battered boat, stumbling a little in the soft sand. There was nothing left in the hull except worn ropes. If Arisilde had left anything behind here, it had long since washed away. She nodded to herself. "So we found where he started. We just need to find where he finished."

* * *

Ilias waited, watching the circle, arms folded to conceal the fact that his palms were sweating. *It gets harder every time,* he thought. Maybe he had never properly appreciated what Karima and Halian felt, or what Irissa and Amari had felt, watching him and Giliead go off into the unknown over and over again. Nearby, Giliead paced impatiently.

The older Aelin were mostly sitting around on the floor a little distance away, talking among themselves now that the only Rienish who could speak their language had gone. Balin sat near enough to listen, but didn't speak to them. She stared at them as if they were some strange thing she couldn't quite fathom, and they, apparently tiring of the rude scrutiny, were ignoring her. Aras stood nearby, the shooting weapon still over his shoulder, seeming more lost in thought than on guard. Cletia and Cimarus were more alert. Ilias knew Cimarus, at least, still stung from the critique of his performance as a guard that Ilias and Giliead had given him after he had let Balin walk out of the mountain caves.

Giliead stiffened suddenly, reaching for his sword, spinning to face the center of the chamber. "That circle—"

Ilias felt the hair on the back of his neck stand straight up. He shouted to Cletia and Cimarus, "Gardier!" After an instant of startled hesitation, both bolted for the nearest doorways. Aras hesitated, lifting the rifle, and the Aelin stared in confusion. Ilias drew his sword, saying hopelessly, "It can't be. Gerard broke the circle we came through."

"It's a different circle, it's that one over—" Giliead started forward, just as a dozen Gardier popped into existence in a circle not twenty paces away.

Ilias plunged forward but something struck him with all the force of a charging bull. It knocked him backward and he hit the floor, losing his grip on his sword as his head banged into the stone. Dazed, he thought, *They were prepared this time.* It was that damn curse, the one that blasted the strength from your legs, except this time it had struck his whole body. His chest felt heavy and he could barely draw in a breath. He heard a thump next to him and managed to turn his head enough to see Giliead sprawled nearby. *It didn't work on him, it couldn't work on him,* he thought, horrified. Then he saw Giliead's chest move as he breathed, far more freely than Ilias could; he closed his eyes briefly in relief.

Ilias heard cries of fear from the Aelin and managed to crane his neck to see past Giliead. Some of the Aelin who had been standing closer were sprawled helpless on the floor, but Aras was still on his feet; the Capidaran man had been too far away for the curse to reach him. But he held his weapon uncertainly. Craning his neck further, Ilias saw why.

The Gardier had spread out and one had caught the Aelin boy, Lomin, and held one of the smaller shooting weapons to his head. Elon suddenly started forward, speaking urgently. A shooting weapon fired, a sharp crack echoing off the stone, and Elon staggered backward and fell.

The Aelin cried out in horror. Ilias gritted his teeth as he remembered vividly what those weapons could do. One of the other Gardier had the small crystal that translated Gardier words to Rienish; he shouted at Aras, "Put the weapon down, now!"

The Gardier must not want to use their curse to destroy the shooting weapon. *They think he's Gerard,* Ilias thought. *They don't want to risk killing him.* Cletia and Cimarus, concealed in the shadows of the doorways, could only take two of the Gardier with the bows. The others would have plenty of time to kill several of the Aelin. Aras seemed to realize this as well; he carefully lowered the weapon to the floor, holding up his hands.

Another Gardier moved forward, standing over Ilias, between him and Giliead. Ilias saw that the man held one of the big melon-sized crystals, the ones inhabited by the dead soul of a wizard, which controlled the gate curses and the flying whales. The man holding it was young, barely older than Cimarus, with an almost boyish face. Or it would have been boyish, except for the glint of small crystal fragments embedded in his forehead and cheek. Ilias winced, his stomach wanting to turn. The flesh around the crystals was only a little green, so the boy hadn't had them long. With a bored expression, the young Liaison looked around at the Aelin, the frightened adults, the children huddled in terrified silence; he spoke sharply, gesturing with his free hand.

What is Gil waiting for? Ilias thought in exasperation. They had to do something, whatever it was. Tremaine and Gerard could return any moment. He saw Giliead staring up at the large wizard crystal cradled in the Liaison's arm. His face was set in a grimace of effort, as if . . . *He's talking to it?* Ilias wondered. *Oh, no, not again.*

Ilias heard more incomprehensible shouting in the Gardier language and twisted his head to see Balin on her feet, hands out in a placating gesture, speaking rapidly. Another Gardier asked a sharp question and Obelin shook his head, giving back an angry answer. The old woman Eliva, obviously more canny, interrupted with a softer response, trying to seem baffled and helpless. Balin spoke in appeal again and the Gardier hesitated, looking back toward the Liaison. Ilias fervently wished Obelin would shut up and let Eliva do the talking; it looked as if the Liaison wanted to simply kill the Aelin, and that Balin was trying to stop them. He noticed none of the Aelin had pointed to Cletia's or Cimarus's hiding places, or to the passage that led to the room where Vervane watched over the injured Meretrisa.

The Liaison didn't look as if he was persuaded. He started to speak, then frowned, one hand going to the crystal in his temple. His gaze swept the room suspiciously. Giliead's eyes narrowed in concentration, and if the man glanced down at him, surely he would notice. Ilias made a frantic effort to move and just managed to heave himself over onto his side. The Liaison made a sharp exclamation and kicked him in the stomach. Grimacing, Ilias rolled helplessly away from the blow, unable even to double up around the pain.

But it was the Liaison who cried out, staggering back suddenly, his hand going to his head, clawing at the little crystal. And every shooting weapon in the room suddenly burst into pieces, the Gardier shouting in alarm, dropping the steaming-hot fragments. The curse pinning Ilias to the floor was suddenly gone; he rolled to his feet, snatching up his sword on the way. He hamstrung the nearest Gardier and finished him off with a slash across the throat. He looked around in time to see the Gardier running, falling with arrows in their backs as Cimarus and Cletia advanced. Aras was grappling with another one. The Aelin, apparently in no doubt about whose side they were on, chased and tackled the others, shouting angrily. Giliead was on his feet, just pulling his sword out of the Liaison's chest.

Ilias killed two more Gardier stupid enough to run from the Aelin and blunder into him, and Giliead killed another, then it was over. They had seven Gardier prisoners whom the Aelin rapidly trussed up with Cimarus's help, Vervane hurriedly bringing rope from their supplies. Elon was alive, though bleeding badly from the stomach; Davret and Eliva crouched beside him, trying to stanch the wound. There were a few other wounded on their side, as two of the older Aelin had broken bones from being flung to the ground by the falling curse. The boy Lomin had a burned cheek and singed hair from when the shooting weapon had burst apart so close to his face, but Ilias counted him lucky.

Aras took a chunk of rock and began to rub out one of the symbols on the circle the Gardier had come through; Ilias thought it would buy them some time, but not much. He moved back to Giliead's side, just as Giliead lifted the big wizard crystal and smashed it on the floor. Ilias grimaced, skipping aside as the white light trickled out of it, flowing across the blue-gray stone in rivulets, vanishing into the cracks. Giliead pushed to his feet, absently brushing the fragments off his hands. "I made a deal with it," he explained. "I told it if it helped us, I'd kill it."

"That's what it wanted?" Ilias circled around the fragments to stand next to him. It was certainly what he would want if he was trapped bodiless inside a rock, slave to the Gardier, even if he was a wizard.

Giliead nodded, his mouth set in a grim line. "I think it used to be Rienish. It wasn't like the woman, the one in the crystal we took from the Gardier world. I think it remembered who it was."

Ilias winced in pity. Then he took a sharp breath, looking up at Giliead. "The crystals can't do curses on their own. You did it. You made the Liaison's head hurt, you made the shooting weapons break. It just helped you." He hadn't forgotten about the judgment looming over them, but he had pushed it to the back of his mind. For the past few days he had been more worried about whether they would ever find their way back to a familiar place again.

Giliead nodded slowly. "The god can only reject me once."

Ilias swore, shaking his head, though he supposed Giliead was right. Giliead gave him a quick smile and ruffled his hair, telling him not to worry. Ilias glared at him, planning to worry anyway.

Giliead started to speak, then flinched, turning to face the other end of the chamber. Alerted, Ilias looked back in time to see Tremaine and Gerard reappear in their circle. He took a sharp breath in relief. In the puff of foreign air that had come with them he caught the strong scent of the sea and a lingering foul odor that was oddly familiar.

"We found the island!" Tremaine called out. "The Isle of Storms. There's a circle, hidden in a blocked-off part of the city—"

Ilias stared; he thought he had been prepared for anything. He looked at Giliead. "Did you hear that?" The island was only half a day's sail from the mainland, from Andrien, from Cineth. From the god. Now they were nearly home, and he wasn't ready.

"I never thought I'd be glad to see that place again," Gerard was saying.

"Me neither," Tremaine told him, stepping out of the circle. "Hey,

Gerard and I were trying to think if we should all go to the island immediately, or wait until we can send to Cineth for some help and—" He saw her face change abruptly as she took in the dead Gardier, the live Gardier prisoners, and the wounded Aelin. "Go immediately, right."

They scrambled to gather their supplies and Giliead carried the injured Elon to the circle, while Cimarus brought the still-unconscious Meretrisa. The Aelin, frightened and shaken, didn't have to be persuaded to leave their belongings in the flying whale behind. Obelin spoke to Tremaine, who translated, "He says now he sees what we mean about the Gardier."

They all barely fit in the circle. Tucking an Aelin girl in behind him, Ilias found himself standing next to Balin. Her eyes were intent, and he knew she was thinking of bolting at the last instant. "Go ahead," he told her, though she wouldn't understand the words. She looked at him, her pale eyes as startled as if a goat had spoken to her. "Run from the truth." She had seen these people, heard their story, and seen what her own people were willing to do to them; she had to realize she had been lied to or she was a bigger fool than all the other Gardier put together.

Balin tensed, then subsided.

The chamber winked out, darkness closing in abruptly. Ilias winced in anticipation and the smell hit him an instant later. *This is the Isle of Storms, all right,* he thought in relief. Nothing produced that odor like generations of death and curses and putrefaction.

Over the startled murmurs of the Aelin, Giliead turned to Gerard. "They can hear us using these circles. They were listening for it, and when you used this one, they knew it. They weren't sure exactly where we were, but they were close."

Wiping the sweat off his forehead, Gerard nodded slowly. "I very much believe you're right."

Chapter 12

Tremaine sat on a rock on the cave's little beach, watching Aras examine what was left of the sailboat while Gerard paced. His boots crunching on the gravelly sand, he muttered, "I don't understand this. I can see how they're able to detect etheric gateways opening nearby when we use the mobile gates. Opening one in the same area several times again, or moving something the size of the *Ravenna* through even once, will cause a huge etheric disturbance. Yet they were able to track us through the point-to-point gates."

Tremaine nodded. "So the Gardier were at another junction, listening or whatever it is they do, waiting until we used a point-to-point circle again so they could narrow their search down."

Gerard gestured helplessly. "At least this makes it less likely that they captured a copy of the new circle Arisilde gave us."

"Wait, wait." Tremaine wearily pushed her lank hair out of her face. After so many hours without real sleep she was beginning to fade, and nothing was making much sense anymore. "We know Meretrisa told Gardier spies about it in Capistown—"

Aras, thoughtfully kicking the boat's battered hull, looked up, affronted. "We know no such thing. There is no proof against Meretrisa but your word. No one associated with the Ministry would be so disloyal."

Gerard stopped pacing to regard him silently. Tremaine lifted a brow. Aras eyed them both, realized he had called Tremaine a liar, and said, "I meant only that this supposedly happened right before you were attacked and injured."

Tremaine rolled her eyes, saying dryly, "Because I'm so hysterical."

"I didn't say that." Aras gestured, sounding reasonable. "Perhaps she did say something of the kind to you, but it was part of a misguided attempt to draw out these Gardier spies."

Gerard stared wearily at the ceiling, apparently unable to comment. Tremaine thought she understood Aras now. He was one of those lucky individuals for whom the whole world was painted in black and white, with no shades of gray. Meretrisa was a Capidaran and therefore on the side of right and so nothing she did could be wrong. There was no point in antagonizing her own intelligence and Gerard's patience by attempting to discuss this with Aras. One of them would just end up killing him.

The Aelin, at least, had finally settled down after Gerard had tended their wounded. Elon was now resting comfortably, or as comfortably as Meretrisa, up in the circle chamber with Vervane. The Gardier attack and the swiftness of their escape from the fortress had left most of the Aelin stunned, though the younger ones had wanted to explore the island. Fortunately, Ilias had found a heap of howler skeletons in the jungle not far from the little stone house that sheltered the top of the stairwell, and that had firmly convinced them that roaming was a bad idea. Balin sat nearby on another rock, her head propped in her hands, half-asleep herself.

Cletia, on guard up at the surface entrance, was the only Syprian still here at the moment. Ilias and Giliead had taken one of the underground ways to scout the Gardier base, to see if there was any unfriendly activity there. Cimarus had gone for help.

"I thought it took a few hours to sail to Andrien in the big galley," Tremaine had asked dubiously earlier in the day, standing beside Ilias on the gravelly beach. She had thought at first they meant to repair the little sailboat and send Cimarus to the shore in that. "Isn't that much longer in a little boat like this?"

"He doesn't have to reach Andrien," Ilias had explained, "Just get past the mist out to where the waterpeople are. Normally they love caves and rocks like these, but the island's too wizard-haunted for them, and the curselings kill the babies and the old ones that can't swim fast anymore." He scratched his beard stubble thoughtfully, looking out over the mist-shrouded water, eyes distant. "I think he will need a raft, at least to get back."

That was when it dawned on Tremaine that Cimarus would actually be swimming out to these waterpeople, to ask them to carry a message to Cineth. She had decided she didn't want to know any more about it.

Even though Gerard had carefully copied a couple of key symbols off the circle, then used the sphere to burn them off the rock, Tremaine still didn't feel safe. They didn't know yet if the Gardier had had a chance to reestablish the base. With the invasion force moving across Ile-Rien and able to construct circles wherever they wanted, the Gardier didn't need the island, except to keep the Rienish in the staging world off it. But Tremaine wouldn't be able to stop her nerves from jangling until Ilias and Giliead returned.

Now Aras climbed out of the boat, dusting off his hands. "So we've been following the footsteps of your friend Arisilde in reverse. He found this circle on the island first, after he separated from Valiarde. He used it to go to the fortress, marked the circle he arrived in with a coat button, chose another—how?"

Tremaine looked up wearily. "Arisilde's random choices aren't as random as other people's. He probably had a feeling that was the right one to take."

"Yes," Gerard agreed. "He was—is—rather known for that. So he arrived at the circle cave in the lower chamber of the mountain, didn't bother to mark the circle because it was only one of seven."

"But why did he put up the illusory wall?" Aras wondered, planting his hands on his hips.

"If he felt something was following him . . ." Tremaine hesitated. Following Arisilde's thought processes had never been easy. She still thought he had planned, if he didn't return himself, for Nicholas to follow him, and that he thought Nicholas would have easily found the trick of the false wall. "I bet the wall looked just as solid from the other side. Or he thought he might be leaving in a hurry and wanted to confuse pursuit."

"He drew the arrow to let us know he went upstairs, and marked the circle again with a coat button and a note." Gerard paused, took a deep breath. "So we know he didn't arrive via the circle he gave us in Capistown, he left the mountain through it." Gerard shook his head, pacing on the hard-packed sand. "All these new circles have to have two circles to work, one to leave from and one to arrive in. Once our copy of the circle in Capistown was destroyed by Nicholas to keep it out of Gardier hands, its counterpart in the mountain ceased to work. Yet the Gardier were able to arrive through it."

Tremaine nodded, her mouth twisted grimly. "Because they came from the original counterpart. If it was broken until they realized we were using the circles, and they fixed it so they could come after us . . ."

Gerard lifted his brows. "And it may have been intentionally broken, because at one point a very powerful Rienish sorcerer came through it, and though he was injured and driven off, even if he left his body behind—"

"They weren't sure where he was, if he was coming back." Tremaine took a deep breath. "Now they know."

It was sunset when Ilias and Giliead returned, the sky darkening to a stormy blue-gray past the perpetual mist and cloud cover that hung over the island. Cimarus had arrived an hour or so ago, bedraggled, though not drowned, and reported that he had encountered water-people out past the rocks, and that they had promised to take the message to Cineth. They were supposed to take it to Giliead's father-in-law, Halian, but apparently they had a great deal of trouble recognizing individual humans, and would just tell every Syprian they encountered in Cineth harbor, so the message was bound to get to Halian eventually. Tremaine hoped "eventually" meant soon; there wasn't much in the way of food or potable water on the island and they had a lot more mouths to feed now.

She went up the stone-cut steps to the surface to meet Ilias and Giliead, finding them in the little clearing just outside.

The stairs opened into a square shelter, dusty and empty, made of the long black stones that looked so much like logs. They showed no signs of mortar or anything else holding them into place except their own weight. Outside, the remnants of a small stone plaza were shielded by overhanging trees and vines, twisted and dark-leaved and faintly foul-smelling. His scabbarded sword propped on his shoulder, Ilias was telling Cletia, "Nothing there but howlers and bones. We didn't go too far in—"

Tremaine came out of the shelter, violently shaking out her hair after an encounter with a cobweb, and Giliead summarized the situation with, "No Gardier, for now."

Tremaine nodded. That was one small relief, anyway. The circle the Gardier had built in the base to transport their airships to Ile-

Rien had been destroyed before they had left the island the first time; unless there were other ancient circles hidden somewhere, or unless an airship or sailing vessel arrived with another mobile circle, they were temporarily safe. *Right, keep telling yourself that.* At least there would be nothing to stop a Syprian ship from coming to their rescue and taking them back to Cineth where they could wait for the *Ravenna,* if she was still unscathed. And find out what had happened in Capistown. And tell the Capidarans about Meretrisa's treachery, if Aras didn't manage to squelch that. And tell the Syprians how Arites had been killed at the Wall Port. And Giliead could confront the god. Finding herself with the sudden need for outdoor air, no matter how unpleasant, Tremaine told Cletia, "I'll take over for a while. Go get some rest."

Cletia lifted her brows, then shook her head, grimacing a little. "I'll stay out here. The cave smells like dead things."

Giliead fixed her with a look that was slightly colder than the ruined ice city. He said pointedly, "You've been out here all day. Take a rest."

Tremaine observed this thoughtfully. In Capistown, Ilias had been the one who had hated Cletia, so much so he could barely stand to have her at the house, while Giliead had been willing to bury the past and try to be friendly. Their roles seem to have reversed, and considering Cletia's behavior in the fortress, Tremaine thought she had an inkling why. *Oh, good. Add that to the list.* Ilias, for his part, stared absently up at the sky through the blue-green canopy of leaves.

Cletia bridled, then glanced at Tremaine. Tremaine had meant to keep her expression noncommittal but had the feeling it had just slipped a little into something more dangerous. Cletia looked uncomfortable and retreated back into the cave without further comment.

Giliead threw Ilias what could only be described as a dark look and followed Cletia. Ilias rolled his eyes.

Tremaine sat down on a broken chunk of stone, by habit checking to make sure Gerard's pistol was loaded. Ilias sat next to her, laying his sword across his knees. He shifted a waterskin off his shoulder and handed it to her. "We found a fresh stream, so we won't lack for water, even if we're stuck here for more than a few days."

"Good. So what's going on between you and Cletia?" Tremaine found herself asking, then realized she could have phrased it better. Fortunately, the connotations in Syrnaic weren't quite as accusing as they were in Rienish.

"She apologized for acting the way she did, about the curse mark."

He shrugged, as if he hadn't quite decided how he felt about it yet. "Nobody ever did that before."

Tremaine felt a bitter twist in her stomach. *Very clever, Cletia. I wouldn't have thought you had it in you.* What seemed a lifetime ago, Giliead had told her that Ilias wanted somewhere to belong, even before the curse mark. She could see how approval, from someone who had always withheld it, could be tempting. There wasn't much she could say to that, so she changed the subject. "Is Giliead worried about the god?"

"No." Ilias shook his head wearily, looking out over the darkening forest. "He's leaving that to me." He hesitated, frowning. "I'm beginning to wonder . . . When Ixion cursed me, and the curse went away when Gil cut his head off . . . We know now Ixion wasn't really dead, no more than the wizards in the crystals are dead. I think it was Gil that made the curse go away, he just didn't know he was doing it."

Tremaine nodded slowly, trying to drag her attention away from her own problems and the half-formed plan to murder Cletia at the earliest opportunity. "He could have. Or you know, Ixion might not have been able to keep up any other spells when the one that sent him off to the new body in his vat was triggered." She shrugged helplessly, fiddling with the waterskin. "At least we should have beaten the *Ravenna* here. Giliead can tell his side of it before Pasima can flap her big mouth."

"That should help." Ilias nodded, but he looked glum rather than reassured. "It's just . . . I wish we knew what the god will do." He propped his chin on his hand, poking at a tuft of grass with a stick. "I don't suppose . . . if the god turns Giliead away, you'd want to marry him too?"

This statement caught Tremaine just taking a drink from the waterskin. She choked and sputtered, nearly dropping the skin. Wiping the water off her chin, she eyed Ilias, who was watching her hopefully. "Was that a yes or a no?" he asked.

Tremaine took a deep breath. Sometimes she forgot just how different Syprian attitudes toward marriage were. It added another world of complexity to her feelings for Ilias, which needed more complexity like Ile-Rien needed more Gardier. She held up a hand. "Let's worry about that after we find out what the god does, all right? We'll . . . think of something."

Ilias subsided, poking at the grass again, obviously not satisfied. Tremaine could tell she had disappointed him. *What, you disappoint someone?* she asked herself with a sardonic twist of her lips. *What a surprise.*

The other chamber in the upper part of the sea cave had a canal running through it, and Giliead found Cletia there. She was retrieving one of the younger children, who had managed to fall in.

He asked her bluntly, "What do you think you're doing?"

Waist deep in the green water, Cletia looked up with a frown. "You wanted me to leave the boy in here?" She handed the dripping child off to Eliva, who carried him away, scolding him and drying him off with a corner of her shawl.

"With Ilias."

Her frown deepened and she climbed out of the water, wringing out the hem of her shirt. But she didn't meet his eyes. "Nothing." She started to brush past him.

He caught her arm, saying deliberately, "I'm a Chosen Vessel until the god says otherwise. Don't lie to me."

She pulled free, standing stubbornly, still not looking at him. "It's not a real marriage," she said through gritted teeth. "Everyone knows that. She lets him do whatever he wants."

He lifted his brows. "Everyone's different, Cletia. If you ever really talked to anyone outside the upper rank of families in Cineth, you'd know that." He eyed her for a moment, reminding himself she was younger than she looked and acted, that Pasima and her mother had kept her closer than they should, trying to make her into their own image. "You're telling me you want Ilias? Or you just want to make Pasima angry?"

Now she did look at him, her eyes furious. "I'm not a child." She started away, still dripping dirty water.

"Tremaine knows that, and she won't treat you like one when it comes to it," he said after her. She didn't stop and he shook his head at himself, grimacing. He hadn't handled her particularly well, but her interference made him angry. Ilias and Tremaine had a hard enough road in front of them, they didn't need this. And knowing he might not be there to help them on that road just made it all the worse.

Florian bit her lip in concentration, carefully rolling the small toadstone in the saucer of dried salamander's blood. Niles only had half a jar of salamander's blood left, and she couldn't afford to waste any. And just looking at the powdery substance made her want to sneeze.

She sat at the writing desk in the room assigned to her, which she hadn't slept in once yet. It was one of the smaller First Class rooms, with a bed, a small seating area with a set of overstuffed armchairs, and a dressing area and attached bath. It was also bare of any of her possessions, with the somewhat depressed air of an unused hotel room, and far too quiet. But she couldn't do this in the suite in front of Kias and Gyan, no matter how enlightened they had become about Rienish magic.

Frowning in concentration, Florian lifted the now dust-covered stone and wrapped the wool thread around it, setting another word of the charm each time the strands crossed. This was the tenth one she had done and she no longer had to glance at her notes to make sure she was getting the pattern right. *I don't know why I'm making so many—chances are I'll only be able to use one, if that.* She wasn't looking forward to taking those chances.

Tying off the last strand, she put the little stone on a square of colored foil borrowed from a discarded candy packet and wrapped it neatly, setting it aside with the others. Checking the clock above the bed to see if she had time for any more, she winced. The electric clock had never been reset for time in this world, but she knew how many hours it was off. Outside, past the dark green curtains and the metal dead lights that covered the portholes, the sun was setting over the sea.

Florian was starting to dread the evenings. She pushed her chair back, rubbing her aching neck, and got to her feet. Despite everything, her stomach grumbled and she realized her throat was dry. She went to the attached bathroom but there was no cup or carafe, so she drank enough from her cupped hands to survive until she got to the dining room. Pocketing the foil-wrapped stones, she hesitated. *I have to convince Nicholas to take some.*

Of all the defensive spells and charms she had researched that she felt she could perform, this was the one that would most likely be of use against Ixion. It also didn't require her to obtain anything that belonged to the sorcerer or to be in contact with him at any time.

The charms were called turnbacks, meant to turn any spell back against the caster. The best thing about them was that the charm was all contained within the toadstone, ready to be released at the first touch of hostile magic, so they could be used by people who had no magical ability. They were a traditional magic of Rienish hedgewitches, who had used them against Bisran Priest-Sorcerers in the old wars, and kept the art of making them concealed until this century. The only disadvantage was that they worked only for a limited amount of time, so you could only use one just before you thought someone was about to cast a spell on you. Florian had to admit that it was a pretty sizable disadvantage.

Surely she could talk Nicholas into carrying a few with him. She cast the familiar concealment charm on herself, then stepped out into the quiet corridor, locking the door behind her. She knew Nicholas's room was down one deck, so she went to the nearest cross corridor and down the narrow flight of stairs to the deck below.

Florian heard voices somewhere up the stairwell, but this corridor was also empty and too quiet, the lights too dim. Suppressing a shiver, she dropped the concealment charm and knocked at the door. She froze as it drifted open at her touch.

For a moment she thought the room was empty. She could see Nicholas's black overcoat, thrown over a chair, so she was sure she had the right room. Then the shadow by the dressing table moved and Ixion was suddenly there, watching her.

She backed away into the corridor, cursing herself for dropping the concealment charm too soon. "What do you want?" It took every ounce of willpower not to drop a hand to the pocket where the turnbacks rested, but she couldn't let him see her do it.

"Now what do you think?" He stepped out into the corridor, tugging the door shut behind him. "I want you to bring me one of the spheres. Every wizard on board has one except for me. It seems unfair." He smiled at her, showing perfectly even teeth. "Tell your friend Niles you wish to practice with it."

Oh, I knew that was coming. Florian took a sharp breath, knowing this was it, that there would be no putting it off this time. Because his coy manner infuriated her and she wanted it out in the open, she said, "Or you'll kill one of my friends, correct?"

His expression went blank. It was more frightening than the smile, than shouting, than threats. "Would you like me to?" he asked quietly. "I'm not playing a game, like your friend Valiarde."

Florian swallowed in a dry throat. *Where is he? What did you do to him?* she wanted to ask, but knew it was a mistake. She had told Nicholas she wouldn't make any more mistakes.

"Yes, I know you speak to him. I have those on board now who tell me things. They don't know they tell me things, but they do." Her expression must have given away her shock. He shook his head, mouth twisted in annoyance. "Oh, your little man in the sphere is not so powerful as you think. He can't see everything I do."

"How do you know he isn't just giving you enough rope to hang yourself?" Florian tried. *I hope that's what he's doing.*

"What a clever expression." Ixion gestured back toward the room, adopting the smile and the teasing manner again. "I was hoping to find Valiarde here, you know. I wanted to witness the results of my afternoon's work."

Oh, no. If he had done something to Nicholas, she had to get to Niles immediately and pray it wasn't too late. Florian stepped back, gesturing sharply and mouthing the last word of the illusion charm she had prepared. It was only a brief obscuring of the lights, just enough for her to bolt up the corridor to the nearest cross passage, ducking down it.

Behind her, as she pounded up the stairs, she heard Ixion laughing.

An alarm blared through the ship's loudspeaker as Florian reached the top of the stairs, punctuating her urgency. It was the one that meant "go back to your cabin or station and stay there," which was confirmed by a hurried announcement immediately afterward. She ran down the corridor to the foyer where First Class passengers entered the ship and bolted up the stairs into the main hall.

She slid to a startled stop. A few Capidaran and Rienish sailors, some men and women in civilian clothes she didn't recognize, and a couple of men from the Viller Institute were clustered around a makeshift stretcher made from a bed mattress. They were taking it forward, toward the other stairwell that would lead downward to the deck with the ship's hospital. They were speaking in an anxious angry mutter and between the men supporting the mattress she saw something half covered by a blanket, something with dark scaly ridges . . .

Oh, God. Her stomach trying to turn, Florian bolted down the corridor toward the First Class smoking room. Reaching it, she stumbled to a halt in the open doorway.

Niles stood beside the table in his shirtsleeves, flipping through a book with an annoyed expression. Giaren sat in one of the chairs, writing in a notebook, and Nicholas was sitting on the edge of the worktable, eating an apple. Beside him the sphere was serenely quiet, not even spinning. Niles glanced up, took in her frazzled demeanor, and said in alarm, "Florian, what is it?"

Stepping into the room, Florian flinched as the ship's alarm blared again from the loudspeaker not far above her head. She had assumed the figure on the stretcher was Nicholas, but Ixion must have done whatever he meant to do to someone else first. "Nicholas, Ixion knows I told you about what he said to me—"

"Said what?" Niles demanded. "What did he say—Wait, when did you see Ixion? He's supposed to be under guard—"

"He's been slipping past his guards and running around the ship at night," Florian told him impatiently. "But, Nicholas, he said he'd take care of you."

Nicholas nodded, imperturbable. "Good. You found him in my cabin?"

She blinked. "Yes. But—" The telephone on the desk interrupted with a shrill ring and Giaren moved hurriedly to answer it. He listened for a moment, an expression of increasing consternation on his face. He turned, covering the receiver, and said urgently, "It's Colonel Averi. He says Lord Chandre's been injured— He's not clear on specifics but he says it's obvious it's a sorcerous attack."

Niles frowned in confusion. "What sort of sorcerous attack?"

Florian's jaw dropped as the light dawned. She stared at Nicholas in horror. "You didn't."

"Didn't what?" Nicholas lifted a sardonic brow. He set the apple core on the coffee tray and dusted his hands. "I believe you'll find Ixion used strands of Chandre's hair, taken from a brush or comb on his dressing table. I talked to Giliead about Ixion, back in Capistown. All of Ixion's favorite transformation spells for people who inconvenience him use hair from the victim."

Florian just stared at him. She had seen Nicholas go into Chandre's rooms. *He took the hair from Chandre's brush and planted it in his own room, then antagonized Ixion. So Ixion took it, thinking it was Nicholas's.* "That's just—" She couldn't think of the right word.

"Oh, God." Niles shut the book, looking appalled. "What did he do to Lord Chandre?"

"What have you done?" Ixion's voice, breathy with rage, echoed the question right next to Florian's ear. With a yelp she spun around, backing away.

"Funny, I was going to ask you that." Nicholas sounded unperturbed, but he slipped off the desk, facing Ixion. Florian darted a look at Niles, who stood calmly, the book still in his hands, watching Ixion. Giaren, she saw with relief, had simply removed his hand from the telephone receiver, so Colonel Averi, hopefully still on the wire, could hear everything.

While Ixion's gaze was locked on Nicholas, Florian put a hand in her pocket, twisted the foil off one of the turnbacks and palmed it as she pulled her hand out. *Let this work the way it's supposed to, please,* she thought fervently, not certain who she was appealing to.

"You tricked me." Ixion's voice was a low growl, his face twisted with fury. He took a step into the room, and the telephone wire suddenly sparked and burst into flame. Giaren dropped the receiver with a gasp and gripped his hand, grimacing in pain. "You foreign motherless bastards tricked me. How dare you—"

Florian used the opportunity to clap a hand over her mouth, apparently in horror, and popped the turnback in. Swallowing it was unexpectedly difficult and it scraped her throat painfully. After a moment of struggle she got it down. *Don't cough, don't cough,* she begged herself silently.

"How dare I?" Nicholas said mockingly, stepping away from the table. "It was easy. You fooled yourself." He added, as if it had just occurred to him, "Having your head cut off must not be very conducive to constructive thought."

"Let's see how you like it," Ixion snarled, lifting a hand. But Niles struck first.

Florian staggered backward, shoved by an invisible force, buffeted until she tumbled over the chair behind her. She landed hard, pushing herself awkwardly into a sitting position. She saw Nicholas thrown back against the table and slammed into the hearth, and Giaren lay on the floor and Niles reeled against the table, teeth gritted, face red with the effort of keeping on his feet. Ixion staggered back and gripped the doorframe to support himself.

Florian took a gasping breath, suddenly aware the air had been sucked right out of her lungs and the room was freezing cold. She knew what had happened: a flurry of spells and counterspells from Niles and Ixion had charged the ether in the air, temporarily giving it a physical presence. If Ixion and Niles were both incapacitated . . .

Then Ixion shoved himself free of the doorway and pointed toward Nicholas, who was still struggling to stand.

Florian gasped, scrambled forward and threw herself in front of Nicholas. She heard someone shout in horror and felt the spell hit like a blow to her chest, knocking her back so she sat down hard on the floor. She felt the turnback move in her stomach, a weird sensation that made her yelp. Something formed in the air just in front of her, made out of the gathered force of the spell. For a heartbeat she saw an impossible creature with no head and several gaping maws, writhing in midair, flailing with far too many clawed hands. Then it flung itself back toward Ixion.

His shocked expression as it shot toward him made it all worthwhile.

The spell struck him with full force, slamming him into the table, jarring it backward on the floor, spilling and breaking bottles and jars, sending papers flying. The sphere shivered, spinning like a top. Ixion reeled across the table, gasping for air, red suffusing his face. He struggled, clawing at his throat, and Florian felt a confused surge of triumph and horror. *He did this to himself,* she thought. *He chose the spell, not—* Gathering himself, Ixion shook his head violently, pushing up off the table, taking deep breaths. The red color faded from his face as he leaned over, spitting out something dark that hit the floor and steamed like hot tar.

Ixion straightened up, wiped his mouth off on his sleeve. He smiled grimly at Florian. "Why, flower, I didn't think you had it in you. Too bad I'll have to rip it right out."

Oh, hell. Desperate, Florian looked around, spotting Nicholas's pistol on the floor. Nicholas was just pushing himself up, shaking his head, still dazed. She stretched, grabbing for the gun.

Ixion turned and snatched up the sphere, lifted it even as it spun and threw off sparks in a paroxysm of rage. He whispered a word and cracks shot across the tarnished copper surface. It spun faster and Florian could see light streaming through the metal. She cried out, lurching forward, but light and sound coalesced into an ear-shattering crack and Ixion's hand suddenly held a steaming collection of metal fragments, broken wheels and gears.

Breathing hard, Ixion turned his hand, letting the fragments trickle out and fall scattered to the floor. He looked at her, eyes still furious. "Now what will you do?"

Staring past him, Florian barely heard. There was a man standing framed in the doorway behind Ixion. He was tall and slender, dressed in a somewhat grubby brown sweater and light-colored canvas pants. He had white hair, long enough to just brush his collar and too wispy and soft to be the white of age. His eyes were a soft blue that looked violet in this light.

He caught her eye and winked. "Ack," Florian managed, the most coherent noise she was capable of at the moment.

Ixion must have read her face. He twisted around, staring. The man fixed his gaze on him, his eyes hardening, his smile taking on an edge of contempt. He looked at the broken metal fragments still clutched in Ixion's hand, and said, "Oh, it's far too late for that."

Ixion cocked his head, fascinated. "So you've come out of hiding."

The man didn't move. He said, "It's the pettiness that always surprises me. You would think the powerful would have the luxury of not taking offense."

Ixion grimaced. "You can't—"

Florian felt a surge of etheric energy that sucked any remaining warmth out of the room and made the electric lights flicker. Ixion's eyes rolled back and he dropped to the floor, banging his head on the table on the way down. He sprawled limply on the floor, unmoving.

Florian looked toward the doorway again, but Arisilde was gone. The dank cold in the room made her shiver. "Did I see— Was that really—"

Niles pushed a broken chair away, managing to struggle upright. A cut on his forehead was bleeding freely but he threw a sharp look at Nicholas, saying, "Was it him, Valiarde?"

"Yes." Nicholas stumbled to his feet. "He looked exactly as I last saw him, when I left him on the island." She could tell by the tightness in his face and the way he kept looking away that he was fighting an uncharacteristic surge of emotion. "I thought for a moment— But when he disappeared, it was obvious I was looking at a ghost."

"A very powerful ghost," Niles added grimly, going to help Giaren extricate himself from a shattered side table.

Florian cautiously approached Ixion, looking down at him. She had expected burns maybe, or some monumental alteration. But Ixion was only white and still, like any other dead man. *Huh?* She frowned, leaning over to look more closely. "He's breathing."

Nicholas moved to her side, gazing down at Ixion with lifted brows. "Of course. Arisilde isn't a murderer. Unlike some of us."

Chapter 13

The next morning a galley arrived at Dead Tree Point, the nearest safe anchorage on the island. Tremaine stood on the bluff with Obelin, watching with arms folded as Ilias swam out to the ship. They quickly lost sight of him; the headlands and the sea were obscured by mist, the galley seeming to float in a pool of white vapor.

The waves lapped on the tumbled black rocks sheltering the cove and the ship rolled gently. It was a big galley, bigger than the *Swift* had been, with a double bank of oars and olive green sails currently rolled up against the spars. It also had a much more prominent prow, painted with the stylized eyes that graced every Syprian ship. Tremaine thought she was looking at a war galley, though she had only seen them beached and lying in their sheds at Cineth harbor. There was something low and dangerous about its shape that the Syprian merchant and fishing ships lacked. She hadn't been able to pick out Halian, but other Syprians milled on the deck, waiting impatiently for Ilias to arrive.

Beside her, Obelin shifted and scratched the gray stubble on his chin, asking, "These people will accept us, you think?"

Tremaine took a deep breath, considering. That was another problem to add to the increasing list. The Aelin had been torn out of their time and place, so isolated they might as well have been trapped in one of the Gardier crystals for the past twenty years. They would need a place where they could find a home, and if the Syprians wouldn't accept them, then they would probably end up in Capistown, just in time for the next big Gardier invasion. Obelin had learned enough by now that she suspected he might be thinking along similar lines. She said wearily, "I think they'll at least give us lunch, and that's about as far ahead as I'm willing to plan for right now."

When told earlier that the galley had arrived, Giliead had pointed out that the waterpeople must have managed to deliver the message late last night and been lucky enough to actually catch Halian in Cineth. *Lucky is a good word for it,* Tremaine thought wryly. Despite rationing, they had run out of food that morning and Tremaine and Ilias and Gerard had been debating the notion of how palatable roast howler would be and could they separate one from a pack and get its body to the surface without being eaten themselves instead. Tremaine was mostly relieved they had been able to table that idea. She was deliberately not thinking about anything else. The galley, even as fast as it looked, would take most of the remaining morning and the afternoon to reach Cineth, and she didn't plan to get there nearly hysterical with worry.

Obelin nodded. "Perhaps you're right. Our luck has brought us this far, we can trust it a little further."

Ilias was climbing a net up the galley's side. Tremaine grimaced. Ilias had said once that she lived on luck. *But luck runs out. . . .*

Florian sat in a chair in the office area of the ship's hospital, one hand on her roiling stomach. "Are you sure?" she asked a little desperately. "You can't use a spell to fix it?"

The hospital was a small maze of green-painted metal-walled wardrooms with a dispensary, operating theater and tiny cabin-offices for the doctor and nurses, with the office area in the center. It had been fairly empty so far this trip, occupied only with the usual minor ailments and injuries caused by sea travel and people going up and down unfamiliar stairways on a rolling ship. Now Nicholas was leaning against one of the wooden filing cabinets along the wall, holding an ice pack to his head, and Giaren was in one of the wardrooms having a broken wrist tended.

"No." Niles, rather bruised and bedraggled himself, gave her a forbidding look. "It's the nature of the turnback, Florian, I can't use a spell on it. I'm afraid it has to come up the same way it went down. I assure you, if left to its own devices, it will choose a far more painful method of exit."

"Right." Reluctantly, Florian took the basin and the bottle of ipecac he handed her. She still felt gratified over how well the turnback had worked, though it had been Arisilde who had dealt the final blow to Ixion. They just weren't sure exactly what that final blow was.

"So Arisilde Damal is no longer in the sphere, he's in the ship itself." Colonel Averi rubbed a hand over his face. He was gray with fatigue. "How is that possible?"

"I've been asking myself that question over and over again, and I have no idea," Niles told him wearily. The cut on his forehead had been closed with sorcerous healing, but Niles was still in his shirtsleeves, his hair disarrayed, and he looked angry and out of sorts.

Averi's brows drew together in consternation. "He's made no attempt to communicate?"

"Not . . . coherently." Niles gestured helplessly. "He was in the sphere for a long time and never made direct attempts to talk to us. I'm not sure his situation in the ship would change that. It may be that he's simply forgotten how to speak on our level."

Nicholas cleared his throat. "That may or may not be the case. Before all this, Arisilde did go through prolonged periods where he was very difficult to communicate with. On any level."

Averi stared at him. "But he isn't dangerous, correct?" At Nicholas's faintly incredulous expression he amended, "Not dangerous to us, I meant. He's still in his right mind."

Nicholas sighed, set the ice pack atop the cabinet and dropped into a chair. "I've known Arisilde Damal most of my life. He hasn't been in his right mind since his early twenties, and thinking back on it, I have my doubts about him before that. But while his behavior has occasionally been disturbing, he has never been violent. Even when he was being attacked by someone or even some creature, he never seemed to take it personally."

Florian lifted her brows, startled. *Tremaine said he was eccentric, but ...* To Florian *eccentric* meant a rather absentminded scholarly sort of person who perhaps dressed unfashionably. She liked eccentric people. Or at least those kinds of eccentric people. *I should know by now that Tremaine's definition of eccentric is ... eccentric.*

Niles frowned, considering this. "When he was in the sphere, he did seem to be rather . . . ferocious in our attacks against Gardier ships." He shook his head, admitting, "Though that could just be the way it appears to us, because the sphere itself increases the speed at which spells are performed."

Nicholas leaned back in the chair and lifted a brow. "Or that considering what the Gardier did to him, he does take them personally."

"Valiarde, for God's sake, decide which side of the argument you're on." Averi shook his head wearily, turning back to Niles. "What about Ixion? Do you know yet what Arisilde did to him?"

"Not really." Niles looked toward the closed door of the wardroom where Ixion now lay. "The etheric signatures I can detect are complicated, and all center around his brain, his nerves." He shook his head, annoyed. "The fact that Lord Chandre returned to normal after it was done—"

"Yes." Nicholas interrupted with a dry comment. "Pity that."

Niles frowned at Nicholas as if he suspected him of ill-timed levity, but Florian knew by now that he was serious. Ixion hadn't been the only one Nicholas had meant to eliminate with his little trick. She still wasn't sure how she felt about that. Niles continued resolutely, "It makes me think whatever it was, it was something fairly . . . devastating."

"Ilias said that after Giliead killed Ixion the first time, the transformation spell Ixion put on him just stopped, and Ilias went back to normal," Florian put in, absently tucking her basin under her arm. "Just because Ixion's still breathing doesn't mean . . . you know, that he's still in there."

Niles lifted his brows. "True."

Averi frowned. "I don't think any of us believe for a moment that whatever Ixion was doing with that vat was actually meant to create a body for the sorceress trapped in the Gardier crystal."

Niles nodded, lost in thought. "I'll be very interested to see what Kressein finds when he examines the contents, and—"

The ship's alarm went off, startling Florian so much that she dropped her basin. *Oh, no,* she thought wearily. She had been about to point out that the howlers and the grend and all the other curselings created by Ixion hadn't died or vanished with the sorcerer's first "death," and that whatever was in the vat probably wouldn't either. *That's got to be—*

Nicholas pushed away from the cabinet with a tired grimace. "I think your curiosity is about to be satisfied, Niles."

I still can't believe the Gardier came from these people," Halian said thoughtfully, leaning back on the rail and looking across the deck. He was a big man, weathered by sun and sea, his long graying hair tied back in a simple knot. He had married Giliead's mother, Karima, some years ago, a second marriage for both of them, for love rather than land or family influence.

Ilias turned to look, the wind tossing his hair. They had gotten everyone bundled onto the ship and escaped the haze of mist surrounding the island. Now the older Aelin were up in the bow, drinking in the limitless blue vault of the sky, the warm sun and the sea. It made Ilias remember what Obelin had told them, that before the Aelin were trapped they had lived a wandering life, traveling long distances from their home. They had been imprisoned in the fortress so long they must have forgotten what it was like to move. "I don't think they believe it yet either," he said ruefully. After their time in Capistown, Ilias had missed the open sea himself. Sailing on the *Ravenna* had been very fine, standing at mountain height above the water, but being close enough to catch the spray was good too. It was almost enough to let him forget what they were heading into.

Halian had told them the waterpeople had climbed up on the dock at Cineth and practiced their usual method of passing on a message, which was to tell everyone in earshot until someone took action. The word had reached Halian quickly, and he had borrowed this ship, the *Importune,* to come after them. It also meant that everyone would know they were back.

The younger Aelin were everywhere, down in the hold trying to talk to the rowers despite the language barrier, up in the bow, atop the steering platform. Halian had had to pull a few crewmen off the oars over the objections of their rowing mates and give them the job of making sure no one fell overboard. Aras was trying to help at this task, and Vervane was sitting with Meretrisa and Elon in the stern cabin. Tremaine and Gerard were both asleep back there as well, which Ilias was glad of, as they both looked as if they needed it. One of the crew was guarding Balin, giving Cimarus a respite.

"They truly have nowhere to go?" Halian asked, watching Davret catch one of the younger boys and swing him around in pure glee, her skirt twirling around her.

"Not that we know of," Giliead told him, looking out over the waves. They were making for Cineth, following the forested hills of the shoreline. "The Gardier who came after us were ready to kill them all, even the children. There's something about this man, this Castines, the one who trapped them in the fortress. If he's as important as we think, the Gardier would probably kill them just for knowing he ever existed."

Halian nodded grimly, looking out over the sea. After a moment he shot a look at Giliead. "You want to tell me now what's wrong?"

Ilias took a deep breath. They had already told Halian briefly about the *Ravenna*'s voyage to Capidara, about Arites's fate and their discoveries on their odd journey back. They hadn't told him what had happened during their escape from the Gardier world.

Giliead hesitated, his eyes still on the not-so-distant shore. He shifted to face Halian. "I used curses."

Ilias managed to keep himself from looking guiltily around to see if anyone else was in earshot.

Halian tilted his head, as if he hadn't heard right, his brows drawing together. "What?"

"We were trapped in the Gardier world, with no Rienish wizard to get us out," Giliead told him, his face bare of any emotion, as if all this meant nothing. "I could hear the dead Gardier wizard, trapped inside the crystal we had captured. She told me a curse to make the Gardier stop firing on us, so we could reach the flying whale tethered to the roof. I made it work. Then she gave me the curse to let us take the flying whale back to our world, so we could get back to the *Ravenna*. I made that work too. When the Gardier found us in the fortress, when Tremaine and Gerard were gone, I talked to their crystal and it told me the curse to make the Gardier weapons break, in exchange for killing it."

Halian had said "But—" three times during that short speech. Now he shook his head, aghast, his expression sickened. "I don't understand, how is that possible?" He looked at Ilias, who just looked away. *This is not going well.*

Halian stared at Giliead for a long moment. "You know what they're going to say, don't you? That you've been too lenient in the past with people accused of cursing, that you let people go when you shouldn't have, that that's why Ixion tricked you into bringing him to Andrien. That it's corrupted you."

Ilias swore. *This again.* Angry past bearing, knowing he should keep his mouth shut, he said roughly, "We didn't bring Ixion to Andrien, we brought a man named Licias whose family had been killed by a curseling. We were tricked, fine, but corruption had nothing to do with it. And we were right about the Rienish wizards, the god said so."

Halian ignored him, still watching Giliead. He asked quietly, "What do you think the god is going to say about this?"

"I'll find out." Giliead faced him directly, his eyes giving nothing away, but the tension in his body belied his calm tone. "What do you say about it?"

Halian watched him for a moment more, then shook his head and walked away.

Ilias gripped the rail, looking out at the sea. He felt sick. He had thought he had been anticipating this all along, but the truth was that deep down he hadn't believed in it. He had really thought Halian and the others would stand by them. Stand by Giliead. "You think that's . . . that?"

Giliead took a deep breath. "He'll wait for what the god decides."

"Why should he wait?" Ilias said through gritted teeth. The sick sensation of being punched in the gut was rapidly turning into something else. *All we've done for them*, he thought, seething, *all those years of fighting and killing to keep them safe, can't that count for something?* "Why can't he trust you?" he burst out, caught between grief and rage and the pure pain of betrayal. "Why can't he trust me?" He flung a hand in the air. "Does he really think you'd—" He sputtered, unable to put it into words. Participate in the kind of corruption that led wizards to kill indiscriminately, driven by nothing but greed and lust, feeding off fear and pain. "And that I'd help?"

Giliead shook his head. For a long time he didn't answer, then he just said simply, "We don't have anywhere to stay in town."

Ilias opened his mouth, closed it again, stopped by the faint catch in Giliead's voice. *We can't go home.* If Karima, if the others, felt as Halian did, they didn't have a home.

Ilias had faced that before, when he was a child and his family had left him out in the hills to die. He knew that to a certain extent he had never trusted anyone in the same way again, never felt as secure about his adopted family as those born into it. But Giliead hadn't faced this before. And Giliead had prepared himself for this, was trying very hard to stay calm. Ilias took a deep breath, and another, until he could speak without shouting or snarling. "We can stay in the god's cave."

Giliead said nothing for a moment, looking away, the wind whipping his hair around to shield his face. Then he just put an arm around Ilias's shoulders.

Tremaine woke, startled, at the thump that vibrated through the hull when the oars were shipped. She sat up on the floor of the cabin, bleary-eyed and feeling as if she had missed something important. Elon lay on the bench built into the wall, cushioned by pillows and blankets, Eliva seated on the floor next to him. Most of the rest of the space was taken up by baskets used for provisions and a rack of red clay amphorae. "I think we're there," Eliva said a little nervously, bracing herself against the cabin floor.

Tremaine grabbed her bag and stumbled out into the brilliant sun and a view of Cineth's harbor.

The long curve of land was sheltered on one side by a high promontory. Atop it was a stone pyramid tower that acted as a lighthouse. On the other side of the harbor was a long breakwater of tumbled blocks. Above the stone docks, Cineth sprawled across a series of low hills, the buildings mostly white stone with red tile roofs, none taller than two stories, with a few round fortresslike structures that Tremaine now knew were granaries crowning the hills. The whole was dotted with shade trees, standing in the gardens and market plazas.

Along the waterfront there were stone stalls with wooden roofs, where men and women haggled over cargoes or hauled boxes and baskets back and forth. Gray gulls wheeled overhead. Most of the fishing boats were docked at short stone piers, and the war galleys like this ship were stored in long wooden sheds along the far bank. But as she studied the harbor front, she saw something new had been added: at regular intervals there were heavy wood scaffolds draped with ropes, with various-shaped levers sticking out and rocks piled on their wooden bases to stabilize them. Tremaine recognized catapults of different sizes, and several onagers, all aimed toward the harbor. If the Gardier came to Cineth again, the inhabitants were a little more prepared this time. But even the naphtha jugs wouldn't be much help against artillery or bombs dropped by airships. And Cineth had no spheres to protect it against the Gardier magic.

The sails were down and their galley was already being hauled into place along one of the docks. The rowers were coming up from below, stretching and calling greetings to the people waiting ashore. Even though Halian had reported that the Gardier attacks had been further down the coast, it was still a relief to see that the place looked undisturbed. Only the Arcade, a long stone building housing shops, still bore the smoke stains and signs of damage from the Gardier gunship that the *Ravenna* had destroyed outside the harbor.

The Aelin were in an excited clump in the bow, pointing, talking to one another, the children bouncing with hysterical excitement, as if they were on an excursion boat. *Oh, God,* Tremaine thought, clapping a hand to her forehead. *This is going to be a circus.* As soon as their feet touched the dusty stone of the harbor front, the Aelin would all be wandering off in a dozen directions. Fortunately, Cineth wasn't exactly a bustling metropolis and it should be fairly easy to round them up again.

The Capidarans stood along the rail near the Aelin. Meretrisa was actually on her feet, Aras and Vervane supporting her. Gerard was nearer the bow, speaking to Obelin, who looked bewildered from too many new sights and sounds, his face and balding head reddened from too much sun.

In all the milling around, she finally saw Giliead and Ilias, standing down the rail from the others, isolated. She shouldered her bag and went to join them, grabbing the rail to steady herself as the boat sloshed and bumped toward its place along the dock. Ilias glanced at her. Even when they had been about to storm a stronghold in the middle of a Gardier city and steal an airship with which they had no guarantee of being able to create a world-gate, he hadn't looked this tense. Giliead's expression was as implacable as stone, though she could see the tension in the line of his jaw. She swallowed whatever comment she had been about to make, since there was nothing to be said, and just leaned against Ilias.

The galley slid into its slip, and as the men along the dock hurried to tie it off, Giliead vaulted the rail, landing on the stone platform and striding away. Ilias squeezed Tremaine's arm and leapt the rail after him.

"Damn it." Tremaine pushed away, elbowing through the crowd of sailors. "Gerard," she said as she reached him. "Ilias and Gil already went ashore, I'm going after them."

Gerard glanced at her, nodding absently. Then he paused, frowning. "They've gone to see the god?"

"Yes. I want to—"

He touched the bag that hung at his side, the one that held the sphere. "Perhaps I'd better come along."

Tremaine considered that for half a moment but shook her head reluctantly. "No. I think you'd better stay back here with the Aelin and the Capidarans."

He looked down at her, concerned. "Are you certain?"

"No, but they need to stay out of this. And hell, you're a sorcerer, you need to stay out of it too." The god had given both Gerard and

Florian its approval on their first visit here, but if Giliead was going to be repudiated by it . . . Tremaine didn't want to take any chances.

Gerard nodded reluctant assent and Tremaine clambered awkwardly over the rail, one of the dockworkers catching her arm to help her down. As she hurried after Ilias and Giliead, Gerard called after her, "Be careful!"

She caught up with Ilias at the Arcade and followed him and Giliead up the hard-packed dirt path through the town, past white clay-covered houses with fruit trees leaning over the walled courtyards. Children played around the fountain houses in the communal courts, dogs barked, people recognized Giliead and called out or pointed or stared, surprised to see him back, or just surprised that no one had told them about it yet.

If the god repudiated Giliead, he would be disgraced in front of all these people, the entire extended Andrien family, everyone he had grown up with. Trudging up the dusty road, Tremaine had the sudden realization that her own problems before the war had been minuscule compared to this. Being kidnapped into a mental asylum and branded by gossip as a madwoman, no matter how degrading she had found it at the time, had been barely an inconvenience in the larger scope of life. No one whose opinion she had really cared about had been affected by it, not Nicholas certainly, and not Gerard or Arisilde; Arisilde, in fact, wouldn't have particularly minded had she actually been raving mad. And it hadn't changed the opinion of her friends or acquaintances in the theater world; with all the quarrels, affairs, satirical newspaper columns, drunken sprees and being caught in opium dens with high-ranking members of the Ministry, they had barely noticed.

They reached Cineth's central plaza, a large area of open ground where spreading trees shaded little markets of awnings and small colorful tents. The markets were crowded today, with men and women buying and selling pottery, baskets of fruit and vegetables, fleeces, chickens, goats. The plaza was bordered by several long two-story buildings with columns and brightly painted pediments. The large one with the pillared portico was the town Assembly, the smaller round one with a domed roof was a mint and the one with the square façade was the lawgiver's house. The city fountain house was next to it, a low square structure with sea serpents carved along its pediment.

Near the center of the plaza was an old oak with heavy spreading branches that had long ago sunk to the ground under their own weight. The goat skull was still there as a warning that the god had inhabited the tree; it was stuck up on the same post but now sprouted dozens of colored ribbons tied to the horns as well as flowers and strings of beads and copper disks.

Tremaine looked around for Nicanor or Visolela, the city's appointed lawgiver and his wife, who wielded more power than he did. The only person who seemed to be expecting them was a young man waiting beside the goat skull. His hair was a dark blond, tied back in a multitude of braids, and he was nearly Giliead's height, his olive skin contrasting with his light hair and silver armbands. He wore a leather jerkin and a sleeveless yellow shirt over his pants and boots and a sword strapped across his back.

Giliead and Ilias halted a few paces from him, and Tremaine stopped well behind, sensing that this would not be a good moment to draw attention to herself. She wiped sweaty palms on her shirt and resolved to keep her mouth shut for once. This close, she could now see the man's face was lined by more than sun and weather and that he also had an old burn scar on his shoulder. She thought he was still young, but life had obviously aged him prematurely.

"Herias," Giliead greeted him, his voice even, that stonelike calm making him seem almost indifferent. Tremaine knew him well enough by now that the more impenetrable his expression the more upset he actually was. And she could tell from the tense line of Ilias's back that he was nearly ready to explode from worry.

Herias flicked a wary glance at Ilias, then his gaze settled on Giliead. "You smell like curses."

God, no, Tremaine thought, sickness settling in the pit of her stomach. This man had to be the Chosen Vessel of Tyros, the one who had watched over Cineth while Giliead was gone.

"It's because of the Rienish wizards," Cimarus said suddenly, and Tremaine jumped. Intent on the confrontation, she hadn't realized he stood beside her. She glanced back, seeing Cletia hurrying toward them. Both must have followed them up from the harbor and Tremaine had just been too preoccupied to notice. "Their curses got us home. But the god met their wizard before we left, so that must be all right." Cimarus threw an uncertain look at Tremaine, asking for her support. "Right?"

"Uh, yes, that's right," Tremaine agreed hurriedly, just as Cletia stepped up beside Cimarus.

"Yes, that's true," Cletia said, but her grim expression told

Tremaine that she didn't think this was going to work either. "We must all smell of curses, but it's—"

"Cletia," Ilias interrupted quietly, not looking at her. "Don't."

Cletia subsided uneasily. A crowd was gathering, merchants from the market, men and women who had come to the city center to buy olive oil or trade cattle and sheep, or who had followed them up here from the harbor. Tremaine saw Halian, watching with a kind of sick horror. She recognized other crewmen from the *Swift,* including Dannor, who on the Isle of Storms had objected so strongly to boarding the *Ravenna* that the delay had almost gotten them killed. She also recognized some faces from the council; among them was Pella, a lean spare man who was the lawgiver's deputy and also the leader of the political opposition to the alliance with Ile-Rien. They were all quiet, so quiet all she could hear was the breeze in the tree leaves, the crunch of the dry grass underfoot, the lowing of a cow in the distance. *A mob should make noise,* Tremaine thought, the back of her neck prickling with unease. Rienish mobs always made noise. Gerard's pistol felt heavy in the back of her belt. *Please, don't anybody make me use it,* she begged silently.

Giliead stared past Herias, his eyes on the heavy shadows among the tree branches. "The god isn't here," he said, a faint frown line appearing between his brows. It was the first sign of distress he had shown. It would be better if he showed his emotions, Tremaine realized suddenly. If he revealed how anxious he was for the god's reaction, how worried he was for what might happen to himself and Ilias. That what had happened might change his family's feelings toward him. If he showed that this frightened him as much as it did everyone else. But she knew she and Giliead were alike in that; the worse things got, the more likely they were to hide behind a blank façade. Or in her case, a sarcastic one.

"I don't know where your god is," Herias replied quietly. "I haven't seen it for two days."

A tremor ran through the crowd. It wasn't quite an audible murmur of alarm, but Tremaine could sense fear replacing the confusion and uncertainty. These people knew gods could simply vanish, leaving their territory at the mercy of wizards and curselings and whatever other supernatural terror might choose to move in. They knew when it happened that it was always someone's fault. Ilias had told her about a city whose people had killed their Chosen Vessel, and how their god had abandoned them. But if the god was already gone . . . Tremaine realized she was gritting her teeth so hard her jaw ached.

Giliead just stood there for a moment, then started to turn away. "Where are you going?" Herias demanded sharply, stepping forward.

Giliead paused, eyeing him. The other man's stance had changed from wary to aggressive. He said quietly, "I'm going to the god's cave."

Herias regarded him narrowly. "Why?"

Giliead snorted in derision, a flicker of contempt in his expression. "Why do you think? I want this over with."

Herias drew his sword, a broad flat horn-handled blade like the ones Ilias and Giliead carried. Tremaine put a hand on her revolver, her throat tight, and felt the crowd behind her tense in startled antici-pation. But Herias just rested the flat of the blade on his shoulder. Giliead watched him, his eyes narrowing. Herias said, "I think I don't want you out of my sight until I find out where the god is."

Ilias swore, shaking his head and looking up at the sky, apparently making a tremendous effort to keep his mouth shut. Giliead faced Herias squarely. "What are you saying?"

"Yes, just what the hell are you saying?" Tremaine echoed under her breath.

"I don't know what you've done to the god, if it's fled because of you or not. But you're not going anywhere until I find out." Herias spoke in what Tremaine thought was a deceptively even tone.

Ilias couldn't contain himself anymore. He burst out, "That's ridiculous! We just got back. Ask Halian, ask the waterpeople. We were on the Isle of Storms, and we didn't even get there until yesterday. That's past the god's reach." He stepped forward impulsively, putting himself between Herias and Giliead. "If you don't—"

Herias stepped forward as if he was going to speak, then suddenly swung his sword. Tremaine saw it strike Ilias, saw him stagger side-ways and fall in a heap. She shoved forward but someone grabbed her arm. She swung her hand, backhanding him, not aware until he stag-gered away that she had the revolver in her hand and had struck him with it across the forehead. Peripherally she saw Giliead leap on Herias, slamming the sword out of the other man's hand and seizing his throat. Giliead was utterly silent. It was Halian who shouted in rage, suddenly surging out of the crowd to fling himself on the man who had grabbed Tremaine. Someone else grabbed Halian, Dannor hauled him off, and in the next instant the entire plaza had exploded into a brawl.

Tremaine plunged forward, reaching Ilias just as he made a dizzy effort to stand and collapsed over on his side, lying in the dirt.

She grabbed his shoulder and rolled him over, sick with fear. But while there was blood running freely from his nose, the huge gaping wound she had dreaded to see wasn't there. She put a hand on his face and felt that he was breathing. He flinched away from her without waking. *Herias hit him with the flat of the blade,* she realized, so dizzy with relief she almost fell over on top of him. *Not the edge.* She looked up to see Herias bowl Giliead over backward, slamming him into the trunk of the oak. *Giliead doesn't know that.* She drew breath to shout at him but gave it up. Everyone else was shouting and he would never hear her.

She looked around as the fighting, yelling mob surged closer. Andrien supporters attacking Pella supporters and vice versa, moderates trying to separate them and an undecided faction attacking all the others indiscriminately. It was mostly fists and makeshift clubs but it could turn deadly any instant. And if someone had a bow he could pick them off from the edge of the plaza before anyone could make a move to stop him. The revolver was still in her hand, but she couldn't shoot these people.

Shouting, Cletia hauled away one of the men trying to attack Cimarus. Another man, staggered by a blow to the head, barreled blindly into her, knocking her back a few paces and nearly into Tremaine. The man threw an apologetic look at Cletia and Tremaine realized that though there were women in the crowd, some angrily shouting, trying to separate combatants, others punching and kicking right along with them, the men were trying to avoid them. Suddenly inspired, she let go of Ilias, pushed to her feet and grabbed Cletia, wrapping a forearm around the other woman's neck.

Cletia caught her arm and swore in surprise, snarling, "I'm trying to help—"

"Then shut up and help," Tremaine said through gritted teeth. She fired twice into the air, two explosive blasts that brought the fighting to a startled halt. She shoved the pistol into Cletia's side, surprising a gasp out of her, and shouted, "Stop or I'll kill her!"

Everyone stared. Cimarus, on the ground a few paces away, his arm wrapped around another man's throat, looked vastly confused.

"Better do as she says!" Cletia called out, adding under her breath to Tremaine, "You are completely mad."

"I know that," Tremaine snapped at her. She became aware that someone was behind her, his back to her and Ilias. He was holding a fallen branch as a club and was obviously helping her because he hadn't hit her yet. She couldn't see much of him out of the corner of her eye and didn't dare turn her head, but he was too short to be Giliead. *Must be one of Halian's crew,* she thought, watching the mostly baffled crowd.

Halian, his nose bloody and his shirt torn, dropped the man he had been pummeling and lifted his hands. "Wait! Just wait, we need to stop this—"

Suddenly the crowd surged again as men and women were shoved from behind, stumbling out of the way as Herias slammed through them, heading right for Tremaine and Cletia.

Tremaine tensed to shove Cletia at him, hoping the other woman would have the sense to fling herself at him and slow him down at least. Then Giliead flung himself on Herias from behind, dragging him back and slamming a punch into his face.

Herias staggered but ducked the next blow and tackled Giliead to the ground.

A thunderclap rattled Tremaine's teeth and she winced away from a bright flash of light. Cletia stumbled back against her, and Tremaine was suddenly supporting her rather than pretending to restrain her. The other woman's hair in her face, Tremaine blinked hard, shaking her head, trying to clear her dazzled vision.

A cloud of bright lights hovered not far in front of her, like a swarm of unusually angry fireflies on a summer evening. The nearest people gasped, swore and scrambled hastily away. Herias and Giliead froze, staring at it.

"It's the god," Cletia said, regaining her feet. Tremaine released her, watching the lights warily. She had seen the god in its cave, and when it had come out to the *Ravenna* to explore the ship and Ixion's prison. Whatever the god meant to do, if the situation went against Giliead, she needed to get Ilias out of here. She shoved the gun into her belt and knelt on the dusty ground beside him, keeping one wary eye on the god.

Ilias lay still, crumpled up on the oak roots. She felt anxiously through his hair, sudden fear that the sword blow had broken his skull making her stomach nearly turn. Gerard was only as far away as the harbor but there was only so much even sorcerous healing could do in those circumstances.

The man who had guarded her back was crouched over them, asking, "Is he all right?"

"I think so." She couldn't feel anything but firm bone. Ilias flinched away from her again but still didn't wake. She focused on her ally for the first time. He was stocky and blond and looked vaguely familiar. "Who are you?" she demanded.

He jerked his chin at Ilias. "I'm Castor, his brother."

The crowd murmured, shifting back in alarm. Tremaine looked up to see the god's cloud swirl, giving an impression of agitation and anger. It drifted sideways, settling inside the goat skull, making the empty eye sockets glow. Giliead pulled away from Herias, pushing to his feet, his eyes on those lights as if nothing else existed.

Herias staggered up, standing next to him. Both their faces were intent as they listened to something no one else present could hear. Tremaine held her breath.

It was Herias who reacted first. He threw a startled look at Giliead, his tense posture shifting into something that conveyed apology and confusion. He put a hand on Giliead's arm. "I—"

Giliead stepped away from him. Still breathing hard, he said thickly, "Get out of here. We don't need your help." He pushed through the crowd and people made way for him, falling back in silence.

Herias shook his head, shoved his tangled braids back, saying in urgent appeal, "Giliead, I'm sorry. You have to understand—" He started to follow and the god lifted off the skull suddenly, expanding, that humming buzz rising again.

Looking hurt, Herias backed away and the god reluctantly settled again. It was angry and the message was clear; it wanted Herias gone as well.

Giliead dropped to his knees beside Tremaine, looking down at Ilias, his face ashen and etched with fear. "He's all right," Tremaine told him hastily. "He just got knocked out."

Giliead nodded, but she wasn't sure he had heard her. Herias turned away, disappearing into the thinning crowd. Guilt and fear of the god's obvious anger had caused much of the opposition to depart rapidly, though she could see a shoving match had broken out somewhere in the back. Halian was standing over them now, with Cletia and Cimarus, Dannor and others she recognized from the *Swift*.

More people scattered and suddenly Visolela was there, holding a rich purple stole wrapped around her shoulders, her dark hair disordered. "What is going on here? Have you all gone right out of your motherless minds?" she demanded. Raising her voice to a shout, she added, "Anyone else who fights in the plaza today will be fined four days of harvest labor and they can explain themselves in front of the council!" The shoving match abruptly broke up.

She turned to them, stopping abruptly when she saw Giliead, the expression on his face giving her pause. "What's happened?" she said more softly, looking down at Ilias uncertainly.

"He's hurt," Halian told her. "Can we take him into the lawgiver's house?"

"Yes, yes." Visolela gestured impatiently.

Halian stepped around Tremaine, leaning down to pick up Ilias. Giliead moved abruptly, knocking aside his arm.

"Hey!" Tremaine caught his chin and turned his head to face her. His eyes were flat with anger; it was a look Tremaine had seen in the mirror often enough. "It's over," she said sharply. "Now let's take Ilias into your sister-in-law's house and calm down. All right?"

He blinked, seemed to see her for the first time. He nodded and she pushed back out of his way as he carefully lifted Ilias.

Giliead carried him over to the lawgiver's house and Tremaine hurried to hold the door open. They passed into the dark foyer and out onto the wide portico that surrounded the central atrium. It had a square reflecting pool down the center of the open space, surrounded by cyprus trees and bright flower beds; it was quiet and cool and seemed a completely different world from the confusion and turmoil of the dusty plaza outside.

Visolela stopped Tremaine on the portico, demanding, "Tell me what happened."

"What, I—" She looked around, but Giliead was taking Ilias farther into the house, Castor had faded away somewhere outside and Halian brushed past her, hurrying after Giliead, followed by Cletia. Cimarus was the only one who stayed on the portico with her, nursing an already swelling jaw from the fight, and Visolela demonstrated her desire for his opinion by waving him off after the others.

"Right." Tremaine rubbed the bridge of her nose, gathering her thoughts. This was a chance to tell the whole story, including their side, before Pasima could; it was an opportunity not to be wasted.

Giliead carried Ilias into the house, finding a smaller room off the portico sitting area that had a couch and laying him down on it. He sat next to him, watching until he made sure Ilias was really breathing, that his eyelids flickered in a sign he was near to consciousness.

He realized he was holding his own breath and let it out, feeling the tightness around his heart ease. *Ilias is alive, and the god didn't refuse you.* It would take a little time to really believe it. He could feel the god now, still out in the plaza, disturbed and angry that Herias had attacked him, as baffled by human violence as it always was. It had accepted the knowledge that he had done curses with hardly a ripple in the familiar waters of its mind.

One of Visolela's younger cousins brought a bowl and cloths, setting it on the table beside his knee, and Giliead looked up to realize Halian was standing over him. He looked gray and tired, someone else's blood smeared on the shoulder of his shirt. He said, "I'm sorry I doubted you. I should have known."

Giliead just nodded. It wasn't until just this moment that he realized what he had to say, what he had to do. "There're some things. . . . My copies of the Journals, and Ranior's sword. Both Priases's colts belong to Ilias. I don't know what else. I'll send for it when I know where we'll be."

Halian took his meaning, his face going still. Peripherally Giliead was aware of Cletia slipping out of the room, the cousin hurriedly withdrawing. But after a moment, Halian said nothing; he simply nodded and left.

Tremaine stood out on the portico and told Visolela the whole story. The last thing the woman had heard had been that Halian had gotten a message from the waterpeople to go to the island to pick up Giliead and Ilias. To her credit Visolela listened without interruption, the lines on her face deepening as she frowned, one hand half buried in her dark hair as if trying to suppress a headache. Partway through the story, Cletia came to join them, hovering a little uneasily.

When Tremaine told Visolela that Arites had been killed by the Gardier, the woman winced, but didn't add the recriminations Tremaine felt she deserved. Visolela only asked, "But the others were well when you left them?"

"Until we were separated, yes."

When Tremaine finished, Visolela said with grim finality, "So the riot was started by the Chosen Vessel of Tyros and my father-in-law, during which you held my cousin hostage."

Tremaine shrugged; the riot was the least of her worries. "That's pretty much the case."

Cletia folded her arms, her face set in stubborn lines. "She's a rank-ing woman in my house, she can hold me hostage if she likes."

Visolela eyed her skeptically. "You've changed your tone."

Cletia looked away, uncomfortable. "I changed my mind."

It was Tremaine's turn to eye her skeptically, wishing Cletia would also change her present location. "Could you go to the harbor and tell Gerard we all survived?" she asked.

Cletia nodded sharply, as if grateful to escape Visolela's scrutiny, and headed for the door.

Visolela watched her go, her lips thinning. She said, "When she was still a child, she told her mother she wanted Ilias for her first husband. We told her no, that there were better prospects."

Tremaine felt a distinct stabbing sensation in the gut but didn't let her face change. She said evenly, "I didn't know."

Still looking after Cletia, Visolela shrugged. "Few know. She has al-ways kept her feelings close. Perhaps too close." Grimacing, she shook her head, as if she already regretted the confidence. "All this . . . The god obviously has no objection to it. For the rest, Karima was coming to town this evening anyway, to meet your ship. She can deal with you all."

"Fine." Tremaine took this as the dismissal it was meant to be and went down the portico. Cletia's feelings hadn't changed, she had just grown up and become independent enough of Pasima's influence that she was venturing to show them.

And Visolela did nothing by accident. She had definitely been giv-ing Tremaine a hint of warning. Maybe after the continued harass-ment by the Gardier remaining in the area, Visolela's feeling about the Rienish alliance had changed. Maybe the marriage being a fait ac-compli, she felt it was her duty to support it whatever her personal feelings on the matter.

Still deep in thought, Tremaine went through the room that opened onto the portico, past columns painted with red and black bands. The mosaic floor had stylized waves along the border and flowers and vines entwining through the center panel. She found the small room off the sitting area, where Ilias lay curled on a low couch, Giliead sit-ting next to him. The floor was still a mosaic, a repeat of the pattern of flowers and vines and waves from the larger room, and the walls were painted a dark blue.

Tremaine couldn't see Ilias's face for all the bloody hair but he was starting to twitch and make groaning noises, a sure sign that he was coming around. Giliead had one hand on his shoulder to keep him still. She sat on the cool tile floor beside the couch, asking quietly, "So what happened out there? Did Herias really think you kidnapped the god or something? How would that work?"

He shook his head a little helplessly. "I don't know. He must have worried because it had been gone so long. It had been out at sea, that's all I could tell. It doesn't usually go that far away. It might have been looking for me, or maybe the *Ravenna*, it was hard to tell." He gestured in annoyance, seeming more like himself. "Gods don't get mad often, but when they do they make even less sense than usual."

"But it was mad at Herias, it made that kind of obvious." Tremaine thought that was the important point. She hesitated. "It wasn't upset about the whole spell thing?"

"No." Giliead brushed one of Ilias's braids off his shoulder and Tremaine thought for a moment that that was all he would say. "It knows. As soon as it sees me, it knows everything I know. But it didn't . . . seem to care." He grimaced. "Herias . . . I can't imagine what he thought. He could smell the curses on me. He had to really believe that I'd done something terrible, because he knows as well as I do that the gods hate it when Chosen Vessels fight. We're the only people besides wizards they can really see clearly."

Tremaine frowned, thinking it all over. Gerard had to be right, the connection between the gods, the Chosen Vessels and the wizards was magic, whether any of them wanted to admit it or not. "Why was it looking for the *Ravenna*? If they left Capistown after the attack, they should be here soon, but how does it know that?"

Giliead squeezed his eyes shut for a moment, concentrating, then gave up with a helpless gesture. "I can't tell. It thought the *Ravenna* would be here soon, and that there was trouble aboard."

"Great." Tremaine didn't know how to take that. Did gods worry needlessly like people? Or did it know something?

Ilias groaned and rolled onto his back, then flung out an arm, nearly managing to smack Tremaine in the head. She shifted to the top of the couch, a slightly safer vantage point, as he blinked and opened his eyes. "What . . . Where are we?" He had a dark greenish spot on his forehead that was developing into a really horrendous bruise and dark circles under his eyes.

"The lawgiver's house," Giliead told him, one hand on his chest to keep him from sitting up, which Ilias immediately tried to do.

"What?" Ilias struggled to push himself up on his elbows and

Giliead leaned in, using his greater weight to prevent him. "What are we doing here? Are you crazy?"

"The god showed up and kicked Herias out of town. We won," Tremaine said hastily. "Will you relax?"

"No. I don't care. I don't want to be here." Ilias subsided with a snarl. He touched the bruise and winced, squeezing his eyes shut. "What did you do to Herias?"

"We had a fight," Giliead admitted. "The god stopped it."

Tremaine knew Herias must have thought Giliead was either under a spell or had somehow been corrupted by wizards; he had obviously knocked Ilias out to remove him from the conflict. She could understand the necessity, even if it made rage simmer. Ilias wouldn't have stood by while Herias attacked Giliead, and Herias wouldn't have had a chance against the two of them together. "Doesn't Herias have anybody with him?" she asked.

Giliead shook his head, still absently holding Ilias down, his face pensive. "He did. His younger sister and brother. But they were killed a few years ago."

"Will you get off me?" Ilias demanded.

"Fine." Exasperated, Giliead released him, and Ilias sat up with a lurch, nearly falling off the couch. Tremaine lunged forward in time to catch him, steadying him and plopping down on the couch next to him as Giliead shifted over to make room.

Ilias wrapped an arm around her and buried his face against her shoulder. Tremaine felt a surge of emotion powerful enough to make her grit her teeth, love and affection mixed with a strong anger at Herias, at the stupidity of the Syprians' prejudice, at the wizards that made the prejudice necessary for survival. Until Ilias made an *oof* noise in protest she didn't realize she was squeezing him around the ribs. She swallowed, took a deep breath and said over his head to Giliead, "Visolela said that Karima should be here soon. Nicanor is up the coast, checking out reports of another Gardier bombing at a gleaners' village."

Giliead rubbed his eyes. "I doubt Mother will come here. I told Halian we weren't going back to Andrien."

Tremaine felt Ilias go still. She held her breath and bit her tongue. This wasn't the time for questions. After a moment, Ilias muttered into her shoulder, "Good."

Giliead nodded, looking weary. He added, "We need to talk to a poet."

Tremaine stared, her brows drawing together. "We need to do what?" *Either he's lost his mind or I have.*

But Ilias lifted his head long enough to ask, "About Castines?"

"Oh." Tremaine shook her head at herself. *Right, I've lost my mind.* "About whether Castines was a Syprian? The poets would know?"

Giliead nodded, distracted and thoughtful. "If he was a Syprian wizard, his name might be in the Journals. I don't remember it, but there are so many names, and it's been a long time since I read the earlier accounts." He glanced at Tremaine. "You'll stay here?"

"I will. Go ahead," she told him. He pushed wearily to his feet and she watched him as he stepped out of the room.

Ilias watched him too, worried. "You can go with him," he told Tremaine. His eyes were focused but he still sounded a little vague. "I'll be fine."

Tremaine shook her head. She had realized that no matter how eager she was to pursue the mystery of Castines, this was where she wanted to be.

"Good," he admitted, and slumped over to rest his head in her lap. Absently she picked at one of his braids, thinking of when Nicholas had said Ilias might do something to Ander out of jealousy. But Nicholas had been wrong. Ilias came from a society where polygamy was normal; he didn't see Ander as a threat, except possibly to Tremaine's sanity and temper. *No, I'm the one who comes from the place where people kill for jealousy,* Tremaine thought.

She could see why. It did seem the most expedient method of dealing with the situation. She buried her face in her hands.

Stop that.

Chapter 14

"Y ou sure it's here, miss?" The big Parscian sailor was actually one of the engineering officers, but he wasn't wearing his uniform jacket and his white undershirt was as covered with boiler room grime as that of any of the ordinary seamen. Florian wouldn't have known he was an officer at all, if the woman sailor following behind her, armed with a large heavy wrench, hadn't called him "sir." He flashed a torch up into the dark maze of pipes overhead, raising his voice to be heard over the constant hum of machinery. "The others jumped out at us as soon as we were close enough."

Dark machine shapes rose up around them on all sides, hemming in the narrow walkway, and Florian wasn't even sure where they were anymore. Circulating pumps, condensers, turbines, switchboards, it was all the same to her. Florian found the *Ravenna*'s engine rooms and other inner workings more unnerving than the long empty corridors; they were all either too hot or too cold, and with all the noise, something could easily creep up behind you. There were also infinitely more crannies to hide in.

She held a small metal bowl with a fragment of wood floating in it, a quick locator spell that Niles had made for all the searchers. The wood held a drop of the gooey substance that had been all that was left of the contents of Ixion's vat. That is, the contents that hadn't escaped and were now rampaging around the ship. Her attention split between the floating splinter and the heavy pipes above them, Florian said, "This one's been out longer than the others, I think, and I'm a little afraid they get smarter the longer they're—" The wood spun, twirling into the center of its own little waterspout in the bowl; she yelped, "Look out!"

They had an instant to brace themselves as something gray and scaly with three eyes and a profusion of teeth leapt silently out of the shadows above. The water slopping on her hands, Florian flung herself out of the way, muttering the illusion charm she had prepared. Fortunately the creatures were as susceptible to illusions as people, and a lot less likely to see through the deception. The creature huddled on the walkway for a startled moment, believing itself inexplicably trapped by metal walls, giving the officer a chance to throw a canvas bag over it and the sailor to leap forward and pound it with a wrench.

Prior experience had taught them to wait until green fluid actually leaked out through the canvas. The officer found a prybar and poked the bag over, until they could see that the thing's head had been smashed. Then he gathered it up with a sigh.

"Join the Rienish navy," the woman sailor remarked, watching this process with distaste. "See unusual sights. Never sleep with the lights out again."

"This is nothing," the officer told the woman wryly, holding the bag out at arm's length. "You should have seen the man-thing with the crystals all over it. They're still finding bits of him."

Florian grimaced. "Sorry about that." She consulted the locator spell again, frowning absently. "I think that's it for this area. I guess we can go back up now and see how the others are doing."

The temporary headquarters for the search was one of the crew dining rooms. The whitewashed compartment was much smaller than the passenger dining areas, low-ceilinged, with little in the way of decoration, but it had chairs to sit in and tables to spread out maps of the ship, and it was near the storage room where Ixion had been allowed to set up his vat. Now it was more than half full of crewmen in various stages of dishevelment from killing Ixion's creatures.

Florian left her team to dispose of the creature's body and to grab a quick drink from the serving counter—Captain Marais had doubled the wine-and-spirits ration for the duration of the search—while she took a seat at the table with Niles. "Another one?" he asked her, marking it off on his chart. "Very good. I think we must have gotten most of them. There can't be more than three or four left. Once Kressein finishes his examination of the vat, we should know exactly how many were released."

"Good." Florian pushed sweat-soaked hair out of her eyes. It felt as if they had been doing this forever; she had no idea if it was day or night outside.

Nicholas, a long trail of green slime on the shoulder of his dark coat, took a seat opposite them. "Two," he told Niles, pulling one of the maps over to indicate the spot. "In the Number 5 Boiler Room. The engineering mate tells me we should do the tunnels that house the engine shafts next, and that that will be, in his words, a nightmare." He lifted a brow at Florian. "Florian, I believe you wanted more responsibility?"

She nodded, her mouth twisted ruefully. "I'll take the engine shafts."

Niles frowned at her. "Have you still got that turnback in your stomach? Do you have the ipecac I gave you?"

Florian grimaced at the memory. That, at least, was one problem she didn't have anymore. "No, the first time I saw one of the vat-things close-up, I got ill and it came up without help." She looked up as Kressein, the Capidaran Ministry sorcerer, entered the room, wiping his hands off on a towel. The old man was coatless, his gray hair tied back and his shirtsleeves rolled up, revealing thin arms corded with long stringy muscles and marked by scars from what were probably old alchemy experiments. Florian caught a whiff of carbolic as he walked up to the table. "There were thirty-two of them." Kressein handed the towel off to the quiet apprentice who followed him, then leaned wearily on the back of a chair. "He obviously meant to set them loose on the ship. What I don't understand is why."

"Because that is one of the things that Syprian sorcerers do," Nicholas answered, a little impatiently. "Giliead described the process in detail. The sorcerer approaches some small community on the outer edges of a god's protection, either in hiding or in disguise. He creates curselings to reduce the population to an acceptable level, casts spells on the rest to enslave them, then takes them away out of any god's reach before help can arrive. Eventually they all die or he tires of the game and kills them, then he goes off to look for trouble somewhere else." He made a careless gesture. "Syprian sorcerers learn their craft by apprenticing themselves to madmen. Presumably the ones who survive the process without losing their sanity escape to take up some more sensible occupation."

"Yes, Gerard had explained that, and Florian had already indicated some earlier suspicions of Ixion as well," Niles said, going back to his chart.

Kressein, turning to go, added dryly, "It's too bad Lord Chandre chose not to listen."

Contemplating another cup of coffee before she collected her crew and went out hunting again, Florian watched Niles cross off sections on the map. But maybe it was better to get it over with as quickly as possible. Nicholas was just getting up to leave when a crewman, his coat torn and his hat missing, hurried over to their table, telling Niles, "Sir, they want you to come down to the hospital immediately. A Capidaran soldier got mauled by one of those things on D deck." He wiped at the blood on his neck, wincing. "Almost got all of us."

"D deck?" Niles pushed to his feet, brow furrowed. "It must have gotten past our barrier. Did you kill the creature?"

The man nodded. "Yes, the sorcerer there got it."

Niles accepted that with a nod, preoccupied with gathering up his bag, but Nicholas frowned, looking around the room. A moment later Florian realized what he was looking for. "Sorcerer?" she asked, worried. Niles, Avrain, Kevari, Kressein and his apprentice. . . . "What sorcerer? They're all here."

Niles stopped, blinked and faced the crewman, demanding, "What did this sorcerer look like?"

The crewman gestured in confusion, obviously not expecting this question. "Tall, thin, white-haired, nice enough fellow but a little vague—" He stared as Niles and Nicholas bolted for the door. Florian shoved her chair back and hurried after them.

Giliead left the lawgiver's house through the dining portico at the back of the atrium, which opened into a small outer court facing the street behind the house. He wanted to avoid meeting anyone but after the fight in the plaza it was impossible; everyone who hadn't participated was now out in the streets trying to find out what had happened. He nodded to polite greetings but didn't stop for questions, making his way through the dusty streets to a white clay-walled house at the base of the nearest granary hill.

Bythia's younger son opened the door, stepping back and smiling, wiping his hands on the tail of his shirt. "Giliead. We heard you were back. But the big ship isn't in the harbor?"

"No, she's not here yet." Giliead stepped inside, glad to avoid any more difficult questions. Bythia's house was far enough from the plaza that the noise of the fight wouldn't have reached it, but the news would have been carried here immediately.

The front room was cool, the walls painted dark green, with an archway opening into a small atrium with a crowded vegetable patch. Giliead could smell baking bread and suddenly remembered they had been short enough of food this morning to consider howler meat. It seemed a world away.

The boy led him along the narrow portico, to an open room where Bythia sat beside a low table spread with scrolls and parchments, littered with pens and ink cups. On top of the pile of scrolls was a drawing someone had done of the *Ravenna*, trying to show how large she was by contrasting her with the lighthouse and one of the war galleys. It looked oddly flat to his eyes, after having seen the way the Rienish drew such things.

Bythia was a small neat woman with long white hair, dressed in a blue cotton shift, her still-handsome face lined with age. She held out a hand to him, smiling a greeting. "Giliead. I'm hearing the strangest stories of a fight in the plaza. Is Ilias all right?"

"He's fine." Knowing poets, he suspected Bythia knew far more about what had happened than just rumors. He took a seat as she sent the boy away to bring wine and some of the fresh bread. As she faced Giliead again, her eyes bright with anticipation of hearing his adventures, he knew what he had really come for. He took her hand and said, "Bythia, Arites is dead."

Bythia had been Arites's teacher when he had first decided to be a poet. When Giliead had told her the story and she had wiped her tears away, she said, "He saw the Walls of the World, Gil. If you had asked him if he would give up his life for that, he would have said yes."

I would have made sure not to ask him if I'd had the choice, Giliead thought. He just shook his head, looking away, and told her about the Aelin they had found, and the fortress and what he had come here for.

"Castines," she repeated thoughtfully when he had finished. "Twenty or so years ago. That would have been when Aricadia was Matriarch in Syrneth and Doliead was her poet. But we don't know where he was from?"

"We don't know if he was even Syprian or not."

"Yes. And you know the wizards don't all end up mentioned in the Journals. Well, having a rough idea of the time helps." She sat back in her chair, studying the wall of scrolls thoughtfully. "I'll start looking for it now."

"Thank you." Giliead pushed reluctantly to his feet.

Bythia stretched out a hand, halting him. Looking up at him with concern, her eyes still red from weeping, she said, "Careful, Giliead. There's a story Arites and I always dreaded to tell, and I know I'd rather put it off as long as possible."

He nodded, though he couldn't help the slight twist in his smile. "I'd rather put it off too, believe me."

The boy walked out with him, pausing on the door stoop to wave.

Walking down the street, distracted, Giliead took moments to realize the god was trailing along after him, a haze of pinpoint lights stirring a flurry of dust in its wake. He stopped abruptly, staring at it in consternation, as it climbed the grape arbor framing the doorway of the nearest house and clung to the shadows under the vines. Startled, he said, "What's wrong?" then glanced up and down the street self-consciously. Only very new Chosen Vessels spoke to the gods aloud, but fortunately nobody was in earshot.

The god was already trying to push an image at him and after a moment of concentration he had it: a view from the stern of the *Ravenna*, as the ship sailed across a choppy day-lit sea, puffs of white cloud streaming up from her three chimneys. The image also conveyed distance, and that it was not something the god had seen itself. There was a confusing jumble of impressions attached to it, and even once he managed to sort them out, they made no sense. Flashes of one of the *Ravenna*'s beautiful wood-paneled rooms, light and garbled sound, one clear picture of Florian's startled face.

Florian's alive. Giliead's heart leapt. The only way the god could have seen this was if it had touched the mind of someone on the *Ravenna*, which meant all their friends were hopefully safe and heading this way. The god was only supposed to be able to touch the mind of a Chosen Vessel, but . . . *A lot of things aren't what we think they are,* he reflected grimly.

Trying to ask the god how and why it knew this just got him the same jumble of images again, but then the god was never good on questions that started with how or why. Leaving the god settled comfortably in the grapevine, he started down the street again, relieved to have good news to report for once.

*   *   *

Visolela had extended a grudging invitation for Tremaine, Ilias and Giliead and the others to stay in the lawgiver's house. But Ilias refused point-blank, Giliead looked horrified at the prospect and even Cletia seemed less than thrilled. Tremaine, finding herself relegated to the unaccustomed role of the tactful one, had explained that there was no room for the Aelin and that they should all stay together.

Tremaine wasn't sure what other options there were. She knew there was nothing like a hotel; apparently the closest equivalents were a couple of establishments on the edge of the city that were basically caravansaries that catered to traders. According to Cimarus, the only member of the immediate group who was actually trying to be helpful, neither would be large enough to accommodate the Aelin either. Tremaine was beginning to wonder if she could get somebody to rent her a warehouse on account; anything of value she had to trade had been left back in Capistown or on the *Ravenna*.

But Visolela, apparently fed up with the situation and anxious to be rid of them, offered the home of one of the less influential branches of her family, packing the current inhabitants off to stay at the lawgiver's house or with other relatives. Tremaine, relieved, had accepted immediately.

The house, which was down toward the harbor and near the edge of town, was apparently only a few streets uphill from the beach and the boat sheds for the war galleys. *Not exactly the best spot to be in case of Gardier attack,* Tremaine reflected wryly. *Near a prime target. Is that Visolela's nonexistent sense of humor?* Still, the Gardier hadn't fired on the galleys in their first attack, only on the fishing boats and merchant craft tied up at the docks; she wasn't sure they realized the fastest and most dangerous Syprian vessels were stored out of the water in the long narrow sheds. Apparently only the galleys needed to defend the city were still here anyway; the others had been moved to less obvious coves along the coast.

The long twilight had fallen by the time Gerard, the Aelin and the Capidarans had been fetched and they all reached the house together. The day's heat had settled into a comfortable warmth and it was a quiet part of town with big trees leaning over courtyard walls to shade the street. The house's entrance was just another wooden door in a white clay-covered wall. But once Giliead opened it and they walked into a large cool tiled foyer that led into a brick-paved court with a fountain and flowering trees, Tremaine decided it would be ideal. The rest of the house rambled off to the back and both sides, much larger than it had appeared from the street.

"Well, this should do nicely." Gerard, with his shirtsleeves rolled up and his coat long abandoned, motioned for the Aelin to hurry in. He looked frazzled from the long day and Tremaine knew that keeping the badly overstimulated Aelin together, even with the help of Aras and Vervane, had not been easy.

"Hard day?" she asked, as he did a quick head count of the Aelin who were milling in the court, pointing and exclaiming appreciatively. A couple of the older men helped Elon in. The younger children had already leapt into the fountain.

"Not really," he admitted. "There was an open-air tavern establishment that was quite accommodating under the circumstances, and Halian was very helpful." He glanced down at her, wiping the sweat from his brow. Ilias passed through the foyer just then. He had recovered quickly, though Tremaine suspected he still had a raging headache. Except for the bruises and the dried blood, he looked normal. In fact, she thought the blow to the face had actually straightened his nose a little. He disappeared into the bowels of the house with the air of someone who didn't want to discuss anything. "I suspect you had a much harder time."

"It had its moments," Tremaine agreed ruefully. She shut the heavy wooden door, wishing they could just forget about the Gardier, forget about Ile-Rien, shut the world out and stay here forever. Even if they had to live with twenty-odd noisy and wildly curious Aelin. "So Halian was with you?"

"Yes, I was surprised, I thought he would be anxious to catch up with Giliead and Ilias."

"They had a . . . disagreement. Giliead said he and Ilias aren't going back to Andrien." She took a deep breath. "I don't know. Karima's on her way here."

Gerard looked weary for a moment, the lines around his mouth more pronounced. "I see."

Gerard located a room with a door and retreated with his notebook and the sphere to work on etheric calculations. Aras had retired to sleep, Vervane was looking after the still-recovering Meretrisa, but Tremaine found herself unable to settle anywhere. She wandered the house, finding it had large rooms, with mosaic or tiled floors, and another atrium toward the back, with a cistern, vegetable patch and flower beds. All the personal possessions had been removed, though from the dusty corners and the arrangement of the remaining furniture—couches, wide beds and the low tables Syprians preferred—Tremaine thought most of it had been unoccupied anyway. The empty corners smelled of wool and incense, and the dried herbs the Syprians stored their clothes in. Maybe this was the house Visolela, Pasima and their other brothers and sisters had occupied as children, before everyone had grown up and gone away to their own establishments. It made a contrast to the Andrien family house, where instead of growing up and out, the family had dwindled through death and disaster, so despite all the marriages and births the comfortable old house still had plenty of room for visitors. Now thoroughly depressed, she made her way back to the atrium.

The sky was blue purple now and crickets sang in the trees. Shrieking children ran through the rooms opening onto the portico. Obelin, Eliva and the other older Aelin had brought couches out onto the grass and were basking in the warm twilight, still a little dazed by their abrupt change in circumstance. One of the older boys was moving along the portico, lighting the olive oil lamps with careful concentration. Tremaine found her way down to the kitchen, a big plain clay-walled room at the end of the garden.

Giliead was there, building a fire in the cooking hearth, and Ilias was sitting on a stool, helping by poking randomly at the kindling with a stick. Cletia was hovering, arms folded, chin set stubbornly, while Davret and two other Aelin girls and a boy were unpacking baskets of food, handling the rounds of brown bread and goat cheese curiously. Balin was there too, poking through a basket, and Cimarus was leaning in the doorway, apparently guarding her. The Gardier woman was wearing one of the Aelin's bright-patterned scarves around her neck. "Dinner?" Tremaine asked hopefully, the sight of the food making her aware how hungry she was.

"Visolela sent some food over." Giliead jerked his head toward the baskets the Aelin were unpacking. He sat back on his knees, having gotten the fire started despite Ilias's help.

"That was unexpectedly nice of her," Tremaine said dryly. Ilias snorted amusement, then winced and gingerly touched his nose.

"They should throw a festival for us," Cimarus put in suddenly. As everyone regarded him with varying degrees of doubt, he bristled a little. "We made a great voyage—not that we had a ship for the last part—but the poets will tell stories about us."

"Maybe so," Giliead agreed with a shrug, not sounding enthused by the prospect. Ilias, apparently on the verge of regaining his sense of humor, poked him with the stick instead of the kindling.

Davret lifted a hunk of cheese, wondering, "How do you cook this?"

"You don't have to, you can eat it the way it is," Tremaine told her.

"Ah." She waved to get Ilias's attention. "Name this?" she said in halting Syrnaic.

Tremaine lifted her brows as he told Davret the Syrnaic word for cheese. He caught her eye, smiled faintly and said, "They don't have a problem with learning our language."

Davret listened to this exchange carefully, as if trying to puzzle out the words. She told Tremaine in Aelin, "You've said we can't go back, and after what happened when the Gardier came, and what Balin has told us, we all know it to be true. We discussed it this afternoon and wish to stay here. They have trading clans, or something like it. We saw at the port today."

Balin, a bag of green fruit sitting forgotten in her lap, stared. "These people are savages," she protested, blank with astonishment.

Davret made a derisive noise and the other Aelin gave Balin admonishing looks. "Don't be rude," Davret said. "They have goods, they trade them and trade knowledge along the way. That's not savage. That's what we do. Or what we're supposed to do."

"What are they saying?" Ilias asked. The Syprians were watching Balin's shocked reaction with interest.

"They want political asylum," Tremaine said. At Ilias's upraised brows, she clarified, "They want to stay here."

Giliead shrugged. This was obviously one problem that he didn't consider his. "That's fine."

Cletia frowned, not sure if this was a joke or not. "They're Gardier."

"It's dangerous to travel here," Tremaine told Davret in Aelin, feeling they should at least be warned. "There are bad sorcerers who kill people, and monsters. And the Gardier might attack here too, if we don't stop them at Ile-Rien."

"You mean we might end up trapped in a stone prison for twenty years?" the Aelin boy interposed, wide-eyed, before Davret could answer. "Oh, no!"

Tremaine stared at him, then laughed so hard she had to support herself on the wall. Davret and the other Aelin girls collapsed in hilarity, leaving Balin uncertain and a little affronted. Cletia was frowning while Ilias, Giliead and Cimarus impatiently demanded to know the joke, when the Syprians abruptly went silent.

Tremaine looked to see Halian and Karima standing in the doorway. *Ouch,* she thought. Karima only had eyes for Giliead, and the look on her face was like a punch to the stomach.

Giliead stood, absently brushing his hands off, his face closed and impossible to read. He threw a glance down at Ilias that drew him reluctantly to his feet.

Tremaine meant to stay in the kitchen and tell the Aelin about cheese. She had spent a great deal of her life avoiding emotional confrontations and she didn't want to be a part of this one. But Ilias caught her arm as he passed, pulling her out onto the portico after him.

The atrium was cloaked in blue twilight, the flickering lamps on the pillars making it seem even darker. Tremaine stepped out after Ilias in time to hear Karima say, "It's never mattered. You know none of it ever mattered."

Tremaine winced again, wishing she could edge off into the shadows and make her escape, but Ilias was still holding her hand. He had stopped in the shadow just outside the kitchen door so she couldn't see his face, but she could feel the tension in his arm, hard as a rock and tight as piano wire. The Aelin had sensed the charged atmosphere and all seemed to be finding things to do in other parts of the house. Eliva had gotten up to herd the children away.

Giliead stopped by the nearest pillar, his face caught in the lamplight. He shook his head, not looking at her. "The *Ravenna* is coming back. The god can see her somehow, feel her coming. When she gets here we'll go to the other world again, to Ile-Rien, to help free their wizards. I don't know what will happen, what I'll have to do. If we come back, everything will be different. Everyone will know I've used curses—"

Karima put a hand on his arm, her face drawn and urgent. "The god accepted you. That's all that matters."

"That's not all that matters," Giliead said, his teeth gritted.

"This is all my fault." Halian's voice was hard, but the pain under it made Tremaine's head hurt. "If I—"

"No." Giliead looked at him directly for the first time. Tremaine knew that even if Giliead wouldn't admit it, Halian's reaction to the story on the ship this morning had wounded him to the core. "But I know how people will react. Many of them are still afraid of the *Ravenna* and the Rienish. Once they know what I've done, they won't accept me, even if the god does." His expression softened as he looked down at Karima. "I don't want to bring that down on you, on Andrien House. Not after everything else."

Tremaine knew he meant his sister, and Halian's daughter and Ilias's cousin, the women of the family who had all been killed by Ixion. The curse that had lived in the house until Gerard had rooted it out on their first visit here. "We've weathered everything else, we can weather this," Karima said, suddenly angry. "It's our choice—"

"It's not your choice to make." Giliead gestured impatiently, angry now too.

"Herias accused him of doing something to the god, Karima," Ilias put in reluctantly. "If Herias can think that, what will everyone else think?"

Giliead persisted, "It's time, and you know it. I've been there too long as it is. Ilias is married now, and you know I never will. It's time we left."

Karima tried to stare him down, her mouth set in a thin line. "Chosen Vessels have married before."

Giliead lifted his brows. "Chosen Vessels who did curses?"

Karima glared, then took a sharp breath and looked away.

Giliead said again, quietly, "It's time."

Tremaine rocked on her heels, watching the moths flit around the lamps, until Karima said, "Do you agree?" She didn't realize the question had been addressed to her until Ilias nudged her with an elbow.

"Oh, what? Yes, sure." Tremaine nodded rapidly.

Karima was still looking at her in the darkness. "Where will you stay?"

"Here, until the *Ravenna* arrives. After that—" She could feel Ilias watching her, willing her not to point out that they might not come back. "After that I don't know."

Karima nodded reluctantly, resigned. "There's no reason to be strangers to us." Her voice was thick but she made herself sound firm. "I'll stay in town until the *Ravenna* comes back with Gyan and Kias. Send someone to me when you come back from Ile-Rien." She stumbled over the name, and Tremaine realized that nobody needed to tell Karima that there was a strong possibility that they wouldn't return.

They walked Karima and Halian to the front gate, and Karima hugged Giliead, Ilias, then Tremaine, so hard Tremaine feared for her ribs. She had the feeling that Karima had just passed the responsibility for her son and her foster son's well-being to Tremaine. It was an emotional reality this time, and not just a means to an end as it had been at the wedding. Halian hugged them too, then he and Karima left for the walk back up to the lawgiver's house.

Giliead leaned in the doorway, watching them go, and Ilias pulled Tremaine into an embrace, burying his face in her hair. She took a deep breath, trying to think of something to say. In the end, all she said was, "Was there wine in those jars in the kitchen? Let's drink it."

They ended up down on the stretch of wide sandy beach, near the boat sheds. The moon wasn't quite full, but it was bright enough to illuminate the white sand and the foam cresting the rolling waves. The boat sheds were guarded by four or five young men and women who stayed within the light of their shielded lamps, watching with wary bemusement.

A wineskin slung over her shoulder, Tremaine stood up above the water line, her bare feet in the still-warm sand, watching as Ilias tackled Giliead into a large breaking wave. The wind was cool, tugging at her hair, and she just hoped the two men weren't drunk enough to drown each other. Starting to feel mildly euphoric herself, she doubted her ability to navigate the waves without falling over, let alone haul anyone out. The younger Aelin had followed them, and were running in and out of the shallow surf, shrieking with delight at the water, at the foam, at finding shells with little creatures still inhabiting them. They were acting as if they had never seen open water before today, let alone played in waves, which of course they hadn't. The ones who had been children when Castines betrayed them would have seen the seas of their home, but that must be a dim memory now. Tremaine kept trying to do a head count of the smaller ones, mindful of the giant crabs the Syprians hunted for food, but Ilias had assured her that those creatures would flee from people.

She could see the lighthouse up on the promontory from here, the blazing fire on the top platform of the pyramid a guide for any ships coming in. It would also be a guide for invading Gardier, but Visolela had told them that a few days after the *Ravenna* had left, the god had begun to inform Herias whenever it sensed Gardier within range of the coast. Gods couldn't usually detect activity by Syprian sorcerers unless it was fairly close; apparently they learned quickly how to avoid drawing the gods' attention, or they didn't live long. The god's ability to detect Gardier was an advantage the Syprians were going to need.

The Gardier here were still just the remnants of the force that had occupied the Isle of Storms and the ships that had arrived to relieve them. The *Ravenna* had destroyed one vessel before leaving Cineth but they knew now there was at least one more. They had no airships yet, but some would surely arrive soon, when the Gardier had subdued Ile-Rien to the point that they could remove the blockade on the coast and send those ships to this world.

Tremaine heard someone behind her and glanced around to see Gerard strolling down the beach, still without his jacket, his hands in his pockets and the moonlight glinting off his spectacles. She shifted the wineskin off her shoulder and handed it to him as he stopped beside her.

He took a drink and coughed. "There are many beautiful things here, but I have to admit, their wine is not one of them," he choked out.

"It's mostly water and some kind of spice. You have to drink a lot of it," she advised him.

Gerard made a disgruntled noise and handed it back. "Cimarus told me they broke with Karima and Halian. I was rather hoping that wouldn't happen."

Cimarus and Cletia hadn't followed them down to the beach, for which Tremaine was grateful. Cimarus had still been nominally in charge of making sure Balin didn't kill anybody, and Cletia, after Cimarus had glared at her and cleared his throat pointedly in brotherly rebuke, had stayed behind. "It wasn't quite that bad. Giliead just told them that he won't be going home to Andrien afterward." She ran both hands through her hair, scratching vigorously. "When the *Ravenna* gets here . . . I've still got those gold coins in the safe. If there's time before we leave, I should buy a house or something." She hadn't discussed this with anyone yet, as she was still tentative about the whole idea. But the more she thought about it the more it seemed like the right thing. "It would give the Aelin a place to stay until they figure out what they're going to do. And if we make it, it would be good for Ilias and Gil to have someplace to come back to."

"And you?" Gerard asked quietly.

Tremaine took a deep breath, feeling the wine thrumming through her veins but not clouding her head. The Aelin teenagers were splashing in knee-deep surf, their clothes soaked. She recognized Davret from her laugh but she didn't know the others well enough to pick them out in the moonlight. The younger children were digging holes in the sand and trying to bury each other. *In a way, you've been planning this since you first saw Cineth.* It was impossible, and probably crazy, and she knew what she would be letting herself in for. But when she thought of going back to Coldcourt, if it was still there at all, and carrying on as if nothing had happened, Nicholas's presence or absence notwithstanding, she knew what she had to do. And she wasn't giving Ilias up to Cletia. "And me," she told Gerard.

He nodded. "I see." She thought he might argue, or list all the obvious disadvantages, but he didn't. He was still looking toward the water and she saw he was watching as Giliead and Ilias wandered up the beach toward them, weaving a little. Giliead paused to rescue an Aelin girl who was getting buried a little too deeply, pulling her out of the sand and brushing her off. "I suppose there are really no firm plans to be made until after we deal with the Lodun situation. That will completely change the character of the war."

Tremaine nodded, wishing she was a little more drunk. *For the better or for the worse,* she thought, understanding intimately for the first time why some people were so afraid of change. They would either gain the upper hand over the Gardier or give them an easier victory, and her stomach wanted to turn at the thought. "I— Oh, no, don't you—" Lost in dark thoughts, she hadn't noticed that Ilias's unsteady progress was a trick until he darted forward and grabbed her around the waist.

Hauled down toward the surf despite protests and struggling, she had to be content with the impotent statement "You're going to get it later!"

"Promise?" Ilias replied, laughing, and dived into a wave with her.

Tremaine had just enough time to hold her breath as they went under, but as he pulled her to her feet, she faked coughing and sputtering. But she was still too tipsy to fake it well, and he just gave her a long salt-water-tinged kiss. As soaked and dripping as he was, Tremaine leaned against him, and it was just cool enough for her to feel his warmth through the wet shirt and pants plastered to his body. Breaking the kiss as another wave washed around them, he spoiled it by nuzzling her ear and saying, "You needed a bath. Everyone agreed."

"You're as big an ass as Giliead," Tremaine told him, winding both hands in his hair and pulling his head down again.

A sound, booming across the harbor like some great bass-voiced giant, made them both flinch. "What the—" Tremaine began, then she recognized it. Gerard was already waving frantically from the beach, Giliead was looking out to the harbor and the Aelin had frozen in place like startled rabbits. "That's the *Ravenna!*"

It was sometime later that Tremaine stood on the stone docks near the Arcade and saw the battery lamps on one of the *Ravenna*'s covered lifeboats crossing the harbor toward them. A moment later she heard the diesel chug of its engine. "Finally," she muttered.

"They must have anchored fairly far out from the harbor mouth," Ilias said, watching the approaching lights intently.

He was more sober too, as was Giliead, who added, "Makes sense. She needs room to maneuver if the Gardier come after her."

Tremaine was also more sober but still barefoot, her feet covered with sand, and her clothes were still damp, though no longer dripping. Gerard hadn't bothered to retrieve his coat and with his few days' growth of beard he looked a little rakish, like a desert island survivor. Standing a short distance away with a few of their followers were Visolela, Cletia and Pella, the lawgiver's deputy. Cimarus was still back at the house guarding Balin, and they had decided to let the Capidarans sleep. The other group was far enough away that no one had to make awkward small talk, not that Pella would have spoken to them anyway.

Behind them on the harbor front, a small crowd had gathered, many of them merchants or sailors who lived nearby or on their boats, hoping to see the *Ravenna*. As they were about most everything, the Syprians were of two minds about the great ship, with one faction superstitiously afraid of it and the other fascinated by it. It was members of the latter group who had gathered in the harbor tonight, and some had brought pillows and blankets, ready to camp out all night for a glimpse of the ship at dawn. Tremaine was reminded of the people who had practically lived at the stage door of the opera and the bigger theaters, hoping to see their favorite performers come and go.

The dark shape of the lifeboat drew closer, the light revealing the people standing in the bow. "It's Florian and Nicholas," Ilias said, giving her a relieved smile.

"And Gyan and Kias and the others," Giliead added, sounding as if that was a great load off his shoulders.

Tremaine felt a tight little knot somewhere in her heart relax. *The god was right.* The boat was about forty feet long, painted gray to match the *Ravenna*'s war camouflage, its canvas canopy meant to protect the occupants if it had to travel a long way to reach safety. It looked oddly prosaic next to the painted Syprian galleys and fishing boats.

"Thank God," Gerard said, and turned to help Ilias and Giliead light the torches along an empty stretch of the dock to guide the boat in.

Tremaine waited impatiently as it drew near, waving back when Florian spotted them and waved wildly from the bow. The boat bumped the dock and Ilias caught the rope one of the seamen tossed him and Giliead helped tie it off. Florian was already trying to climb out and Tremaine caught her arm, hauling her up. Florian hugged her tightly, saying in a rush, "We knew you were all right, Arisilde told us."

Ready to demand answers to a dozen questions, Tremaine sputtered to a halt. "Who told you?"

Gerard, in the middle of giving Nicholas a hand up onto the dock, stared in shock. "What?"

Florian answered but Pasima, Sanior and Danias had already climbed out the stern and were noisily being welcomed by Visolela, Cletia and the others and Tremaine couldn't hear what she said. Kias and Gyan had followed Nicholas out, and in the confusion of their greeting, Gyan clapped Ilias on the shoulder and explained happily, "Their god took human form and destroyed Ixion."

"What?" It was Giliead's turn to stare.

"We've had some interesting developments," Nicholas said dryly, cutting through the babble of voices. "I think you'll want to come back to the ship with us."

Chapter 15

Wincing at the bright lights, Ilias followed Tremaine down the *Ravenna*'s wood-walled corridor. After days of firelight, candlelight and the little floaty puffs of wizard light that Gerard used, he had forgotten how harsh even the *Ravenna*'s glass-covered curse lights could be when you came in from the night.

The outer part of the ship was shrouded in darkness and curses to keep the Gardier from seeing her from the air. They had survived the perilous act of being in a small boat winched up the wall of the great ship to the boat deck one more time, then blundered through the dark to a hatch, following a sailor with a small curse light. Tremaine, intent on their goal, had practically jittered with impatience the whole way, and Florian was just as excited. Ilias wasn't so sure he was looking forward to this. He threw a worried look up at Giliead, who was frowning in thought as he listened to Gerard and Niles.

Gerard was shaking his head, frowning. "But what did he do?"

Niles sighed with the air of a man who had been asked that question far too many times. They had gotten through the explanation of Ixion's being let loose on the ship to make curselings on some flimsy pretext and Arisilde leaving the god-sphere to save Florian and Nicholas and the others, but they still weren't clear on what had happened to Ixion. "We're not certain. He hasn't really said, and Ixion—I suppose he could be faking, but—"

"I don't believe he's faking." Nicholas, dressed in black and trailing them like a sinister storm cloud, had a dry little preoccupied smile.

Giliead lifted a brow, doubtful, but Ilias knew that Nicholas was as unlikely to be fooled by Ixion's games as Tremaine.

They turned through a half-lit foyer lined with stacked furniture, their steps oddly muffled by the dark-patterned carpet. Ilias saw the big double doors, padded with leather embossed with a design of squares and circles, that led to the ballroom where the ship's curse circle lived. Something about the place gave him prickles up the spine even without Giliead's ability to smell curses.

Still flushed from excitement, Florian fumbled in a pocket, bringing out a ring of Rienish keys, saying, "He's shown up other places today but mostly he's—"

A click inside the door made Ilias start slightly. He stepped back hastily with the others as the two doors swung slowly open. Cold air wafted out, the same damp chill that shades brought. "Here," Florian finished. Tremaine plunged into the shadowy expanse beyond without hesitation, Florian only a step behind her. Gerard and Niles followed, still deep in conversation, and Nicholas after them.

Giliead and Ilias exchanged a wary look. Giliead had a weary "here we go again" expression. Ilias agreed; Arisilde had been easier to accept when he had just acted like a particularly idiosyncratic god, trapped in a little metal ball or not.

Bracing himself, Ilias followed Giliead inside.

The cut-glass sculptures that surrounded the curse lights were lit but the room was still dark, shadows clinging to walls cloaked with wood and rich red drapes, the red-enameled pillars. The curse circle the *Ravenna* used to take her between worlds was painted onto the marble floor, encompassing most of the room.

The spectral cold raised tiny bumps on his arms but Ilias couldn't see anything different from the last time they had come to this room. The others stood near the edge of the curse circle, looking around expectantly. Tremaine radiated tension, her arms tightly folded. He glanced at Giliead, wondering if the new human god would appear after all, and saw Giliead had his head cocked, listening intently, a faint frown on his face. The silence seemed as supernatural as the cold, so palpable that even the constant distant rumble of the *Ravenna*'s insides was inaudible.

"You found some more pieces. I thought you would."

Ilias whipped around, backing into Giliead. The voice had come from just above his left ear. He found himself facing a tall thin man, dressed in Rienish clothing, though it was ragged and the worse for wear. He had white hair and very odd eyes. But the oddest thing was that his form seemed faintly translucent; there seemed no weight at all to that light body. Ilias stared, only realizing he had frozen in place when Giliead took his shoulders and shifted him off the foot he had stamped on. His only consolation was that everyone else had flinched violently as well, even those who had seen Arisilde manifest before.

Tremaine stepped forward, moving to Ilias's side, fascinated. "What pieces, Uncle Ari?"

"Pieces of the puzzle." He shook his head, a faint smile playing about nearly colorless lips. "Questions can be difficult, as I seem to be missing pieces myself. I think I put some bits of my memories into different parts of the sphere for safekeeping, and then you know what happened."

"When Ixion destroyed the sphere," Niles explained quietly.

"Yes, we didn't like that, it gave us all quite a fright." Arisilde looked quizzically at Ilias, then at Giliead. He said gently, "I should have liked to tell you not to worry. It thinks the world of you, you know, and wouldn't let a little thing like a spell or two get in the way. It does understand the difference between magic used in a benevolent fashion and magic for gain or ill."

Ilias looked up at Giliead, startled. Giliead blinked, his face still, a red flush creeping up his neck. Tremaine said urgently, "You mean the god, Arisilde? Our god? Cineth's god?"

"I made the wall because I felt I was being followed. But I was wrong, you know. Or right, actually. Just not the way I thought I was," Arisilde explained earnestly, though the answer had nothing to do with her question. "You know, if you destroy the master, you free the slaves. But the whole structure will collapse as well. I shouldn't have minded it, you know. Being stuck there. Wander around a bit, meet new people, if I survived the fall. Certainly would have saved us all a lot of trouble. But I didn't realize it was the crystal that was important, and not the bodies, until it was too late. And then I had to leave my body there. I know, silly of me. You go and do it then. I'll come and get you when you're done." That odd violet gaze settled on Tremaine. "You found my boat, you and Gerard, that was clever. Remember, that was three o'clock tomorrow afternoon."

Ilias heard Gerard ask quietly, "What does he mean?"

"That's the time he told us would be best for using a modified world-gate to reach Ile-Rien," Niles replied. "He said you'd have 'the rest of the pieces.' "

Gerard lifted his brows. "He's right."

Arisilde told Tremaine, "That was where I met the god, before I died, you know. Not there, of course, it can't quite reach the island."

She turned to meet Gerard's baffled gaze, then looked at Arisilde again. Ilias shifted uncomfortably. They knew Arisilde had met the god somehow, or he wouldn't have been able to pass along stories about them to Tremaine, before she had come to this world. But hearing how it had happened somehow made it all too real. Hearing someone other than Giliead talk about what the god said and did felt . . . wrong. Oblivious, Arisilde continued, "I could hear it, though, after Nicholas had left. I heard it singing to itself. It gets very lonely, when you're not there." This last was addressed to Giliead. "But there's no help for that, is there? So I took the boat and sailed toward the singing, until it heard me singing with it and came out to see me. It told me all about you." For an instant his vague eyes went even more distant. "Its memories go very deep, back into dark places it no longer wants to visit. It has lived for a very long time, finding bright little mortal lights it can talk to, and then losing them to the dark. It feels it more than you know. It has forgotten more of its past than it willingly remembers."

Ilias tore his gaze from those eyes and looked at Giliead again. Giliead's face was utterly shocked, as if the words had just peeled his soul bare.

"After you met the god, Arisilde," Nicholas said carefully. Ilias realized this was a tale they must have been trying to get out of Arisilde since they had first been able to speak to him.

Arisilde blinked and seemed to become a bit more aware, but his eyes moved up to a shadowy corner of the ceiling. "I was going back to the island but the boat got a bit out of hand in the wind and I landed in the wrong spot. Those things always happen for a reason, you know. It mightn't be a good reason, of course. But I found the circle in the cave, quite different from the one Nicholas and I had found in Adera. So I gave it a whirl. Hello there, I expect you'd like to see Ixion."

Giliead started, turning to follow Arisilde's gaze. Ilias looked to see familiar sparkles of light high up in the shadows at the top of the room. "It's the god," Giliead said quietly.

"So it's true—" Ilias turned back to face Arisilde, but he was gone.

* * *

Giliead waited while the Rienish guard unlocked the door. This was a room in the place called the Isolation Ward, at the stern of the ship. It was a warren of small rooms, all with dingy white walls, where the Gardier had been held prisoner on their voyage to Capidara. Now the only prisoner was Ixion.

"You know you don't need to do this," he told Ilias. Despite the cool air that came from little holes in the walls, Giliead felt sweat soaking the back of his shirt. He couldn't imagine how Ilias felt.

Ilias just gave him an annoyed glare. "I know I do need to do this."

"Me too," Tremaine put in. They both looked at her and she flung her arms up in exasperation. "Oh, come on. This ship has half a dozen sorcerers, plus Arisilde. And you two. He's not going to do anything, even if he is faking. You need to stop acting like he's some kind of bogeyman and see him for what he is—an opportunistic manipulating bastard."

"When I said that to you about Ander, you ignored me," Ilias told her testily. "And what's 'bogeyman' mean?"

Tremaine craned her neck to look into the front room, obviously trying to see if Gerard and the others waiting there had heard Ander's name. "I did not ignore you. And don't change the subject," she snapped.

Giliead rolled his eyes wearily. *Cletia must be out of her mind to think this isn't a real marriage.* "Fine, all right. The door will be open, just stay outside." He nodded to the guard, who had been regarding the Syrnaic conversation with impatience.

The man opened the door and stepped back.

The room was small but clean and the air wasn't stale; the Rienish had always treated their prisoners better than the Gardier. There was a small bed with cushions and blankets, and Ixion sat on the edge of it, watching them with a puzzled expression. Giliead's first startled thought was *It's not him.* Then he looked more closely, stepping forward into the room. The wizard's hair and eyebrows had grown in more fully, disguising the unnatural smoothness of the body he had grown like a curseling in one of his vats. He had beard stubble now too, and it made him look younger, innocent. And somehow less like his original body. Or maybe that was his expression, baffled and a little worried. Ixion said in Rienish, "Who are you?"

Giliead had discovered the hard way that he couldn't tell someone was a wizard unless they had recently made a curse. He couldn't smell or see any curses around Ixion now, but that meant nothing. He

glanced back at Ilias, who was leaning in the doorway, warily fascinated. He was holding Tremaine's hand, either for reassurance or to
keep her from following Giliead inside or probably a combination of
both. Tremaine just looked fascinated. Making his voice even, Giliead
told Ixion, "You know who I am."

Ixion shook his head. "No, I don't know anyone here." He sounded
as if he was weary of saying it. "I don't know where this place is, or
how I got here." His eyes moved from Giliead to Ilias and Tremaine.
Giliead realized suddenly why he had thought this wasn't Ixion. The
wizard's eyes had been dark brown in his old body and his new one.
Now they were blue. "Why does this building feel like it's floating?"

Giliead saw Ilias's eyes narrow and Tremaine lift a skeptical brow.
He knew they thought it was a trick, but Giliead wasn't certain. Ilias
asked suspiciously, "What do you remember?"

Ixion gestured helplessly, unaware that his audience had tensed at
the movement. "A farm, I think, the forest. A city . . . ? It's all in fragments."

Giliead felt the god's presence again as it worked its way through
some inner conduit inside the ship's structure. Relieved that it had decided to follow them here, he looked up in time to see it climb out of
the curse light in the ceiling of the room. Arisilde's words came back
to him again: *It feels it more than you know,* unsettling and warming, all
at the same time. He had always told himself that the god didn't feel
toward him the way he felt toward it, that it didn't have emotions as
people did. But maybe all it lacked was a way to communicate those
feelings. The haze of light drifted into a corner, and he could feel it
studying Ixion intensely. *Is it true?* he asked it. *Did Arisilde take away
his memory?*

It pushed images toward him and Giliead concentrated, his eyes
widening as he realized what the god was telling him. He told Ixion
hastily, "It'll be all right. You're on a foreign ship, an ally's ship, in the
Cineth harbor. Just give us time to talk it over."

Ixion nodded uncertainly, though hope had leapt to life in those unfamiliar eyes. This was possibly the most solid information he had
been given yet. Giliead stepped out, having to shift Ilias and Tremaine
out of his way, and the guard closed the door again. "What?" Ilias demanded. "Is that all? How can you tell—"

"Arisilde took away his ability to cast curses, and all his memories
of ever using them," Giliead interrupted. The god had followed him,
popping out of the curse light in this room and drifting down to settle

under the table the other Rienish guard was sitting at, somewhat to the man's consternation.

Gerard had come into the room with Nicholas in time to hear. "He took away his magic?" he repeated, sounding shocked.

"I thought he was different but I couldn't tell how. But the god is certain of it," Giliead told him. Arisilde had shared the knowledge with the god just like a Chosen Vessel would. It had seen Arisilde blast the curses out of Ixion's body and mind, scouring him clean like sand out of a shell.

Nicholas lifted his brows. "I'd say that sounds like a permanent solution. And very like Arisilde."

Ilias was staring at Giliead, almost as confused as the rootless man that was all that was left of Ixion. "You're sure? The god is sure?"

"We're sure. It's over." They just stared at each other for a long moment. Giliead felt light-headed suddenly, from relief, from the shock of finally being able to close the door on Ixion forever. He put a hand on Ilias's shoulder to steady himself, then pulled him into a tight hug. He felt Ilias gasp a half sob against his shoulder as the realization sank in. "It's over."

Tremaine commandeered a ride with one of the lifeboats back to Cineth as the sun was rising over Cineth's hills. The Gardier boy Calit was with her, standing in the bow next to the woman sailor who was piloting the boat.

The fresh wind cleared her head, though drinking the stewed coffee available in the wheelhouse with no food to pad her stomach had made her a little queasy. *Queasy*, she thought, disgusted with herself. *Not exactly the right way to start a mission behind enemy lines.*

At least she was going, apparently on her own merit as one of the few people with experience with the Gardier. She mentally amended that; a large number of people had experience with the Gardier, very few of them had actually survived it. The other members of the party were Gerard, Nicholas, Ilias and Giliead; the other top four in the list of Gardier survivors.

After a frantic meeting in the officers' chartroom in the wheelhouse, Averi had finally agreed to the plan to try to liberate Lodun, though it was a little different from the major military operation that the council and the Capidarans had originally conceived back in Capistown.

Leaning on the battered and coffee-stained surface of the chart table, Gerard told them all, "During our adventure, I've been able to put together a new modified gate circle, using the point-to-point circles we discovered and tested along the way. Now those circles only operated within this world, apparently as a quick method of travel for some of the ancient inhabitants. Though this new circle can't take us from here to Ile-Rien, it can—theoretically—transport us up to approximately five miles, within a single world. The short distance is because there is no receiving circle on the other end. If the distance is any greater, my calculations show that the spell would simply dissipate."

Averi, his skin sallow and yellow with illness and his eyes hollow and exhausted, had nodded. "You're thinking of creating the circle just outside Lodun, and using it to transport a group inside the barrier. A group with spheres for the sorcerers trapped inside."

Gerard inclined his head. "Exactly. The next problem, as we all realized, was to get to Ile-Rien past the blockade. The Gardier have the coast of Ile-Rien completely locked down, and they have been showing an increasing ability to detect and focus in on our use of the world-gate circles. The more we use them, the more adept they become at locating us. But Niles has a solution."

Niles took up the explanation: "I've been working on the problem using the circle Arisilde gave us in Capistown." Captain Marais had a look of thunderous confusion, so Niles elaborated, "Arisilde altered it to create a gate from any point in our world to the circle in an ancient ruin in a mountain range somewhere in this world. I was trying to alter it so that we could gate directly into Lodun from a point of safety in this world, such as Cineth, or the *Ravenna* herself. I had to eliminate the *Ravenna* as apparently any movement whatsoever, even if the ship was at anchor, would change the parameters. Possibly fatally. But the other problem is finding the destination site. I don't have any parameters for Lodun, as a circle has never been drawn there. I do, however, have perfect parameters for Port Rel and for the old Viller Institute site outside Vienne, where the first test circles were created."

"But those circles were both destroyed to keep the Gardier from using them," Averi pointed out.

Niles spread his hands. "But we still have their full parameters. And Arisilde has indicated that with a few adjustments, he can make my circle work." He cleared his throat, and added, "He's also indicated that three o'clock tomorrow afternoon is the best time to attempt this."

Averi and Marais exchanged a look indicating something of a lack of confidence in Arisilde's indications, but Gerard nodded. "We use your world-to-world circle to gate from Cineth directly to Port Rel. The Gardier near there are sure to notice our arrival in Ile-Rien, so we'll have to move quickly. We'll make our way to Lodun and use my point-to-point circle to gate inside the barrier. And give the sorcerers trapped there a selection of the spheres we've made."

Niles nodded. "In the meantime, I'll create a point-to-point circle on the *Ravenna*. The *Ravenna* will then gate to Ile-Rien, using its conventional circle. Once you establish the other point at Lodun, we can evacuate the civilians back to the *Ravenna*. Since both the starting-point circle and the destination circle will be within the same world, the ship's movement shouldn't matter. Again, the Gardier will probably detect the activity, but we're counting on the *Ravenna*'s speed and the spheres to hold them off during the process." He made this sound easy.

Averi had shaken his head, doubtful and conflicted. Tremaine hadn't remembered until then that his wife was trapped in Lodun, that Niles had a brother in the medical college there. Gerard said with quiet emphasis, "I think we all know what will happen if we don't get those people out before the Gardier lift the barrier and push through whatever defenses Lodun has mounted. We may already be too late."

So it had been decided, and Tremaine was mostly relieved that they had a plan, even if it was based on jury-rigged spell circles and weeks-old intelligence of the situation in Ile-Rien and Port Rel.

The Capidarans had been ferried back from Cineth earlier this morning, with Aras still maintaining Meretrisa's innocence. Tremaine didn't suppose the woman would face any punishment, and at the moment, she couldn't find it in herself to care. There had been so many spies, so many traitors, what was one more?

Now she just wanted to get this done before it was time to get ready for the mission. Gerard, Niles, Giaren and the other Rienish sorcerer Avrain had already landed a short distance down the coast, between Cineth and Andrien village, at a spot Kias had guided them to. It was sheltered, secluded and safely within the god's territory; an excellent place to construct the new circle. Everyone was working quickly to meet Arisilde's deadline.

Ilias and Giliead had stayed behind. While Tremaine had caught a few hours of sleep, then gotten Calit ready to leave, both men had been conked out exhausted on a bed in the Syprians' stateroom. They had been too unconscious to give her an opinion on whether they wanted to come along or not. Tremaine felt they were not only sleeping off the past few days, they were sleeping off weeks of anxiety and anger over Ixion's return to life.

The engine cut and the boat bumped into place along the dock. Tremaine hauled herself to her feet as the pilot and the other sailor scrambled out to tie it off. Calit climbed out immediately, standing on the stone dock, surveying the boats with their colorful sails and the eyes painted onto the hulls. Tremaine clambered out, feeling old. The woman pilot was looking around too. "I haven't been ashore here before," she said to Tremaine. Her hair was carefully tucked up under her cap and she looked as young as Florian. Possibly because she was as young as Florian. "The others said the natives don't bother you."

"They don't," Tremaine told her, shouldering her bag. Syprians had strict rules about how guests and visitors were treated, even guests and visitors who came in stinking curse-powered lifeboats. The other Rienish crews had been mostly ignored, except by the Andriens, but since the pilot was female she might get more polite attention. "There might be marriage proposals."

Unexpectedly, the girl laughed. "Like Kias? I can handle that."

Tremaine snorted in amusement. "Yes, he does get around." She steered Calit up the dock. Gyan had reported that the boy seemed to be doing better on the *Ravenna*. They had taught him a smattering of Syrnaic and Rienish, though he didn't have the same gift for languages as most of the Syprians. He had been sleeping in his bed instead of under it, and the only worrisome symptom was a tendency to overeat, which Gyan wisely attributed to an early life spent not knowing where his next meal was coming from. However Gyan was handling the situation, it seemed to be agreeable to Calit. When Tremaine had asked him if he wanted to stay with Gyan for a while, the boy had actually looked enthusiastic.

They reached the lawgiver's house, were let inside by Sanior, and Tremaine waited in the atrium for Visolela to appear while Calit fished for shiny rocks on the bottom of the reflecting pool. Tremaine could smell the grainy porridge Syprians preferred for breakfast and it was making her stomach rumble. She was beginning to wonder if it was a mite early for a meeting when Visolela appeared, wrapped in a dark purple stole, and demanded wearily, "What now?"

Before Tremaine could answer, Nicanor came out, his dark hair still mussed with sleep and dressed in a silky dark red robe. He said, "There's trouble?"

He must have arrived late last night. "No," Tremaine said hastily. "Actually there's news, good news for once. Ixion won't be back. He's taken care of—permanently." She didn't want to give specifics, in case Giliead wanted to tell them the story himself. "Also, I wanted to ask you something. I'd like to buy the house."

Still startled by the news about Ixion, Visolela frowned in confusion. "What?"

"I need a place for the Aelin to stay." She decided not to mention Ilias and Giliead and other assorted Andriens who might also be occupying it eventually. "I don't have time to look for anywhere else, so I wanted to buy the one you loaned us." She pulled open the leather flap of the bag, fishing through Calit's possessions for the wallet she had retrieved from the ship's safe this morning.

Nicanor's brows lifted when Tremaine produced the handful of gold coins. Syprians didn't use gold coinage but they traded it to foreign merchants. She had no idea what a house of that size in Cineth was worth; her only reference point was that she had paid three gold Rienish reals for Ilias. From Nicanor's expression she thought her guess might have been close enough.

Visolela eyed the gold a moment, her brows drawing together. She said finally, "The house has a plot of land that goes with it, outside the city."

Tremaine inclined her head, and drew out five more coins.

Visolela nodded. "Done."

The next stop was the new house. There was no deed to be filed; the lawgiver had to be notified and the change of ownership announced in the plaza on market day. Since Nicanor was the lawgiver, that was already accomplished, and he had agreed to arrange the announcement himself.

Tremaine found the front door open and Gyan, Kias, Gyan's foster daughter Dyani and all the Aelin sitting down to breakfast in the atrium. Before Tremaine could open her mouth, Dyani yelled with delight, jumped up and flung herself on her. "You're back! Everyone thought you might leave without stopping here." Davret and the other Aelin waved delightedly and called greetings.

Tremaine staggered under the effusive welcome, feeling as if she didn't deserve it. "Yes, I just came by to . . . I brought Calit to stay."

She prodded the boy forward. He was eyeing the Aelin children warily, though she didn't think he recognized them as his own people.

Gyan smiled at her. "Dyani, don't hang on Tremaine's neck. Have you had breakfast yet?"

"Not yet, and it smells wonderful." She took a seat on the sparse grass next to Gyan and accepted the plate and cup Kias brought. Calit got handed a plate by one of the Aelin women and plopped down next to Kias, still eyeing the other children with uneasy fascination.

Breakfast was porridge sweetened by dark sticky honey and bread. Tremaine ate half of it before she managed to say conversationally, "I bought this house for you all."

Gyan blinked. "What?" Dyani looked up, startled, and even Kias stopped eating to listen.

She shrugged, feeling incredibly self-conscious. "You know, Giliead told Karima he won't be living at Andrien House, so we don't have anywhere to stay when we're in town. And the village got burned down, and everything. So stay here as long as you want, or while it's safe in Cineth, anyway, and if you could keep an eye on them, and help them get out of here if the Gardier attack again." She nodded at the Aelin, who were unable to follow the Syrnaic conversation and were talking among themselves.

Gyan watched her for a moment, then smiled, his eyes warm. "That was very well done. We'll stay."

"Oh, good." Tremaine cleared her throat. She switched to Aelin to say, "Obelin, this house belongs to me now, and you can all stay here as long as you want. There may still be Gardier attacks, but while it's safe to be in town, you can stay here."

The old man looked at the others, got a consensus of nods and told her, "We would be honored to stay here, and to give you any help that we can."

A fter breakfast, Tremaine sat in the sun in the atrium, nursing a second cup of tea, mentally gearing up to return to the ship. She needed to prepare for the trip to Ile-Rien, to change clothes and to renew her supply of ammunition. And say good-bye. She took a deep breath, feeling her stomach tighten with anxiety. *These things are easier when you're suddenly flung into them.* She knew a part of it was that she didn't want to see what the Gardier had done to Ile-Rien. *At least we'll be in Rel and Lodun, and not Vienne.*

Most of the Aelin had wandered off. Dyani was going to teach them how to shop at a Syprian market and give them a tour around the city; how they had come to this arrangement when the Aelin knew only about twenty words of Syrnaic, most of them food-related, Tremaine wasn't sure. But then she and Ilias and Florian had managed to navigate the Isle of Storms with only three words in common, so she supposed it wasn't as hard as it sounded. She hadn't told the Aelin where she and Ilias and Giliead were going; the fewer people who knew, the better.

The Aelin children were fascinated by a new playmate who spoke their own language and were desperate to drag Calit into their games whether he liked it or not. He was still a little standoffish from what she could tell, but he was beginning to make overtures by splashing fountain water on one of the younger girls, so she suspected he would do fairly well.

Then she realized Cletia was standing over her. Tremaine glanced up with a frown, and Cletia said, "I want to speak to you in private."

"Oh, fine," Tremaine said, with a deliberately poor attempt at good cheer. She pushed to her feet, wondering if it was some message from Visolela. She wasn't sure how much Cletia had seen of Pasima since the *Ravenna* had returned. She followed Cletia to the portico and one of the disused sitting rooms directly off it. The red tile floor had collected dead leaves and dust, and the room was bare of furniture. "Well?" Tremaine asked impatiently.

Cletia threw a look out the wide doorway, checking to make sure Gyan and Dyani were out of earshot. She said a little stiffly, "I want to speak to you about Ilias."

Tremaine folded her arms and put on an expression of faint boredom. She did not want to encourage this conversation. "You know, I don't think he's any of your business."

"Everyone knows you only married him for the alliance, even if you are bed friends now," Cletia said, obviously fighting to keep her expression calm. Tremaine felt her face go tight. "But the alliance is sealed now. Visolela knows how dangerous the Gardier are to us, she won't let Pasima or Pella or anyone else argue with Nicanor's decisions." Cletia hesitated, as if hoping Tremaine would agree, then added more firmly, "You don't need Ilias anymore."

Tremaine held her gaze, feeling rage simmer. Apparently more lack of encouragement was going to be necessary. "I'm still not hearing anything that's any of your concern."

Cletia's face hardened in annoyance. "You saw us in Capistown. You know he could never live in one of your cities."

"I know that," Tremaine said through gritted teeth. She remembered a promise to Karima, before they had sailed for Capidara, that she wouldn't make Ilias come back to her world. But the idea of severing the tie between them was as attractive as the idea of cutting off her arm. She should tell Cletia that she meant to stay here, but for some reason the words didn't come out. "The chances that any of us are going to live past the next few days are low, so why bother to talk about it."

"You said that before." Cletia gestured impatiently. "You use it like an armor, so you don't have to think about the future. I want to talk about what happens if you all live. He could be happy with me, you know that."

Rage bubbled over. Almost without her conscious volition, Tremaine said, with no particular emphasis, "You know, I'd just hate it if anything happened to you."

Cletia stepped back, wary. "I don't want to fight with you."

"You really don't," Tremaine agreed. It just infuriated her more that Cletia was being so reasonable. It also infuriated her that she recognized the fact that Cletia was being reasonable.

Cletia seemed to realize the conversation wasn't going to get any better. With a gesture of frustration, she turned to go. "We don't have to be enemies."

"It's a little late for that," Tremaine told her retreating back.

She listened to Cletia's footsteps recede along the portico and stood in the room for a long time, taking slow deep breaths, despite the dust. It had occurred to her why she had avoided every opportunity to talk to Ilias. *I can't say it. I can't say it like I'm supposed to.* All the ridiculously emotional phrases of love. She remembered the last play she had seen before the war had closed the theaters, a romantic drama with people draping themselves languorously on couches and saying things like *Oh, darling, my wife will surely understand. She knows a love like ours extends past destiny and reason* and *You're the only one in my life and you fill it completely.* She couldn't imagine how drunk she would have to be to say something like that. Whenever she had tried to write a romance in her plays, the audience could never tell if the characters were in love or not. She clapped a hand to her forehead in despair. Killing Cletia seemed like the best solution. *Yes, for a crazy person,* she thought in disgust. *We were trying to give that up, remember?*

And Ilias couldn't live in her world. Not in the cities, the places they would have to fight the Gardier. Even if the fighting didn't kill him, he would be badly ill within the year. And Giliead couldn't leave this world for long periods of time, and the separation would probably kill them both. *And I can't stay here. If we don't stop the Gardier at Parscia and Capidara, they'll take the rest of the world. Then this world.* That cold fact settled sickly into her stomach, turning the bright morning gray. *I can't stay here.* That was why she hadn't told Cletia of her plan to come back to this house.

Someone stepped into the doorway, blocking the fall of light. She looked up to see Balin, standing uncertainly. The Gardier woman said warily, "I need to speak to you. I want to talk."

"Oh God." Tremaine pressed the heels of her hands to her eyes. "Not you too."

Balin looked a little affronted. "You don't need my information anymore?"

"What?" Tremaine stared, trying to drag her mind back from the abyss of her personal life. "Oh, you want to talk? Finally?"

Balin stepped further into the room, saying, "I want to stay with them."

"With who? The Aelin?" As Balin nodded, Tremaine lifted her brows. "Even here, with the savages?"

"The Etara don't seem to mind." She shifted uncomfortably, folding her arms tightly and looking away. "I can see why Command would want to kill me. I've been with you too long, I could have told you anything, been corrupted. . . . It's a chance I took willingly. But the Etara, they were trapped in that place for a generation, they knew nothing, except one name." Her mouth hardened. "And they aren't soldiers."

Tremaine nodded slowly. "Talk, and I'll speak to Averi about letting you stay here, in Obelin's custody."

Balin took a sharp breath. "I heard the name Castines before Obelin spoke of it. In Maton-Command. I've heard the Liaisons say it to one another. I didn't know who they meant, but I thought it must be someone in a very high position. Your spy will have told you that we don't know the names of our leaders, only our immediate commanders." She hesitated but looked out into the court again, where Eliva and two of the other women were cleaning up after the meal, and Gyan was bringing a bucket of water to sluice down a wooden table. She let out her breath, sounding defeated. "Your people showed me maps, but I would tell you nothing. But there was one—it was near a place in your world that they called Kathbad—that showed Maton-Command. I have been there several times, but only the Liaisons go to Maton-First."

"Maton-First is different from Maton-Command."

"It is near to it." Balin seemed to be making a genuine effort to explain and make herself understood. "I'm not sure where. Only Liaisons go there. The ones I heard speak of Castines . . . they spoke as if he was at Maton-First."

Tremaine rubbed her temples. It was an odd bit of information, and confirmed some of their theories about Castines, but she didn't see that it changed anything having to do with the mission. "Right. You'll have to come back to the *Ravenna* and talk to Colonel Averi."

E ven after waking up and cadging a quick meal from the *Ravenna*'s dining room, and making small talk about how the people making the food on this trip weren't nearly as good at it as the ones on the voyage to Capidara, Ilias still felt as shaken as if he had had a hard blow to the head. Besides the one Herias had given him.

The sorcerer Kressein had agreed to take charge of Ixion, to continue to watch him and to take him back to Capistown if he proved to be as innocent as he appeared, and as the god had said. Ilias wasn't sure how he felt about that, but he did know that releasing him anywhere in the Syrnai would mean a quick death. People didn't know Ixion's face, but they knew his name, and the poets would spread the story everywhere.

Ilias realized he was actually looking forward to sneaking through captured Rienish territory and fighting the Gardier. It would distract him from what had just happened, and give him time to put it in perspective. If he wasn't killed.

Ilias and Giliead had been given Rienish clothes to make them less conspicuous, though the idea was for no one to see them until they reached the wizards trapped in Lodun. It was also going to be colder in Ile-Rien and they would need the extra protection. The clothes didn't feel right, and Ilias rejected outright the boots, which felt heavy and gripped his feet in distracting ways. They decided to settle for what they had mostly done in Capistown, and wear the heavier wool shirt and long coat over their own clothing. Then they had then spent some time figuring out where to put a slit in the shoulders of the coats so they could get to their swords.

"We're going to a whole city of wizards." Ilias sheathed his sword and sat down on the bed, laying the leather scabbard across his knees. It hadn't been so long ago that the idea would have been laughable. Or, actually, screamable. Now they were here in this room with curse lights in a floating metal mountain of a ship. He pulled at a loose piece of leather braid, looking up to ask Giliead, "Are we crazy?"

"It seems like the best explanation," Giliead agreed. He plopped down next to Ilias.

"Fortunately the god's crazy too."

"Apparently." He added dryly, "I guess that shouldn't be as big a surprise as it was, at least according to Arisilde the bodiless wizard god."

Ilias lifted a brow. Giliead sounded jealous of Arisilde's connection with the god. Pointing this out, or pointing out how unsurprising this was, would probably provoke a fight, so he decided to save it for later. "And Ixion doesn't remember any of it," Ilias said, just to test how the words sounded. "He's sane now."

"I wish I was." Giliead let out his breath, shaking his head. "At least they're Rienish wizards. It won't be like the city I saw from the curse circle in the Barrens." He twitched, shaking off the memory.

Considering where they were going, Ilias didn't want to talk about places where wizards ruled and kept people like cattle. He knew Rienish cities weren't like that, but he would just rather not start this trip with those images in mind. "Where's Tremaine? She should be back by now."

After searching around the *Ravenna* for Tremaine and finally being told that she had just arrived back, Ilias ran her to ground in Florian's cabin. She was throwing a collection of clothes around the room, apparently in an effort to select what she wanted to wear. Florian was sitting on the bed, one of the new spheres in her lap, with a disgruntled expression. He knew she was upset that she wasn't going with them. The idea that she was much younger than Gerard and Niles, and that they wanted her to grow old and do curses for her people instead of ending up in a Gardier wizard crystal didn't sit well with her. Ilias understood; he had been a young warrior once too and had had even less concept of his own mortality than Florian.

He leaned in the doorway, brows drawn together, watching Tremaine fling things around the cabin. "What's wrong?" he asked her finally.

She threw an opaque glance at him. "Balin told me she heard

Castines mentioned by two Liaisons in Maton-Command, that he's in a place called Maton-First, but that's all she knew. And that it's on the same side of their world as Capidara, so we won't be going there any-time soon."

Ilias nodded. She seemed to have settled on a pair of dark-colored pants and a heavy wool shirt, not unlike what he and Giliead had been offered. As she bent over to wrestle her boots back on, the tightness of the pants was extremely attractive, but he didn't think commenting on it would be a good idea at the moment. "And that upset you?"

She tossed her hair out of her eyes, fixing a glare on him, as if she had read the other thought anyway. "No."

"Oh." His frown deepened. "All right." Giving in, he asked Florian, "What's wrong with her?"

Florian shrugged, shaking her head. "They'll let me go down in the engine shafts—which is the scariest place I've ever been in my life, thank you very much—after a disgusting and really hungry curseling, but I can't do this."

"If a curseling rips your guts out, Niles can fix that," Tremaine replied laconically, struggling with the last boot. "He can't get you out of a Gardier crystal. Unless it's the hard way."

Florian rolled her eyes. Ilias decided talking to either of them at this point was a waste of time. He left the cabin to find Giliead waiting for him in the dim corridor. He reported wryly, "Don't go in there, it's dangerous."

"What did you do?" Giliead asked accusingly.

Ilias stared at him, offended. "I didn't do anything. I've been with you all day."

Giliead just frowned suspiciously and stalked away. Ilias flung his arms in the air in frustration and followed.

Kias had picked a good spot for the curse circle. It was an open grassy clearing, near the ocean but sheltered from the sea wind by a ridge of rock and stands of heavy pines. The remains of an old house, a fallen-down tumble of stone, lay just under the trees where the ground flattened out. Giliead remembered this had been some-one's land once, but the family had died out and no one was left to claim it.

The circle had been painted onto small flat stones, laid out in a ring in the center of the clearing under the bright afternoon sun. Gerard and Nicholas were waiting for them, along with Gyan and Kias. There were also a couple of Rienish sailors and Avrain, a young Rienish wizard who had come with the *Ravenna* from Capistown. He had reddish hair and a face Giliead would have said was good-humored, if it hadn't belonged to a strange wizard. Avrain shook hands with Gerard, telling him, "Good luck. When you reach Lodun, I hope—" He gestured a little helplessly. "I just hope."

Gerard nodded, looking away uncomfortably. "I know."

It reminded Giliead that these people had friends, family trapped in this place, who could end up as slaves imprisoned in Gardier crystals.

The god, which had settled into the remains of the ruined house's hearth, was fascinated by the circle. It kept pushing images at it, as if trying to talk to it, and Giliead kept seeing the circle's symbols in the god's thoughts. *As if it's talking back,* Giliead thought, baffled. The whole thing should have been deeply uncomfortable, but the god seemed to be enjoying it. Arisilde's words went through his head again, that he had heard the god singing and sang back to it.

They had assembled a supply bag with the little packages of Rienish travel food, maps, more ammunition for the Rienish shooting weapons that Tremaine, Gerard and Nicholas would carry, and other necessary items. This was sitting next to the pack that held the spheres.

Tremaine sat on the ground to open it now and Giliead leaned in to look over her shoulder. Six new spheres, each wrapped in a thick cotton cloth, were nestled inside. A couple had come a little unwrapped, and he could see things moving inside their copper bodies, and an occasional spark of white or blue. None of these had an actual living wizard inside, like Arisilde's late sphere, but he could hear them whispering to themselves, a background hum of words just on the edge of audibility.

"Some of these look a little active," Tremaine told Gerard dubiously. "Is that good?"

Looking over a sheaf of papers, he replied, "I think it's due to being transported on the *Ravenna*—being exposed to Arisilde seems to have an enlivening effect on them."

Giliead's mouth twisted ruefully. He noticed Gerard hadn't answered her question as to whether this was good or not. Tremaine had obviously noticed too, and frowned into the pack before folding over the top and buckling it closed again. She wasn't saying much to Ilias, but then that wasn't unusual on the eve of a battle. But Giliead would have given a great deal for a chance to cross-question Cletia about what had happened while Tremaine was in Cineth this morning.

As Giliead straightened up, he saw Bythia, standing with Gyan and Kias a short distance away in the shade of the trees. No one else was supposed to know about this, but then poets tended to know everything anyway. She came forward to meet him, saying, "I had news and Gyan said it shouldn't wait until you got back."

"He was right." Not the least because as dangerous as this was likely to be, they might not be coming back. "What is it?"

"I found mention of a wizard called Castines in the Journals. There's not much, just a story about how Dinias—he was Chosen Vessel for Essanum back when you were a boy—hunted him up into the mountains at the edge of the Hisians' territory."

Giliead nodded. That put Castines in the right area. He thanked her, returning to the others in time to hear Gerard explain, "In order to create the gate into Lodun more quickly, we've already drawn the necessary symbols on corkboard. It will still take some time to ritually join the symbols, but considerably less time than it takes to draw them out."

Looking out to sea, past the curtain of pines, Giliead could see huge puffs of steam rising into the air, the white breath the *Ravenna* made as she prepared to depart.

Gerard looked around, a brisk air masking what Giliead could easily read as weariness and anxiety. "Are we ready to go?"

"No," Tremaine replied before anyone else could, "but let's go anyway."

Chapter 16

They stepped in the circle, Gerard used the sphere, and sunlight abruptly gave way to darkness. It was night, as they had expected, but they stood in a damp cold forest clearing, the winter-dead trees just looming shapes in the dark. Tremaine squinted, trying to make her eyes adjust faster. *Something's wrong,* she thought. Beside her Ilias pivoted slowly, whispering, "We're not at the port. I can't smell the sea."

"No, this isn't Rel," Gerard agreed slowly. Tremaine heard dead leaves scrunch underfoot as he took a step forward. *Not Rel,* she thought grimly. *Well, we're off to the usual bang-up start.*

"But these were the parameters Arisilde gave you?" Nicholas asked quietly.

"Yes." Gerard added ruefully, "Of course, he never did confirm that he would actually send us to Rel."

Nicholas sighed in weary annoyance and Tremaine heard Giliead snort with disbelief. But this place had an oddly familiar feel, and Niles had said that the modified circle could take them anywhere as long as it had the parameters. Arisilde must know the parameters for all the places the sphere had previously opened a gate. She had a bad feeling about this. "Ilias, Giliead, can you smell a city?" she asked.

It sounded daft, but they knew what she meant. The diesel and coal smoke odors were as distinctive to them as good perfume was to her. "Yes," Ilias said immediately. "There's one all around us."

Uh-huh. That's what I was afraid of. Tremaine rubbed her forehead with a silent groan. "Nicholas, when you and Arisilde opened a gate circle for the first time, you were in Vienne, weren't you?"

"Oh, bloody hell." Silhouetted by starlight, she saw Nicholas clap a hand over his eyes.

"I take it that was a yes." Gerard sounded grimly resigned. "We're in Vienne?"

Tremaine felt Giliead standing at her elbow. "Where's that?" he asked quietly.

"It's our capital city," Tremaine explained, biting her lip in thought. "We could have gone cross-country to Lodun from Port Rel and mostly avoided occupied territory. But now we'll have to get out of Vienne first." She looked around, squinting into the dark. *This is going to be a problem.* She was starting to feel glad that Nicholas had half a dozen explosives in his coat pockets. "I think we're in a park."

"We're in the Count Castillion Gardens," Nicholas said, still sounding disgusted. He stepped past her, finding a path between the trees. "The first time Arisilde and I tried the gate spell, it was in one of the houses I own on Ivory Street." He hesitated. "Yes, I think I know what we can do."

Tremaine hurried to follow him, stumbling as a fallen branch trapped her feet. "And what's that?"

"There's a manhole a few streets over—"

"Oh God, not the sewers." She could hear the others following, a faint clink of metal as Giliead shouldered the pack with the spheres.

Nicholas said repressively, "No, not the sewers. The maintenance tunnels for the underground rail system."

Tremaine nodded, trying not to feel disgruntled at Nicholas's typical omniscience regarding Vienne's public works. The maintenance tunnels had been built parallel to all the underground train lines, so workers could easily repair the rails. They were entered by manholes in the streets that looked nearly identical to the sewer manholes, but the train tunnels were dry, mostly safe and easily navigated, at least compared with the sewers. Vienne's sewers made the passages under the Isle of Storms look safe and easily navigated.

Following Nicholas, they reached the edge of the park so abruptly Tremaine walked into the waist-high wall that bordered it. She hopped back, rubbing the knee that had collided with the stone. The street before them was dark, the buildings tall shapes etched against the lighter darkness of the sky. *No streetlights, no noise,* she thought uneasily. It wasn't unlike Vienne's normal blackout conditions, but there was a quality to this silence that made the back of Tremaine's neck prickle. Those shapes across the street were old town houses and blocks of flats. There should be some feel of movement, people returning home late, artists staying up to work or drink. She realized they had all come to a halt and heard Ilias ask Giliead quietly, "Curses?"

"No." But he added, "It feels like . . . people have been hunted with curses."

Tremaine felt that cold chill go right down her spine. "Thanks," she murmured, "I feel very confident now. Let's go get them, hurrah."

Somebody, probably Giliead, thumped her in the back of the head. But her comment seemed to have broken the spell cast by the silent city, and Nicholas said, "An illusion charm, Gerard? Or not?"

Gerard shook his head, still studying the street intently. "I'd rather not risk it, unless it's absolutely necessary. There's too much of a chance of detection."

Tremaine nodded to herself. They had crossed the Gardier's home territory without illusion charms. Of course, that hadn't been by choice. "Very well." Nicholas swung over the low wall. Gerard tucked the sphere into the bag under his coat and Ilias and Giliead returned their swords to their scabbards. Tremaine doubted that would help much if they were seen; there was probably a curfew, if the Gardier hadn't simply killed all the civilians who hadn't been able to escape the city.

They made it across the dark canyon of the street and found an alley through to the next safely, but had to go down to the end of the next block to take the cross street. At the corner, Ilias hissed a sudden warning. An instant later, Tremaine saw the glow of electric torches down the block and heard boot steps on the cobbled street.

Tremaine swore mentally, flattening herself back against a gritty stone wall, Ilias beside her. There was no shelter, not even a nearby door to force. Running would just draw attention. "Gerard, I think it's absolutely necessary," she whispered.

"I concur," he muttered. He didn't say or do anything, but she knew he didn't have to cast a concealment charm.

Tremaine held her breath as the patrol approached, trotting down the street. She caught flashes of brown Gardier uniforms in the torch-light and heard someone give a breathless order in Aelin, but the words were too distorted by distance for her to understand.

A torch flashed across them and Tremaine winced, but there was no outcry. The patrol continued down the street and she heard Ilias take a deep breath of relief. As the light vanished at the corner of the next cross street, Giliead said quietly, "They didn't have a sorcerer crystal."

"They obviously detected the gate opening, and sent the nearest patrol to investigate," Nicholas said grimly, pushing off from the wall. "The next group will be considerably larger and will have a crystal."

Ilias and Giliead were already moving ahead and Tremaine hurried after them. Behind her, Gerard said with some asperity, "Yes, that was why Rel would have been a better choice. But obviously Arisilde didn't agree."

They crossed the next old cobbled street to the promenade, where the houses were bordered by ornate wrought-iron railings and empty flower beds. Nicholas led the way swiftly down the walk to a break in the houses. He opened the gate and they passed rapidly through another little park attached to one of the sets of flats. Even in the dark, Tremaine could tell it had gone untended. The fountain was still and no one had cut away the dry winter growth to prepare the beds for spring. Following Nicholas's back, Tremaine didn't realize they were being watched until Ilias stopped abruptly, his sword half-drawn. Tremaine saw movement in a doorway, heard a faint noise, and Giliead said, quietly, "Stop." The command had been for Ilias, who returned the blade to the scabbard without hesitation.

Tremaine peered uncertainly at the shape in the doorway, her hand on the pistol in her pocket, but she trusted Giliead's indication that a weapon wasn't necessary. Both Syprians could see in the dark far better than she could. Gerard was beside her, hand half lifted to cast a spell. Nicholas stepped forward to look, flashing a pocket torch on the figure.

It was a woman, wrapped in a dark green shawl, her face smudged and dirty. She winced away from the light and Nicholas switched it off.

"It's all right," Gerard said quietly. "We're not Gardier."

Tremaine heard the woman take a sharp breath, almost a sob. Sounding dazed, she said in a Vienne accent, "I can't get in. I've lost my key."

Tremaine recognized that tone; the woman was a little mad. Maybe she had been driven that way by circumstance, but she was no longer quite connected to reality. She would have said the same thing to the Gardier if a patrol had caught her here.

Tremaine looked at Nicholas, barely able to see him in the dark. She half expected him to argue that there wasn't time to help random survivors, especially slightly demented ones. But he must have anticipated her argument that it would take less time to just do it than it would to argue about it; he stepped forward swiftly, pulling something out of his coat pocket. The woman edged away to give him room and he worked at the doorknob. Before Tremaine could even gather her wits to offer to hold a pocket torch for him, the knob clicked and the door swung open. The woman pushed to her feet, breathing fervently, "Thank you."

Nicholas stopped her with a hand on her arm. "Where are the Gardier?"

The woman spoke in a hurried hush, and Tremaine got the impression of information learned by rote and passed swiftly to strangers encountered in alleys. "They're in the palace, that's their headquarters, I think. They're all along Saints Procession Boulevard, the Street of Flowers. They're staying in the center part of the city, where the streetlights work. The army broke the others in the rest of the city and cut the telephone and telegraph wires, but the Gardier fixed the ones in the palace quarter."

"Is the Rienish army still here?" Gerard demanded, startled.

"Some, for a while." The woman shook her head a shade too rapidly. "Not anymore." Tremaine grimaced. That must have been the remnants of the troops forced to retreat from the Aderassi border. They had been too far from the coast to make it to the mostly doomed evacuation ships and too late to get on the last trains across Bisra to Parscia. And some at least must have tried to make some kind of half-assed defense of Vienne. *Stupid, crazy . . .* Tremaine gritted her teeth, fighting the well of emotion that made her want to cry or kill somebody. Mostly kill somebody. The woman was still talking. "Garbardin and Riverside and Redroyal Hill are a little safer. They don't like narrow streets or the big tenements. It's too easy for people to shoot or throw things and run away."

Nicholas nodded, and held the door for her as she slipped inside. "Not everybody in the city is dead," Tremaine said, not realizing she had spoken until she heard the words. Ilias squeezed her shoulder.

"I suspect there's still thousands of people here," Gerard said slowly. "The survivors are simply hiding very carefully."

They found the hole in the next street and Ilias was never more relieved to be climbing down into a black pit underground. Even though he knew it would be nearly impossible to see anyone moving through the dark street from one of the looming buildings, it still made him mortally uncomfortable to be in the open.

Giliead and Nicholas went down first, just in case something lay in wait below. Tremaine and Gerard followed, and Ilias climbed down last, planting his feet on the narrow metal ladder and bracing against the rock-lined wall to nudge the heavy cover back over the hole.

This shut out what little light there was, and Ilias fumbled down the ladder. He heard the others below, their voices distorted by stone and metal. As he reached the bottom, one of Gerard's curse lights formed in the air, the little wisp of illumination revealing a narrow tunnel just wide enough for two men to stand abreast. The walls were lined with brick and he saw there were even Rienish trail signs painted beside the ladder. It was cold and damp, colder than it had been up on the street, and the air was full of strange metallic odors. But the tunnel seemed empty of anything bigger than vermin that fled squeaking from Gerard's curse light.

"Well?" Tremaine demanded, looking at Nicholas.

"We can take these tunnels all the way over to the north end of Cabellard Street," he said. "That's as far north as the underground rail extends. At that point we'll have to return to the surface, but we'll be fairly near the city gate."

"The Gardier have to be guarding the gates. Granted, most of the city is outside the old wall, but still," Tremaine persisted.

Nicholas eyed her. "There are a number of houses and business establishments built up to the wall at the Cabellard Gate. With Giliead to find the Gardier wards, we should be able to get over the wall easily. I did choose this way for a reason."

"If you share the reason with us," Tremaine pointed out, mock-innocently, "then the rest of us would understand it too."

I could have told him that one was coming. Ilias exchanged a dry look with Giliead. At least Tremaine was turning her ire on her father rather than him.

"Tremaine, Nicholas," Gerard said sharply. "That's enough. Nicholas, when you make a decision, please briefly indicate how you arrived at it. Tremaine, please exercise your considerable self-restraint. Agreed? Then let's go."

Nicholas said, "This way," and strode off down the tunnel as though he knew exactly where he was going. *Of course, he always does,* Ilias thought wearily. Tremaine let her breath out in annoyance, exchanged a jaundiced look with Gerard, and followed. Giliead, already concentrating to listen for curses and curselings, moved after them and Ilias fell in behind to guard their backs. He couldn't help saying under his breath, "I got married to get away from family fights."

Working his way to the front of the group to look for curse traps, Giliead threw him a darkly amused look.

They walked for some time, Gerard's soft wizard light drifting along, revealing the dusty bricks and the dark cross passages, the trail signs Ilias wished he could read. He recognized many of the same symbols from the trail signs on the *Ravenna,* but frustratingly these were all arranged in different patterns. Nicholas, still leading the way with Giliead beside him, would stop occasionally to consult one of the signs, then take another passage. They also passed a great many metal doors, set back into the walls and touched with rust, though the locks looked heavy and strong. Tremaine explained in a whisper that they were the doors into the train tunnels. Ilias still had only a vague idea of what a train was, but it didn't sound as impressive as the *Ravenna.* From what she had said, they should be able to hear the things moving in the adjacent tunnels, but there was nothing. The Gardier didn't seem to be using them, and Ilias found himself wondering if they would have any more idea of how to make a train work than he would. For all their pretensions to superiority, the Gardier city he had seen from a distance had seemed much inferior to this one, and even to Capistown.

They came to a junction of three passages, one curving smoothly away, and Giliead flung out an arm to stop Nicholas.

Brow lifted, Nicholas asked, "A spell?"

Giliead nodded, sitting on his heels, holding one hand over the dirty brick floor. "A curse trap, right through here. I can't tell what it's meant to do."

As Gerard moved up beside them, Tremaine said in disgust, "Well, that's great. So the Gardier know about these tunnels?"

"It's not Gardier," Giliead said, shaking his head. "It smells like your curses. Rienish curses."

Gerard lifted his brows, studying the innocuous stretch of brick thoughtfully. "Let's see." Taking out the bulky contraption with glass lenses that he used for seeing curses, he fit it into place over the smaller lenses he normally wore, then put a hand inside the sphere's bag.

He muttered some words Ilias couldn't understand and couldn't really hear well enough to tell if they were in Rienish or not. But Giliead pulled back a little from the cursed spot, frowning. Startled, he said, "Can you read those symbols?" Ilias craned his neck to look, but to his eyes, there was nothing there. He leaned against the wall, a little disgruntled, but not much. It would have made things easier on occasion to be able to see curses as Giliead did, but he knew it just wasn't worth all the trouble the ability brought with it. *At least Herias wasn't accusing you of doing something to the god.* Ilias had always had enough trouble all on his own.

"Yes. This is a ward, cast by a Rienish sorcerer, within the past month. It's very subtle, obviously in an attempt to avoid Gardier attention." Gerard pulled off the bulky glass thing, blinking, and put it away. "It's designed to alert the casting sorcerer if anyone passes this way, specifically down this left-hand passage, which appears to lead to—" He gestured for Ilias to move. Ilias shifted sideways, realizing he had been leaning on the painted trail sign. "The west end of the Street of Courts. There's an addition to the standard ward structure that's attempting to set another alarm if the person who breaks the ward is Gardier. But it's a bit clumsy and I'm not sure if it works." He tapped the sphere absently, his brows drawing together. "You know who this structure reminds me of?" he asked Nicholas. "Old Berganmot. His spells were very idiosyncratic. But he died two years ago, on the Aderassi front."

Nicholas lifted his brows. "Interesting. You realize what's on the west end of the Street of Courts?"

Gerard nodded, intrigued. "One of your safe houses was down there, wasn't it?"

"Yes." Nicholas's eyes narrowed in thought. Tremaine sighed, took the little round gold case out of Gerard's pocket that the Rienish used for measuring time and studied it impatiently. Gerard recaptured it from her with an annoyed frown. "Can you disarm the ward without alerting the sorcerer?" Nicholas asked, ignoring the whole performance.

Gerard touched the sphere again and gestured with his other hand. "Did that work, Giliead?"

Giliead pushed to his feet, nodding. "There's a path through it now."

"Very good." Nicholas gestured for Giliead to proceed down the passage to the Street of Courts. A little warily, Giliead led the way, showing them where the curse was so they could avoid it.

"Who was Berganmot?" Ilias asked as he fell in behind Tremaine, still keeping an eye on the passages behind them.

"He was a Rienish sorcerer who came to our house sometimes, so he must have done things for Nicholas," she told him. She raised her voice to ask the others, "We know Berganmot is actually dead? There's no chance that he's—" She gestured vaguely, indicating something about the size of one of the big Gardier crystals.

"He died in an airship bombing," Gerard replied repressively, as they passed a cross corridor. "I doubt there would have been any opportunity—"

Ilias heard a faint sound and sensed movement in the corner of his eye. He clicked his tongue to alert the others, stepped to the wall beside the opening and flattened himself against it. Tremaine and Giliead both stepped to the wall, Tremaine ducking down beside Ilias, her shooting weapon suddenly in her hand. It was a little tight in the passage to draw his sword; Ilias slipped the knife out of the back of his belt. Nicholas threw them a glance and drew Gerard further down the passage, continuing to speak in the same quiet tone, "Of course, it's quite out of the question . . ."

When the figure peeped cautiously around the corner Ilias slammed him in the head with his knife hilt. The intruder made a strangled noise and staggered, but Ilias had already seized him by the shirt and jacket. He knocked the shooting weapon out of his hand and flung him against the far wall, pinning him and setting the blade at his throat.

The man was young, dressed in rough gray and brown, with narrow features and greasy dark hair. Ilias felt him reach for another weapon in his belt and growled, "Don't," pressing the knife in a little harder. Tremaine had already collected the shooting weapon from the floor, and now reached under Ilias's arm to pull a second one from the man's belt.

Nicholas stepped up beside her, scrutinizing the man carefully. The captive's eyes flicked from Ilias to Tremaine, to Nicholas, to Giliead and Gerard standing behind them. He saw the carved horn handle of Ilias's sword hilt where it poked up through his coat above the shoulder. His wary expression turned a little incredulous. He said in Rienish, "You're not Gardier."

"You should realize by now that that isn't an assumption you can safely make," Nicholas told him deliberately. "You're using the hidden cellar at number 12, Street of Courts?"

Now the man's eyes widened. He was sweating in the chill air. "Who are you?"

Giliead had slipped past them to investigate the passage the man had come down, one of Gerard's curse lights drifting along after him. Now he ducked back to report softly, "There's another Rienish curse down here, a big one, not so subtle. I think it's hiding something. And the ground shows recent signs of people coming and going through here."

Giliead had spoken Syrnaic so the man couldn't understand him, but his face tightened with suspicion at hearing an unfamiliar language.

Nicholas stepped back from the captive, his eyes hooded. "Bring him."

Ilias threw an inquiring look at Tremaine, who rolled her eyes and gestured for him to follow Nicholas.

Giliead and Nicholas went down the passage first, cautiously, with Giliead checking for curse traps. Gerard and Tremaine followed. Ilias hauled the captive along, still keeping the knife to his throat, as they continued down the passage. He couldn't tell whether Nicholas meant to kill the man or not, so he knew the prisoner himself couldn't have a clue. Personally, Ilias hoped not; unless the man had one of those implanted crystals, his gut said this was a Rienish survivor and not a Gardier spy.

Within only a short distance the soft white curse light fell on smashed blocks of stone and broken beams, some charred by fire and still stinking of smoke. Then the passage ended abruptly in a wall of broken brick and rock, as if a Gardier bomb had caved in the buildings above. *As if*, Ilias thought, watching Giliead carefully. But these were the people who had curses strong enough to make the *Ravenna* look like a stretch of empty water.

Giliead stared at the wall, his expression tight with concentration. "Is it an illusion?" Gerard asked quietly.

"Part of it. There was a cave-in here." Giliead's arm lifted as if he was in a daze and he pointed to a section of the collapsed wall. "But there's also a door . . . there."

Nicholas stepped forward, reaching for where the handle should be, even as Gerard and Tremaine both drew breath to protest. Ilias had just enough time to clap a hand over the captive's mouth.

Between one blink and the next there was a wooden door in the wall, the brick framing it rough and broken. Nicholas produced a shooting weapon out of nowhere, giving the door a hard shove.

Ilias nearly had his arm wrenched out of the socket by the young man's attempt to struggle free, and missed what happened next. Occupied by restraining his captive and muffling his attempt to cry out without either strangling or stabbing him, Ilias was only peripherally aware of the door swinging open and the startled shouts of those inside. Giliead reached back and caught the captive's arm, helping Ilias haul him forward as hostage.

Past the door was a big stone-walled room, large beams overhead, with a faint odor of damp earth and the bitter scent of the oils the Rienish burned for fuel. There were no curse lights here, just a couple of glass-shielded lamps giving off a warm glow of firelight. There were five men inside and one woman, all dressed roughly in drab Rienish clothes. One of them had a shooting weapon pointed at Nicholas, but he hadn't fired because Nicholas and Tremaine were both pointing their shooting weapons at him.

For a moment no one said anything and Ilias felt his skin prickle with tension. Their captive had stopped struggling, breathing hard with exertion, and the silence was taut with expectation. Then the woman stepped forward into the light, and Ilias saw Tremaine twitch with the effort not to fire at the abrupt movement. He felt a flush of relief; if Tremaine had fired her weapon, they would have all killed each other in the next few heartbeats.

The woman had gray hair pulled back from a strong-featured handsome face, and wore a gray-blue dress with a brown shawl over it. Ilias could tell from the way she held her arm that she had a weapon concealed under the shawl, but she was staring incredulously at them. No, not at them. At Nicholas.

Giliead flinched suddenly, turning to face another door half-hidden in a shadowy corner. "Gerard!"

Gerard turned sharply, gesturing, one hand on the sphere's bag. Light burst for an instant, scourging shadows. Ilias caught sight of a man in the doorway before the brightness forced him to wince away. Something banged and an odor like burned air, as if lightning had struck nearby, came to him in a puff of breeze. Ilias looked back to see a man, short and sharp-featured, stagger out of the other doorway and fall to his knees, coughing. "That's enough, young man," Gerard said sharply. "I could have killed you. And you should realize that genre of attack adjuration is useless against the Gardier. Save your strength for illusions and charms."

The man looked up, his face white in the blending of firelight and curse light, and Ilias realized he was barely out of boyhood. Staring at Gerard, he choked out, "Who the hell are you?"

But the woman was still regarding Nicholas with an almost reverent expression. She said slowly, "God above, is it your ghost?"

Ilias heard Tremaine swear under her breath, and mutter, "I knew it."

"I'm all too solid, and ghosts don't age." Nicholas smiled slightly, though it was a smile that gave nothing away. He nodded toward their baffled hostage. "Your son, Madame Cusard?"

"My nephew, Ricard," she said, then urgently, "But how—"

Nicholas interrupted, "I recognized him. He has his grandfather's nose." Though Ilias didn't think that was the question the woman meant to ask, and he thought Nicholas knew that as well.

The woman blinked. "God, it is you." She told the men with her, "Put the guns away, boys." More sharply, as they hesitated, "Now."

As the wary men complied, Nicholas pocketed his shooting weapon and said in Syrnaic, "Release him."

Tremaine didn't object, though she hadn't put her weapon away. Ilias glanced at Giliead, who gave him a resigned shrug. Ilias turned the young man loose, propelling him forward just enough to keep him from grabbing a weapon from any of the others.

Ricard stumbled, caught his balance, and joined the woman, demanding, "Who is he?"

She threw a look at him, her mouth a tight line, but something about her spoke more of elation than dread. "Who do you think it is, turning up here, back from the dead, with a real Rienish sorcerer—"

"Hey!" the young wizard, still on the floor, objected.

"You're one of Berganmot's apprentices, aren't you?" Gerard said to him, still sternly. "Found and trained on the battlefield?"

"Yes." The wizard studied him suspiciously. "What have you got in the bag?"

"Take care or you'll find out," Nicholas told him, with a lifted brow. The words could have been a joke but Ilias was sure they weren't. These people might know him, but Nicholas was only trusting them so far. *I hope,* Ilias thought worriedly. Nicholas eyed the woman again. "We need reliable transportation, a safe distance outside the Cabellard Gate. Tonight."

She nodded, businesslike. "You'll have it. At the old mews on Vintner's Row, in two hours."

Nicholas inclined his head to her. Tremaine, obviously having had enough of this, said tightly, "We need to go."

Nicholas nodded. He told the woman, "The Gardier will be concentrating on Castillion Gardens tonight. Avoid it for the next few days," and swept out of the room. Gerard, with one more severe look at the young wizard, followed. Ilias and Giliead backed out with Tremaine. Ilias tried to keep an eye on the door as they retreated down the passage, but the shadows closed in and he couldn't see if the illusory part of the cave-in had returned or not.

"Come along," Nicholas said from the corridor, deadpan. "We're wasting time."

Tremaine jammed her weapon back into her coat pocket with a snarl.

"One of those men was wearing an army fatigue jacket, and Berganmot's apprentice must have been with the retreat," Gerard pointed out quietly.

"Yes. Madame Cusard and her nephew were the only ones I recognized," Nicholas admitted. "I left her in charge of part of my organization when I left Vienne last. It wouldn't surprise me if she was recruiting the retreating soldiers, but it will make her vulnerable to spies. She will realize that herself, of course. I don't expect any of the other remaining members of the organization to have contact with anyone but her."

"Oh, that's jolly," Tremaine muttered. "So who do we think is going to be at the Vintner's Row mews?"

"The Gardier will be there, of course," Nicholas said with a faint air of impatience. "The person we actually want to contact will be waiting for us near there."

Tremaine swore under her breath, and said to Ilias, "Do you understand why I'm like this now?"

"I understood before," he told her, and got a suspicious glare in response. *That didn't help.* He resolved just to look blank if she asked him something like that again.

They started down the corridor and Giliead asked Nicholas quietly, "Will you give them a sphere?"

"That boy may have some natural talent, but he's a bit undisciplined," Gerard objected.

"If the right person is waiting for us at Vintner's Row," Nicholas answered obliquely, "they'll get their sphere."

Tremaine had to admit the rail tunnels had been a good idea, even with the encounter with Nicholas's old gang. The tunnels had allowed them to rapidly leave the Castillion Gardens area without being seen. But once they climbed up to street level again, the situation hadn't changed much. From a vantage point down the dark street they could see there were Gardier at the Cabellard Gate. A large party with spotlights and a sorcerer crystal was camped out to one side of the two-story stone arch that framed the giant gate. But past the patrol's lights the night was silent and intensely dark.

The old city wall wound off on both sides, with inns, shops, a garage and even a tumbledown block of flats built right up against it. For decades the wall had been nothing but a quaint historical obstruction and some of the buildings leaning familiarly against it had been there since the previous century.

Giliead and Ilias went ahead to scout a way over, while Tremaine, Nicholas and Gerard waited in the shelter of a looted grocer's shop, safely out of sight of the gate. Ilias returned after a short time to guide them down Cabellard Street to a set of flats that had been artists' studios. The artists had had a little patio atop the flat roof, and it was an easy climb from there to the broad top of the city wall, and from there a slightly harder climb down to the roof of an inn.

Once they got down to the ground, Nicholas led the way through the maze of smaller avenues to Vintner's Row, barely hesitating in the dark. It was a good distance from the gate, and Tremaine's feet were beginning to hurt by the time they reached the street. They took cover in a Martine-Viendo Wire office that had lost its front façade in some small explosion. "The mews is the building down toward the end, the one with the three arches," Nicholas said, taking a cautious look around the edge of the empty doorway. The bay window and most of the storefront was blasted out, with piles of broken brick and shattered glass mixed with plaster dust. Nicholas had chosen it in particular; Tremaine felt he had a reason, but wasn't going to oblige him by asking for it. "It used to be a large stable but was converted to an automobile court. There may still be a supply of gasoline there. I rather hope so. It will make a handy diversion."

Behind her, Tremaine heard a faint movement as Giliead twitched. Quietly grim, he said, "There's a Gardier wizard crystal up there somewhere. I just felt it."

"They're going to blow that place up, aren't they?" Tremaine asked quietly. "Not the Cusards, but whoever Madame Cusard reported to."

"What about the Gardier?" Ilias asked, keeping his eyes on the back entrance while Giliead watched the front. "Can't their crystal stop the building from blowing up?"

"It could, if the Gardier knew there was a bomb," Gerard answered softly. "But I suspect they don't know, and even if they've done the mechanical disruption spell as a precaution, it won't work on a few sticks of explosive and a long fuse."

Nicholas turned his back, using his hand torch to look at his pocket watch, shielding the light from the street. "We should know in the next—"

The explosion from the far end of the street made Tremaine flinch back against the brick and clap her hands over her ears. Plaster chips and dust rained down from the ruined ceiling above and the ground trembled. Fire lit the night, making the area around the ruined telegraph office even darker. She shook the plaster dust out of her hair and over the not-so-distant roar of fire, heard Nicholas say with satisfaction, "Yes, I think the gasoline was still stored there."

A dark-colored automobile roared out of a side street, executed a hairpin turn in the center of Vintner's Row, and screeched to a halt beside the office. Startled, Tremaine pushed off from the wall, aiming her pistol. Ilias whipped around and Giliead and Gerard backed rapidly away from the opening. Nicholas just looked over his shoulder, one brow lifted.

It was a big black touring car. Nicholas took a step forward, standing in the red glow of the fire now illuminating the street, deliberately showing himself to whoever was driving the automobile. Tremaine hesitated, wondering if he was mad, then realized it was a highly unlikely motorcar for the Gardier to be driving. The front passenger door flung open and a man leaned out. The firelight revealed the face of a handsome older man with long gray hair and Tremaine recognized Reynard Morane. "Get in," he snapped.

Nicholas strode to the motorcar. Gerard followed, saying under his breath, "I should have known."

I did know, Tremaine thought, rolling her eyes and hurrying to pull open the back door. She climbed in, scrambling across the broad bench seat to make room for Giliead and Ilias. The two Syprians moved quickly enough, though Ilias made a disgusted noise. He hated automobiles.

As Nicholas made room for Gerard, Morane said, "Good God, it is you. What took you so long?" Tremaine had met Reynard Morane for the first time in Vienne, while the city was being evacuated. She had known before then that he was Captain of the Queen's Guard; she hadn't known that he was one of her guardians and a former crony of Nicholas's.

"I was unavoidably detained," Nicholas told him. As soon as the last door was shut, Morane slammed the motorcar into gear and sped off.

The headlamps weren't lit as the automobile tore through the dark streets. Morane took the next turn, tires squealing, and Tremaine grabbed the back of the seat, swaying over into the door. The interior smelled of the fine glove-soft leather upholstery and faintly of old cigar smoke. Morane said, "Damn it, Nicholas, tell me where you've been."

"How did he know where we were?" Ilias demanded in Syrnaic.

"To certain members of my original organization, 'Vintner's Row mews' is a code for 'Martine-Viendo Telegraph Office,' " Nicholas answered in Rienish, sounding vastly satisfied with himself.

"Of course it is," Tremaine said under her breath, as Ilias swore in disbelief. The car jolted, throwing her against the door. *God, he drives like me.* She hoped Morane knew what he was doing. In the front seat, braced for an impact, Gerard said thickly, "If you'd like, once we're far enough away from the Gardier patrol at the Cabellard Gate, I can cast an illusion so that no one outside the car can see the lamps."

The motorcar took another turn and Tremaine heard Ilias swear softly, though Giliead was stoically silent. Her eyes had adjusted again and she could dimly see a street like a cavern, buildings leaning in close on either side. "That would be handy." Morane sounded intrigued. "I didn't have time to get our sorcerer to prepare anything— I only found the car half an hour ago." In rising exasperation he added, "Nic, if you don't tell me where the hell you've been—"

"I was spying on the Gardier, what did you think I was doing?" Nicholas's dry voice was annoyed.

"I thought you were dead, obviously, the more fool me." It came to Tremaine that Morane was, in his own way, nearly giddy with relief at seeing Nicholas. "Where are you all going, by the way? Not Parscia or Bisra, as I presume you came from there."

"We came from Capidara," Nicholas said. There was something in his voice Tremaine couldn't quite define, but it made the hair on the back of her neck prickle. "We're going to Lodun."

Reynard hit the brakes and the big touring car slammed to a halt. Tremaine, clutching Giliead's arm to keep from smashing her face into the front bench, saw Morane staring at Nicholas. "The *Ravenna*," Morane said, his voice quiet but with a suppressed emotion underneath that made Tremaine's breath catch in her throat. "She made it."

"And now she's back," Nicholas said, and this time Tremaine recognized the tone in his voice. It was pure menace, and pure certainty, all at once. "With a vengeance."

Morane drove out of the city, past the outskirts of deserted houses and commercial buildings, some of them burned-out shells, passing automobiles and trucks abandoned by the side of the road. Despite the darkness, Tremaine could tell some of the fires were recent; the bitter smell of smoke still hung in the air. When the fields and deserted estates gave way to heavy woods, Morane took an old farm track off the main road and followed it until they were deep into the forest. The heavy touring car took the ruts in stride, rumbling over every obstacle easily. He pulled off the road finally, into the deep shadow under a stand of big pines, the tires crackling on fallen cones and needles.

As soon as the engine cut, Ilias bailed out and staggered into the shadows to be ill in private. More dignified, Giliead climbed out slowly and walked deliberately over to lean weakly against the nearest tree.

. "The illusion will keep anyone from seeing the car lamps, from above or from the road," Gerard was saying. "It's more complicated than the charm that conceals people, so it will take some time to cast."

On the way out of Vienne, Morane had told them that they could take the automobile, that he could find another one to get back to town. "We have something for you in return," Nicholas had told him. "A handy tool for a sorcerer, if you have one."

"At the moment I've got a frightening old biddy of a hedgewitch and an octogenarian Aderassi academic, so any help would be greatly appreciated." Morane had thrown a glance at Nicholas, causing the motorcar to sway dangerously close to a wrecked omnibus. "I presume Gerard has been constructing more Viller spheres? If you've got a spare one for me, I'll kiss you."

"If he stops this thing," Ilias muttered in Syrnaic, from somewhere close to the floorboards, "I'll do anything anybody wants."

"Take deep breaths," Tremaine advised. Giliead, who hadn't moved except to brace himself against the motorcar's sway, reached down to sympathetically ruffle Ilias's hair.

"Tremaine's married," Nicholas told Morane, as if he expected the news to shock him as much as it apparently had Nicholas.

"Is she?" Morane was startled. "Good God, I'm old."

Now, standing in the dark quiet clearing, Tremaine watched from a little distance as Gerard circled the touring car with the sphere, weaving the illusion. Behind her, Morane said quietly to Nicholas, "You realized there was a strong possibility Madame Cusard's group was compromised, of course."

"Of course. I hope she used this opportunity to pick out the traitor."

"I'm hoping for good news when I get back. I hope it's not Berganmot's boy—we could use another sorcerer, even a half-trained one." Morane was still looking at Nicholas, and in the dim light Tremaine saw him shake his head suddenly.

So did Nicholas. "Don't get sentimental," he said, but he had a smile in his voice.

"Bastard," Reynard retorted, sounding fond. He looked away for a moment, regaining his composure, then continued, "If you've got maps, I can mark a path that should keep you out of the way of the major Gardier occupation areas. They're keeping to the cities, ignoring the countryside, for the most part. But one of the last reports we had was that a large Gardier detachment was bypassing Vienne and was apparently headed straight for Lodun."

Nicholas nodded, taking a folded map out of the inside pocket of his coat. "That's not surprising. They have a use for the sorcerers there."

Tremaine turned away, not wanting to hear it again. Reynard Morane had stayed here by choice, to fight this to the bitter end, and she hadn't. She found Ilias, who had recovered enough to walk a perimeter of the clearing, sword propped on his shoulder. She thought Giliead might be scouting further off in the trees, nearly invisible in the shadows. She paced Ilias long enough to say quietly, "Watch out for fay." They didn't usually come this close to Vienne, but all the chaos and the lack of sorcerers would surely attract them.

He tilted his head, telling her he didn't understand the word, and she clarified, "Like curselings. They can't stand cold iron." His sword and her pistol both qualified.

He nodded, and knowing she was making too much noise, she returned to the others. Morane had found a reasonably flat spot of ground to spread the map and was using a small pocket torch to see as he carefully marked a route with a pen.

Tremaine stood beside Nicholas. The light was reflecting off the map just enough for her to see his expression clearly, and she caught an unguarded look on his face. "You want to stay here, don't you?" she asked him. She could understand it. Reynard's information would give them a mostly clear path to Lodun. Getting there, and making the circle once they were within range of the town, was all Gerard's job, and she, Ilias and Giliead were more than enough to guard him while he did it. Nicholas's talents would be wasted. He belonged here in Vienne, where he could gather the threads of the organization that Reynard and the Cusards had kept alive and pull them back into a deadly web. "You should stay. We can handle it from here."

The unguarded expression disappeared. Nicholas said dryly, "Why, thank you for your permission, Tremaine."

Tremaine made a derisive noise, unimpressed. "Somebody's got to give you permission, if you won't give it to yourself." She shook her head. "Knowing Arisilde, he probably sent us here because he had a feeling this would happen. Maybe he didn't know that we would run into Captain Morane, but he knew that things would go better for us if he sent us here and not to Port Rel. If he did, and this is it, you can't waste that."

Still carefully marking the map, Reynard said, "She's right, Nic."

Nicholas didn't reply. The forest was intensely quiet, not even a wind stirring the trees. The small sounds of Gerard's spellcasting and the scratch of Reynard's pen on the waxed map paper seemed loud by contrast. Ilias and Giliead, moving through the brush not so far away, were entirely silent. Tremaine felt they should have been able to hear something from the city, even out here, but there was nothing. As if it had been wiped from the face of the earth. Then Nicholas said, "I should never have left Arisilde alone."

He sounded regretful, guilty. Hearing Nicholas express guilt was unexpected, but Tremaine didn't need to think about her response. She countered, "I'm not Arisilde."

Reynard glanced up at her, his face lined and drawn in the torch-light, and gave her a quick wink. Nicholas looked away a little. "What?" Tremaine demanded suspiciously.

"By God, you're all grown up." Nicholas shook his head, almost wryly. "And your mother predicted I'd kill you by your next birthday."

Tremaine went still, staring blankly. She didn't want to hear what her mother had said to Nicholas on her deathbed. She wasn't ready for that. Or at least, she had never been ready before, not that he had ever demonstrated any inclination to tell her. Morane had paused now to watch Nicholas too. Uneasily fascinated, she asked, "Did she really say that?"

He threw her that opaque look again, but instead of dodging the question, he said, "It was in the nature of a challenge to me, to make sure I'd feel sufficient motivation to take care of you. It was part of the way we always spoke to one another."

Tremaine realized she had her arms wrapped around herself under her coat. She dragged the subject firmly back where it belonged. "So, will you stay?"

Nicholas looked into the distance, his eyes narrowing. "Yes, I'll stay."

Chapter 17

You were awfully quiet around Morane," Tremaine said to Gerard, sometime later. It was late into the night and she was driving the touring car, its lamps illuminating the dirt road ahead. They were cutting around the edge of a large forest, the trees just half-sensed shadows towering on either side of the road. They had been driving for hours, and the last time Gerard had consulted the map, he had estimated that they were about halfway there.

So far they had spotted the lights of three distant airships, but Gerard's illusion had held and none had demonstrated any sign of noticing the automobile's lamps. The route Morane had outlined bypassed any villages or small towns that might hold Gardier troops or spies, so except for the airships, they might have been traveling through deserted country. *Dead country,* Tremaine thought, remembering the ancient ruins around the circle cave, and the ice city. Maybe someday in the future more travelers would come through a gate circle and find the ruins of Vienne. *That's right, cheer yourself up,* she thought dryly.

It was too dark to reliably read expressions, but at the other end of the front bench, she heard Gerard shift uncomfortably. "Was I?" He sounded casual. "I don't recall."

Ah ha. Tremaine lifted a brow. "I recall." About the only thing Gerard had said was a brief explanation of how to use the sphere for Reynard to pass along to his sorcerers.

Ilias was in the back, curled up in the corner asleep, apparently as a defense against nausea. Giliead seemed to have gotten used to the motion; now he shifted forward, leaning against the back of the front bench to listen.

Gerard sighed in annoyance. "I met him many years ago. And as I told you before, I knew he and your father knew each other, but I wasn't sure of the extent of their connection, though I had my suspicions."

"And?" Tremaine prompted inexorably.

She could feel him glaring at her. "All right, fine. When I was a very young man, I used my magical talent for confidence games."

"You what?" Tremaine's jaw dropped. She stared at him in the dark, until Giliead prompted, "Ah, the road?"

"Oh, sorry." Tremaine steered away from the approaching ditch. "You did what?" she asked Gerard again.

"I was foolish, I had no money, and I was . . . somewhat unscrupulous," Gerard admitted reluctantly.

"Really." Tremaine bit her lip, trying to keep the laughter out of her voice, but she didn't think she succeeded.

Gerard continued, speaking through gritted teeth. "Unfortunately—or fortunately, as it turned out—I attempted this on a man I did not realize was Reynard Morane. He was in the Queen's service at that time, but this was before he became Captain of the Queen's Guard, so he wasn't well known. At least in my circle of acquaintance. He caught me out, of course, but instead of turning me in to the Magistrates, he took me to your father. Nicholas offered to pay for my education at Lodun if I would work for him after I became more proficient." He added, grimly, "Are you happy now?"

Tremaine was flashing back to Nicholas telling her *Gerard was not chosen as your guardian for his status as a paragon of propriety.* "I'm ecstatic," she told him.

Gerard fumed in silence for a moment, then said deliberately, "At this point in time, when the entire fate of Lodun is resting on my jury-rigged spell, I really don't need any reminders of my insalubrious past."

"Oh." *Well, if he puts it that way.* She heard Giliead shift uncomfortably and knew he was about to ask for a definition of *insalubrious.* She firmly changed the subject.

★   ★   ★

They stopped just as dawn broke to let Gerard adjust the illusion for daylight. Tremaine had pulled the motorcar off under an old railroad bridge so Gerard could alter the illusion without worrying about an airship suddenly passing overhead. Gerard had pointed out that the lead in the bridge would help block any etheric vibrations and hopefully keep any Gardier sorcerer crystals from noticing their presence. The spot was also sheltered by low hills crowned with sycamore, oak and ash trees, the leaves turned to a whole spectrum of reds and yellows by the fall and the early-morning light.

The night's cold had gathered under the bridge, ground mist floating spectrally over the grass. Ilias and Giliead were pacing the dusty ground with the impatience of caged animals, cramped from the long time in the automobile. Tremaine's stomach was grumbling so she dug some dried fruit and tinned meat out of their supply pack. Giliead accepted some fruit with a faint expression of distaste but Ilias just shuddered and looked away.

Driving at night, far from Vienne's dangerous environs, had lulled Tremaine into a sense of security. The dawn revealed they were about to enter the area of gently rolling hills and open fields that surrounded Lodun, and the automobile seemed huge and obvious on the wide dirt road. They had also come to the end of Reynard's recent information on Gardier troop movements near Lodun. The map also didn't show many of the little country lanes that would be safer than the main roads; fortunately, Gerard knew the area well enough to navigate it. Still, the danger of staying near any road at all had increased a hundredfold.

Ilias thought so too. "We should leave it," he told her, arms folded as he watched Gerard circle the touring car. "We can run the rest of the way."

Tremaine rolled her eyes. She had been obsessively studying the map to see how much further they could safely go, and knew just how far away the town still was. "You two could run. Gerard and I can't."

"You can't?" Ilias glanced at her, frowning. "Seriously?"

"It's easy," Giliead added encouragingly, "You just pace yourself."

Having seen the amount of ground Syprians could cover on foot on the way to the Gardier stronghold of Maton-devara, Tremaine knew the two of them could probably go cross-country and reach Lodun before the touring car. The fact that it would be infinitely safer just made it more annoying that Tremaine couldn't do it. "Just stop it, all right? We're not running." She could feel them exchanging a look over her head but ignored it.

"That's done," Gerard said, tucking the sphere back into the bag. He threw a worried glance up at the sky. "Let's get moving."

They drove for another hour and counted six airships, the black predatory shapes clearly outlined against the gradually lightening sky. "That's more than we've seen all night," Gerard said, worried. "Averi was right, they must be getting ready to move on Lodun."

"If they're moving troops into the area, at least it means that they're expecting resistance," Tremaine put in. The fields to either side were fallow, though whether their owners were still alive to replant in the spring was debatable. They were neatly divided off by low mounds planted with stands of trees, and Tremaine had seen an occasional farmhouse or outbuilding in the distance, though there was no sign of chimney smoke or other indications of life. Now the rutted road was curving up to the top of a low hill, crowned by a stand of oaks. "They must know the people inside aren't all dead."

Gerard flicked a wry look at her. "Your brand of optimism is truly unique."

"People keep telling me that and I have no idea why— Shit." As the car topped the hill, Tremaine saw a long section of road, cutting through fields and running alongside a wide streambed. Also revealed were six large trucks, one of which had its hood propped open and its engine issuing puffs of steam. Milling around them were dozens and dozens of Gardier, their brown uniforms plain under the bright morning light.

Slamming on the breaks would just make noise; Tremaine let the car drift gently to a halt on the side of the road, in the shadow of one of the leaning oaks. She saw the trucks had been looted on the Gardier's progress through Ile-Rien; one had side panels with the name of a Vienne furniture factory, another had the open sides of a truck meant to haul livestock.

"Get out or stay with the wagon?" Giliead asked quietly in the appalled silence.

"Stay in the car," Gerard said. "The illusion is tied to it. If we climb out here, they might see us."

"Right," Tremaine muttered. She shifted into reverse, felt the gears grind in the big metal body, and carefully backed out of sight.

There was a collective breath of relief as the hill rose up between them and the Gardier. Tremaine put the brake on as Ilias asked, "What about the gate curse? Are we close enough yet?"

Gerard dug out his notes and consulted the map carefully. He thought about it for a moment, looking out the window, eyes narrowed in concentration. "Another few miles—it'll mean the difference between success and disaster."

Tremaine nodded. Trying to make that distance in the automobile would mean backtracking for ten miles, probably more, and they had bypassed that alternate route because it went too close to the main road. It was time to abandon the touring car. "We can do that on foot. Everybody get out, I need to hide this thing." Gerard had said earlier that the illusion wouldn't last more than a few hours without being renewed, and she didn't want the Gardier to wander back over the hill and suddenly notice a large black touring car that certainly hadn't been there when they had come down the road earlier.

The others bailed out and Tremaine released the brake, easing the big automobile down off the road and back through the ditch, between the oaks. Acorns cracked under the tires and she brought the car gently to rest deep in the grove. She cut the engine and climbed out. Hiding it completely would be better, but the next nearest stand of trees was too far across the field and the automobile would just become mired in the soft dirt and mud trying to reach it. Here, at least, if the Gardier found it they might assume they had passed it without noticing. If someone with a sorcerer crystal checked it for etheric traces, however, the game was over.

Giliead shouldered the pack with the extra spheres, Gerard took charge of his bag and Tremaine took the provisions and ammunition, letting Ilias take the heavier bag with their canteens. She checked to make certain the explosives Nicholas had tucked into the bag before leaving with Reynard were on top and easy to get to.

The birdsong seemed hushed, as if even they were reluctant to attract Gardier attention. After a moment's thought, Tremaine dropped the key to the touring car on its front seat and rolled up the window. If the war ended in their favor and the owner of these empty fields returned, he would at least find a pleasant surprise in his oak grove.

"Tremaine, come along," Gerard whispered harshly.

"All right, all right." She hurried back through the trees, trying not to trip on the roots buried in the dead leaves. Ilias was already ranging ahead, scouting, and Giliead strode along, scanning the countryside for movement. They didn't stop until they were well away from the road, with two more low hills and several scattered stands of trees between them and the Gardier.

The air was cold and crisp but as Gerard consulted the map and the compass, Tremaine already found herself sweating. The wind brought them snatches of voices speaking Aelin, and the grumble of truck engines. The daylight and the lack of tree cover made her feel terribly exposed. *If we'd moved faster, got to this point while it was still dark . . .* But that was pointless. If they had moved faster, they would still have come up on the Gardier troops.

"Right." Gerard nodded briskly, folding up the map. "We need to head that way."

As soon as they were far enough from the Gardier, Gerard cast the illusion charm that would conceal them from casual view. It made Tremaine feel a little better, but not by much.

The sky was clear and the tall grass wet from dew. Tremaine reflected that you might almost be fooled into thinking this was a country hike on an ordinary day, except for the strange hushed quality to the birdsong and the occasional scent of smoke on the wind. Ilias and Giliead took turns ranging ahead, finding a route that wound through the low hills and small pockets of trees and undergrowth, then backtracking, making sure they weren't being followed. *If they could do this alone, they'd be in Lodun, have handed out the spheres, and be eating lunch by now,* Tremaine thought dryly. They crossed through an untended apple orchard and skirted a vineyard that had been burned down to the scorched ground, but the Syprians kept their route well out of sight of any houses.

Tremaine had an abundance of nervous energy so wasn't really noticing the distance, but she saw Gerard was turning a bit red, and it wasn't from the sun. Finally, he paused, breathing hard, to consult the map. Tremaine peered over his arm and when Giliead came jogging back for a report, Gerard told him, "We're just within the range. Please start looking for a sheltered spot for the circle."

Giliead nodded thoughtfully and took off again. Gerard wiped sweat from his brow and folded the map. "You all right?" Tremaine asked, eyeing him. She was sweating too, despite the cool air, and the singlet she was wearing under her sweater was damp. But she didn't think she felt anywhere near as bad as Gerard looked.

He gave her a glare. "I'll be fine."

After they had gone a short distance Giliead came back to lead them to a low spot near a stream with a little footbridge, sheltered by brush and saplings and a large willow. The ground was mostly flat and strewn with gravel from past floods. As Gerard dropped his bag and immediately began pacing off the circle, Tremaine peered through the screen of brush. She saw the stream wound through a field to pass near a group of thatched cottages and a couple of larger fieldstone houses, all silent and deserted. Some distance past that she saw yet another Gardier airship, floating above a hazy dome of storm clouds. *It's going to rain over there,* she thought stupidly, then felt a shock that made her scalp prickle as she realized what she was looking at. That was the barrier.

The cloud was light gray on the edges, shading down to dark and roiling in the center, and a flash of lightning streaked across it as she watched. She retreated from the brush, a thorny branch catching at her sweater, feeling a chill that had nothing to do with the cool air. "Damn," she commented to Giliead. He stood nearby watching Gerard as he started to lay out the first of the cork pieces with the circle symbols. "Did you see that thing?"

He grimaced. "I've been able to smell it since before dawn. It smells like a thunderstorm, and like death, all wrapped together."

"Gah." Tremaine rubbed both her hands through her hair, her scalp already itchy with sweat and dust. She had a bad feeling about this. Even more so than usual. *If we're too late, if the Gardier have been inside and everyone's dead . . .* But no, they would hardly be amassing troops and airships here if they knew there was no one inside capable of resistance.

Giliead deposited the pack of spheres beside Gerard's bag, then took off to tell Ilias where they were and to scout the area. Tremaine paced, checked her pistol three times to make sure it was loaded, and paced some more.

Gerard had nearly half the cork squares laid out, held down with river pebbles, when Giliead returned, striding through the tall grass, ducking under the low branches of the willow. "What?" Tremaine demanded immediately. Giliead looked urgently worried.

"This curse circle is much louder than the others," he told her.

Gerard looked up, frowning at the interruption. "What?"

"The one on the *Ravenna* was noticeable, once I got near it, but the one you made in Capistown, and all the others we found after that, were quiet. I don't know about the one at Cineth—the god kept trying to talk to it so I couldn't hear anything else—but this one—" He winced, gesturing to the half-finished circle. "This one is shouting. And the scent is strong too. It's not a bad scent, but still—"

Gerard stared at him, then down at the cork squares, in disgust. "Oh, damn."

Tremaine swore more succinctly. "Because it's different from the other spells, because it's cobbled together, it puts out more etheric vibrations."

"Exactly," Gerard agreed grimly, putting down the next square and making the ritual gestures to connect it to the others. "There's nothing to be done about it."

Giliead shook his head, giving Tremaine a frustrated look, then he went back through the trees to keep watch.

Tremaine paced again, snarling under her breath. *We should have tested it,* she told herself. *Oh right, when was that going to happen? And how were we going to test this?*

She realized she was distracting Gerard and went to sit near the base of the willow. Rocking back and forth, gritting her teeth with anxiety, she suddenly caught movement out of the corner of her eye.

Tremaine turned her head, reaching for the pistol tucked into her jacket pocket.

Something was crouched in the grass on the bank of the stream, not two paces away from her. Its face was brown and wizened, like that of a ruinously old man, but a man that thin and skeletal would surely be dead. The hands were gnarled but the nails looked long and sharp, and it was dressed in ragged brown pants and a shirt that hung off its bony shoulders. Rank strings of gray hair were collected under a grimy badly dyed red kerchief. . . . *Cap,* Tremaine corrected herself sourly. *It's a goddamn Red Cap.* She thought of the old fieldstone houses standing next to the cottages down by the stream. Red Caps were traditionally drawn to stone ruins and those houses had been left standing empty. Red Caps also ate travelers, dying their caps with human blood. It said, in a grating voice with a thick country accent, "You look tasty, little girl."

Tremaine had never seen a real fay this big before, only the tiny bright flower fay that sometimes inhabited gardens. It leaned toward her, gray lips drawing back to reveal a mouthful of brown-stained fangs. All the advice for dealing with fay Tremaine had ever heard or read flashed through her mind. Don't look in their eyes, don't listen to them, don't antagonize them, run away. Instead, she went with her first instinct. She looked into the black pits of its eyes, drew the pistol and aimed for its head, saying in a level voice, "So do you."

Its eyes widened. It hesitated, seemed to sense her sincerity, then drew back slowly. It grumbled, "Bloody humans."

Gerard had ignored the interruption, if he had even been aware of it, methodically continuing to lay out the squares, whispering the words that made them a Great Spell rather than just a collection of cork and ink. A noisy Great Spell. Tremaine kept her hand on her pistol and one eye on the Red Cap. It crept back down the streambed and settled at the base of a stunted tree at the edge of the clearing. She wanted to just shoot the damn thing, but the noise would surely attract the Gardier.

Tremaine sat there, trying not grind her teeth, trying not to count each symbol of the circle, until Ilias slipped through the bushes at the far side of the clearing. There were leaves caught in his hair and his queue had come mostly unraveled, as if he had been pushing or crawling through brush, and from his harried expression the news wasn't good. Tremaine pushed to her feet, striding across to meet him. He told her, "Three patrols, coming up all around us."

"Great," Tremaine snarled. She looked at the circle again. Gerard had about a third of it left to go.

Ilias nodded, his mouth set in a grim line. "Each group must have wizard crystals—" His eyes narrowed as he spotted the Red Cap, and he stepped toward it, sword suddenly drawn.

"Hold it." Tremaine caught his arm to stop him. She looked at the Red Cap thoughtfully. It had recoiled in startled fear from the three feet of gleaming steel blade. Obviously, it was more used to people who ran away, not people whose first impulse was to attack. "I've got an idea."

"What?" Ilias glanced at her doubtfully. "An idea for that thing?"

She took a couple of steps toward the Red Cap, which eyed her uneasily. "I'm not doing nothing," it muttered. "I never hurt nobody—"

"Shut up and listen," Tremaine interrupted. "There's a bunch of people in brown uniforms over that way. If you go eat a few of them, I promise not to cut you into little pieces and our sorcerer probably won't set you on fire."

The Red Cap considered this dubiously, its mad dark eyes confused. She had read once that the average fay's intelligence, for all their ability to talk and their cunning, wasn't much better than the average dog's. "What'll you give me for it?"

Tremaine swore. "What do you want?"

It considered, an expression of almost comic concentration on its face, much at odds with the sharp fangs. "A spindle."

She clapped a hand to her forehead. "I don't have a damn spindle, we're in the middle of the woods, you stupid— All right, all right." She dug into her pocket for the remains of her hastily eaten breakfast. She found a still-intact package and pulled it out. "How about some dried orange pieces?"

For a moment she thought that was going to be too rational an offer for a creature who wanted a spindle. But its long nose twitched as it sniffed toward the package. Then it nodded. "It's a bargain."

She tossed it the package and it clutched it tightly, still eyeing Ilias warily as it circled around him and skittered for the brush. "Will it really help?" Ilias asked, following after it at a careful distance.

"I think so." Tremaine nodded, ducking under the branches he held aside for her. "Making deals with them is dangerous, but getting killed by Gardier is dangerous too. And I think it was more afraid of us than hungry." She was aware she wasn't making sense but Ilias seemed to get the gist.

The Red Cap vanished into the brush, at least to Tremaine's eyes, and Ilias led the way up the slope to a slight rise, where Giliead stood in the cover of a stand of big ash trees, worriedly surveying the vista of tree-dotted hills and fields. Moving up to stand next to him, Tremaine saw the first group of Gardier almost immediately.

There were about a dozen of them, about two fields over, spread out, their brown coveralls blending into the bare earth and weeds. The sun gleamed off the blue steel of rifle barrels and struck sparks off the chunk of crystalline rock the man in the lead held. *If I had a rifle, I might be able to hit that from here,* Tremaine thought, eyes narrowed. *Or hit him. Of course, that would tell them exactly where we were.*

"Tremaine made a deal with a curseling to distract the Gardier," Ilias was telling Giliead, with the air of someone who was washing his hands of the whole matter.

Giliead frowned down at her. "What?"

"It was worth a try. Maybe they'll even think it was the fay the crystals were hearing." She tried to remember if fay left etheric traces, but she had no idea. Of course, the Gardier probably didn't either.

Giliead twitched and a moment later Tremaine heard a distant outcry and a scatter of gunfire. "I just heard a wizard crystal. That must have been your curseling," Giliead said. He nodded as the Gardier patrol they could see broke into a run, going to the aid of the patrol that was invisible past the trees and the rise of the ground.

"That should buy us a little time." Tremaine nodded to herself.

"I don't know." Ilias winced, looking back toward the deserted houses, the rooftop of the tallest stone building barely visible through the trees. "The third group is over there. If they come to see what the others found, they could cut right through here."

"Oh, great," Tremaine muttered, aghast. *Now I know why they say not to bargain with the fay. They bugger everything up even when they don't intend to.*

Giliead stepped away from the tree trunk. "I'll see where they are."

Ilias frowned at him. "Draw them off? They've got shooting weapons, Gil."

Giliead threw him a repressive look, already fading back through the brush. "I know that."

Ilias looked after him, conflicted, then muttered something under his breath, watching the Gardier patrol again. Tremaine grimaced and turned to go back down to Gerard.

In the clearing, Gerard, his face gray with fatigue, had perhaps ten more symbols to put into place. Tremaine collected the provision bag and Gerard's pack, putting them next to the bag with the spheres so they could be quickly tossed into the circle when it was ready. Then she paced, trying not to tear her hair out. They were so close. The thought intruded that what they might be close to was an imprisoned town that had been dead since the beginning of the war, but she shook it off.

Ilias came through the brush at a run, telling her, "They're closing in. It's either make it work or run away."

Tremaine looked at the circle again. Gerard had three symbols to go. It was either now or never, and running away meant never. "We'll make it work."

Ilias glanced over the circle, nodded, and bolted off in the direction Giliead had taken. Looking after him, Tremaine felt her stomach cramp with nerves.

Gerard laid down the last symbol, and though he made no move or gesture, she knew he was drawing the complicated gate spell to a close. Gunfire rang out and she flinched, spinning around, but there were no Gardier crashing through the trees. Yet. *God, that was close,* she thought, her heart pounding.

Gerard pushed to his feet, the sphere tucked under his arm, moving as if his entire body ached. "It's ready. Where are—"

"On their way." *I hope*. Tremaine grabbed the pack with the spheres, carefully depositing it inside the circle. "The Gardier are all around us, Gerard. They're going to find the circle."

He looked around almost vaguely, utterly exhausted, but said, "I'm prepared for that."

Looking up as she dumped the other two bags into the circle, Tremaine saw there were pronounced hollows under his eyes and his face was pale. "You look awful."

Gerard mopped the sweat from his forehead with his handkerchief, saying dryly, "Thank you, Tremaine."

Shots rang out, close enough to make Tremaine duck reflexively, and Ilias and Giliead tore through the brush, breathing hard. They leapt into the circle. "The Gardier will find these—" Giliead began, pointing toward the corkboard pieces.

Gerard stepped into the circle, gesturing and speaking. Just then a dozen brown-uniformed Gardier pounded up the streambed, shouting. Shots rang out but Tremaine felt a breath of heat and saw the air waver. The grass around the spell circle fizzed into flame like candlewicks. Ilias started and Giliead grimaced in pain, falling back a step. "There won't be a circle," Gerard said calmly. He lifted the sphere and Tremaine felt her stomach lurch as the clearing vanished in a wash of fire.

Ilias winced away from the heat and the bright flare, then it dissolved into storm cloud light. He took a startled breath. The air was damp and warm now, and smelled of wet earth and pasture. They stood on a grassy lawn only a few ship's lengths wide, under a cloudy gray sky. It was surrounded by big stone three- or four-story buildings in the Rienish style, with round and square towers and elaborate carving and colored glass in the windows. Their arrival had caused a scorched circle to form in the turf, the curse symbols visible as outlines of ash. A small herd of black-and-white cows, larger than the ones in the Syrnai, had been grazing nearby and were staring at them in faint amazement.

Also staring in amazement that wasn't faint at all were several Rienish. They stood on a stone terrace, at the base of a set of steps leading up into the largest building, an imposing structure with huge carved wooden doors framed by crystalline windows that stretched up nearly to the roof.

Gerard handed Tremaine the sphere, then his knees buckled and he started to fold up. Ilias reached to catch him but Tremaine deposited the sphere in his arms and caught Gerard herself, easing him to the ground.

Warily watching the group of Rienish, who were now hurrying toward them across the field, Ilias felt the sphere suddenly turn warm and shiver as something spun inside it. *That can't be good.* "Gil," he said, distracted, "something's—"

Swearing, Giliead stepped back, drawing his sword. "It's a curse!"

Tremaine looked up, startled, then collapsed as if she had been struck with a club, slumping down in a heap beside Gerard. Heart pounding, Ilias dumped the sphere on the ground and dragged his sword free of the scabbard, putting his back to Tremaine and Gerard.

They were already surrounded by a group of men and a few women, some old and some young, staring at them with different degrees of startled consternation. They were dressed as the Rienish normally were, in jackets and pants of dull browns and grays, some of them in rougher work clothes. The women wore knee-length dresses in brighter colors, with the slim skirts that always looked so difficult to walk in. A few men wore open robes of black-and-purple silk over their clothes, something Ilias had never seen the Rienish do before. One of the younger men dressed that way said, "Drop your weapons. We're sorcerers and you can't harm us."

Ilias snorted derisively. *If Tremaine's hurt, I'll kill that one first.* He could hear clanking and spinning from the bag of spheres, as if they all agreed, and the one at his feet threw out a brief shower of sparks. In a tone of even menace, Giliead told the young man, "The next curse you throw at us will be your last."

He looked taken aback, but started to reply. Then an old man, balding with a short fringe of crinkly gray hair, pushed to the front of the crowd, saying, "Everyone, quiet!" He wore one of the silk robes over dull brown pants and a jacket, and a dark green striped cloth knotted at his neck. Ilias tensed as he fumbled for something in a pocket, but it turned out to be a pair of glass lenses like those Gerard wore. He got these fixed over his eyes, then gave Ilias and Giliead a sharp glance, stepping to the side a little to peer down at Tremaine and Gerard. Then he asked, "Who are you?"

It was a reasonable question. Careful to speak the Rienish words clearly, Giliead answered, "We're sent to help you. What did you do to our friends?"

"Good question," the old man said grimly. He raised his voice to ask the others, "Now who did this and what is it?"

"I'm sorry, I'm sorry, it was me." A dark-haired young woman pushed to the front, out of breath and red-faced. "It's only a sleep adjuration. I saw them appear from my window and thought— Sorry. But it'll wear off shortly, no harm done."

Ilias threw a glance at Giliead for confirmation, feeling sweat run down his back. Giliead lowered his sword and knelt to make sure Tremaine and Gerard were breathing. Ilias made himself keep his eyes on the men in front of him. After a tense moment, Giliead said in Syrnaic, "She's right, they're both just asleep. I'll try to wake Tremaine. I think Gerard was struck ill before the curse hit."

Ilias took a breath, the relief sharp enough to be painful. Shaking it off, he replied in the same language, "He fell before the sphere started to spark. Don't let Tremaine kill anybody when she comes to." He realized the curse had missed him because he had been holding a sphere; good to know the thing still worked, even if it didn't have a wizard inside it.

The old man was watching them alertly, head cocked as he listened to them talk. One of the other men tried to speak to him and he motioned him to be silent, saying to Ilias, "Well, we can all see you aren't Gardier. Who are you?"

"Are you a wizard?" Ilias countered.

Being Rienish, the man didn't find this an objectionable question, and replied as readily as if Ilias had asked him if he came from Ancyra. "No, I'm the Master of the History College. I'm Arise Barshion."

Still in Syrnaic, Giliead confirmed, "I don't think he's lying. I don't smell any curses on him and I do on some of these others."

Ilias lowered his sword, enough not to actively threaten Barshion. *Great, that means the robes aren't a good way to tell which ones are wizards.* Even with Rienish wizards, he would prefer to have a way to tell. He said carefully, "We're Syprians. We're sent by—" *Who?* he thought suddenly. He couldn't remember the name of the Rienish Matriarch's daughter. "We're sent by Warleader Colonel Averi. And Lady Aviler and Count Delphane." Those were the highest-ranking Rienish he knew, and he hoped he was pronouncing the names well enough to make them understood.

Apparently he was, because there were awed murmurs and exclamations from the people surrounding them. "But how did you do this?" one of the other men asked, gesturing helplessly at the ashy remnants of the circle.

"Gerard did it," Giliead told him. "It's . . . a long story."

Another old man stepped forward, far more haggard and infirm than Barshion. Giliead watched him suspiciously but let him step close enough to lean down to look at Gerard. He straightened up, saying in astonishment, "Guilliame Gerard? Good God, it is him. You'd better call for a stretcher, Barshion, he doesn't look well."

That appeared to settle things for Barshion. He nodded to himself, telling the others, "Summon the Masters. Chani, go and run to the Lord Mayor's house, tell him to gather the city council." He turned back to Ilias, eyeing him thoughtfully. "Young man, if you'll put up that weapon, we can all go to my home and talk this out."

He was right, Gerard needed tending and these people had no reason to hurt him. And Ilias wanted badly to put his sword down so he could see for himself that Tremaine was all right. He cast a quick glance at Giliead to make sure they were in agreement, then returned his sword to the scabbard.

Barshion turned away, calling orders to someone as Ilias knelt beside Tremaine. She was breathing well, as Giliead had said, and just looked asleep. Giliead was keeping a watchful eye on Gerard, and just in case, Ilias nudged the sphere over so it lay against Tremaine's side.

The crowd around them kept milling, new people coming and going as the word spread. They were bringing the stretcher, which turned out to be a heavy canvas sling supported by two poles for carrying, when Tremaine woke. She groaned, blinked, and her hand jerked toward the pocket that held her shooting weapon. Alert for this, Ilias caught her wrist before she could drag it out. "It's all right," he said quickly in Syrnaic. "They took us for Gardier and cursed you to sleep by accident. It didn't get me because I was holding the sphere."

Tremaine swore in Rienish, violently enough to startle the people still surrounding them, and pushed herself upright. "That's just fantastic," she added bitterly, clutching her head and wincing. "What the hell's wrong with Gerard?"

Two of the younger men were helping Giliead lift him onto the stretcher. She had spoken in Rienish and one of them answered her, "We don't know yet." He gave her a suspicious glance, reminding Ilias of Ander. "Why are you here?"

Ilias rolled his eyes. *Very like Ander.* Tremaine snarled, "We're rescuing you, you idiot."

★   ★   ★

Some of the Rienish still seemed suspicious of a trick, but Tremaine used Rienish words Ilias had never heard before, and this convinced the others. Apparently they thought a Gardier spy trying to persuade them to trust her wouldn't talk to them that way.

Barshion led them out of the park to his quarters, a small vine-covered house of amber brick tucked between the larger stone edifices. It had a sharply peaked roof and colored glass windows, and was entered through a garden court. The rooms were cavelike and cool, with walls covered in dark wood and a slate stone floor, and little of the gray daylight leaked in through the windows. A few dim wisps of wizard light floated near the ceilings, revealing that the walls had the colored glass holders for curse lights, but none of them were lit.

They wanted to take Gerard off to a bedchamber; Tremaine didn't so much hesitate as stop dead, blocking the narrow hall and looking thoughtful in a threatening way. Barshion gave her a sharp glance. "I take it you're the leader?"

"Yes," Ilias said immediately.

Tremaine threw him a dark look. "Yes," she told Barshion.

"He'll be all right. I've sent for the Master Sorcerer-Healer."

After eyeing the old man, she nodded and stepped out of the way. They carried Gerard to the other room and Giliead followed to keep an eye on him, pausing to pass Ilias the pack of spheres. The room Barshion led them to was just down another short hall, and seemed to be a place for dining, but with the flat Rienish books stacked on almost every available surface. There was a small fire in a heavily carved wooden hearth surrounded by dark green tiles. The wispy wizard lights drifted in with them but Barshion took a spill and lit several candlelamps, saying, "I can't stand those damn things—always wander off just when you need them." He poked at the fire and added some wood to it.

Tremaine glanced around the room. "I take it you haven't had electricity or gas since the barrier went up."

"Yes. We rationed the coal and oil, but they've run out now too. Fortunately, the amount of unnecessary furniture in a town and a university this size is staggering." As Barshion spoke, he pushed books and papers aside to clear a space on the table, and set out cups of a delicate pottery with a blue-and-white pattern. Ilias saw that his hands were shaking, and knew the old man was maintaining his calm demeanor with effort. "We've only recently had to start cutting down trees. The large number of cottage gardens and householders who had their milk cows, sheep, goats, chickens and so forth within the town limits have kept us supplied with food, and we've converted most of the open land to agriculture. Again, fortunately, the barrier does not succeed in keeping out rain, nor has it affected the wells and groundwater. We are feeling the lack of coffee and other essentials." He opened a cabinet in the bookcase and took out a tall green bottle. "But, considering the occasion, I think I can afford to serve the last of the Ananti Red while you tell me how you came here." He gestured for her to take a seat.

Tremaine hesitated, then took a chair at the table. Ilias took a seat on a padded couch against the wall behind her, so he could keep an eye on Barshion and watch the two doorways in the other half of the room. Instinct told him to trust Barshion, but he wasn't sure if the old man was the leader here or not. He deposited the pack of spheres next to his feet, close enough to keep him from falling under any curses. As the pack shifted against the floor, he heard the contents clank and hiss.

After a moment of gripping the table, apparently to focus her thoughts, Tremaine started to tell the story. It was the brief version, concerned mostly with the spheres and the curse circles and how they had managed to get here, leaving out the personal parts. A few other people, two older men and a young woman, came in quietly and stood in the shadows of the other half of the room or shifted books aside to perch on the dusty furniture. Ilias could just glimpse others listening out in the hallway. He heard the murmurs of dismay when Tremaine told them of the Rienish cities that were occupied by the Gardier. When Barshion poured the strong red Rienish wine, he refused it with a shake of his head, feeling terribly out of place. This was a Rienish place, a Rienish moment, and he had no part in it.

Tremaine finished with, "So it's up to you, if you want to evacuate or fight. Or both. We have five spheres to give you now. The Gardier are getting ready to drop the barrier. Do you have anything that's keeping them out or was that just wishful thinking on our part?"

"Our wards were augmented shortly after the barrier appeared." Sitting at the table, listening intently, Barshion shook his head, as if waking from a dream. He sat up, his face drawn. "It was closing in on us, and if the wards hadn't held—" He gestured tiredly. "At first the Gardier made occasional forays just inside—to the no-man's-land between the barrier and our wards—to communicate with us and to test our resolve. For the last year they've been content to simply wait us out. But we can tell the wards are beginning to fail. That's undoubtedly why they're preparing to drop the barrier."

"The palace wards lasted for a long time too, but they're some of the oldest magic in the country." It was Tremaine's turn to eye him sharply. "How did you 'augment' your wards?"

One of the men on the other side of the room shifted uneasily. Barshion said, "Our Master Sorcerer used necromancy; he sacrificed himself to keep the Gardier out."

"There were times I considered that, but Niles just couldn't be persuaded to make the sacrifice," a dry voice said wearily from the doorway. "Also, I think it's going to make it damn difficult to shore up your ward structure with the spheres. I suspect we'll have to dismantle it, then build another one from the ground up."

Ilias looked up, sharply relieved to see Gerard upright and conscious and sarcastic, and even more relieved to see Giliead follow him in. An older woman came after them, saying with exasperation, "This is ridiculous, you must rest. You are completely exhausted—"

Gerard looked completely exhausted. In the candlelight his face was as white as bleached bone and his eyes were dark hollows. Tremaine grimaced but didn't comment. Ilias lifted his brows at Giliead, who cast his eyes up in a gesture of defeat. Ilias nodded, getting the message that Gerard couldn't be in a worse condition to do curses, but that there was nothing to be done about it. Gerard added, "The sooner we start the better. Our gate spell must have punched a hole right through your already weakening warding structure. If the Gardier realize it's there—"

"Gerard." Barshion stood up, regarding him seriously. "I believe we owe you and everyone else here a great deal of gratitude."

Gerard shook his head, leaning on the back of a handy chair, and trying to make it look like a casual gesture rather than a need for support. "I believe we'd all prefer to wait on that. Now if you have a spot where I can begin constructing the circle—"

Chapter 18

Again, Tremaine found herself with nothing to do except wait and feel her nerves slowly disintegrate from tension. The spheres had been given to five cautious sorcerers, who were now using them to build new wards around the town. Gerard had been right, the Master's act of necromancy had made the wards powerful enough to keep out the Gardier, but also impossible to do anything else with. Magic involving death, even a voluntary death, was terribly powerful but also tended to distort and corrupt any other etheric structures associated with it. Gerard had had a more involved and technical explanation, but that was all Tremaine had bothered to listen to. The other Lodun Masters had apparently known this; the Second Master had already taken certain texts out of the locked section of the Aldebaran Library and been boning up on the technique for his sacrifice.

For some time Gerard had been at work building the circle in the east quadrangle, a park surrounded on three sides by the pillared galleries of the Philosophy College and on the fourth by a narrow avenue that led out toward the Medical College. Gerard, using the sphere, was marking the circle out with paint on the paved area on the center of the green. He was paced by Adel Kashani, a Parscian sorceress who was trying to learn the spell, and several students. Giliead was down there with him, watching the Rienish sorcerers with enigmatic caution.

Gerard was nearly finished, though he was moving much more slowly now. Building the circle in the conventional way was slower but apparently much less physically taxing than connecting the premade symbols. And Barshion, with the Master Physician, had at least persuaded Gerard to drink a glass of wine and eat some cheese and bread before beginning. Now he looked like death warmed over instead of just death.

The Lodun town council and the university Masters were having a meeting under the gallery of the Philosophy College, with more people, from Masters and Scholars with university gowns over their battered and much-mended suits to students in shirtsleeves and summer dresses to farmers, laborers and merchants, all coming and going and spreading the news. To avoid questions she was in no mood to answer, Tremaine went up the gallery stair to the open portico that ran along the college roof. There was a good view of the court from there and part of the avenue.

The university was a maze of interconnected college courts, with houses and private gardens for the Masters and Scholars as well as student halls scattered among them. Buildings of old stone, with ancient round towers or more modern spires or green-stained copper domes stood next to the newer brick constructions. Past the low and mostly useless university wall were the houses and shops of the town, and past them the barrier.

Ilias had followed her, leaning against the balustrade to look up at the frieze carved into the pediment of the roof above. It was something about the advance of philosophy, and mainly showed a lot of old men handing each other significant objects too small to really make out. Tremaine thought the profusion of gargoyles on the Medical College more interesting.

The barrier made the air perpetually warm, giving the whole town a hothouse quality. Tremaine had dumped her jacket down on the gallery and rolled her sleeves up, though she still kept her bag over her shoulder, not willing to leave the explosives and ammunition unguarded. Ilias and Giliead had abandoned their coats as well. Ilias's queue was still coming apart and he was bare-armed and nearly bare-chested in the wine-red shirt she liked, with her ring on a thong around his neck. He was a colorful contrast against the gray stone, with the patterns stamped into the leather of his boots and pants, the curved horn hilt of the sword slung across his back, the copper in his armbands and earrings. He and Giliead both made exotic figures, and in the comings and goings below she could see Giliead was drawing almost as much attention as the circle.

Ilias turned around, looking down at the court. She hadn't thought he would say anything, but after a moment he asked, "What's wrong?"

This time Tremaine couldn't make herself answer "Nothing." There was no point in putting it off any longer. They had brought spheres to Lodun. If the *Falaise* and the *Ravenna* reached Parscia, the spheres they carried to the sorcerers there would keep the Gardier from crossing the borders. But the war would go on, possibly for years. It would surely take at least that long to convince Castines or whatever was driving the Gardier on that it couldn't get what it wanted in Ile-Rien, not anymore. There was no point in Ilias continuing to risk himself. And she knew if a stuck-up prig like Cletia was willing to unbend enough to admit she wanted him, there had to be other Syprian women willing to do the same. And all of them would be better for him than her. Not looking at him, she put her hands on the balustrade, feeling the old stone grit against her skin. "We both know this isn't going to work."

Somehow, in the back of her mind, she had assumed that he would take the easy way out as soon as she offered it. Every other man she had ever offered it to had certainly taken it. Not counting those who had bolted before she could indicate the exit. Instead, Ilias stared at her, then demanded, "What 'this'? I don't know what 'this' you mean."

He was so agitated his command of Rienish had slipped. Still not looking at him, Tremaine switched to Syrnaic, and continued doggedly, "You know what I mean. Us this. I mean, us. It's not going to work."

"I don't understand." This time he sounded more stubborn than emotional.

She made herself look at him. "Yes, you do." He just stood there glaring at her. She pressed her lips together. *He's actually going to make me say it. He's going to stand there and play dumb until I say it.* "We—as in, you and me—are not married anymore."

Ilias took that in quietly. He transferred the glare to the view of the green court below. Then he said calmly, "No."

Tremaine lifted her brows. "What do you mean, 'no'?"

"You can't do that," he explained with annoying patience. "We're still married. Karima can't give back the price, she doesn't have it anymore."

Tremaine felt her jaw tighten. *Surprise, surprise, you knew he was stubborn.* "I don't want the money back. I waive all claim to the money. She can keep it."

"You can't do that. If you don't take it back, we're still married. And Karima doesn't have it. So it's against our laws."

Tremaine flung her arms in the air. "Oh, that's a damn lie. You people have like three laws and they're all about curses. You're telling me in the whole history of the Syrnai nobody ever broke up a marriage without getting the money back."

"Yes. No. Never." Ilias folded his arms.

Tremaine tapped her fingers on the stone, seething. She kept expecting this to segue into "there's another man, isn't there" except Ilias was Syprian and could care less if there were half a dozen other men. She decided to try insults. "Oh, so this is a money thing, is it? You just want to stay married for my family's land and money and . . . things." She tried to suppress a wince. *Oh, that was convincing.*

Ilias appeared equally unmoved. He snorted derisively. "Like the house in Capistown your father was supposed to burn down? Or the land that has the Gardier camped all over it?"

Tremaine pushed a hand through her hair, snarling in frustration. "You can get married again."

"No, I can't," he explained, mock-patiently. "I'm still married to you."

She glared at him. "I'm trying to make this easy."

His expression said plainly that if she thought this was easy, she was crazy. He told her, "I don't know what's in your head, but when you get over it, I'll be here."

Swearing, Tremaine looked away. She saw that Gerard had finished the circle and was sitting on the steps of the college's gallery, his head in his hands. She pushed away from the balustrade and started for the stairs. Ilias, of course, followed her.

As she came down the gallery steps and out onto the grass, Giliead looked up, brows drawn together in worry. "What?"

Tremaine had hoped her expression was under control, but obviously it wasn't. She sensed eye-rolling and gestures going on behind her and clenched her jaw. "Nothing," she said pointedly. It had occurred to her that she would also be losing Giliead, and Gyan and Kias and the others back in Cineth. *You got along without them before,* she reminded herself. *Oh right, and how was that plan for killing yourself going?*

Gerard pushed wearily to his feet, collecting the sphere from the ground at his side. "I'll make a test first," he told Barshion and the others gathered around.

Tremaine came over to stand beside him. "You need a volunteer?" she asked.

"No," he told her, writing something in his notebook. He tore the page out and gave her a brief glance from under lowered brows. "The acoustics in this court are excellent, by the way."

Tremaine grimaced. One of the young students hurried up to hand Gerard a rock and a section of twine. As Gerard tied the note to the rock, she said, "Are you going to say 'I told you so'?"

"I'm considering saying it to Ilias," Gerard said dryly. He tossed the rock into the circle and looked at the sphere thoughtfully for a moment.

Tremaine gazed at the perpetual storm clouds above, counting to ten in Aderassi. She knew the rock had vanished by the excited murmurs from the watching crowd. She managed to say calmly, "I have my reasons."

Gerard lifted a brow, enigmatic. "I don't doubt that you do."

Before Tremaine could reply, a young man shouldered his way through the crowd, breathing hard. He did a double take at the sight of Ilias and Giliead, then stepped up to Gerard. "I'm sorry, they sent for me—They said—I'm Cathber Niles—"

"You're Breidan Niles's brother?" Gerard asked, startled. "He should be here any—"

Niles appeared in the circle to a chorus of startled and gratified exclamations from the crowd. "Hello there," he said, spotting Gerard and Tremaine first and starting toward them. "I see everything is working as—" He stopped, staring as his brother stepped forward. "Cathber?"

"God, you're alive!" Cathber flung himself on Niles in an enthusiastic greeting.

The expression on Niles's face was too personal, too painfully relieved to watch. Tremaine leaned over to ask Gerard, "Did you ask about Colonel Averi's wife?"

Gerard's expression went still. "Yes. When the barrier first appeared, it cut across a number of lodging houses and homes on the north side of town. Everyone in its path was killed. After the Master augmented the wards, the barrier was pushed back slightly and they managed to recover the bodies. She was a nurse, and had been visiting a patient in one of the lodging houses."

"Goddammit." Tremaine rubbed her eyes. She had to find some way to avoid being the one to pass that news along. At least with Ilias and Giliead back in Cineth, she would never know when they eventually tackled a wizard they couldn't kill. Unable to help herself, she broke her rule and looked at them.

Ilias was staring off toward the people still gathered on the portico, managing to appear completely unaffected. So Tremaine was the first one to see Giliead, who had been frowning absently at him, stiffen suddenly and spin around, looking toward the open end of the court. "Gerard—" Tremaine began, the back of her neck prickling with unease. Ilias turned, watching Giliead worriedly.

Giliead said, "There's a Gardier circle, I just felt it."

"Where?" Gerard shouted. Tremaine could see the sphere in his hands twitching and sparking.

Giliead moved further out into the court, head lifted, listening. "Back there somewhere!" He pointed across the left wing of the Philosophy College, to the towers behind it.

Swearing bitterly, Tremaine bolted down the court. She didn't know Lodun at all, except for brief visits years ago. She hoped someone was following her who would know the shortcuts and byways of the college courts. Behind her she could hear Gerard shouting, Barshion and Kashani echoing him, people running in all directions.

She reached the end of the gallery where an alley ran back between the Philosophy College and the wall of the women's college. She ran down it, hoping it went where she thought it did. It opened into another court, smaller and shaded by half a dozen trees, where someone had strung up an entire laundry's worth of sheets. Giliead caught up with her at that point, seized her arm and dragged her back behind him. Tremaine flattened herself against the wall. Beside her, Ilias glared. "If you try to get yourself killed, I'll— I'll—" He finished with a snarl of frustration.

"Yeah, you and who else?" Tremaine shot back at random, desperate to ignore that insight into her character. She leaned out past him to see that several students had followed them: a couple of young men in Scholars' gowns over their suits, a few men and women in battered work clothes stained with mud, as if they had just come in from gardening, and one wide-eyed young blond woman in a flower print dress. None of them seemed to be armed, but firearms were problematic where the Gardier were concerned anyway. "Nobody brought a sphere?" Tremaine asked. "You know, the thing we need to fight the Gardier?"

Giliead nudged her, showing her the copper metal ball tucked under his arm. "Gerard gave me his. The others are with the wizards working to make the new barrier."

"Right." Gerard was without a sphere, and Tremaine didn't like that, but he must realize he wasn't up to running and dodging through these courts. "Are any of you sorcerers?" she asked the students hopefully.

"All of us," one of the young men assured her.

Giliead held up the sphere, saying urgently in Rienish, "I can smell and see the Gardier curses, but I can't make this do things to stop them. Which of you is the best wizard?"

Everyone turned to the young lady in the flowered dress. She looked around at the others, and shrugged. "I suppose that's me."

Great, Tremaine thought, trying to ignore Ilias where he was pressed against her side. *Our lives are in the hands of someone who looks like she should be organizing the First Year Play or charity dinners for the Old Students' Club.* She heard bells start to ring, an urgent peal of warning. As Giliead handed the sphere to the young woman, Tremaine pulled her pistol out of the back of her belt, chambering a round. "You listen to him, you understand, all of you? To both of them. They've been doing this a long time. What's your name?"

The young woman blinked at the sudden appearance of the gun. She accepted the sphere meekly. "Yes, madam. I'm Alissa, madam."

Giliead nodded and slipped around the corner. Tremaine followed with Ilias, the students hurriedly moving after them. Alissa took a couple of long steps, catching up to Tremaine. She was wearing pumps, and the half sleeves of her dress were frayed and grubby, not that that was necessarily a by-product of Lodun's captivity; every young woman student Tremaine had ever met had been a little grubby.

Giliead led them through the court, using the drying sheets moving gently in the breeze as cover. *Why can't I hear gunfire? Where the hell are they?* Tremaine wondered, gritting her teeth. On the far side of the court they found a rambling old house made of fieldstone, with delicate leaded windows and tiny little cupolas. Giliead jerked his head, telling Ilias to go around the far side. Ilias motioned for four of the students to follow him and ran around the side of the house. His soft leather boots were silent on the grass and paving but the students' shoes made noise and Tremaine's nerves jumped. Giliead led them rapidly along the other side, through an untended flower bed. Ahead high garden walls cut off the view. Above them more college buildings loomed, heavy stonework blocking the light. "This is a lodging house for tutors—there's another quadrangle behind it," Alissa whispered. "Is that where they are?"

Tremaine flicked a look at Giliead's intent face. "Yes."

"Isn't that gun useless against them? Can't they blow it up?" one of the young men behind Tremaine asked.

She tapped the sphere in Alissa's hands. "Not while we have that."

Footsteps on grass gave them an instant of warning. Tremaine pulled Alissa back and Giliead surged forward, reaching the corner just as two Gardier came barreling around it. He slammed one in the head with his sword hilt but the second dodged sideways, lifting his rifle.

Tremaine aimed for his forehead but Alissa muttered and gestured, the sphere sparked and the man dropped the rifle with a cry, stumbling away, his hands knotted in pain. Two of the students tackled him, another grabbing up the weapon. "Damn," Alissa muttered in awe, looking down at the sphere. "You lot weren't kidding."

"Do that again!" Tremaine told her, pointing to the garden wall. Giliead was already around the corner and she plunged after him.

On the other side of the wall was an open paved court, surrounded by a grass verge and shaded by two large oak trees. A dozen or more Gardier stood there. Alissa's spell hit and most of them threw their rifles down, crying out in pain. One had been just out of range of the spell and Giliead slammed that one's rifle away with his sword. Tremaine heard Ilias shout as his group burst into the court from the far end. She dodged past Giliead, her eyes finding the man with the sorcerer crystal, standing in the center of the court. She fired as the first shots rang out, diving to the ground and hoping the students had the sense to duck.

Nothing changed and, swearing, she rolled over and fired again, mindful of how many shots she had left. This time she saw the flash of light near the crystal as it deflected the bullet. The man holding it was a Liaison, light glinting off the two crystals pocking his face, and he didn't even bother to look in Tremaine's direction. Alissa had come out from behind the wall, talking to the sphere in a low steady voice. The Liaison wasn't talking to his crystal, just holding it and glaring at Alissa as the air seemed to thicken and twist between them, the ether within so agitated it was almost visible to the naked eye.

Alissa winced and set her jaw as some part of what the Liaison was directing the crystal to do leaked through to her. Peripherally aware of fighting, yelling, of the two students with captured rifles shouting at the Gardier to surrender, of Ilias blocking the escape of several others, Tremaine shoved to her feet, willing the thought toward Alissa: *Just let the damn thing help you, don't force it!*

Then Giliead left his sword in a Gardier's chest and charged forward, tackling the Liaison to the ground. The sorcerer crystal tumbled in the grass, a few feet from the Liaison's outstretched hand. Tremaine scrabbled forward but Ilias got there first with a rock from one of the flower beds. He smashed it into the crystal, hastily backing away from the flood of liquid light pouring out of the scattered shards.

Tremaine looked around, seeing most of the Gardier captured by the students, the ones unlucky enough to encounter Ilias and Giliead lying bleeding on the ground. One of the students had managed to get shot despite the various spells, but he was sitting up and cradling his arm.

She stepped toward the Liaison, looking down at him. Giliead had him pinned to the ground, and the man was glaring up at them with a grimace of rage. He was the same one who had come to the ruin in the mountain. Tremaine said, "Remember me?"

His eyes went blank, his face transforming from that of an angry young man's into an expressionless mask. His voice distant, he said, "You're too late."

"Probably," Tremaine agreed, knowing she was talking to it, whatever it was, the thing that spoke through the Liaisons. "But I'm used to that."

"Why aren't they sending more men?" Ilias asked quietly from beside her. "If they were finally able to make a circle in our world to come here, why send this few? Why not a hundred?"

He had a point. Tremaine shook her head, thinking furiously. "The wards must be down—"

Giliead turned his head to say, "They aren't. I can still feel them. They're weak, but they're still there."

"Madam, come and look at this, please," Alissa said, as if Tremaine was her tutor and she was calling her attention to a bad citation in a text. The sphere tucked under her arm, a lock of stray hair falling across her forehead, she pointed at something on the paving stones.

Tremaine moved to her side. Faintly etched on the paving stones in lines and strokes of ash were the symbols of a circle. Tremaine followed the curve of it with her eyes, trying not to see it. "This is our circle. The one we used to get in."

"No." Ilias shook his head, pacing along the line of symbols. "These runes are different. But it burned itself into the ground, just like ours did. Does that mean it came from this world, from outside the city, like we did?" He looked up at her, stricken. "But how could they? Only Gerard and Niles knew the new curse."

He was right again. Gerard hadn't finished the spell to make the gate to enter Lodun until yesterday. *Oh. No. The more we used the circles in the mountain and the fortress, the easier it was for the Gardier to find us.* Tremaine shook her head, in horror, not denial. *What if it isn't the circles the Gardier were somehow tapping into, but the spheres themselves?*

They had known the Liaison crystals somehow communicated with each other. In Maton-devara the Liaison had found Giliead through the captured sorcerer crystal, even though it had only been out of its lead-lined box for a few moments. *Arisilde broke the crystals we found,* she thought, mentally kicking herself. When they had first come to Cineth in the *Swift,* they had put Arisilde's sphere and the small Gardier crystals they had captured in a bucket of water, to try to block the etheric vibrations. And the crystals had come out of the bucket broken and cracked and yellow. *Nicholas thought that Arisilde broke the first sorcerer crystal they found because he was trying to free the soul trapped inside. Did Arisilde know then?* Arisilde had always known things without quite knowing them, done things that turned out to be important later without knowing why he had done them. "Arisilde said the crystals see everything. What if they see the spheres too? Or if Arisilde's sphere was the only one they couldn't see, and when we started using the others . . ." The regular Viller spheres were just tools, without personalities inside them to detect and prevent that kind of spying. *If they can hear the spheres, they know all our new gate spells.* And no matter what adjustments were made to it, no matter how Arisilde or Gerard or Niles manipulated it, the world-gate circle was still a Gardier spell. They had had it the longest, maybe they were the only ones who truly understood it.

Alissa was looking down at the sphere, her nose wrinkled dubiously. Tremaine paced back toward the Liaison. He still wore that blank mask, the face of whatever controlled him. *You're too late.* Her heart was starting to pound, and she was surprised her voice came out even when she asked, "Giliead, did you feel any other circles, in the past few minutes?"

"Yes, but it was our circle, that Gerard made." Giliead looked up at her, suddenly appalled. "I thought it was our circle."

Ilias swore softly, clapping a hand to his head. Tremaine lifted the pistol, telling Giliead, "Move."

Giliead jerked back and she shot the Liaison in the head. Everyone in the court flinched as his body convulsed once and went still. Giliead pushed to his feet, stepping away from the corpse. Tremaine had already turned to Alissa. "Those crystals report everything they see. If you find any Gardier like him, with these things in his face, kill them. Don't touch the crystals. Burn the bodies." She leaned down, grabbed up one of the belt devices the Gardier used, this one a metal canister with something like a clock face, with a small crystal fused to the back. She dropped the device, ground the crystal to powder under her heel. "Break all of these." She didn't wait for an assent, already striding across the court.

Florian paced the *Ravenna*'s First Class lounge impatiently, holding one of the extra spheres, torn between excitement that Lodun refugees were about to arrive and guilt over a lingering resentment that she hadn't been allowed to participate in the mission. That Ixion had somehow sensed her feelings before and tried to exploit them just made it all the worse. *Really,* she thought, *I would have to be completely out of my mind to go along with him on anything. Or just stupidly blind to reality.* But from what Giliead had told them, those were exactly the traits Syprian wizards looked for in their apprentice slaves.

The whole outside wall of the lounge had floor-to-ceiling windows that looked out onto the Promenade deck, filling the long room with shaded daylight. Niles had gated the ship to Ile-Rien perhaps half an hour ago, and Gerard's message had arrived not long after that. Right now Viller Institute volunteers, Capidaran Ministry staff, and nurses and soldier-orderlies from the ship's hospital were standing or sitting around on the couches and chairs, talking excitedly and waiting for the first group of Lodun evacuees to arrive so they could hurry them off for medical treatment or new quarters as needed. The double doors behind Florian were open to the ship's smaller ballroom, where Niles had built his new circle.

Glancing back, she could see that all the lights were on, from the crystal prisms overhead to the milky white glass panels in the walls, etched with garden scenes. The chairs and tables had been stacked up atop the bandstands on each end of the room or pushed back into the adjoining lounge and the movie theater. The open expanse of floor was painted with the symbols of the new circle. And at least now they knew it worked, that the others were safe in Lodun.

On the Promenade outside Florian saw Colonel Averi walking past, with Kressein, several Rienish and Capidaran officers, and Balin, the Gardier woman prisoner. *I wonder if she told them anything more about this Maton-First place and Castines.* Hurrying, she went to the end of the lounge and through the doors, then out onto the Promenade. She walked quickly to catch up to the group. Averi had a map out, and was saying something to Kressein.

Florian felt the sphere in her hands flash with heat. Startled, she stopped, looking down to see it sparking, its insides spinning.

She looked up and her jaw dropped. Hanging in the air, low and threatening over the calm sea, was the massive black shape of a Gardier airship. Instinct made her throw herself to the deck an instant before the guns fired.

Glass shattered, wood splintered as the airship's gun sprayed the ship, someone screamed. Huddled against the wall, Florian looked up. She saw bodies sprawled on the deck, blood. Several of the officers, Averi, Balin . . . Kressein was on his knees, braced against the ship's metal wall, holding his sphere and shouting. Florian saw the airship's nose tip up as it tried to turn away from the ship, red-orange stripes of fire already outlining the shape of the balloon. *He got it,* she thought, starting to crawl toward the injured and the dead.

But above the railing she saw another airship, and another. And another. She made a strangled noise, pointing.

Feet pounded on the deck behind her and crewmen ran past to help the injured.

"Avrain!" Florian yelled to the other sorcerer back in the ballroom. She shoved to her feet and bolted back toward the inside doorway, twisting and ducking to avoid being trampled by the officers and crewmen running out. *They found us, like they kept finding Tremaine and Gerard and the others whenever they used the point-to-point circles.* "Avrain, it's an attack, get out there!"

She almost slammed into him at the doorway to the ballroom. "God, no," he gasped, staring past her out the broad windows. He looked down, saw the sphere she was holding. "Go to Lodun, tell them to wait, don't send anyone through yet!"

The ship's Klaxon belatedly began to sound an alarm. Florian nodded rapidly. "I will." Avrain ran for the lounge doorway and Florian hurried into the empty ballroom. The Gardier already knew about them, using the circle again couldn't hurt. Putting aside her fear of what had happened the last time she had tried to use a world-gate without any help, she stepped into the circle.

Tremaine broke into a run when she reached the gate, heading back along the side of the lodging house, through the garden court with its damp laundry. Giliead and Ilias passed her but she couldn't make her legs move any faster. *They didn't send troops through because this was a distraction. Idiot.* And both times the Liaisons had managed to find them, they had been looking specifically for Gerard.

Back through the alley and she was running around the corner of the Philosophy College. She heard gunfire but it was muffled by distance, and the court was a confusion of running and shouting people, students, townsmen, but no Gardier. Tremaine looked desperately for Gerard but there was no sign of him or Niles either.

Then Florian appeared in the circle. Tremaine skidded to a halt on the grass, demanding, "Florian, what are you doing here?" Ilias had stopped to listen but Giliead was running for the college gallery.

Startled at the confusion, Florian blurted, "The *Ravenna*'s under attack—airships appeared right around us."

"Great," Tremaine snarled. "We're under attack too. Come on." Without waiting, she ran for the gallery. Ilias caught up with her easily and the bells were still pealing urgently as they took the broad steps two at a time. Digging in her bag for more ammunition, Tremaine crossed the portico to the big open double doors. The high-ceilinged hall just inside was dark except for a few oil lamps, smelling of dust and aged wood and books. She saw Giliead, Niles, Barshion, a dozen others looking out the windows in the far wall that opened onto another court.

Niles's brother Cathber glanced back at their arrival, saying grimly, "It's a standoff."

Past the other men, through the wide arched window, Tremaine could see perhaps twenty Gardier. They were all armed, except for a Liaison who still stood within a gate circle, holding a sorcerer crystal. The circle was small, barely ten feet across, and burned into the grass. They had three hostages, a young woman and two men, all dressed as students. The Gardier were holding them with pistols to their heads, making a human barrier in front of the circle. Four other bodies already lay sprawled on the grass, one of them in Gardier uniform. "Where's—" Tremaine started to ask, then her throat closed in shock.

Gerard was a short distance from the other hostages, two Gardier gripping his arms, a third holding a pistol to his head. He looked barely conscious and only the Gardier seemed to be keeping him on his feet.

Niles stood out on the open portico, holding a sphere, Adel Kashani and two student-sorcerers flanking him.

The Liaison spoke, too quietly for Tremaine to hear. She did hear Niles, on the portico, breathe the words "No, damn it, no."

Then the three Gardier dragged Gerard over the edge of the circle and vanished with the Liaison.

Tremaine yelled in pure horror, barely conscious of the shocked gasps and dismayed murmurs of the people around her.

The remaining Gardier looked as horrified by it as she was. A Gardier officer stepped back, lifting his pistol, but with the sorcerer crystal gone he was as good as unarmed. Niles didn't even gesture and the officer dropped his weapon, then fell to the ground, clutching his throat. The other Gardier shifted, still holding their hostages; but they were frightened, uncertain. Niles's face was a stony mask. He started down the stairs, saying in Aelin, "If you surrender, you won't be injured."

In the sudden silence, the officer's gasps for air as he writhed on the grass were clearly audible. Two of the Gardier dropped their weapons, hastily backing away as their hostages pushed free. The last Gardier shouted angrily, but in his agitation he moved the pistol away from his hostage's head, and she grabbed his hand, sinking her teeth into it. The pistol went off but the bullet struck the ground as the other two hostages leapt to help her.

Tremaine pushed through the crowd, ignoring the confusion as more people rushed forward to help. She hurried down the stairs, across the gravel path to the grass and the edge of the small circle. The Gardier had used something similar to Gerard's new circle again; the symbols had burned into the grass, faint lines of white ash, already beginning to disappear.

Tremaine looked wildly around. "Florian! It's going away!"

"Here." Florian stepped into the circle, looking back at her, eyes wide and serious. "I can do it."

"Tremaine, you can't!" Niles shouted from the portico. "We can't risk it!"

"You're the only other one here who knows the spell, you have to stay," Tremaine told him. She stepped into the circle with Florian. Ilias was right behind her and Giliead with him. She wanted to tell them not to come, but she knew she needed the help.

Niles had lifted his sphere, probably about to knock them all unconscious, but if he tried, Florian's sphere deflected it. Then the court and the gray daylight vanished.

Tremaine's stomach lurched and the floor moved under her feet. They were in a sizable room with huge window panels on each side, looking out onto a sea of heavy gray clouds. *Airship*, she thought, lifting her pistol. One of the new prototypes, like the one they had stolen from Maton-devara. The circle they stood in had been hastily inked onto the floor, the cork mats ripped aside to expose the metal surface. Barely ten paces away was another circle, this one larger, more carefully drawn. In it stood the Liaison and the two Gardier with him, an unconscious Gerard hanging limply in their grasp.

Another Gardier stood outside the circle. He spun around, stared incredulously and stepped toward them, just as Tremaine fired.

The bullet struck his chest instead of the Liaison's. As he fell, the Liaison, the other Gardier and Gerard disappeared.

"Goddammit!" Tremaine strode to the other circle, snarling. She dug into her satchel for an incendiary, pushing down the strike lever to arm it. "Come on."

"Quick, before they break the other end," Giliead said as they all stepped over the border of symbols.

Florian took a deep breath. "Ready?"

Tremaine heard shouts and running boot steps from the access corridor, and tossed the incendiary outside the circle. "Ready."

Florian yelped and the room vanished in a blast of heat.

They were in a large stone chamber, lit by the harsh light of a carbide lamp, the circle carved in stone on the floor. A Gardier armed with a chisel and hammer was just stooping over one of the symbols. He had time to look up in horror just before Ilias kicked him in the head, knocking him over backward. Ilias stepped in to finish him off with a sword thrust.

"Tremaine," Florian snapped. "Warn me next time. And that was our escape route."

Looking around for more Gardier, Tremaine threw her a look. "You wanted to escape to a Gardier airship?"

"Point taken, but do warn—"

"We're back in the mountain, in our world," Giliead interrupted. The polished stone threw back reflections from the lamp, the distinctive half columns along the wall arching up the curves of the domed ceiling, the bands of carving that repeated the circle symbols. He was right, they were in the lower chamber of the mountain ruin. It was night and no daylight was showing through the cracks in the far wall that led outside.

"Why the hell did they come here?" Tremaine said to herself. And which circle had they taken? The one they were standing in had been the dud that she and Gerard had tried first when they were exploring the room. The Gardier must have used the circle in the airship to reconnect it, but they had modified it to cross from Ile-Rien back to the staging world, the way Arisilde had modified the circle at Cineth. *They were catching up to us,* Tremaine thought, sick with fear at what they might do to Gerard. *Now they're a step ahead.*

"Quiet." Ilias was standing with his head cocked, listening. Then he and Giliead ran for the stairwell. "They went up!"

Tremaine pelted after him, Florian behind her.

The stairs were pitch-dark and Tremaine kept one hand on the cold stone wall to steady herself. Behind her she heard Florian swear softly. "What?" Tremaine demanded.

"That sorcerer crystal is casting like crazy," Florian reported, breathless as they climbed. The cold was chilling Tremaine's sweat-soaked shirt, making it damp and clammy. "I think the sphere's deflected a dozen spells. If we didn't have it, we'd be paste."

"Can you talk to the crystal?" Ilias asked Giliead.

Giliead sounded bitter. "No, this one won't listen." That didn't surprise Tremaine. Giliead had already talked two crystals into defecting; the Gardier must be onto his abilities by now.

They came to the top of the stairs and Tremaine saw Giliead charge down the passage, Ilias taking the last steps in one bound to follow. She scrambled after them, reaching the passage in time to see the figures of the Gardier and Gerard, etched in the light from another carbide lamp, framed against the jagged black opening in the wall. Then they vanished.

Tremaine swore, running after Giliead and Ilias. They came out into the open chamber, the cold wind off the river filling it with the scent and sound of rushing water. The two men stepped into the circle, and Tremaine followed, turning as Florian hurried after her. The other girl threw one curious look around the big room, then hastily stepped into the circle.

The circle Arisilde gave us in Capistown, Tremaine thought. She was certain now he had given them the last circle he took, before whatever happened had happened, perhaps his last coherent memory before he had fled to the sphere. The circle that had been dead after Nicholas had destroyed the other end in their Capistown house, dead until the Gardier had come through it. Gerard was right, the Gardier must have broken it at its original destination after Arisilde came through, because they were afraid he might come back. *Then when they realized we were here, when they noticed we were using the other circles, they restored it so they could come after us.* "Everybody, be ready," she said, feeling inadequate. "I think this is the one."

Giliead grimaced, Ilias just nodded, and Florian lifted the sphere, saying, "Right. Here we go."

Chapter 19

This time the abrupt vertigo knocked Tremaine down. She shoved herself upright off a cool stone floor, looking around wildly. They were in a round rock-walled room, very like the one they had just left, the walls a mottled dark gray, curving up to meet in a dome high above their heads. There was a small opening in the very center of the dome, letting in sunlight and revealing a small patch of blue sky. She heard a shout and boot steps and twisted around, lifting her pistol.

Three Gardier were just disappearing through an archway in one curved wall, leading into another half-glimpsed room. Still near the edge of the circle, the last man spun around, raising his rifle. Tremaine jerked her pistol up but Giliead had landed near the man and he stood up suddenly, gripping the rifle and shoving it upward. Tremaine winced away from the blast of the shot, painfully loud against the stone.

The man had the sense to let go of the rifle but Giliead slammed him in the head with the butt before he could back away. As the Gardier collapsed, Tremaine scrambled to her feet. She reached the wall just as Florian and Ilias did. Ilias flattened himself against the stone, taking a careful peek into the next room.

He jerked back as two more shots rang out, spraying them with stone splinters from the edge of the arch. Ilias swore, throwing a look back at Tremaine. "Well?" he asked. On the far side of the archway,

Giliead had dropped the rifle, edging close to try to see into the next room without getting his head shot off.

Tremaine grimaced. She couldn't chance throwing an explosive, not if Gerard was in there somewhere. There was no other exit and the Gardier could keep them pinned here indefinitely. "Florian," she said, "do something."

"I've already done a concealment charm, but that's not going to work well in close quarters. I don't want to use the mechanical disruption, not with those around," Florian muttered, nodding toward the satchel slung over Tremaine's shoulder. "I don't trust this sphere like I would Arisilde. I'll make them drop the guns."

"Right." Tremaine had time to notice that the circle was carved into the floor and the walls weren't mottled as she had first thought, they were smooth gray stone covered over with writing in black charcoal or paint that was coming off on her sweaty hands. Looking closely at the wall, she made out some of the more familiar symbols from the circles, scrawled wildly, in no discernible pattern or order, on top of each other. It had the look of something written by a madman, and was not reassuring. *So where the hell are we?*

Firmly gripping the sphere, Florian closed her eyes for a moment. Alarmed shouts and the clatter of weapons striking the floor sounded from the next room. Giliead and Ilias bolted through the archway and Tremaine flung herself after them, making sure Florian was close behind her. The sphere was the only protection for the explosives and her pistol, and she had to keep near it.

Through the archway Tremaine saw another dome-shaped room, another circle carved into the floor. One Gardier already had Giliead's sword through his abdomen; another charged Ilias and got a slash across the throat. Tremaine shot the last one, just as he turned to run.

Florian was muttering to the sphere, distracted, and Tremaine kept a hand on her arm. The back of her neck was prickling; there was something very wrong about this place. It was obviously another ancient ruin, but the Gardier had to be here for a reason.

"This place is familiar," Giliead said quietly, moving to the next archway.

"It's familiar and creepy," Ilias added, following him, his sword held ready. He jerked his head back toward the dead and dying Gardier. "These are all Liaisons."

Tremaine looked at the bodies on the floor, saw crystals embedded in their cheeks, foreheads. *Creepy is right,* she thought. Following the

Syprians' lead, Tremaine and Florian veered rapidly around the carved circle, the blood and still-twitching bodies. Writing covered the walls in this room too, stretching up to more than a man's height. The skylight was bigger and the light let Tremaine see a line of carving, so obscured by the scribbles that her eyes had passed right over it before. The circle symbols were carved into the band, as if in decoration. She said, "It's just like the circle cave in the mountain. That's why it looks familiar."

Giliead threw a worried look at her. "This whole place is alive with curses, like the circles Arisilde makes."

"The place we just came through?" Florian asked, head down, still concentrating on the sphere.

"Yes, this looks like it was built the same . . ." Tremaine followed Giliead into the next room, where he and Ilias stood looking around in wary astonishment. It was a mirror image of the room they had camped in at the mountain, with the same carving on the walls, the same raised border that they had used as a fire pit. It was so like it Tremaine almost expected to see the scattered remains of sava rinds and firewood from their hasty departure. "Exactly like it," she finished in a low voice.

Giliead went to the further doorway, past which Tremaine could see a corridor just like the passage that had led from the mountain's upper circle chamber to the stairwell. From this vantage point it looked identical, though the bright sunlight seemed to be coming from the wrong direction. Tremaine wondered if it looked out on the same view of the river gorge, or a mirror image of it. "Creepy is an understatement," she muttered. Were they somewhere near the mountain ruin, or had there been another part of it they had somehow failed to find?

Giliead said suddenly, "Curse! Back that way!"

Tremaine spun around, just as the floor dipped and swayed, eerily reminiscent of the deck of the *Ravenna,* and she flailed to stay upright. Florian gasped and caught hold of her shoulder; Giliead and Ilias both stumbled but managed to keep their feet.

More Liaisons appeared in the archway they had just come through, these unarmed. They charged, shouting, and Tremaine fired twice into the pack, hitting the one in the lead. He fell back just as Florian lifted the sphere and a black cloud sprang into existence in the center of the room, vapors roiling, shooting off sparks of contained lightning.

"They're gating in behind us!" Tremaine snarled. Shoving the gun back into her belt, she reached into the satchel for an explosive but

Giliead and Ilias had slammed forward into the Gardier, taking advantage of Florian's illusion. *Just as well,* she realized. They had to get back through that circle and she couldn't risk blocking the way with rubble.

"The Gardier shouldn't be able to do that." Florian grimaced, handling the sphere lightly. It must be red-hot from all the spells; there had to be sorcerer crystals here somewhere and there was no telling what attacks it was holding off.

We have to find Gerard and get the hell out of here. Tremaine ducked through the doorway into the wide passage. Halting abruptly, she saw the far end, where the stairwell had been in the mountain ruin, was just a rough jagged opening, as if the stone had been torn away. It looked out into open air, with a glimpse of forest and low hills far below. The forest was the lighter green of the Gardier world. *I have a really terrible feeling about this,* Tremaine thought. The opposite end had a broad stone spiral stairway, but it was leading up.

She had to take a look, she had to be sure. She hurried down the passage toward the opening, past the doors that led into the other rooms, all identical to those in the mountain. She looked into each briefly to make sure Gerard wasn't there, but all were empty. Reaching the edge of the gap, she gripped the jagged stone and leaned out cautiously to look down, the wind whipping her hair.

The ledge was sheared off, remains of broken masonry blocks sticking out of it. Hundreds of feet below she could see a complex of Gardier buildings, stone like the ones in Maton-devara, with the same flat mansard roofs. Two black airships were moored in cleared fields nearby. *This is not a mountain,* Tremaine thought, feeling a little sick. She could see from looking at the ground that the structure was moving a little. Floating.

She turned, heading back toward Florian. Though the other girl was too occupied with the sphere to listen, she said, baffled, "God. We are there. This is the other half of that room in the mountain." *So it didn't fall into the river, it came here?* Then she shook her head, trying to get past her astonishment. *If we can gate the whole Ravenna, why can't they gate part of a mountain? And keep it in the air with a Great Spell, to make sure nobody sees it except the Liaisons they control.*

"Get out of there," Florian shouted at Giliead and Ilias. "I've got a spell!"

Tremaine looked over her shoulder. Now ignoring the illusion, the Liaisons were throwing themselves practically onto the two Syprians' swords, trying to overwhelm them, with no sense of their own survival. More were pushing in from the room behind them. Ilias hamstrung one that tried to jump Giliead from behind, and the two men ran for the door.

Tremaine backed away, giving them room to get through. As the Liaisons started forward, Florian whispered something.

The black cloud abruptly swelled to fill the room. Tremaine retreated hastily from the doorway, stepping on Ilias. From past the cloud she heard abrupt screams, then silence.

Breathing hard, Giliead stared at Florian, aghast. Looking from him to Florian, Ilias asked, "What was it?" He was panting as well, his shirt torn and his chest and sword spattered with someone else's blood. His nose was bleeding again and there was a cut under his eye where a Gardier had gotten in a lucky hit.

"It electrified the air in the room," Florian said evenly. Her face was set but as she turned away, her mouth twisted in pain. "I learned it looking for things to use on Ixion."

Florian was going to feel that later, but they couldn't stop to deal with it now. The Gardier must have taken Gerard up the stairwell at the other end of the passage; it was the only way out of this corridor. "We need to go this way." Tremaine started for the stairs.

The others followed her, and she added, "I think we're in the missing half of the mountain ruin, that they gated the whole thing to the Gardier world, to the place they called Maton-first." She pointed back toward the opening at the far end of the passage. "And I think it's floating in the air." Giliead moved past her to take the lead, casting another worried look at Florian.

Ilias guarded their backs, watching the corridor behind them. He said, "I don't understand. The Gardier stole part of the ruin and brought it here? Why? And what's holding it up?" Tremaine couldn't tell whether he really wanted to know or if he just needed to talk. She suspected the latter.

Giliead said reluctantly, "That would explain why the floor keeps moving, why there are so many curses."

Florian didn't say anything, barely seemed to be listening. She just looked sick. Tremaine was fairly sure she had never done a death spell before.

They started up the stairs and Tremaine had the sinking feeling they had come too far, that the place to rescue Gerard had been back in their mountain, before the last gate.

Each step was a little too high for her, like the stairs in the mountain ruin, like the stairs in the Wall Port, the city under the Isle of Storms, the fortress. The walls were dotted with the small niches. She thought the missing section of the ruin must have been a series of egg-shaped domed chambers, running alongside the cliff for some distance on either side, stretching up all the way to the cliff top. Tremaine couldn't hear any movement; if there were more Liaisons here, they were keeping quiet about it.

The stairs ended in a broad open ledge, looking out onto a large domed chamber, shadowy and vast, nearly as large as the circle room in the fortress. In its old location it must have spanned the river gorge. The walls were studded with the carved half pillars and a short set of steps led down to the floor from their ledge.

The room was dimly lit and it took a moment for Tremaine to pick out the small glass lamps, strung from ropes supported by hooks pounded into the stone walls. The light was green-tinged and odd, and she realized they were glowworm lights, like the one Davret had shown her aboard the old Aelin airship. *Of course, they can't run electricity up here.* As her eyes adjusted to the light, she saw that carved symbols covered the floor, but instead of multiple circles they all formed one big spiral, winding out toward the walls of the chamber. The stone was scribbled over with more symbols, written in chalk, dust, red-brown streaks like dried blood.

And in the center of the spiral, atop a low stone plinth, was a large sorcerer crystal. It was twice the size of the sphere in Florian's hands, yellowed with age, fragments of black rock stuck to it like mold. Tremaine started to spot more crystals, smaller ones, scattered all over the spiral, hundreds of them. There was no movement, no sign of any Liaisons, but they must have all gated to the circles at the other end of the ruin to get in behind them. *Gated from here?* "This thing, I think this is one big gate," Tremaine said softly.

Ilias looked around cautiously, stepping back to suspiciously eye the ledge above their heads. "Those wizard crystals," Giliead said, low-voiced. "Most of them are alive."

"This must be where they do it," Florian whispered. "This must be where they put people in crystals."

Tremaine could believe that; the air was tinged with decay, as if a number of people had died here. "There's Gerard," Giliead said suddenly. Tremaine stepped to his side, scanning the chamber's floor anxiously. In a moment, she saw him. He lay unconscious, half on his side as if he had just been carelessly dropped. He was on the spiral, off to one side in the deeper shadow, his gray suit almost blending with the stone. "I'll get him, you all wait up here," Giliead said, starting down the steps.

The outer edge of the spiral started just at the bottom. Giliead reached it, eyeing it and the writing scrawled across it with distaste, then stepped cautiously out onto it. Beside her, Tremaine felt Ilias shift nervously.

"Hurry," Florian said, anxious. "The sphere is all twitchy, I'm not sure if it's the—" As she stepped forward, something leapt on her from the roof of the ledge above them.

Tremaine had just enough time to realize it was another Liaison. She yelled in alarm, plunging forward, but the force of the man's leap knocked Florian down the stairs and onto the edge of the gate spiral. Florian hit the ground hard, letting go of the sphere. It rolled across the spiral, sparking madly. Ilias dropped his sword to fling himself on the man's back, dragging him off Florian. Giliead spun around, running back to help.

Tremaine flung herself across the floor, reaching for the rolling sphere.

The floor lurched underfoot again and Tremaine fell to her knees, just managing to catch hold of the sphere. The metal was burning hot and as she grabbed it she felt it jerk and shudder as the gears inside spun wildly. *Oh, shit,* she thought. Even she could tell that it had just deflected a spell. Clutching it to her side, she twisted around.

Florian lay crumpled on the floor, Ilias sprawled next to her. The Liaison who had knocked Florian down lay nearby in a spreading pool of blood, Ilias's knife hilt protruding from his neck, but another Liaison stood over them, aiming a pistol at Ilias. It had so many crystals pinpricking its face its features were nearly unrecognizable as human; it looked like some weird fay horror. Giliead stood helplessly, watching the Liaison with the intensity of a thwarted predator. There was no way he could reach it before it shot Ilias. And there was no way Tremaine could drag her pistol out from where it was tucked into her belt, aim and fire before it shot Ilias.

Sprawled on the stone and unable to move, the curse sapping his strength, Ilias swore at his own stupidity. The Gardier must have used Rienish illusions, one of the few curses that could fool Giliead.

And fool the sphere. Ilias knew he had looked at the ledge above their heads and seen nothing, and the second Liaison with the shooting weapon must have been crouched below them next to the stairs, concealed by a curse.

He could just see that Florian's eyes were open and aware, glaring at the Gardier. She struggled to move, gritting her teeth, but couldn't lift her head. The curse holding them both immobile wouldn't work on Giliead and must have been deflected from Tremaine by the sphere. But he didn't think she could make it do anything else to help them. Tremaine must have come to that conclusion herself. "Hey there," she said to the Liaison, her voice even but her eyes flat and angry. "Can we talk about this? I don't see any—"

Ilias couldn't see what happened but there was a flurry of movement, then something grabbed his hair and dragged him half-upright. He felt the cold muzzle of the shooting weapon shoved against his temple and saw Giliead jerk to a halt a few paces away, breathing hard.

Shit, this is . . . bad. Giliead must have tried to take advantage of an instant of distraction on the Liaison's part. Ilias couldn't even make himself wince away from the weapon, couldn't even make his throat move to speak. He didn't know why the thing hadn't just killed them already. *Because it hasn't been told to yet?*

He saw Tremaine eye the Liaison narrowly and wet her lips, though she didn't betray any other hint of nerves. She tried again, "Where's Castines? You know, he's really the one we came to see. . . ."

She let the words trail off as the air shivered and a man stepped into existence near Giliead. He was tall, with the olive skin of coastal Syprians, his hair a matted mane that might have been any color beneath the dirt. He wore the ragged remnants of a filthy Gardier uniform, and there were little crystals pocked all over his face, though the skin around them wasn't infected and discolored, the way it always was with the other Liaisons. Ilias could smell him from here, an odor rank enough to make his stomach want to turn. *And I think we've just found Castines.* In a low rough voice, the man said in Syrnaic, "I told you, that's not him either. That's the Chosen Vessel they brought with them from Cineth."

Giliead stared at him, startled. Ilias supposed the man was talking to the surviving Liaison.

"Hey!" Tremaine said loudly, trying to distract him away from Giliead. "Glad you've finally got that figured out."

The man lifted his head, looking toward her, and Ilias saw he had a crystal about the size of a child's fist sticking out of his temple, half-hidden by his hair. Ilias felt bile rise in his throat. The man's face was blank, as if he was concentrating entirely on something else. Looking at the sphere Tremaine was cradling against her side, he said, "You can't use that. It wants curses, and all your curses are dead."

*T*his is not going to end well, Tremaine thought, feeling cold creep down her spine. He was right that she couldn't use the sphere. It wasn't Arisilde, and she just didn't have enough magic to talk to it. Under the flap of the satchel, she put her hand on something that she would be able to use, but there was no point in revealing it yet. Giliead must have seen her stealthy movement. Watching the man with contempt, he said, "So you're Castines," bringing the man's attention back to him. "You don't look as if this place agrees with you."

Castines's expression changed, coming alive, and his lips curled in a sneer. "Don't speak, Vessel, or I'll kill him. Not a word. You Vessels make this so easy. You think you're so superior because a filthy ball of light gives you orders. Always bringing others with you, afraid to travel alone outside the gods' reach. It makes you so easy to—" Then his face went blank again, and he said more softly in Aelin, "Castines wants to kill the Rien sorcerer. But he's the wrong one, isn't he?"

Giliead pressed his lips together, torn between anger and confusion. Tremaine tried to keep the consternation off her face, wondering if Castines was as barking mad as he looked and sounded or was switching languages to confuse them. In this situation she couldn't see why he would bother. *Right, just . . . keep him talking.* Trying to sort out the sense from the madness, she thought, *He was looking for the Rien sorcerer, someone he mistook Gerard for.* She took a not-so-wild guess. "You were looking for Arisilde." Her voice came out even and conversational, which was a nice surprise.

Castines turned slowly back to face her. Still in Aelin, still with that oddly empty look on his face, he said, "We found him traveling the gates. We see all the gates through the avatars, as well as through the master gate. All the avatars are of the same material, they are all one. But we found we could also see into the metal avatars, whenever they were used to make the gates. So we called to him, showed him how to find the gate to bring him here. He was powerful, and we thought we could use him, make him an avatar and get more of his kind, power our ships and our gates. But he grew angry. He did that." He pointed to the far wall of the dome, and Tremaine saw a spiderweb of cracks that branched through the old stone. "Before he fled, he pulled us apart a little. Castines doesn't like it."

Tremaine bit her lip, trying to follow it. He was talking about himself in the third person, with something innocent and almost earnest about his manner, completely at odds with how he had spoken to Giliead in Syrnaic. Giliead was looking at her with a desperate expression; Ilias still looked angry and Florian just confused. *All right, I just have to clarify this.* She asked him carefully, "You are Castines, right?"

His eyes focused on her. Still in Aelin, he said, "I'm Orelis. Castines found me in Delvan Teal. The High City. The place you call the fortress."

The fortress. The crystal Castines took with him. But this man is Syprian. Tremaine nodded, trying to look sympathetic and understanding. "You were in a crystal?"

"I can hear you talking," Castines said in Syrnaic suddenly, his eyes turning angry, contemptuous. He laughed harshly. "Talking behind my back."

Understanding hit Tremaine in the pit of the stomach. "Oh, hell, there's two of you in there." That was Castines and the crystal, or whoever had been in the crystal, both inhabiting that body, both talking to her. She had spoken Rienish by habit and Giliead, realizing what she meant, looked startled and sick.

The other Liaison, the dead one sprawled on the floor, sat up so suddenly Tremaine flinched. He turned toward her, Ilias's horn-handled knife still jammed to the hilt in his neck, the brown cloth of his uniform soaked with blood. He spoke in Aelin, in a flat even voice, in Orelis's voice, "Listen, listen. I was trapped there longer than I can remember, and I can remember forever. Castines came, running from the gods who were trying to kill him. He found me and tried to use my essence, my power, and I went into him. All the other vessels in the chamber were broken, all but mine, my people were gone, dead, fled. They left me behind."

"That was careless of them." Tremaine wet her lips again. Her throat was dry and she willed herself not to cough. *This is Orelis talking. The crystal. The person who was in the crystal.* "Why did they put you in there in the first place?" She spoke in Syrnaic so Giliead and Ilias could at least understand her side of the conversation.

The Liaison stared at her with blank clouded eyes, as if whatever inhabited that dead body didn't understand the question. Then it said, "It was a great experiment."

Castines laughed, stepping away from Giliead to move toward Tremaine. She could tell it was just him in there now, because his face was alive with hate and his eyes too bright. He said in Syrnaic, "She was a prisoner. That's what I've always thought. Why did they let all the others go but her, if she wasn't the worst of them?" He lifted a brow, the crystals in his face catching the light, except for the big dull one jammed so horribly into his forehead. "Would you like me to tell you what I'm going to do to you all? Shall we start with the little girl?"

"Oh, I think I can probably tell you," Tremaine said dryly. Orelis made her skin creep, but this kind of thug she could handle, crystals or not. "None of you people ever show any real imagination."

Castines frowned, startled. That shut him up long enough for Orelis to take up her tale again. The dead Liaison said, "I was not a prisoner." The words had a certain earnest patience even though there was no inflection in the dead man's voice. "It was a way of extending life, of giving service to others past death. But I did not wake as I was supposed to."

Tremaine considered that, wondering if Orelis actually had some emotions that she could appeal to. "Giving service to others past death" didn't sound too bad. In fact, it sounded almost noble. Surely someone who had volunteered for that, even if it had gone terribly wrong in the end, could be reasoned with. Maybe the war was all Castines's influence. "Orelis, what are you trying to do here? What do you want?"

Instead, Castines answered with a sneer, "She wants to rebuild her world. Remake it. She makes this master gate transport wizards out of their bodies, into the avatars that we make here from hers. Then we throw the bodies away."

"We both wanted that," Orelis corrected him, the Liaison's head turning stiffly to face him. "My world was ruined. We will make it again."

There goes the "reasoning with her" plan, Tremaine thought, inwardly grimacing. "Why Ile-Rien?" she demanded. "Why there, and not here, in the Aelin world, or in the Syprian world?"

Orelis turned the Liaison's head back to face her, to fix the dead eyes on her. With that same hint of earnestness, she explained, "There are no gods in your world. And there are not enough Aelin wizards in this one."

"I see." Tremaine thought she understood what had happened now, at least, or part of it. Fleeing from Chosen Vessels twenty or so years ago, Castines had found Orelis in the fortress, where she had been left behind by the ancient inhabitants, either because she was a prisoner or because it was the only way for the last of her people to escape whatever they had been escaping. She had attached herself to Castines, sharing his body, and sent him to the Aelin world to scout a new home for them. And it had been perfect for them, with just enough people with a talent for magic to be useful, but no advanced sorcery, no defenses. And no Syprian gods to fight them.

Castines had used Obelin and his family to get him close enough to the corresponding location of the fortress so he could use the world-gate to return. Then he had tricked the few members of the family who had enough magical talent for him to use into returning with him to the Aelin world. He had gone on to take over the place with a magic more powerful than anything those unlucky people had ever seen before. Killing their potential sorcerers and putting their souls and power into the crystals, turning people into Liaisons, and eventually convincing their leaders they had been attacked by a place called Ile-Rien, which happened to have a stockpile of sorcerers to place in crystals. At some point he and Orelis must have gone to the mountain ruin and gated these chambers with this master circle to the Aelin world, and established Maton-first.

Castines was staring at the Liaison with bored contempt, as if he had heard this story too many times before. "Your world was ruined because of you," Castines told her. "Once she had me she saw the Syrnai was no good for her purposes. Primitive." Castines pronounced the word deliberately, stressing the vowels. "Too few wizards and all those mad as me, and she was afraid of the gods. She thinks they're her own people, forgotten who they are, but still hating her. She's a god of wizards, a failed god—"

"He's afraid of the gods," Orelis said without looking at him. "I am superior to the gods."

"The gods aren't trapped in a crystal shell," Castines pointed out, saving Tremaine the trouble. Tremaine suspected Castines was no longer happy with the body-sharing arrangement. Even if he had originally gloried in Orelis's power, he didn't sound as if the years together had bred anything but hatred and contempt. *Of course, he's a Syprian wizard. He probably started out with hatred and contempt.*

Orelis was silent a moment, then added softly to Tremaine, "It's not working, is it? I'm not remaking my world."

Lying to her wouldn't help. And Tremaine might need her to believe a lie later, so the truth was best for now. She told Orelis gently, "No, it's not working."

Castines turned away in disgust, then took a few steps toward Florian and Ilias. Giliead tensed but Tremaine didn't want him to move yet. She had to keep Orelis talking, find out if there was another way out of this. Tremaine told Castines sharply, "Hey, shithead. We're talking over here."

He turned back toward her, glaring, but Orelis kept speaking as if nothing had happened. The dead Liaison said, "Arisilde left his body here, but we thought he had found another. He left the pieces of one of your metal balls, but we looked at it and looked at it and could not understand. We traced his progress through the gates. He had seen our great spiral here, the controller, and used his memory of it to make different gates that could reach other worlds, that broke all of our rules. He learned to hide from us, but he had always been with you before." Orelis stared at her with the Liaison's eyes, fixed and dull. "Bring Arisilde to us. Tell him I want him to finish, I want him to pull us apart. I didn't understand that he was trying to help me."

Castines snarled, "He wasn't trying to help us, you stupid bitch. He was killing us."

"He was doing what was best for you," Tremaine said, holding that dead gaze, putting every ounce of sincerity she had into it.

"Best for me," Orelis repeated.

Tremaine nodded. "To help you."

"Yes. Bring him," Orelis agreed. "He can pull us apart. And then he can help me finish the new world."

Oh, hell. We're back to that. "Right." Tremaine dropped the sincerity, fairly sure she had heard enough. "I guess I can't talk you out of the new world thing, can I?"

"Where will I live if not in my world?" Orelis sounded utterly puzzled by this question.

"There's the other option." Tremaine pulled her hand out from under the satchel's flap, showing them the incendiary. She had pushed the detonator down against the floor, when Castines had first spoken to her, and her thumb was on the strike lever. "It's called death."

Giliead made a faint noise, a sharp intake of breath, and Florian blinked in alarm. Ilias actually looked relieved, which Tremaine thought showed either a mistaken level of confidence in her or a high awareness of just what Castines could do to them all.

Castines frowned and took a step toward her. Orelis said, "Stop. No. Look at her hand."

Just to make certain they knew their danger, Tremaine explained carefully, "If I let go, it blows up. If you grab me, it blows up. If you hurt them, it blows up. If you move, it blows up. Do I really have to elaborate further?"

Watching her carefully, Castines said, "We have a curse, to destroy weapons such as that."

Tremaine had to laugh. "Yes, by making them blow up. There are three more of these in the bag, by the way. You must remember what that did to your workshops at Maton-devara." She looked into the dead Liaison's eyes, into Orelis's eyes. "So curse away." The sphere should deflect that spell, but there was no harm in emphasizing the point.

Castines laughed at her, but it wasn't very convincing. "I could turn you into—"

Tremaine widened her eyes at him. She felt a faint shiver from the sphere, and knew he had tried something. "Go ahead. Whatever it is, it better have a thumb to hold this lever down."

"It would kill these others, as well as us," Orelis pointed out.

"They trust my judgment." She deliberately avoided looking in that direction. "You could use this spiral—your master gate?—to take yourselves out of here, but—" She nodded to the big crystal that sat on the plinth at the center of the spiral, yellowed with age. "—I'm guessing that can't leave the spiral. Not if you want to hold on to your control over the gates."

"You don't want to die," Orelis said, blank-eyed, blank-faced. "No one wants to die."

Tremaine could see Florian looking at her, glaring at her really. She was trying to mouth the word "master." Arisilde had said, *If you destroy the master, you free the slaves. But the whole structure will collapse as well, all the gates, all falling down like a house of cards. I shouldn't have minded it, you know. Being stuck there, and if I survived the fall. Certainly would have saved us all a lot of trouble. But I didn't realize it was the crystal that was important, and not the bodies, until it was too late.* It made more sense, once you saw this stolen jury-rigged master circle, and knew that Castines and Orelis could trace the spheres whenever they were used to travel through a gate. It sounded as if Arisilde was saying that if the master circle, or maybe the master crystal, or both, were destroyed, it would destroy all the others. *Other what? Crystals and gates?* "This spiral makes all the circles work, doesn't it? You had to bring it here to the Aelin world, alter it to make the circles go from here to your world to our world."

"Yes," Orelis said. "Castines feared the gods. We had to come here. It is our essence that powers all the gates from here. It is our presence in the great spiral that makes them work." Castines stared at Orelis, brows drawing together suspiciously.

"That was your great work," Tremaine said gently. "The gates were the only way for the others to leave the fortress. They broke the other crystals to let the avatars out, but you volunteered to stay, so the gate would still work and the people could escape."

Orelis tilted the dead man's head. "Yes. That is exactly what happened. Alone, with no one in this spiral, I could only make those nearest to me work. Castines had to bring me here before I could make all the others work."

Tremaine nodded. *That's what I thought.* Orelis died, the gates stopped working. *It's not as if I have anything better to do.* She said, "Nobody wants to die, do they." *That's not true, but we'll leave it for now.* And with so many incendiaries in her lap, Tremaine doubted she would feel a thing. "I can bring Arisilde to you, but only if you send them home—" *Wait. Damn.* If this did work, and the gates stopped functioning, she didn't want Ilias and Giliead trapped forever in Ile-Rien. But they had ordered Gyan to break the new circle in Cineth and Gerard had broken the one on the Isle of Storms. That left the fortress with the only working circles close to the Syrnai. She grimaced to herself, thinking *I hope Ilias was right when he said they could climb down the cliff and walk home from there.* "Send Florian and Gerard back to the *Ravenna*'s circle, and the Syprians to the place we call the fortress, where Castines found you." She added, "Arisilde will check on them first, and if you send them anywhere else, he'll be very, very angry."

Florian made a huge effort and twitched. Giliead looked at her and silently mouthed the words, "Don't send us away. You shouldn't do this alone." He was wrong about that; alone was the only way to do this. Tremaine didn't want to look at Ilias, but did anyway. He was making a tremendous effort to speak. He settled for glaring at her.

Castines snarled in frustration, stalking a few paces away. Orelis turned the dead Liaison's head to watch him. A long moment passed while Tremaine counted her heartbeats. Then Castines gestured sharply.

The sphere sparked in sympathy as the crystal on the plinth pulsed a sick yellow. Florian and Gerard vanished, then Ilias and Giliead. The other Liaison still stood frozen where Orelis or Castines had left him, pointing the pistol at empty air.

That's done, Tremaine thought, relieved and cold all at once. Orelis had turned the dead Liaison to face her again. Orelis said, "You aren't going to bring Arisilde, are you?"

Tremaine let out a breath. "No."

Castines spun around, staring incredulously at Tremaine. "You knew!"

"Knew what?" Tremaine started to ask, but Orelis replied calmly, "I suspected."

Castines lunged at Tremaine and with a yelp she scrambled backward, trying to hold on to the sphere and the incendiary. *Let go, let go, let go,* her mind ordered frantically but some other part of her refused, and she kept her hold on the incendiary's strike lever. She thought Castines would grab for her but instead he snatched the bag of explosives. He flung it away, making another grab for her. Tremaine yelled in pure reaction and flung the incendiary away from her, toward the spiral and the crystal in its center.

Nearby the Liaison's body jerked with Orelis's startled reaction. Tremaine had one breath of a moment to roll over, curling into a protective ball around the sphere. The blast shattered sound; heat washed over her. She felt the sphere hum in her hands; either Castines had tried a last-second spell or it was reacting to the blast, protecting itself and her. Then something struck her, landing heavily atop her and slamming the breath out of her lungs.

Her head hurt terribly and there was a moment of darkness; Tremaine came out of it abruptly when the heavy hot thing atop her moved and she realized it was Castines. He gripped her hair, yanking her up. With a snarl of pain and terror, Tremaine cradled the sphere in one hand and reached up to shove it against his head.

The sphere touched the big crystal in his temple and blazed red-hot. His scream was weirdly muffled and it took Tremaine a moment to realize it was her hearing at fault. She could feel moisture around her right ear and she didn't want to know if it was blood. Grimacing, she pushed the sphere against him, not breaking contact until he rolled off her.

Gritting her teeth, Tremaine moved with him, struggling around, keeping the sphere in contact with the crystal. Something shoved against her and a flaring light blinded her; she shied away from a terrible heat.

Then she was pushing herself up off the floor, the broken remnants of copper and gears caught on her hand. The sphere had shattered. She looked for Castines, shaking the hot metal off her fingers and reaching for her pistol.

But Castines lay nearby and he looked shattered too. The crystal in his forehead was just a blackened hole. His eyes were open but fixed on nothing, and he lay like a broken puppet. Tremaine poked him cautiously with her foot, then eased away.

The nearest crystals were in pieces, or shattered to powder. Tremaine unsteadily climbed to her feet, looking around. The big crystal on the plinth in the center of the spiral was blown to bits, white light puddled around it. As she watched in wary fascination, the light seeped into the stone, gradually fading.

The Liaison who had held the gun lay sprawled against the wall, what was left of his uniform and the skin beneath blackened and burned. The one Orelis had spoken through lay farther away in a tumbled heap. The sphere or Castines or both must have protected Tremaine from the blast.

The place was weirdly quiet, but that must be her damaged hearing. *Nothing's happening. So did it work?* She looked around vaguely for the satchel with the other explosives. Something moved in the corner of her eye, and she flinched away with a gasp. A long dark line was forming in the stone floor, creeping across it. Tremaine stared at it, utterly baffled. It spread out, forming more lines, a spiderweb stretching out. . . . Cracks. They were cracks.

I don't think I'm going to need more explosives.

Ilias rolled over, struggling to sit up as the paralyzing curse faded away. He could see the fall of moon- and starlight through the openings in the high ceiling and it gave shape to the dim outlines of the giant circle chamber. "We're really back here, the fortress," he said incredulously. They were near the spot where they had left the Gardier who had survived the attack; someone must have come for them because both the living and the dead were gone, only bloodstains and the scattered remnants of the ropes they had been tied with were left behind.

Giliead grabbed his arm, demanding, "Are you all right?"

"No. Yes." Ilias shook him off. He was still trembling with rage and an urgent need to kill Castines or Orelis or whatever that thing called itself. "We don't have a sphere, a crystal. We can't go back. She's going to kill herself to kill them, she'd never bring Arisilde there."

Giliead just looked at him, shaking his head helplessly. "Maybe not. Maybe she meant to—"

"Maybe," Ilias snarled, and slammed his hand against the stone floor. "Was Tremaine right? Would breaking that spiral really break all the curses?" If it was for nothing, if it was all for a lie . . .

Giliead gestured in frustration, started to speak. Then his face went still and he slowly turned to look out over the shadowy room, the dusty carvings half-visible in the blue-white shafts of cold moonlight.

Ilias felt his anger freeze, sinking into sick dread. "What is it?"

"The curses are fading away, the curses in the circles." Ilias could barely see him in the dimness but he knew Giliead's eyes were fixed on that distance that no one but Chosen Vessels could see. "They're fading away, dying."

O h, no." Florian struggled to her feet, dazed. Her knees and elbows had been scraped in the fall and for a moment refused to bend right. She was in the *Ravenna*'s empty second ballroom, in the circle they had drawn to reach Lodun. Gerard lay nearby, unconscious, his face pale and bruised, his breathing shallow. Sense caught up with her. Gerard was out, Ilias and Giliead were stuck back in their world with no sorcerer and no sphere, it would take too long to explain the situation to Kressein or Avrain or Kevari, who must all be occupied defending the ship, Colonel Averi was injured or dead, it would take too long to get Niles. She bolted for the doors.

Her heart pounding, she ran out and down the length of the lounge. She glimpsed two airships outside hanging over the sea, another in flames, just settling to the blue surface. A bomb blast went off, somewhere not so distant. She banged through the doors to the stairwell and pounded down the stairs, so frantic she almost missed the landing she wanted. There was someone running after her, calling her name, but she ignored him. She heard another explosion that made the deck under her feet shiver. Out of the stairwell, down the corridor and across the hall, into the main ballroom foyer.

There were two guards there who stared at her in amazement when she flung herself on the embossed leather doors, pounding on them, and shouting, "Arisilde! Arisilde, please!"

"Stop her?" one of the bewildered men asked.

The other shook his head, watching her in consternation. "She's one of the sorcerers, so— I don't know. Miss? Miss, what—?"

Florian couldn't take the time to explain. She pounded on the soft leather again. "We have to get Tremaine! I know she wouldn't kill herself, I know she had a plan. You're the only one who can—"

The door flew open and she staggered through into the dark ballroom. The doors slammed shut behind her, leaving her in darkness for a heartbeat, then every light in the big room blazed into life.

The original circle was still there but new symbols had been painted inside it, branching off from it in a loose spiral like the master gate in the ruin. The symbols were more neatly painted than Castines's master circle, and the entire spiral was much smaller. Florian stared, realizing suddenly what she was looking at. "You made another master circle."

Arisilde stepped around a pillar and came striding toward her, waving his hands excitedly. "No time for questions, we're in a bother." He pointed toward the front corner of the room, where a different spiral of writing spread out across the floor from the main circle and climbed up one of the pillars. "I've connected our circles to theirs, but when the last of their master circle is all gobbled up, this will be eaten too, and no more gates. So you must be quick, like a little bunny rabbit."

"Right." Florian nodded rapidly. *I hope he meant what I think he means.* "I don't have a sphere."

He looked down at her, his violet eyes already going distant. "Just call for me. Be sure to be in the same circle, or I won't be able to find you."

"I will." She started to step into the circle and fell flat on her face.

There was a rough stone floor under her instead of the *Ravenna*'s marble tiles. Swearing in shock, Florian pushed herself up and saw the gray walls with their frantic writing arching up over her. She heard a not-so-distant crash. She pushed to her feet only to stagger sideways as the ground swayed under her. She saw cracks creeping up the walls, and the opening at the top rained stone chips and dust down on her head as it widened. Mentally pleading *Don't fall yet, don't fall yet,* she caught her balance and ran for the archway.

*   *   *

Tremaine retreated hastily from the cracks spidering across the spiral. The stone underfoot shuddered again and a massive bass groan echoed through the chamber; the sound of walls shifting. *You know,* she told herself, hastily climbing the swaying steps, *blowing yourself up when you had the chance would have been quick.* The satchel with the explosives was on the far side of the room where Castines had flung it, on the other side of an inexorably widening crack, so that was out of the question.

The stairwell was shaking, dust falling from overhead, so Tremaine stayed on the ledge, looking out over the chamber. Rienish sorcerers had created Great Spells that lasted for years and years after their deaths; obviously whatever was keeping the ruin intact and airborne wasn't one of them. *Stupid worthless Castines,* Tremaine thought sourly. The gods were right; Syprian sorcerers really weren't good for anything.

Footsteps sounded on the stairs behind her and she yelled and spun around. Florian rounded the corner of the landing just below, sliding to a stop as she saw Tremaine. *Am I crazy?* It looked like Florian, her clothes dusty, her cheek scraped and the sleeve of her sweater torn from her fall. "What the hell—" Tremaine managed, flabbergasted.

"Arisilde sent me!" Florian shouted, gesturing wildly. "Come on, damn it!"

Tremaine plunged down the stairs. She realized Florian must have been shouting for her the whole way up here, but she hadn't been able to hear her. Florian pushed off from the wall and they ran down and into the passage, the stone swaying erratically under their feet. "Arisilde made a spiral in the *Ravenna,* and sort of spliced it into the Gardier spiral, to make a gate to the circle we came in on," Florian panted. "But he's making it work all himself, and protecting the *Ravenna,* so I don't know—"

"Florian, you don't have a sphere," Tremaine pointed out as they ducked back through the fire pit chamber. The electrified air spell must have vanished when Florian was separated from the sphere; the only evidence of it was several dead Liaisons, their bodies twisted and convulsed.

"I know that, he's doing it all himself!" Florian said frantically.

As they ran through the second domed chamber and into the first, Tremaine began, "Yes but—" Just then a thundering crash sounded from behind them. The floor dipped and Tremaine staggered across the line of the circle.

Her stomach lurched and she fell flat on her face. But it was on the tiled floor of the *Ravenna*'s ballroom which swayed only with the welcome movement of the ocean.

Florian slammed into the floor beside her, then rolled over with a groan. Tremaine managed to sit up, saying, "Never mind. It worked." She wished she knew how to faint, but all she could do was sit numbly on the floor. It was deathly quiet, though maybe Tremaine's damaged hearing just couldn't detect the *Ravenna*'s normal noises; there was no sound of bomb blasts from outside the metal hull and she was fairly sure she would be able to hear those. If it was true, if Orelis's death had released the spell that had imprisoned the crystals' unwilling inhabitants, those airships would have no defense against spells or anything else.

"That was . . . close." A dazed Florian pushed herself upright, pulling at her torn sweater to look at a bleeding elbow. "I don't know how he got us there and back without going through the staging world, but if he hadn't . . ."

If he hadn't, I'd be dead, and Florian too for trying to come after me, Tremaine thought. "You rescued me again," she said blankly. Her head throbbed slowly, the pain settling in just above her right ear.

Florian stared at her, cradling her elbow. "I thought this was the first time."

"Really? I—"

"I have to go, Tremaine," Arisilde said. He was suddenly kneeling in front of her. He looked the same as he had before, but his eyes were weary. She didn't think she had ever seen him look tired before.

"You took Orelis's place, and made the circles work." Tremaine wanted to be clear on that.

"Yes. But it was very hard," he agreed with a sigh. "I can see why she was so tired. I've done too much, Tremaine, and it's all going away. I have to go away."

"You mean you have to die." She could see the dark wooden walls through him, and she didn't think he had been that transparent before.

"I don't have a choice anymore, I'm afraid. I've been mostly dead for a long time, I think it's past the point to get on with the rest of it. And having seen an example of what comes of holding on to life for too long—" He waved his slender hands deprecatingly. "We wouldn't want that, would we?"

"No, we wouldn't want that." She could barely see him now and his voice was faint.

"Tell your father good-bye for me. I'll miss him. And when you see the god of Cineth again, tell it Orelis and Castines would never have come to Cineth. They feared the gods more than anything."

"Arisilde," she said, but he was gone.

They sat there in silence for a time. Tremaine pushed sweat-soaked hair out of her eyes and took a deep breath. He had forgotten there would be no gates to Cineth or anywhere else without him or Orelis. She would never know if Ilias and Giliead would be able to leave the fortress and get home safely. *But you couldn't chance trapping them here, away from everything they know, away from the god, to finish a war that no longer has anything to do with them, to be out of place forever.*

Watching her, Florian said hesitantly, "He left a lot of spheres. Maybe one of them is powerful enough to open a gate to Cineth. . . ."

Tremaine just looked at her. She knew it wasn't true. Without a living sorcerer inside them, the spheres were just tools, dependent on whoever wielded them.

Florian groaned under her breath. "I know, I know it won't work. But they'll be all right. And maybe Niles or someone will invent another way to get us there."

"Maybe." Tremaine didn't want to hope. It hurt too much, and she had always been a realist. She struggled to her feet, holding out a hand to Florian.

Nicholas handed off the field glasses to Reynard, saying, "I don't suppose you know where there's a stockpile of arsenic?"

"I thought of that already," Reynard said with some asperity, hunkering down between the crenelations to focus the glasses on the plaza three stories below. "If we poison the water supply, we might as well cut our own throats."

"Hmm." Nicholas wasn't sure he agreed, but there was no point in arguing over it. It had been a long busy night and morning.

The overcast sky made the plaza in front of Prince's Gate fade into a gray dimness; the paving stones, the ancient towers of the old palace wall, the great arch of the Queen Ravenna Memorial, which stood like a prisoner in the center of the plaza, were all of the same gray stone and blurred by the fine rain. The great iron-sheathed doors of the gate stood out in rust-streaked black. Service Gardier armed with rifles, many of Rienish make scavenged on their march to Vienne, were collected in the plaza, readying themselves for another patrol through the city.

The patrol was probably occasioned by the destruction of two generators late last night, the ones that had been powering the streetlamps in this section of the city. Or at least Nicholas hoped it was; that had certainly been his plan. The Gardier were going to make a show of force and use a sorcerer crystal to search for the saboteurs; Nicholas meant to make sure they found them relatively quickly.

He glanced back at Madame Cusard and Berganmot's young apprentice, whose name was Perrin. They were on the roof terrace of the oldest wing of Fontainon House, shielded from view by the wall atop it and also by the bulk of the house's tower behind them. There had been a Gardier sentry up there, but he was dead now, his place taken by a young woman wearing his uniform cap and coat and holding his rifle. Anyone looking up from below wouldn't notice the difference. Madame Cusard's nephew Ricard was below with the other men and women, hastily gathered into the lower levels of the house and readying themselves for their own attack.

The Cusards had identified and disposed of their two traitors after the Vintner's Row mews trick, which had freed the rest of their recruits to participate in this. With the sphere's help, Perrin had been able to get them past the Gardier wards to enter Fontainon House this morning. "Ready?" Nicholas asked him with a lifted brow.

The boy looked up, his eyes alight. The sphere had been a revelation to him. He nodded. "Yes."

"As we said earlier, the important point is to wait for the sorcerer crystal. It's—"

"Here," Reynard interrupted, lowering the glasses and drawing back from the opening in the wall. "He's just come out of the gate."

Nicholas stooped hastily to look. Down below, a Gardier had just stepped out of the shelter of Prince's Gate. The bad light and the distance meant Nicholas couldn't see much detail about the man himself, but the large chunk of crystal he carried was fairly obvious. "Very good," Nicholas muttered, and drew breath to give the order.

Below, the Gardier staggered and fell to his knees as the crystal in his arms shattered, white light bursting out of it in a brief fountain that coalesced into drops, falling to the ground and vanishing. The men around him cried out or recoiled in shock.

Nicholas and Reynard exchanged a startled look, then both turned to stare at Perrin, Nicholas demanding, "Did you do that?"

"No, it wasn't me!" He stepped close to peer past them. "Wasn't the sphere either. But that crystal's a deader."

Madame Cusard craned her neck to see. "Is it a trick? What does it mean?"

Nicholas shook his head slowly. From the reactions of the men below, it didn't look like a trick. But this was a question that would have to be settled later. He said, "It means we need to get started. Give the word to the others. Tell them no prisoners," and reached for the rifle leaning against the wall.

Chapter 20

Cineth, the Syrnai

Giliead and Ilias would have reached Cineth sometime that night, but rain had swelled the river and clouds covered the waning moon, so they decided to camp. Trying to cross the ford in the pitch-dark in high water would be suicidal, and from the news they had gotten from both the last village and the traders they had met, there was no reason to hurry.

They had encountered the last trader along the muddy forest road. She was an older woman with three young husbands, one riding on the wagon with her and two on horseback, probably all acquired to help load and unload the wagon. They were transporting amphorae filled with either wine or olive oil, destined for the villages along the river valley. She had picked up her last load in Cineth, so she knew all there was to tell.

Standing beside the horses in the light drizzle of rain, she had told Giliead, "No, there's been no word of the giant wizard ship, or any of the Rienish wizards, not since the rainy season started. And they said it's been almost as long since they had word of a Gardier attack. A few days ago one of the small metal ships drifted into shore near a Gleaners' village up the coast, but the Gleaners killed all the Gardier before the lawgiver could get there. The Chosen Vessel of Ancyra said she didn't think there had been any wizards among them, but she and the lawgiver were too late, and there was nothing to be done." The woman shrugged, looking curiously past Giliead to where Ilias stood. They were both wearing oiled leather cloaks dyed blue and gray, with the Hisian clan signs ripped off to keep from being shot at, and Ilias had his hood pulled up to hide his curse mark. He had been looking off into the dripping forest the whole time Giliead had been speaking to the trader. She asked, "Is your brother married?"

"Yes," Ilias said, and walked away. Giliead had nodded his thanks to the woman and followed. He had been able to hear the god since they first crossed back into its territory, and though it was too agitated at his return for him to get much sense out of it, he thought it would have shown him the Rienish if any of them had been within its boundaries.

The fitful rain stopped by nightfall and they camped beside a fallen tree, finally managing to scavenge enough mostly dry wood from it to build a small smoky fire. There wasn't much food left, just some cheese and dried pomegranates from the last village, and some tree-eggs, round white fungi that grew on exposed roots in damp weather and tasted a little like bread if you baked them in the ashes long enough. Ilias just poked at the food, anyway.

Huddled in his cloak, Giliead finally said, "It's good news, about the Gardier. If they didn't have any wizard crystals, then breaking the spiral must have worked."

It had been fifty-three days, and they had tried not to talk about it. At first they had speculated so much on what had happened, what might have happened and what could have happened that they were almost telling stories to one another about it, each one further and further from the facts. After that they had been well occupied with climbing down the escarpment to get out of the fortress, then with killing or avoiding Hisian bandits. It was after they had gotten back into friendly territory that the things they weren't talking about had begun to wear on them.

Poking at the fire, Ilias shrugged. "They could have been left over from the Gardier on the island and never had any big wizard crystals."

Right, that's how this is going to go, Giliead thought, suppressing a sigh. He knew Ilias had been counting on hearing something, anything, in Cineth, but from what the trader had said, the two of them knew far more than anyone in the city.

★   ★   ★

They spent a damp wakeful night, but by afternoon the next day they were walking into Cineth. It was a gray day again, and though the sun broke through the clouds sporadically, it did nothing to improve Ilias's mood. They passed through the open gates without a challenge and went down the muddy road toward the plaza.

Most people were down at the harbor or working in their homes or out in their fields. The white houses were quiet in their courtyards, though the smell of bread baking made Ilias's stomach grumble. A few children played around a fountain house but didn't bother to look at the two weary mud-spattered men trudging along the road.

They reached the plaza, where the lawgiver's house and the other city buildings were. The market under the tents was fairly active and people were startled to recognize Giliead; some pointed and a few called greetings. Ilias ignored them all. Giliead had to tell Visolela and Nicanor he was back, then they had to walk on to Andrien to reassure Karima and Halian, but after that they hadn't decided what they were going to do or where they were going to go. They had discussed going back to the Isle of Storms, trying to find any Gardier left behind to see if they knew what had happened in Ile-Rien. Ilias knew in his gut that was a forlorn hope; even if there were any Gardier who had survived there this long, they would have no more idea what happened than Ilias had.

They were walking under the god's favorite oak tree when a voice shouted, "You back!"

Ilias looked up, startled, just as Davret of the Aelin joyously flung herself on him. He staggered sideways as she released him and flung herself on Giliead. "Where you been? We heard nothing for days and days! And see, I speak your language now. Where is everybody else?" Her hair was longer than Ilias remembered and her skin tanned and freckled from the sun. She wore light pants and a red shirt, with strings of beads around her neck and woven through her hair. Except for her accent, there was nothing to tell she wasn't Syprian.

Giliead disentangled himself from her. "We were— It's a long story," he told her, with a glance at Ilias.

Ilias knew Giliead was trying to spare his feelings, but there didn't seem much point in it. Davret had dropped a basket filled with olives and a couple of small rounds of cheese and he sat on his heels to help her collect it. He said, "We ended up at the fortress again, and couldn't use the circles to get back. We'll tell you later. Where's Gyan?"

Davret looked from him to Giliead and back, brows drawing together.

It must be fairly obvious this wasn't exactly a happy homecoming. But instead of asking more questions, she just said, "At your house, where we live."

Giliead nodded, his lips pressed together. "At Andrien?"

"No, no, your house, in town," Davret explained, taking her basket back from Ilias. "The one Tremaine got for us."

"The what?" Ilias stared at her.

"The one we came to when you first bring—brought—us to here. Gyan says Tremaine has it for us." At their increasingly baffled expressions, she gestured helplessly, laughing. "Come and see then. Maybe I explain it wrong."

Ilias didn't really believe it until they reached Visolela's old house above the boat sheds and found Gyan and the Aelin there. Gyan had wept to see them, having nearly given them up for dead after so long, and sent one of the young Aelin men running off to take the word to Andrien.

The house looked the same on the outside, but in the court Ilias could see the difference. Couches and benches with brightly woven cushions were set out on the previously empty portico and the flower beds were now carefully tended. The center one had been replanted as a vegetable garden. After recovering himself a little, Gyan had led them into the dining room, which opened off the atrium. It was now clean and lit with new clay oil lamps, and there was fresh red paint on the walls and columns. Ilias recognized the dining table and the benches from the waterbirds carved on the legs; they were an old set from Andrien House. There was a small fire in the center hearth to drive the damp out of the room before everyone came back for dinner. "Not that we all fit in here," Gyan explained, lowering himself to one of the benches with a grunt. "But the young ones eat at all hours anyway." On the walk here, Davret had explained that the young Aelin had been finding work at the harbor, loading and unloading cargo, or helping the local merchants, while they considered whether they could establish themselves as traders again. "It's mostly me, the children and the elders that keep regular hours. Dyani will be back from the harbor soon. And Kias should hear that you're back and turn up tonight too." He gave Ilias a searching look. "You didn't know Tremaine bought this place? She got it from Visolela the morning before you left. She came here to leave Calit with me, and said she wanted the house for you and Giliead, to have a place to stay in town, and invited us all to live here."

Sitting on the opposite bench, Ilias made a gesture midway between a shake of the head and a shrug, unable to form a coherent reply.

After they had had a cup of warmed wine and taken off their muddy boots, Ilias left so that Giliead could tell Gyan the full story. He wandered around the house, barefoot on the cool tiles. The Aelin were taking up most of the rooms but they had saved a set for Ilias and Giliead, and Halian had brought over their belongings from Andrien House.

Ilias sat down on the bedstead in one of the rooms left for their use. The mattress was still rolled up and tied from when it had been carted here, with folded blankets, linens and wall hangings piled atop it. Their clothes chests were set against the wall, along with Ranior's old sword rack and the long wooden cases for bows and javelins, holding the weapons they had decided to leave behind. The only thing he could think was that a woman didn't buy a house for a husband she was planning to discard. Not here, and surely not in Ile-Rien either, where men were expected to own their own property and shift for themselves.

Vienne, Ile-Rien

Light would help, but Tremaine didn't think Vienne would ever look the same. She stood at the big bay windows of the third-floor lounge of the Hotel Galvaz, looking down into the dark street. The blackout conditions had been lifted last week, but electricity and gas had yet to be restored to most sections of the city.

The lounge she stood in was softly lit by candles in shielded glass lamps, rescued from the old hotel's copious attics. Below in the dark cavern of the street, a party of men with oil lamps and pocket torches were guiding a rumbling truck and a convoy of farm carts, bringing supplies into the city for the growing number of returning refugees and troops.

The Gardier had been unable to hold Vienne without sorcerer crystals, and with several Lodun sorcerers and a combined force of Rienish and Parscian troops landed near Chaire by the *Falaise* and the *Ravenna*, the occupying army had been driven out only two weeks after Lodun's liberation. Adera and anything to the east of Vienne and

Lodun was still considered occupied territory, but Rienish and Aderassi refugees, the scattered remnants of the Rienish armies and allied Parscian troops were pouring back in over the southern borders. The *Ravenna*, the *Falaise* and a dozen or so Capidaran transports had been carrying supplies from Capidara, landing at Chaire, Rel and Portier without incident. With the Gardier supply lines through the staging world completely cut off, the invaders were relying on Adera's resources and the bases they had established there and in the Low Countries. But Adera had always been a poor nation, without much in the way of resources to be had. And word had recently spread that Aderassi rebels were committing violent acts of sabotage at every turn.

It wasn't surprising; the Gardier had relied heavily on the crystals, to protect their airships, to make their wireless sets work, for attack, for communication, for defense, for coordination. Without them, they were left with inadequate stolen machinery they didn't quite understand and captive populations who could smell their invaders' new weakness.

"Tremaine, are you all right?"

She rolled her eyes in annoyance, still facing the dark window. "You have to put a real in the bowl."

"I do not," Gerard said patiently. "The arrangement was that I have to contribute a copper real every time I ask you if you're all right for no reason. I've been sitting here trying to ask you if you want any coffee for a full—" She heard a rustle as he consulted his watch. "Two minutes without a response. Therefore, I'm allowed a bonus 'are you all right?' "

Tremaine turned to glare at him. He was sitting in an upholstered armchair, his feet propped on a stool, reading by candlelight. The book was a novel with a singed cloth cover, salvaged from the mess the Gardier occupation had made of the lending library the next street over. Dr. Divies had absolutely forbidden Gerard to perform spells, read anything pertaining to sorcery or even be in the same room as a Viller sphere for another six months. "I didn't hear you."

"Yes, it's such a great distance to the window." He closed the book with a sigh, adjusting his spectacles. He still looked too thin and too tired, but he was no longer sleeping through most of the days, and his voice had life in it again. "Do you want any coffee? If you don't get downstairs, there won't be any left."

"Not really." She paced away from the window. The hotel had become the temporary headquarters of the Viller Institute, though the opposite wing had suffered fire damage. The lounge was a long room, with bay windows draped with heavy gold curtains looking down onto what had been one of the most fashionable avenues in the city. The hotel was determined to reestablish itself as quickly as possible, and unless you knew, it would have been hard to tell that the couches and chairs in this lounge and the downstairs dining rooms had been scavenged from all over the building. It did leave the small number of usable rooms sparsely furnished. Tremaine would rather have been at Coldcourt, but a stray artillery shell had hit one of the towers, rendering most of the house uninhabitable until it could be rebuilt.

Gerard was eyeing her thoughtfully. "You will be going to the memorial service for Colonel Averi, won't you?"

Tremaine dropped into the other armchair, sighing in annoyance. She had gone to the private memorial, where Florian, Gerard, Niles, Captain Marais, Dr. Divies and several of Averi's officers had locked themselves in the Observation Bar aboard the *Ravenna* and drunk all of the ship's small remaining supply of liquor. Tremaine hadn't known until then that Averi had actually retired from service before the war because of a wasting disease. It wasn't something that could be cured either by surgeons or sorcerer-healers, though Niles had been keeping him supplied with charms and healing stones to keep the pain at bay. In some ways, it had been a mercy that he had been killed instantly when airships had fired on the *Ravenna* during the Lodun evacuation. Balin had died in that attack too, but there had been no memorial for her. She was just one of the dead people Tremaine hadn't been able to keep a promise to.

The memorial being held at Aviler House tomorrow night would be a big public display, more of a demonstration that all was under control in the city than anything else. But there was no point in staying away. It would just elicit more unwelcome inquiries as to her health and state of mind. "Sure, I'll go. Florian will be there too."

"I see." Gerard was still watching her with a faint frown. "I was rather surprised that you agreed to give Arites's papers to Barshion. I thought you'd like to work on the translation for yourself."

Tremaine leaned her head back against the upholstery that still smelled faintly of smoke, despite the hotel's best efforts. She was getting really tired of being treated like an invalid. First, they had assigned her the duty of taking care of Gerard while he recuperated, as if Gerard wasn't perfectly capable of sitting around in the hotel himself, as if there weren't any number of Viller Institute workers within shouting distance at all times.

No matter how much time Niles and the other remaining sorcerers devoted to it, no one knew how Orelis had managed to power the gate spiral. No one knew how Arisilde had managed to power his copy long enough to send Florian there and bring her and Tremaine back, though the fact that it had caused even him to give up his tenuous hold on life implied that it wasn't something an ordinary human sorcerer could do. And considering the small number of sorcerers left in Ile-Rien, it would be a very long time before anyone managed to figure it out.

Still looking at the water- and smoke-stained plaster overhead, she said, "All I had to read the papers with was the Syrnaic-Rienish word list Arites started. Barshion knows people who can do a much better job of translating them than me. And it was Arites's version of what happened on the *Ravenna*. It's a historical document. Who better to have it than the History College at Lodun?" She looked at him directly, tired of dancing around the real issue. "You were the one who told me that shared danger was no basis for building a relationship."

"I remember it clearly," Gerard said dryly. "I do wish I hadn't said it."

Tremaine looked away. The real issue, of course, was that she would never see Ilias, or any of the other Syprians, again.

She didn't even know if they had been able to get out of the fortress. She hadn't ever voiced this fear aloud, but Gerard and Florian and even Nicholas had all seemed to guess its presence. They had pointed out that the teenage Aelin had been able to get in and out several times, and that they had left a large amount of rope, food and other supplies behind. There was every reason to think the two men had made it back to Cineth easily. But it still wore on her and always would. Along with everything else that wore on her and always would.

Watching her as if he could read her thoughts, Gerard sighed. "Tremaine—"

Tremaine was almost relieved when the door opened and Nicholas entered. He greeted them with a nod, taking his coat off and hanging it on the rack beside the door.

"Well?" Tremaine demanded. She had spotted a rolled sheaf of gray paper sticking out of his coat pocket. One of the big printing companies had begun issuing a newspaper again, mostly to help people locate missing or wounded relatives and identify the dead. But it also carried news of the war.

Nicholas directed an opaque glance at her, but didn't pretend he didn't know what she meant. "The War Department won't direct more troops into the Marches. There simply aren't enough men available yet to waste them in police duties."

Gerard made a noise of disgust. Tremaine looked at the dark window, locking her jaw.

The Rienish government was offering amnesty for Gardier Service or Labor caste who surrendered, on the grounds that most of them had probably been forced into the conflict. But that wasn't working out so well. Many Gardier troops near Lodun, caught flat-footed by the sudden retreat from Vienne, had surrendered. An inadequate number of Rienish troops had been holding them in the town of Charven in the Marches, but local rioters had broken into the makeshift camp and burned it, killing many of the unarmed and wounded men and women. Others had escaped and were being killed by the local people, despite the Rienish military's attempt to stop them. Paranoia about Gardier mixing with the population was rampant, despite the fact that the Aelin had never been allowed to learn the languages of the lands they had invaded so that blending in would have been next to impossible. There had been incidents where refugees or freed Gardier slaves from obscure countries who spoke Rienish poorly had been badly beaten or killed by panicked crowds.

For a long moment the only sound was the faint rustle as Nicholas removed the paper from his pocket, leaving it on the sideboard. Tremaine was a little startled when he broke down enough to say, "I agree that it's regrettable, but there's nothing we can do about it."

Tremaine snorted derisively. *So all these people who surrendered on good faith are just going to be murdered. Along with whoever else gets in the way. Regardless of how difficult it's going to make convincing the Gardier troops to the south to trust us.* They had nowhere to go, and offering them an option other than fighting or dying had been the only solution. *And it's not going to work.* "Who said it was regrettable?" she said, hearing the acid tinge in her own voice. "I just don't like having our record for murdering Aelin broken by a bunch of hysterical shopkeepers. We're professionals, after all."

Nicholas shook his head, giving her a dry look. "We're not murderers, Tremaine. We're killers. There's a difference. A small difference, but a difference nonetheless."

Tremaine rolled her eyes. *Yes, that was comforting.* "I'm sure it matters to the dead people. I think I'll go downstairs for coffee after all."

*   *   *

After the door had closed behind Tremaine, Nicholas threw himself into a chair, the first betrayal of irritation Gerard had witnessed.

Standing on the beach at Cineth with Tremaine, when she had all but told him she meant to make the place her home someday, Gerard had thought of all the reasons she shouldn't. The primitive conditions, the danger, the prejudices of the inhabitants. But Ile-Rien was no less dangerous, the war would go on for years and the Rienish were currently giving the Syprians a run for their money where irrational prejudices were concerned. And Tremaine had already done more than her part. And it had simply come down to the fact that this was a chance she would have to take, that she couldn't know it was the right thing until she tried it. Now that chance had been snatched away. Watching Nicholas, Gerard said carefully, "It's very frustrating as a friend, and especially I suppose as a parent, to know the exact solution to a problem, yet be unable to provide it."

For a long moment he didn't think Nicholas would reply. Tremaine tended to be reticent about her feelings, but next to her father she was positively fulsome. Then Nicholas grimaced, and said, "Especially since this is the first time I've ever had the slightest clue what she wanted."

Gerard nodded, resigned. "I think this is the first time Tremaine has ever had the slightest clue what she wanted."

Cineth, the Syrnai

Giliead woke at dawn, his head aching a little from too much strong wine, with the feeling that the god wanted to talk to him.

They had sat up for a long time, Giliead talking to Karima, Halian, Gyan and Kias and the others. Ilias had mostly just sat there. Because of the late night, Giliead hadn't done anything in their new set of rooms except unroll one of the mattresses and unpack a couple of blankets.

Ilias had also tossed and turned in his sleep, finally settling onto Giliead's arm. Now Giliead managed to ease him off without waking him and climb out of bed. He dressed quietly in the dark room, finding a shirt in the clothes chest to replace the one that was muddy and bloodstained and shabby from their long journey.

Out in the atrium no one was stirring except a few sleepy Aelin whose names he didn't know, preparing to go down to the harbor for cargo work. He let himself out the gate and walked down the quiet tree-shaded street, following the ground mist to where the path wound down the hill to the beach. At the top was a large tree, leaning at an odd angle to accommodate the rocks around its roots. He sat on the damp grass, with his back to the trunk, and waited.

After a short time, the god climbed down out of the leaves, wound its way down the trunk and settled into the grass beside him.

Ilias woke when Giliead did, though he pretended he hadn't. He got up after Giliead left, dug out clean clothes and proceeded to wander around the house trying to avoid the other inhabitants. He managed to sit still through breakfast but ended up pacing the atrium afterward, waiting impatiently for Giliead to get back.

There had to be something they could do to get news. It seemed like insult added to injury that Ile-Rien itself wasn't that many days' sail away, yet separated from them by the world's breadth and the lack of a curse gate.

Karima and Halian had come to the house the night before to greet them and it had turned into something of a party. Ilias had spent most of it avoiding people and trying to nod and smile at all the right times. He suspected the word had passed not to ask him questions because no one did.

It was nearly as bad as the first few days after he had gotten the curse mark.

He was standing beside the atrium pool when he heard a soft step on the stone walk and looked up to see Cletia.

She nodded to him, coming forward to stand on the grass nearby. She wore blue and green, with a wrap around her shoulders against the morning mist. "It's good that you're back." She hesitated a moment. "I heard what happened."

"I don't want to talk about it," Ilias warned her. He realized he was going to be saying that a lot from now on.

"I understand. I just wanted to ask you . . ." She took a deep breath, seemed to steel her resolve. "If you would consider marrying again. With me."

Ilias stared blankly at her. He had forgotten that as he was a married man, Cletia could ask him directly without having to negotiate with Karima first. He shook his head, not sure if she meant what she said. "I'm still married to Tremaine, Cletia."

"Giliead told Gyan that it sounded as if the Rienish could never come back here, that killing the Gardier wizard leader killed the thing that made the curse gates work." Cletia shook her head, her mouth twisted. "Would she want you to wait forever for nothing?"

Ilias felt his whole body go tense, but she didn't say that Tremaine was most likely dead. He realized that perhaps Gyan and the others hadn't passed that part of the story along. If they did, if Tremaine was known to be dead, Karima would have to take possession of the house. They probably thought it was just easier to keep quiet on that point for now. He looked away across the court, where Calit and two other Aelin children were digging industriously in a flower bed, wishing it was that easy. That you could make people live again just by skipping the part of the story where they died. He said only, "I'm not giving up yet."

Cletia watched him a moment, frowning. "When will you give up?"

He swore under his breath, then faced her. "I don't want to give up at all. I don't want to look back on the time I knew her, any more than I want to look back on the time I knew Giliead. I want her to be with me when I look back." He didn't think he had fully realized that himself until the words came out. And if Cletia wanted plain speaking, so be it. "It's not just that. When I got the curse mark, you listened to your family and treated me as if I was dead. Or ruined, as Pasima says. Now you've changed your mind, you're sorry for it. But how am I supposed to trust that? This year you want me, what if next year you want Pasima's approval more?" She looked stung, and he said, "I'm sorry," before he walked away.

He went past the kitchen where Gyan and Davret and several of the Aelin were cleaning up after breakfast, then back through the portico and the storeroom and into the back court. It was small, with a spare cistern squatting under a ragged plum tree and a few slop jars. The wall here was only chest height, and looked into the neighbor's goat pen. He leaned on it, fingering the ring that still hung around his neck, not noticing the brown-and-white goats crowding up to see if he brought food.

At least now he knew what was wrong, why this homecoming seemed so off-kilter. *Because they're treating me like a man with a dead wife.* And if that was true, at least he could grieve and learn to live with it and go on. But he didn't think of himself that way. Because in his gut he believed she had found a way out, whether she had intended to when she sent them away or not.

Ilias buried his face in his hands. *Great. How are you going to live with not knowing?* He would be crazy within the year.

He was still standing there, leaning on the wall, when Giliead found him. "Ilias."

"What?" Ilias looked around, startled by the tone of his voice.

Giliead looked as if he had just seen something that had both shocked him senseless and given him hope. "I talked to the god. It told me . . . I knew it talked to Arisilde, that it shared knowledge with him the way it did with me. But I didn't realize— It knows the curse, the gate curse."

Ilias just stared at him. "But they said—Orelis said the circles wouldn't work once she was dead. And we don't have a god-sphere."

Giliead took a deep breath. "I asked the god if it could take us through the gate the Rienish left and bring us back. It said yes. Or at least it showed me pictures that looked like it meant yes."

Hope made Ilias's chest ache. "I don't understand. How can that work?"

Giliead gestured helplessly. "Castines said Orelis was a god of wizards, a failed god. What if that wasn't a lie? What if the gods came from the ancient people too? Orelis was just something that, I don't know, went wrong, like our wizards went wrong, while the gods went right." He shrugged impatiently. "I don't know, but the god thinks it can do it." Giliead put his hands on Ilias's shoulders, saying urgently, "It's worth a try."

Y ou really think we can do this?" Ilias said for perhaps the third time. They were in the forest clearing where so many days ago Gerard and the other Rienish wizards had made the circle Arisilde had given them to reach Ile-Rien. The rock ridge and the pines sheltered the area of flat ground, but the wind was strong and cool, tossing the high tree limbs and bringing sprinkles of rain. Despite this, Ilias was sweating as if they were crossing the Barrens under a noonday sun.

Pacing the perimeter of the circle, Giliead just glared at him. Bythia was following along with him, a blue wrap pulled up over her head to shield her from the rain, reading from the tablet she had made. Her brows drawn together in concentration, she said, "I'm not a Vessel, but it looks as if it's all still here, just the way they drew it." Grass had grown between the stones and in the center, but the painted symbols hadn't faded.

Gyan and Dyani were sitting on the fallen blocks of the ruined house, watching worriedly. "You know what Herias would make of this," Gyan pointed out.

Giliead grimaced at the mention of the name. "Herias can argue about it with the god," he said.

"If you can get there, how do you know Tremaine will want to come back with you?" Dyani asked.

Ilias stared at the sky, gritting his teeth. Gyan shook his head at her, and Bythia paused to throw her an admonishing look, saying dryly, "Don't edge up to it, girl, just speak your mind."

"Sorry, I didn't mean—" Dyani shrugged in confusion. "Well, you know what I mean. We saw how beautiful the *Ravenna* was. Why should she leave a place with things like that for here?"

Ilias saw Giliead glance at him in sympathy, and he managed to take a breath before replying. If he could find out Tremaine was alive, that the Rienish were safe, or at least safer than they had been, he thought he would be able to live with that. The other part he wasn't counting on. He said, "I have to ask her and find out."

Giliead came to the place with the missing symbol, where Gyan had broken the circle on Gerard's instructions, to keep the Gardier from finding and using it. He sat on his heels, contemplating the empty space. It looked as if Gyan had used another rock to rub the paint away, leaving only fragments of the original.

Ilias heard rustling and stepped away hastily as the god crept out, its sparkle of light bright against the dull yellow grass. *It must really want to help us,* he thought, startled. He knew it usually avoided open ground, preferring rocks, trees, eaves of houses, wells, any dark quiet spot or perch. It made its way toward Giliead as Bythia backed away. It passed him, climbing atop the flat rock with the missing symbol. It sat there a moment, a hazy glitter of light, then it crept off toward the center of the circle.

They knew only wizards could draw the circles, that it didn't matter how well you knew the marks that it was made of, that they had to be knitted together with curses. But it appeared, even to Ilias's untutored eyes, that the god had just done something to make the spot ready for the symbol. His eyes intent, Giliead motioned urgently to Bythia. She knelt beside him, holding out the little clay bowl of ink and the tablet so he could see her copy of the missing symbol. Giliead put his fingers in the ink and with sure strokes drew it in.

Ilias realized he had stopped breathing at some point. He took a sharp breath, refusing to ask.

Giliead pushed slowly to his feet. "It worked." He sounded shocked. He held out a hand, as if he didn't quite believe his senses. "The curse is here again. The god made it . . . wake up."

The god had taken a position in the center of the circle, as if ready to go. Giliead looked at Ilias, his face set and serious. "Well?"

Ilias nodded, his stomach tight with tension. "It's worth a try."

Vienne, Ile-Rien

Tremaine walked along the promenade of the Street of Flowers as dusk settled over the city. The broad street had once been lined with fashionable shops, with even more fashionable flats in the upper floors of the old stone buildings. The electricity was still out now and no lights blossomed in the windows. Some of the trees had been cut down, and the ornamental iron railings were twisted and broken, but all the debris and wrecked vehicles had been carted away.

It had been a warm day for this time of year but the air had turned brisk as the sun set, and Tremaine was wearing broadcloth pants, a lighter blouse and a blue jacket. Not exactly appropriate attire for the event she was going to, but she couldn't really care less. She didn't feel as if she belonged here anymore, and didn't feel like making the effort to pretend that she did.

She wasn't the only one having that problem. Florian's mother had returned to town a few days ago, but they still had no idea how many of Florian's brothers had survived. "I'm having trouble talking to her about it," Florian had explained, as they were sitting over two very bad cups of coffee in the hotel's downstairs parlor earlier that afternoon. "I killed a lot of men. Men that were only there because they had been lied to and tricked. And maybe there were even some who had realized the truth, but they had a little crystal stuck inside them that took away their choices." She had shaken her head, looking weary and drawn and older than her years. Tremaine knew from some things Gerard had said that death spells established a connection between sorcerer and victim. The stronger the sorcerer, the stronger the connection. It was probably the reason Arisilde had always tried to avoid them. Florian shrugged helplessly. "Mother thinks I'm a hero. I don't want to be a hero if this is what it means. Killing deluded men who were driven into battle like cattle."

Tremaine nodded, turning her cup around in the saucer. "There are people who will come back here and it will be like nothing ever happened." Her mouth twisted bitterly. "I hate those people."

Florian had nodded glumly.

Later, Tremaine had fled the hotel. Now she had been aimlessly wandering the city for the past few hours. She felt the need to get it out of her system, so she wouldn't simply walk out in the middle of the memorial service tonight.

Some of the city had fallen victim to looting, but on this street the broken glass from the shop windows had been swept up. A small theater had been turned into a station for distributing food and clothing. A large crowd still gathered around it, waiting for supplies to be handed out. They were entertaining themselves with card games. There was even a group of musicians, a horn quartet, playing on the corner.

As Tremaine moved out into the street to bypass the crowd waiting under the theater marquee, the wrought-iron streetlamps flickered and blazed to life. The crowd broke into cheers and applause.

Tremaine reached the corner, heading down the side street to the Aviler Great House. There were soldiers in Rienish uniform posted along here, and a couple of motorcars puttered past her. The streetlamps were only on about halfway down the block, but when she took the turn into the circular drive in front of the massive house, she saw that the windows on the second and third floors were bright with light. Aviler House had been functioning as a sort of auxiliary government building, as the palace was still uninhabitable, so it probably had diesel generators. None of the other expensive town houses and blocks of flats along the street seemed to be lit with anything but candlelight.

Aviler House was one of the oldest remaining Great Houses in the city, and actually predated the Queen the *Ravenna* had been named for. The white façade of the front wing, with the classical figures carved above the large windows and in the pediment under the peaked slate roof, was only fifty years old and was the youngest thing about the house. The other wings were built of heavy gray stone like the oldest city walls, and the windows were small and forbidding and meant for defense. Even in this newer section meant to present an attractive face to the street, there were no windows on the ground floor. It was fitting for a family house that had been attacked by private troops and fay of the Unseelie Court and nearly burned several times throughout its long history.

There were more motorcars parked in the drive, men in suits or dress uniforms and women in evening dresses stood talking on the terrace. The broad steps led up to wide-open double doors, though there were soldiers posted there too.

Tremaine had made her way up to the terrace when she noticed a soldier walking along beside her. He began, "Madam—"

"I'm invited," she told him, though she felt she might get some bitter satisfaction out of being mistakenly turned away. "I'm Tremaine Valiarde."

But he said, "Yes, Madam Valiarde. Captain Morane sent me to look for you," and walked her up the stairs past the others waiting to have their identities checked, past the guards at the door and into the brightly lit foyer.

The marble floor and the columns were pristine, but as Tremaine headed for the grand stairs, she saw empty wall niches where sculpture or vases had once stood. There were two large blank sections of wall above the wainscoting, where faint scuff marks suggested large paintings had once hung. It didn't surprise her that the place had been looted or just simply vandalized.

She went up the stairs behind some Rienish officers and a couple of men and women in the elegant robes and little round caps that Parscians wore to formal occasions. The stairway opened into a large hall, with three archways giving onto a ballroom on the left, and three interconnected formal salons on the right. The light was lower here, to spare the generator. The wooden paneling was polished and the gold silk panels pristine, but again, the furniture and artwork were sparse, and the pieces that were left had a mismatched look, as if they had been scavenged from different parts of the house. Chairs had been assembled in the ballroom, and there was a speaker's rostrum on the dais normally reserved for the orchestra.

Officers and more people in evening dress congregated here. Lady Aviler stood to one side of the hall, formally greeting guests, her son beside her. They were both dressed in black, and the son wore an eye patch. Tremaine knew he had been injured in the attack on the Queen's train, the attack that had killed his father. The Gardier had gained nothing else out of it, however. The Queen had left the train somewhere in Bisra with several retainers and reached Parscia by a combination of farm carts and borrowed motorcars. The Crown Prince had gone a separate route, mostly on foot, with only one Queen's Guard as escort. They were both back in Ile-Rien now with Princess Olympe, who had returned last week from Capidara, and were staying in Fontainon House.

Tremaine mixed with the Parscian group, slipping past into the hall and avoiding Lady Aviler and her son. She had never been good at giving condolences, and there had been so many to give lately.

Tremaine eased toward the salon, hoping for a place to sit down, or to spot Gerard and Florian, when someone behind her said, "Tremaine."

Oh, the delights of the evening begin. Tremaine turned, "Hello, Ander. Where have you been?" She captured a drink off a passing tray to fortify herself.

He was dressed in a well-tailored evening suit. "I just got back into the city today. I've been in the south." He hesitated, watching her, deliberately not making any comment on how she was dressed. "A great many people are going to be disappointed when they release the reports, if they do."

Tremaine nodded. She tasted the drink and winced. It was lemon-flavored water, with nothing alcoholic about it. She felt her chances of surviving the evening unscathed had just dropped dramatically. Ander's chances of survival had probably risen. "They think there are camps, where the Gardier are holding Rienish sorcerers. They're wrong."

He nodded in surprised approval of her sagacity. "Yes. Anyone with any sorcerous ability is dead. If there are any prisoners alive, they're going to be in labor camps." He shook his head, looking away. "Things are never going to be the same here."

Tremaine tasted the drink again, winced again. "No one follows the rules anymore."

"Rules?" Ander lifted his brows.

"To make life less painful."

Ander shrugged a little. "Your father never struck me as a man who followed rules."

Tremaine let her breath out, tired of the game, whatever it was. "His biggest rule was that you didn't involve anyone who wasn't already playing the game. Or, as he phrased it, if you have to kill innocent bystanders, then your planning is at fault and someone should best eliminate you."

Ander smiled indulgently. "He didn't really say that, did he."

Tremaine thought about framing a reply, then decided it really wasn't worth her time. She set her drink down on a marble-topped side table, walking off through the crowd as a nonplussed Ander stared after her.

The next person who called her name was Florian, which was a relief. Tremaine found her standing with Gerard, Nicholas and Reynard Morane. The three men were all dressed in dark suits, Florian in a conservative blue dress. "Were you talking to Ander?" Florian demanded. She craned her neck to look past Tremaine. "Is he still being . . . you know."

"Yes. Surprise, surprise," Tremaine said dryly. She eyed Gerard, but he didn't look overtired. "You didn't walk here, did you?"

"Your father drove," Gerard explained, giving Nicholas a wry look.

Tremaine lifted a brow. "We have a motorcar?"

"We do now. There are a number of them left unclaimed in the street." Nicholas was imperturbable.

Captain Morane snorted in amusement and confided to Tremaine, "It has nothing to do with the war. Your father hasn't actually purchased an automobile since the first horseless carriage rolled out of the factory."

Nicholas ignored him, taking a drink off a passing tray. He tasted it and winced.

"There's no alcohol in the drinks," Tremaine explained. She turned to Reynard. "They aren't serving wine?"

"Are you—" Gerard began. Nicholas cleared his throat and shot him a meaningful look. Gerard subsided.

"I believe we drank it all already," Morane said kindly, answering her question about the refreshments.

People were moving into the ballroom. Through the archway she saw Count Delphane standing on the dais talking to Lady Aviler. Morane gestured them to some seats near the front, but close to the archway. Probably Nicholas's preference, in case someone threw a bomb. Or in case he decided to throw one. Before they could enter the room, one of the uniformed men from downstairs appeared beside Morane, saying, "Sir, someone is asking for you down in the foyer."

Morane excused himself and Tremaine sat on the end of a row next to Florian and Gerard, Nicholas taking the seat behind her.

People shuffled into place, Delphane began to speak and Tremaine propped her chin on her hand. *I should really just go.* She had said good-bye to Colonel Averi already and she wasn't sure he would approve of all this. He had been terribly antisocial with people he didn't know.

"Tremaine," someone whispered.

"What?" She looked at the archway and saw Ilias standing in the hall.

Tremaine thought later that she had actually fainted for an instant, though she didn't lose consciousness or fall out of her chair. She was aware of some agitation occurring around her, but really of nothing else until Captain Morane took her arm firmly, pulled her out of the chair and walked her across the hall with Ilias.

Morane said, "You can speak privately in here," and handed Tremaine into a little parlor down the hall from the ballroom, shutting the door behind Ilias.

Tremaine dropped into an armchair, still unable to frame a coherent sentence.

"You're alive," Ilias said, kneeling beside her. He needed a shave, badly, and his hair was a tangled mess. He looked dirty too, but that could have been caused just by walking around Vienne. "I knew you didn't mean to kill yourself, I knew you had a plan."

"Yes. What?" Tremaine tried to get her thoughts together. "No, I did mean to kill myself, but I flinched at the last minute, and Florian and Arisilde saved me." She gripped her head, trying to get back to the important point. "How the hell did you get here?"

He gestured helplessly, looking as if he was just as shocked to be here as she was to see him. He wasn't wearing his sword—he must have had to leave it with the guards at the front door, who must have summoned Captain Morane to deal with the situation. He was wearing a shirt she hadn't seen before, a dark brown one, and her ring on the thong around his neck. "Giliead talked to the god and found out it knew the gate curse from Arisilde, and it thought it could make it work, so we fixed the curse circle left in Cineth and we tried it and it worked." He paused to take a breath. "That was actually the easy part."

Tremaine was aware that her mouth was open, but she couldn't seem to close it.

"It took us to that forest in the middle of the city, and then we didn't know where to look for you. But after we walked around a while, I found the way back to your house, but it was knocked down. We talked to your neighbor—"

Tremaine managed to speak. "I didn't know Coldcourt had neighbors. That knew us, I mean. That were willing to admit they knew us."

"It was the old man, in the next big house, two fields over. It got knocked down too, but not as bad as yours, and the people are staying there while they rebuild it. His name was Lord Evian-something. He said he thought you would be at a place called Hotel Galvaz because that's where something called the newspaper said the other Viller people were, and he described how to get there. So we went there, and the people there sent us here."

"You can get back?"

Ilias nodded. "Oh, sure. We went back and forth a couple of times to test it. The god can hear Gil when he stands where the gate opens in the forest." He added in a rush, "I had to see if you were alive. And you are, so, I wanted to ask you to come back with us. I know it's different, and not as fine as this, but we thought if you could try it for a while, and if you decide you want to go back, Gil can get the god to make the gate work again."

Tremaine gestured vaguely, having trouble getting the words out. "I have to get—" A coat? A bag? Maybe nothing. "Before we go."

"Before we go?" Ilias repeated, obviously wanting to make sure. "We?"

Tremaine nodded. "Yes." She came to the conclusion that she hadn't brought anything with her that she had to collect from the coatroom. "Definitely we."

She put her hand on his shoulder and as they both stood up, she pulled him into her arms. He hugged her back so hard her ribs creaked and he laughed with relief into her hair.

Giliead was out in the hallway, with Gerard, Nicholas, Florian and Morane, explaining what had happened in a hurried hush. Giliead needed a shave too. Gerard looked quietly elated, Morane was smiling and Florian was actually bouncing with excitement. Nicholas just looked like Nicholas. "And then we came here," Giliead finished.

Gerard nodded, saying, "Yes, I think you're correct about the gods and Orelis. The—" He stopped as Tremaine stepped out of the doorway with Ilias.

"So, I'm leaving," Tremaine announced. "With them," she added in case there was any doubt. She found herself looking at Nicholas.

He just lifted a brow and said, "I'll walk you to the park."